BATMAN™ VS. THE JOKER

Written by Julia March

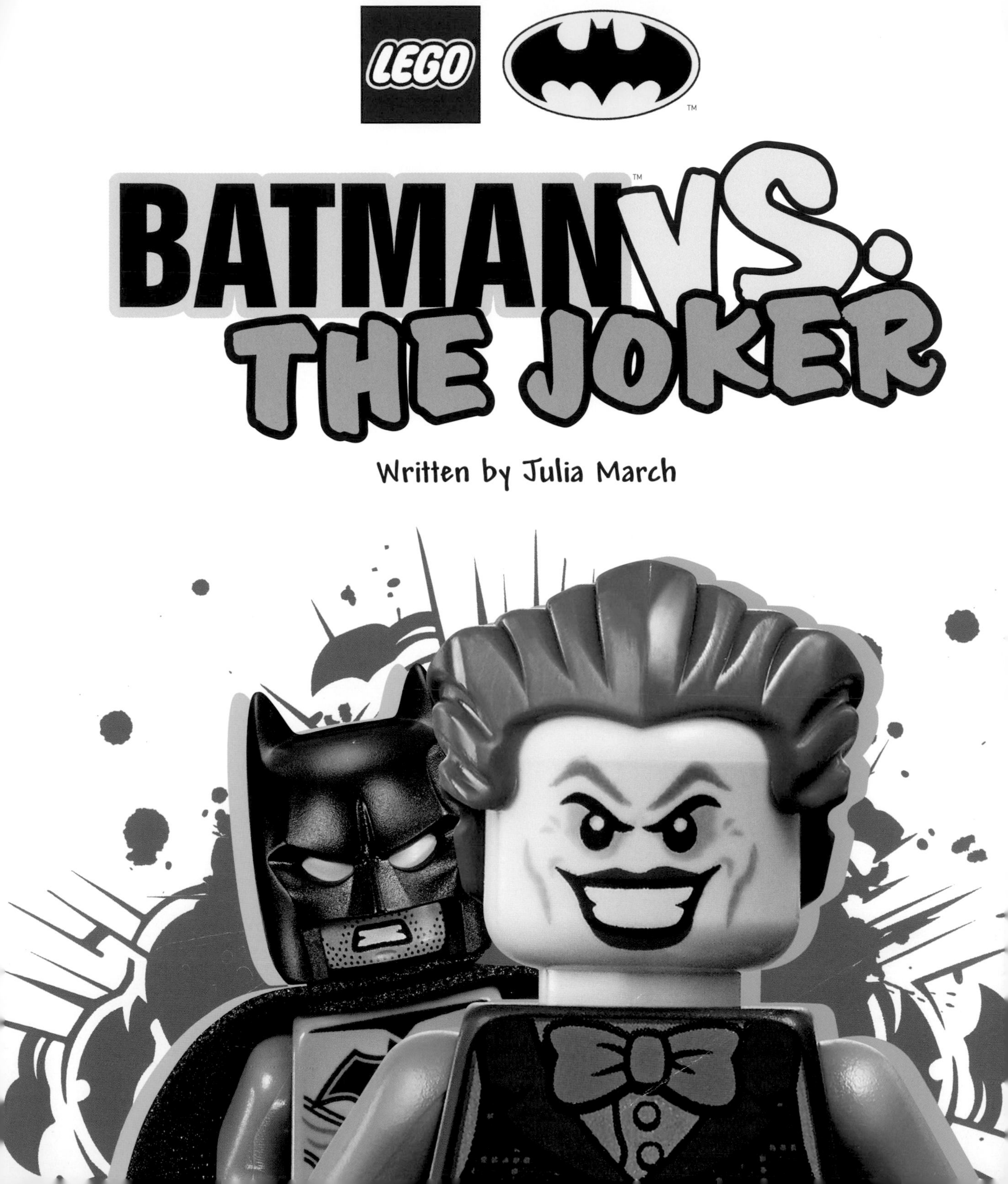

CONTENTS

YOU'LL NEVER BEAT US, JOKER!

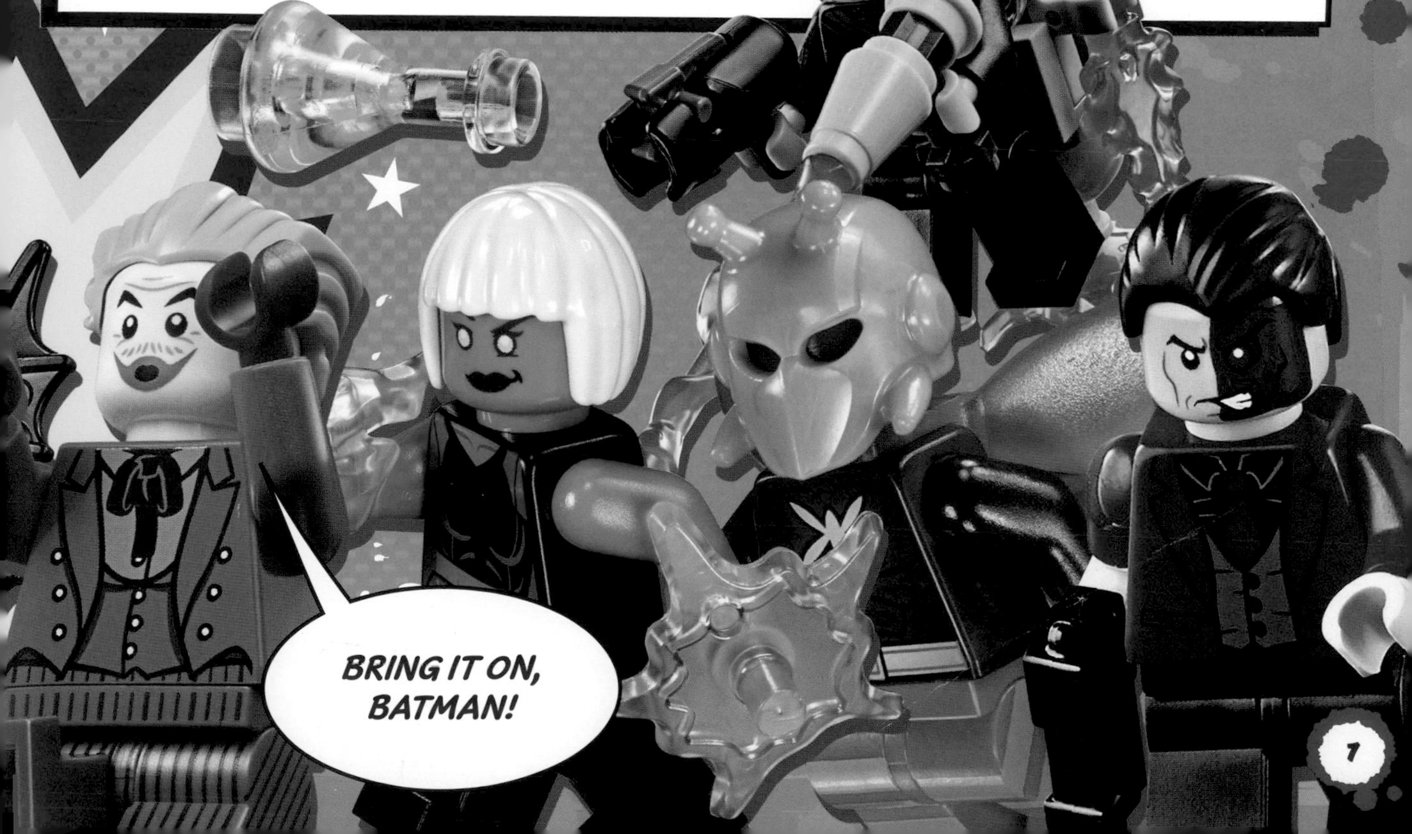
BRING IT ON, BATMAN!

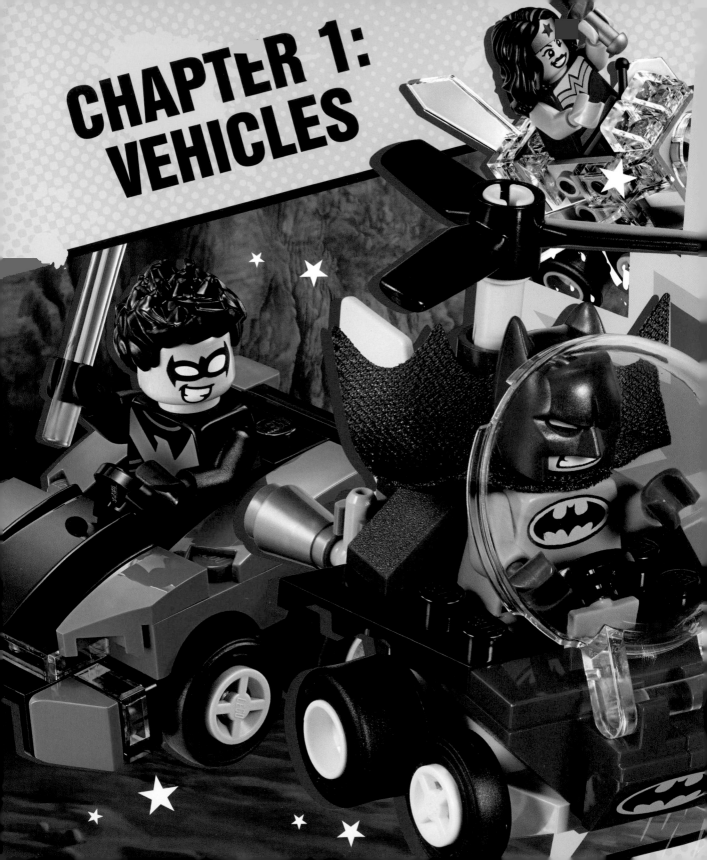

CHAPTER 1: VEHICLES

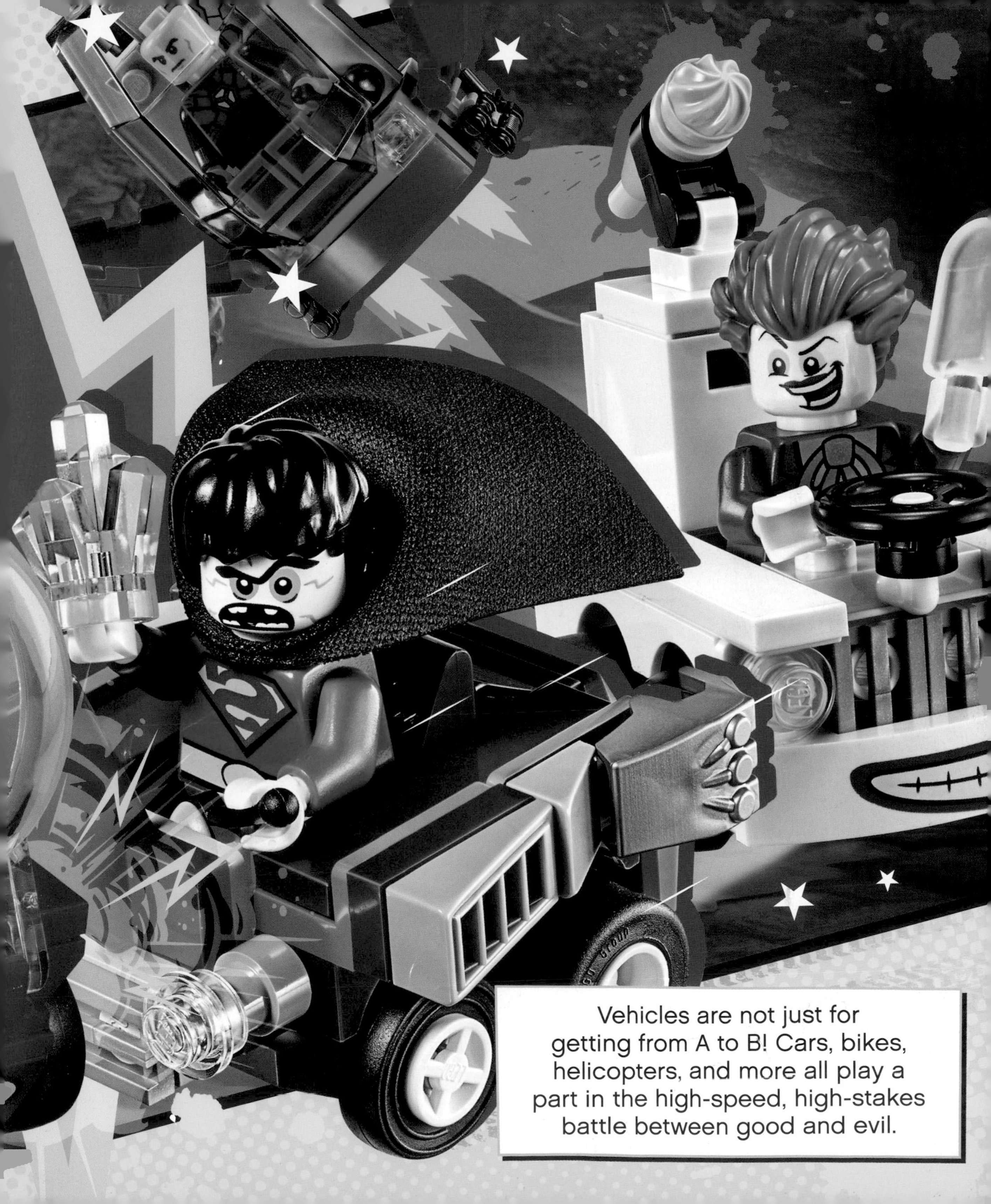

Vehicles are not just for getting from A to B! Cars, bikes, helicopters, and more all play a part in the high-speed, high-stakes battle between good and evil.

BATMAN VS. THE JOKER

Batman and the Joker go head-to-head in their vehicles. The Batwing is fast, but the Joker's ice cream truck is packed with wacky weapons!

When Batman needs to fight crime, he hops into one of his many amazing vehicles! He is ready for anything.

My speedy **BATWING** will leave you in the dust!

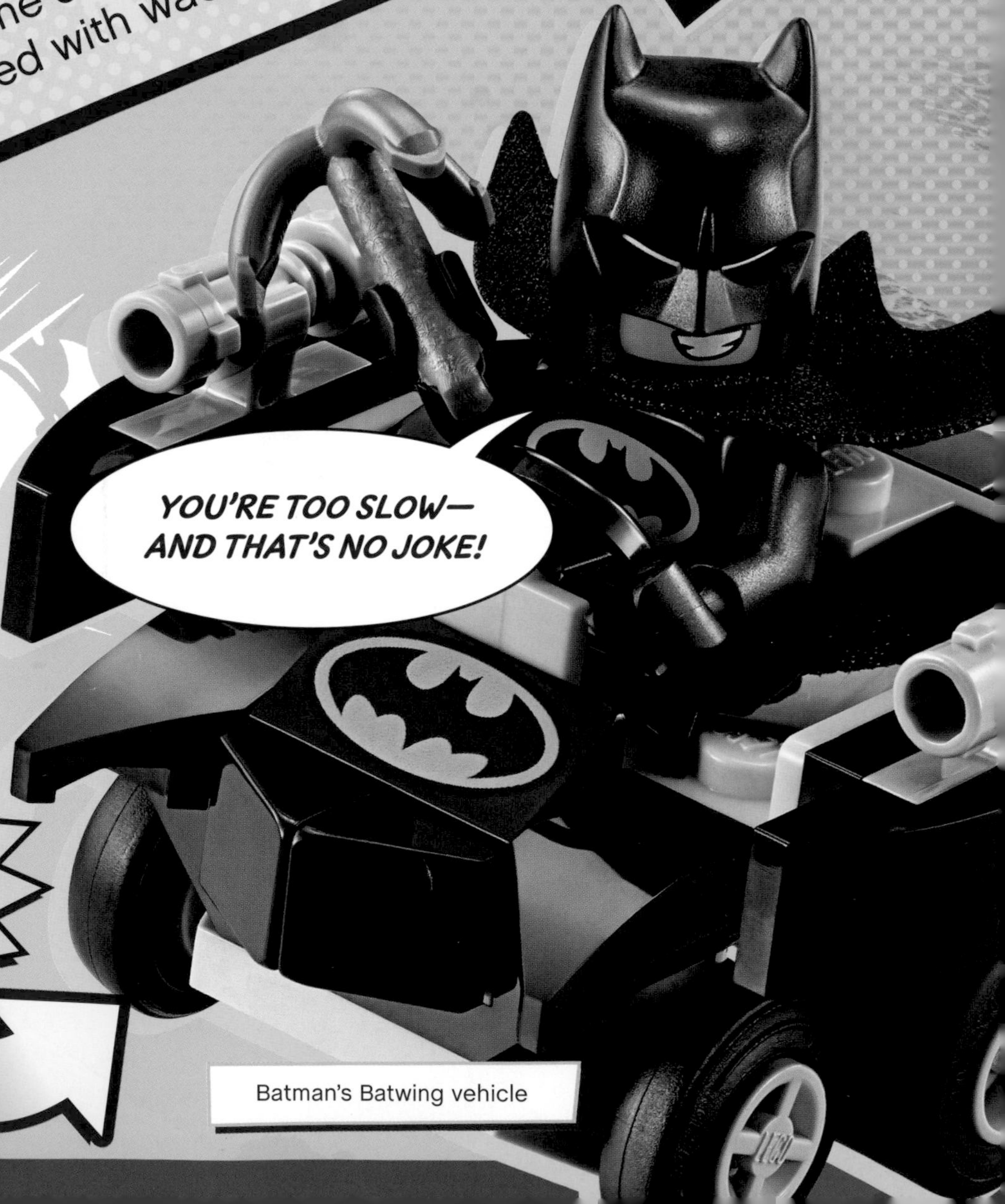
YOU'RE TOO SLOW—
AND THAT'S NO JOKE!

Bat-symbol designs make my ride look **SO COOL**

Batman's Batwing vehicle

The Joker's ice cream truck

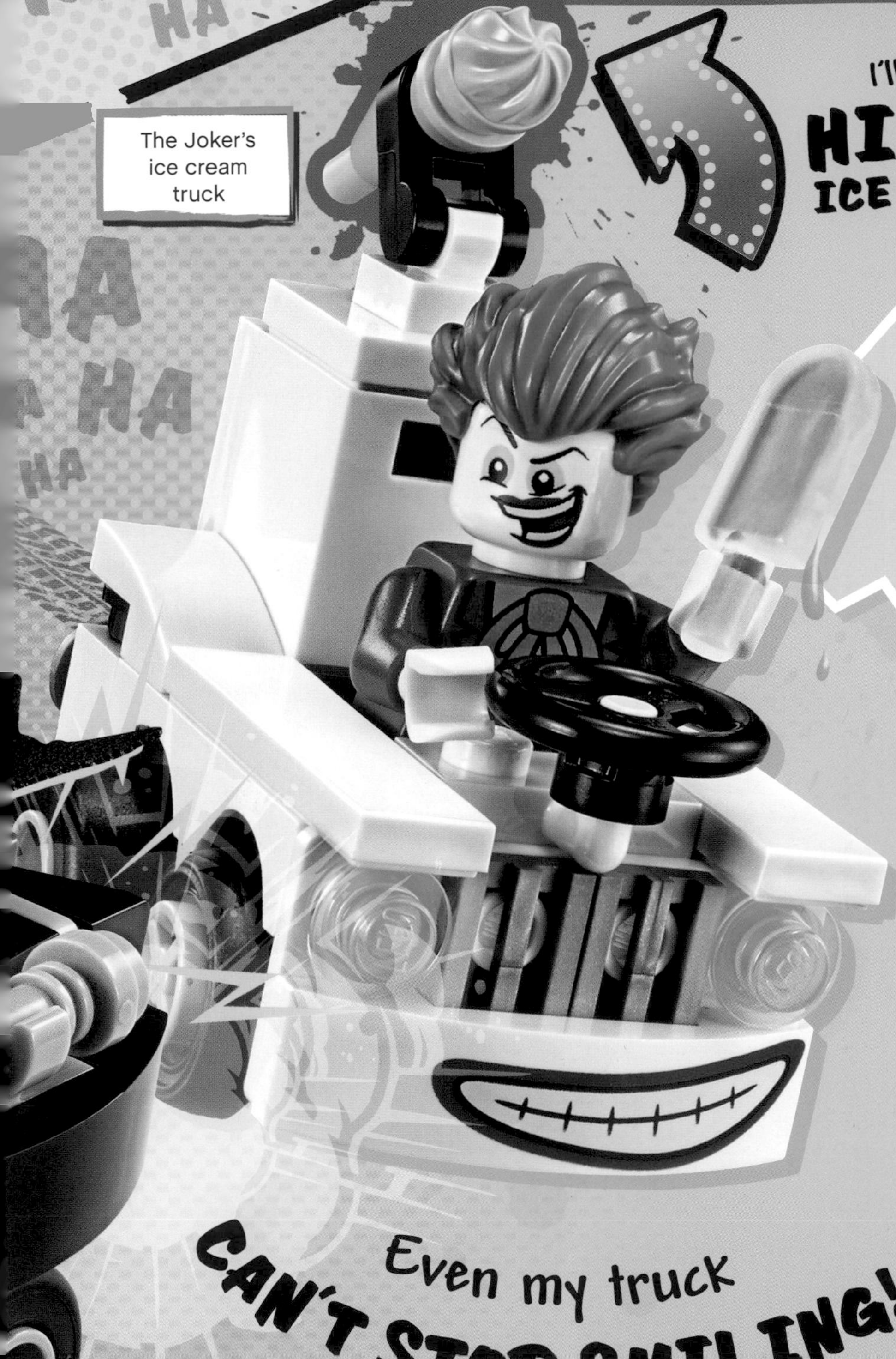

I'll blast you with my **HILARIOUS ICE CREAM CANNON**

This **LAUGHING GAS POPSICLE** will leave you with a smile on your face!

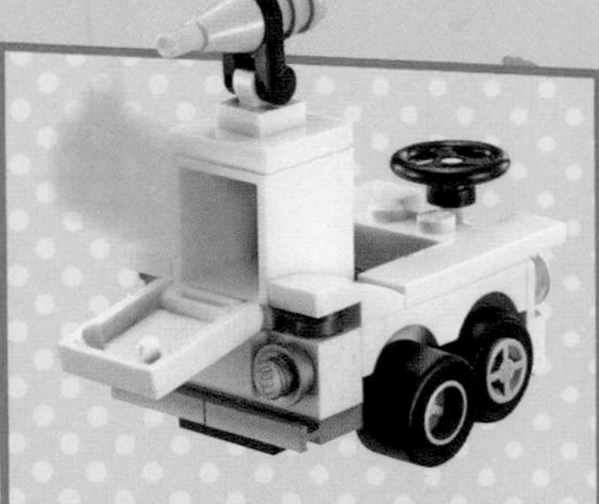

DID YOU KNOW?

The ice cream truck's trunk can store extra weapons. Sometimes the Joker fills it with his favorite—laughing gas!

Even my truck **CAN'T STOP SMILING!**

Which vehicle would you like to drive?

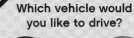

OR

NIGHTWING VS. HARLEY QUINN

The race is on! Nightwing's car is faster than Harley Quinn's, but Harley has plenty of sneaky tricks on board. Will speed or sneakiness win?

I'll use this baton to **JAM YOUR WHEELS**

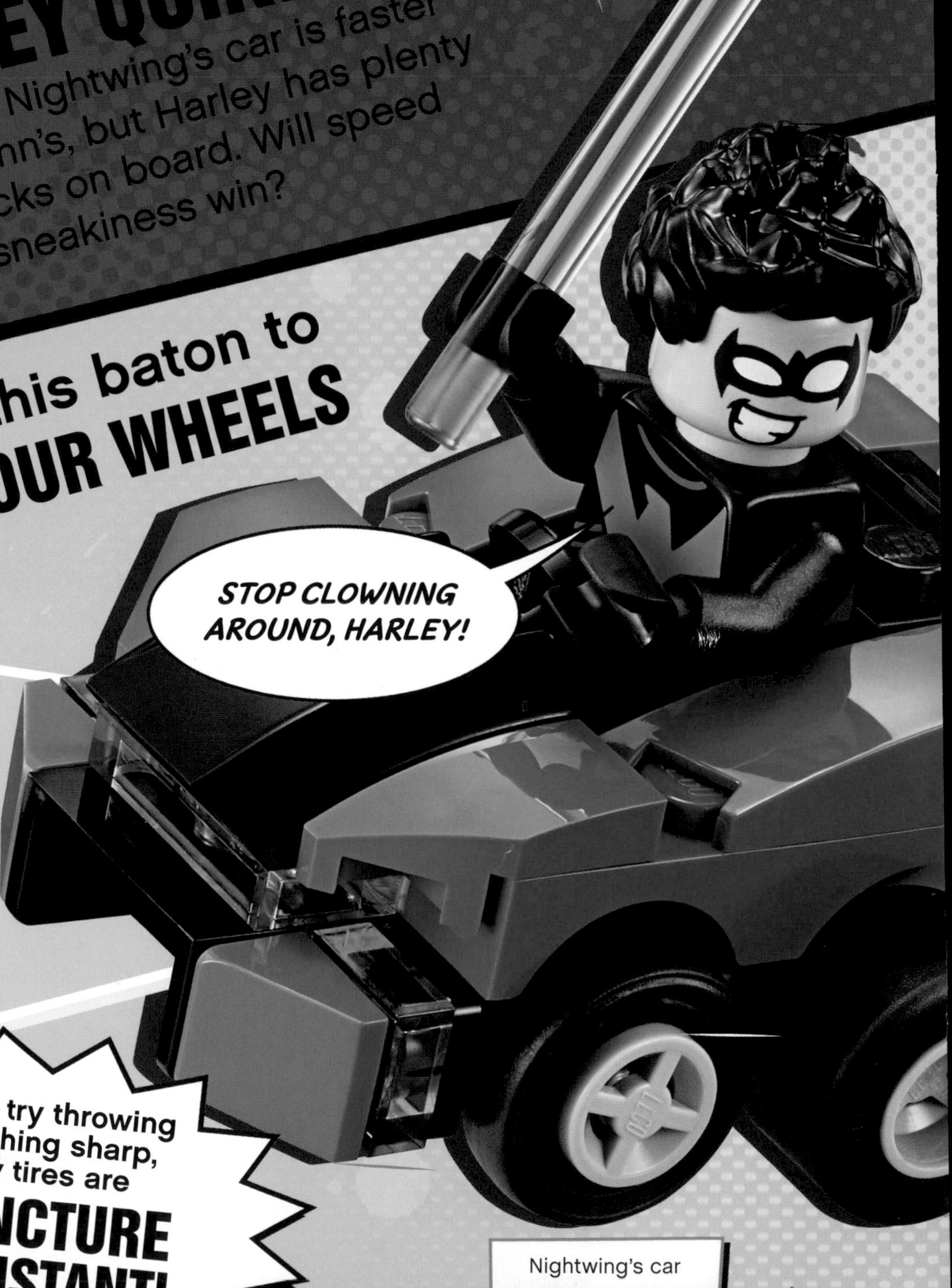
STOP CLOWNING AROUND, HARLEY!

Your tricks won't help you if you **CAN'T CATCH ME!**

Don't try throwing anything sharp, my tires are **PUNCTURE RESISTANT!**

Nightwing's car

Harley's car goes forward, backward, and in circles! It doesn't need fuel—but Harley has to stop to wind it up now and then!

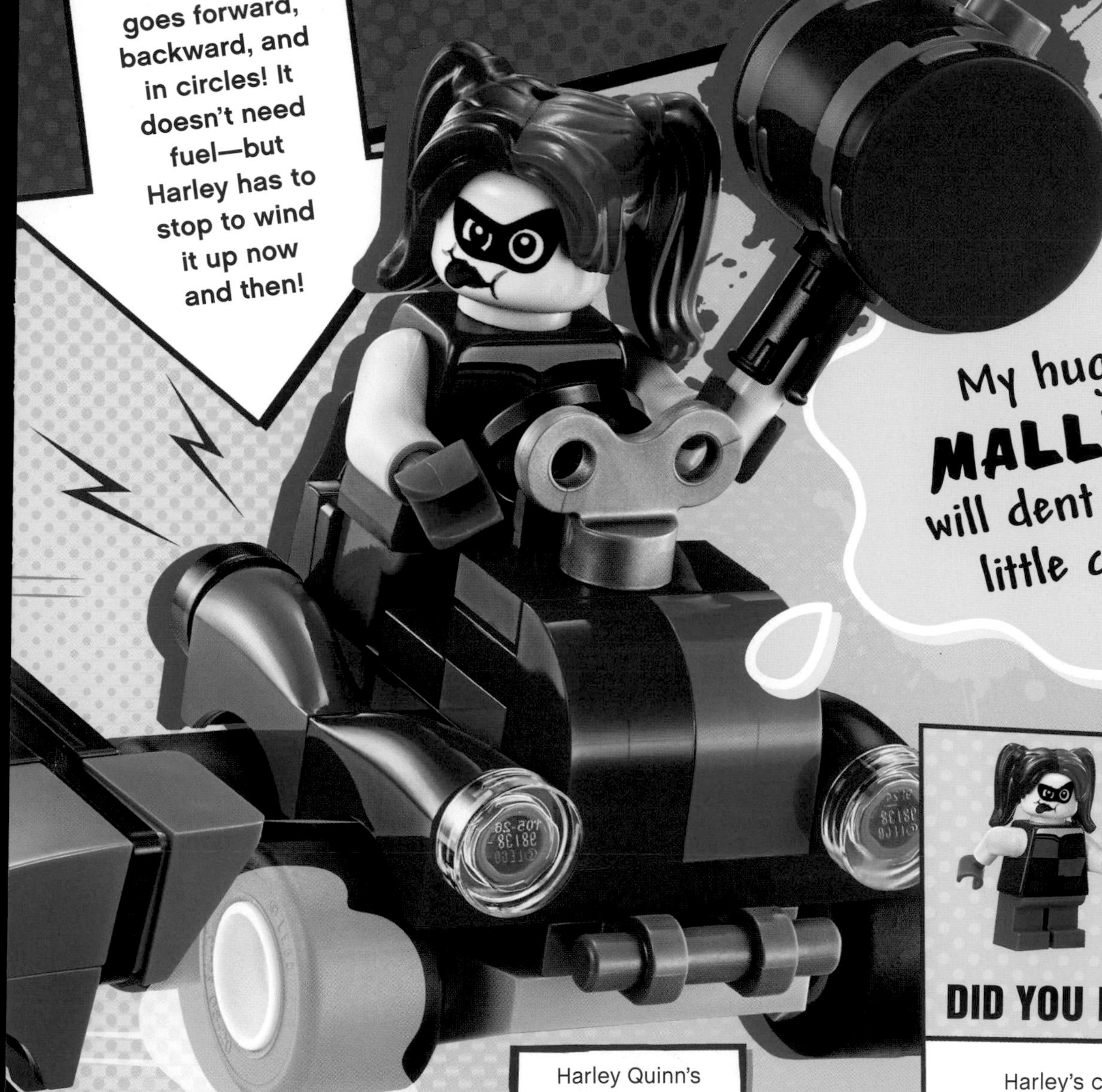

My huge **MALLET** will dent your little car!

Harley Quinn's wind-up car

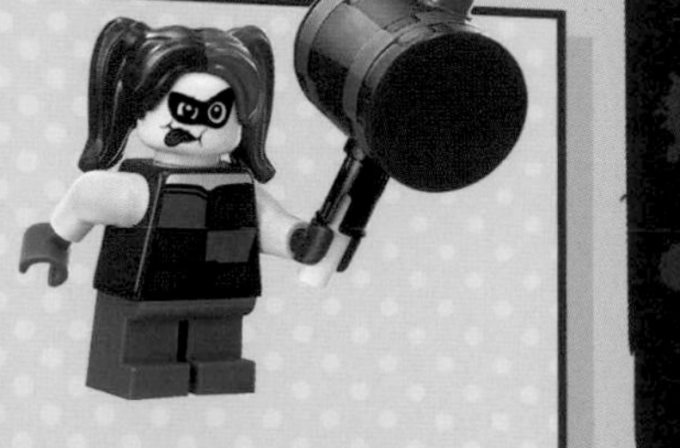

DID YOU KNOW?

Harley's colorful costume is based on the suit of a medieval jester. She dyes her hair half red, half blue to match!

My car is full of **TRICK WEAPONS!**

Who will be king or queen of the road?

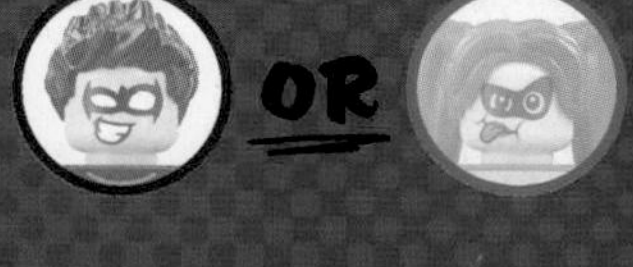
OR

ROBIN VS. CATWOMAN

Catwoman has been on a crime spree! Robin is chasing the Catmobile in his car. Can he catch the cat and send her home empty-clawed?

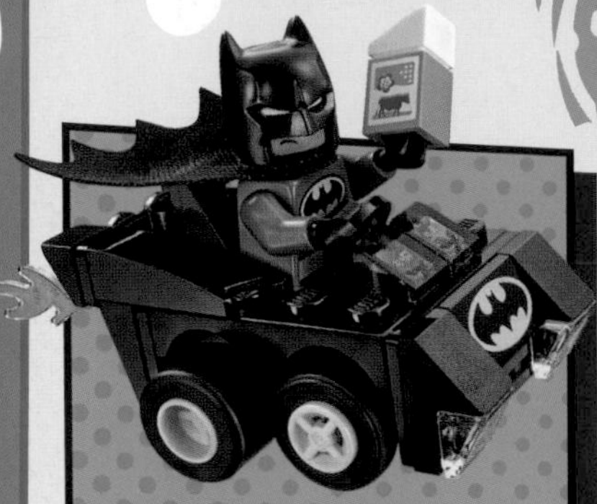

DID YOU KNOW?

After stealing diamonds, Catwoman often steals a carton of milk, too. Crime is thirsty work! Batman is returning this one to the supermarket.

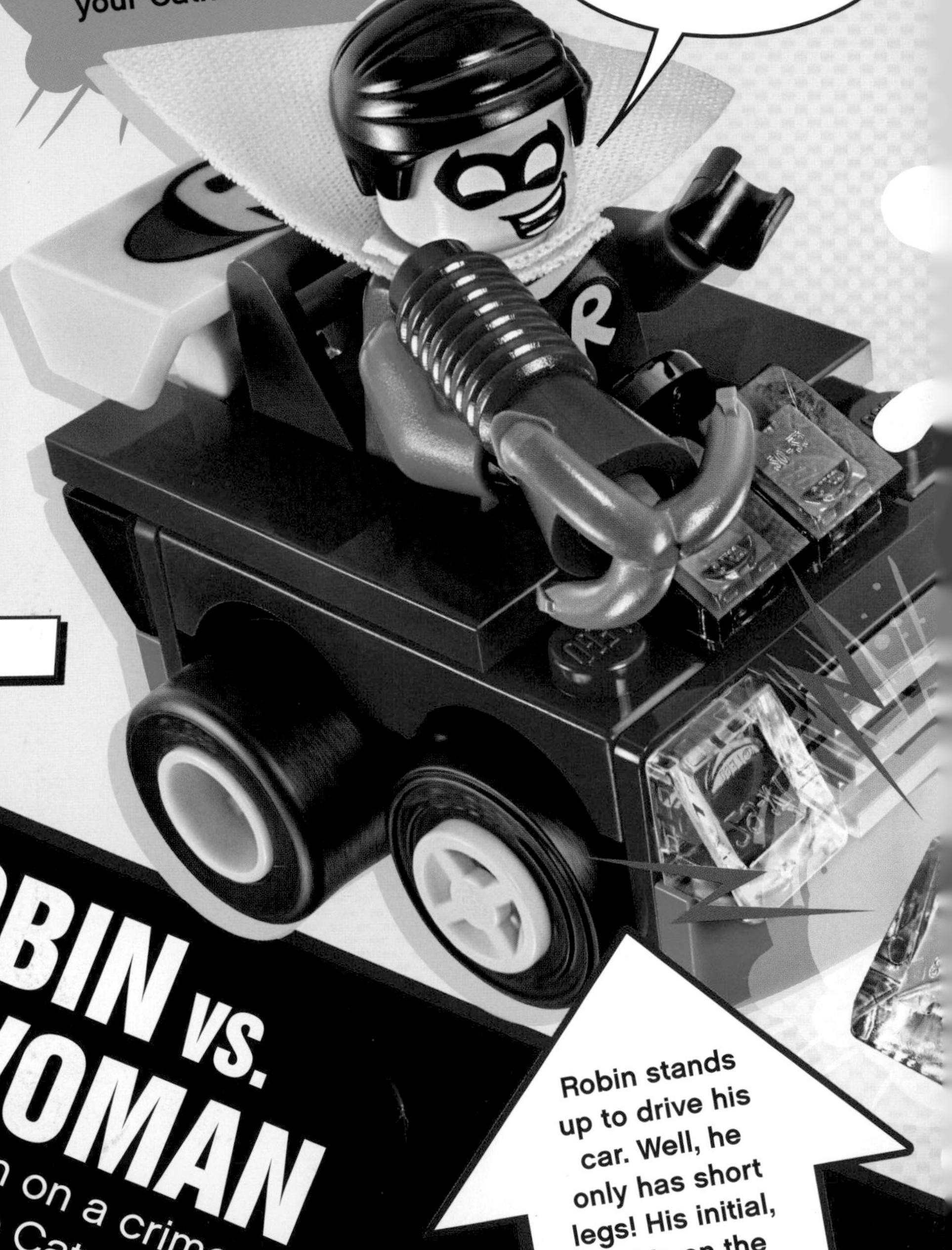

I'll fire this GRAPPLING HOOK and latch onto your Catmobile!
THIS ROBIN IS TOO FLY FOR YOU!

Robin's car

Robin stands up to drive his car. Well, he only has short legs! His initial, "R," is on the rear spoiler to deter anyone who might try to steal it.

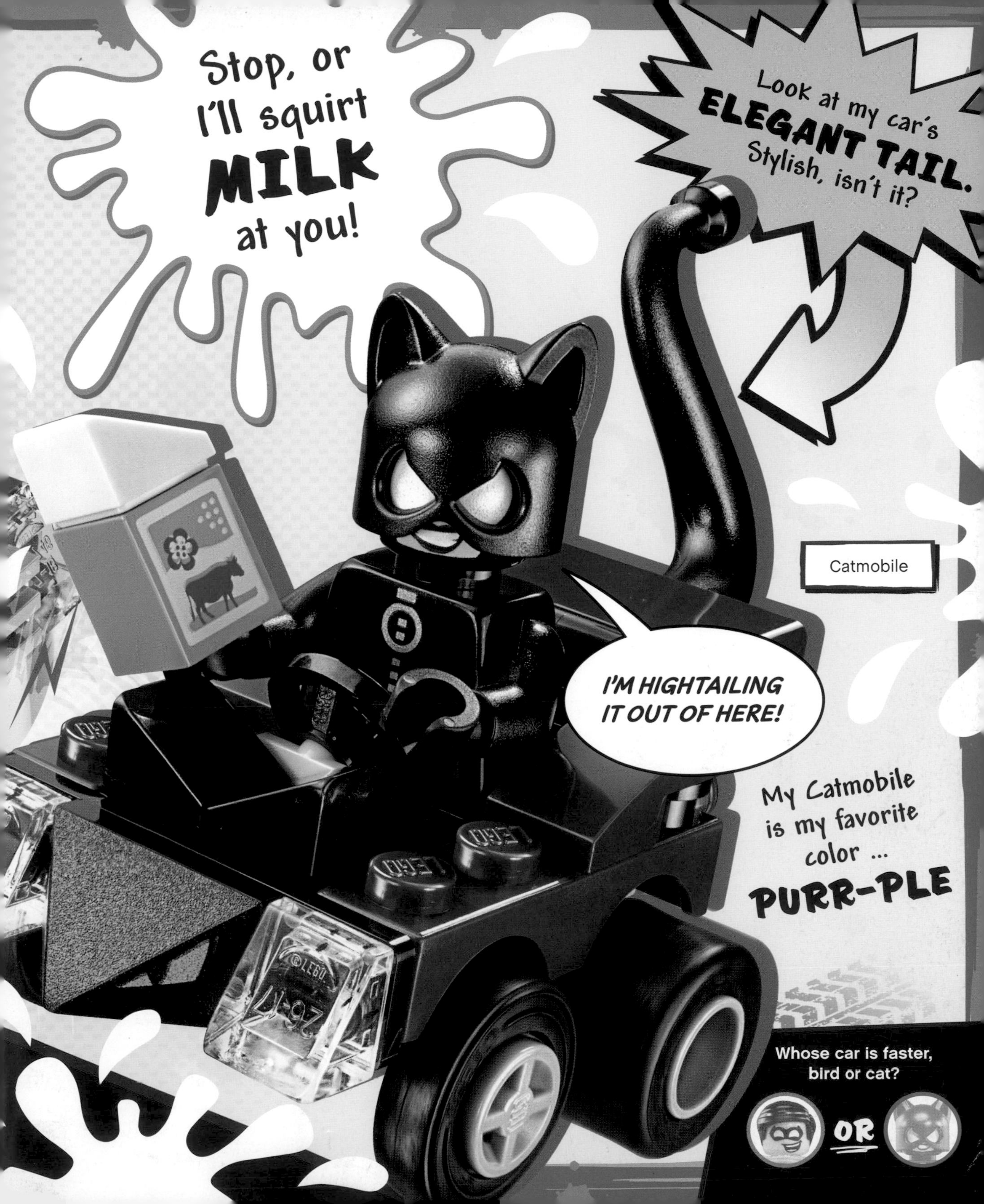
Stop, or I'll squirt MILK at you!
Look at my car's ELEGANT TAIL. Stylish, isn't it?
Catmobile
I'M HIGHTAILING IT OUT OF HERE!
My Catmobile is my favorite color ... PURR-PLE
Whose car is faster, bird or cat?
OR

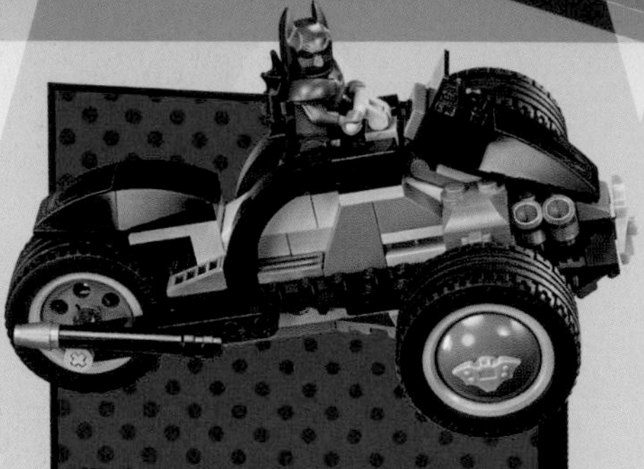

DID YOU KNOW?

Batman's bike has three wheels. It's narrow at the back but very wide at the front—ideal for ramming villains off the road.

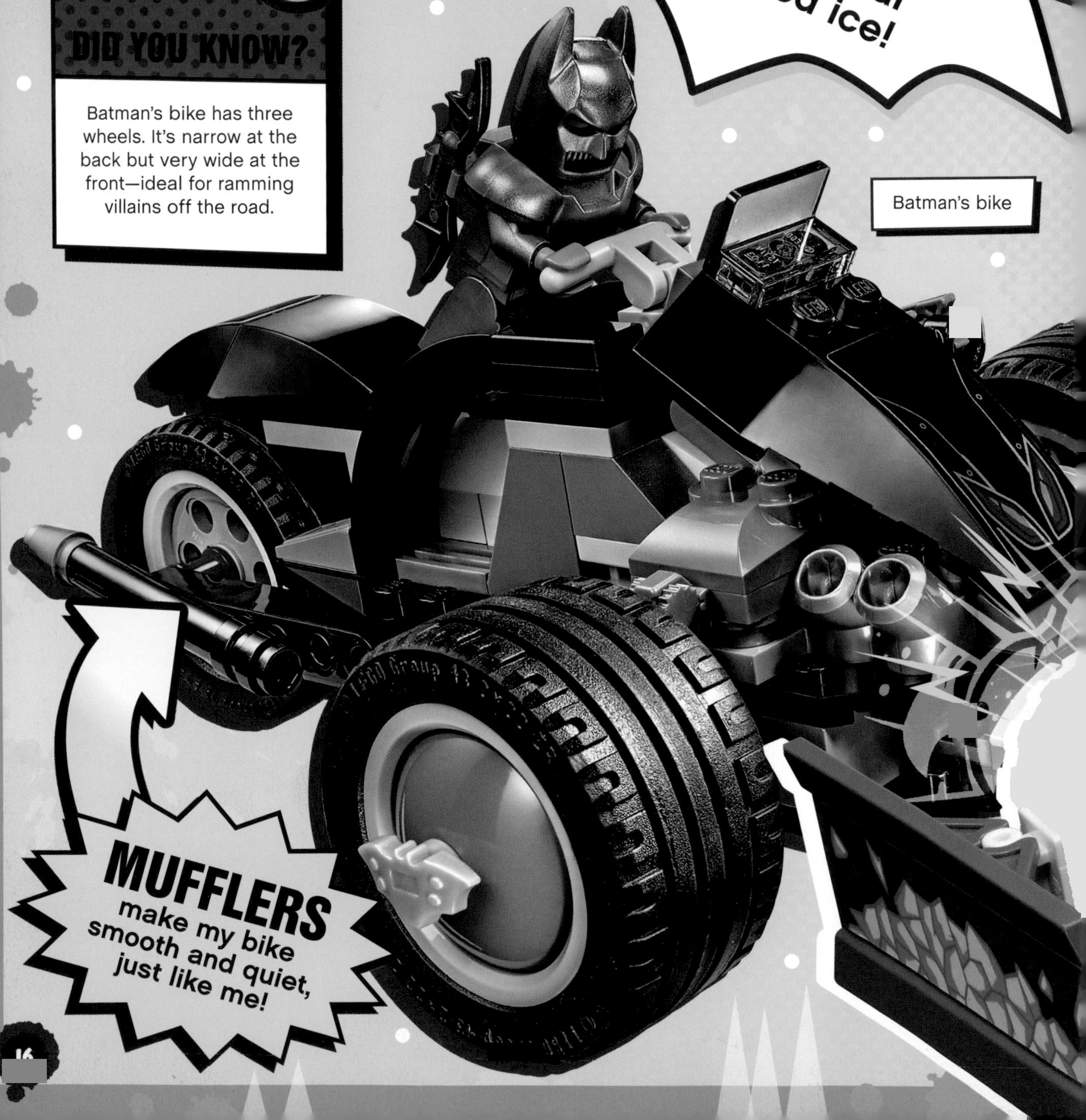
My BIG BIKE will turn your car into crushed ice!
Batman's bike
MUFFLERS make my bike smooth and quiet, just like me!

BATMAN VS. KILLER FROST

Batman is fighting to keep Killer Frost out of Gotham City. If she gets in, she will suck the heat out of the city and power up for a chilling crime spree!

Killer Frost absorbs heat from enemies and converts it into cold. She then uses it to make icy weapons and missiles!

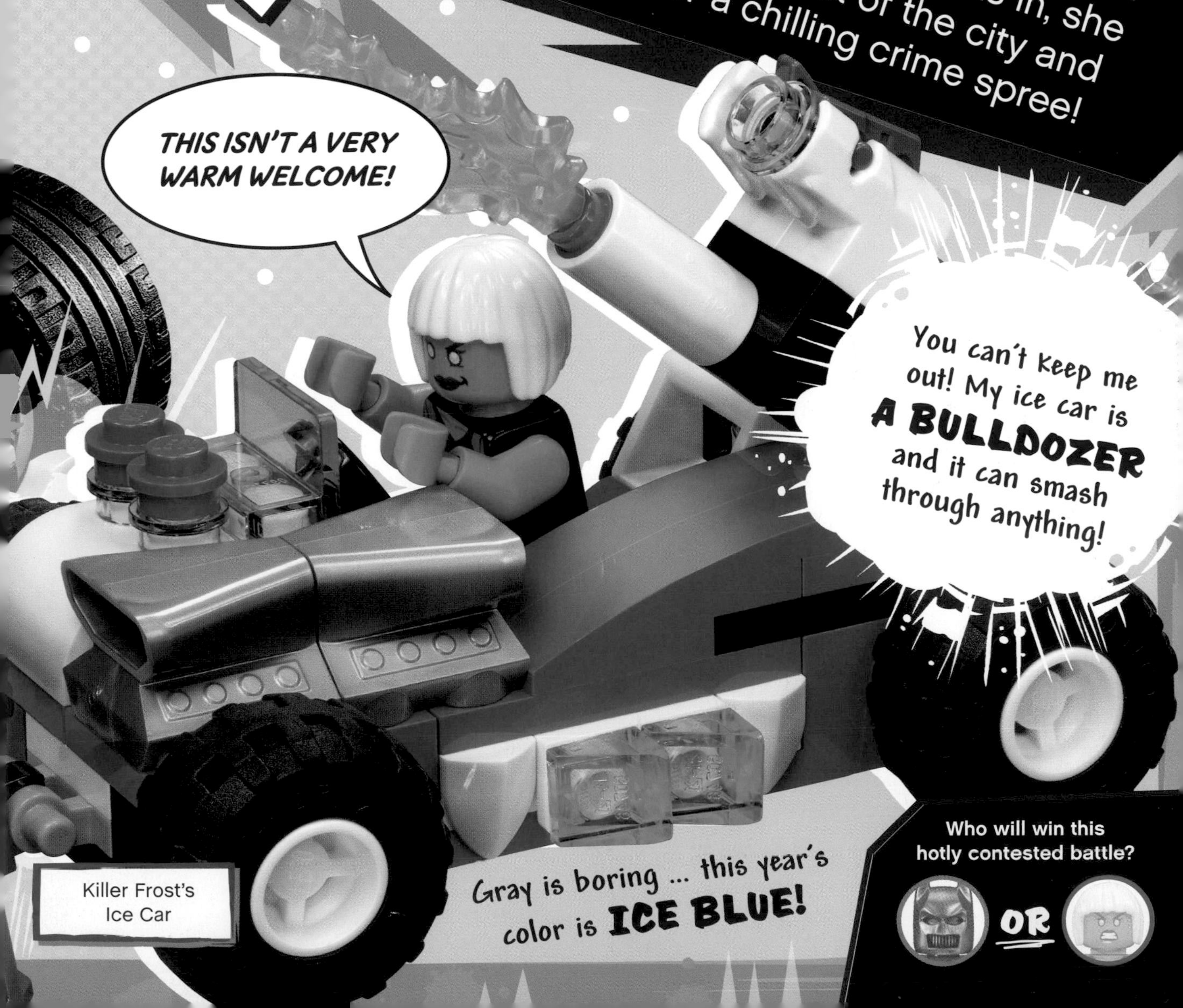

THIS ISN'T A VERY WARM WELCOME!
You can't keep me out! My ice car is **A BULLDOZER** and it can smash through anything!
Gray is boring ... this year's color is **ICE BLUE!**

Killer Frost's Ice Car

Who will win this hotly contested battle?

OR

WONDER WOMAN VS. DOOMSDAY

Doomsday is destroying everything he sees. But here comes Wonder Woman in her Invisible Jet. Doomsday might soon meet his own doom!

Foes don't see the Invisible Jet coming! Wonder Woman steers it with her mind, so her hands are free to use a sword.

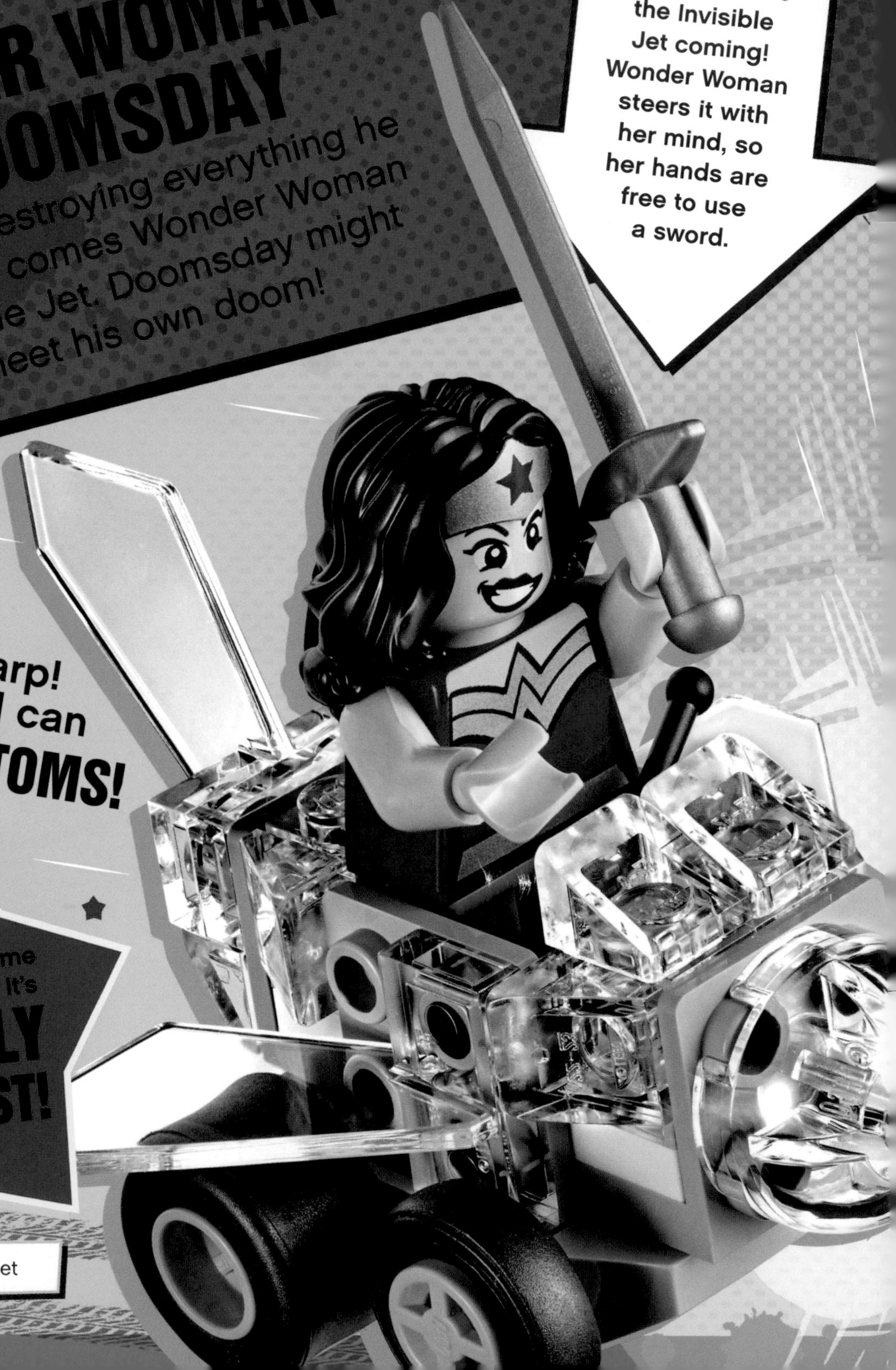

Look sharp! This sword can **CHOP UP ATOMS!**

My jet can become totally invisible. It's **CLEARLY THE BEST!**

Invisible Jet

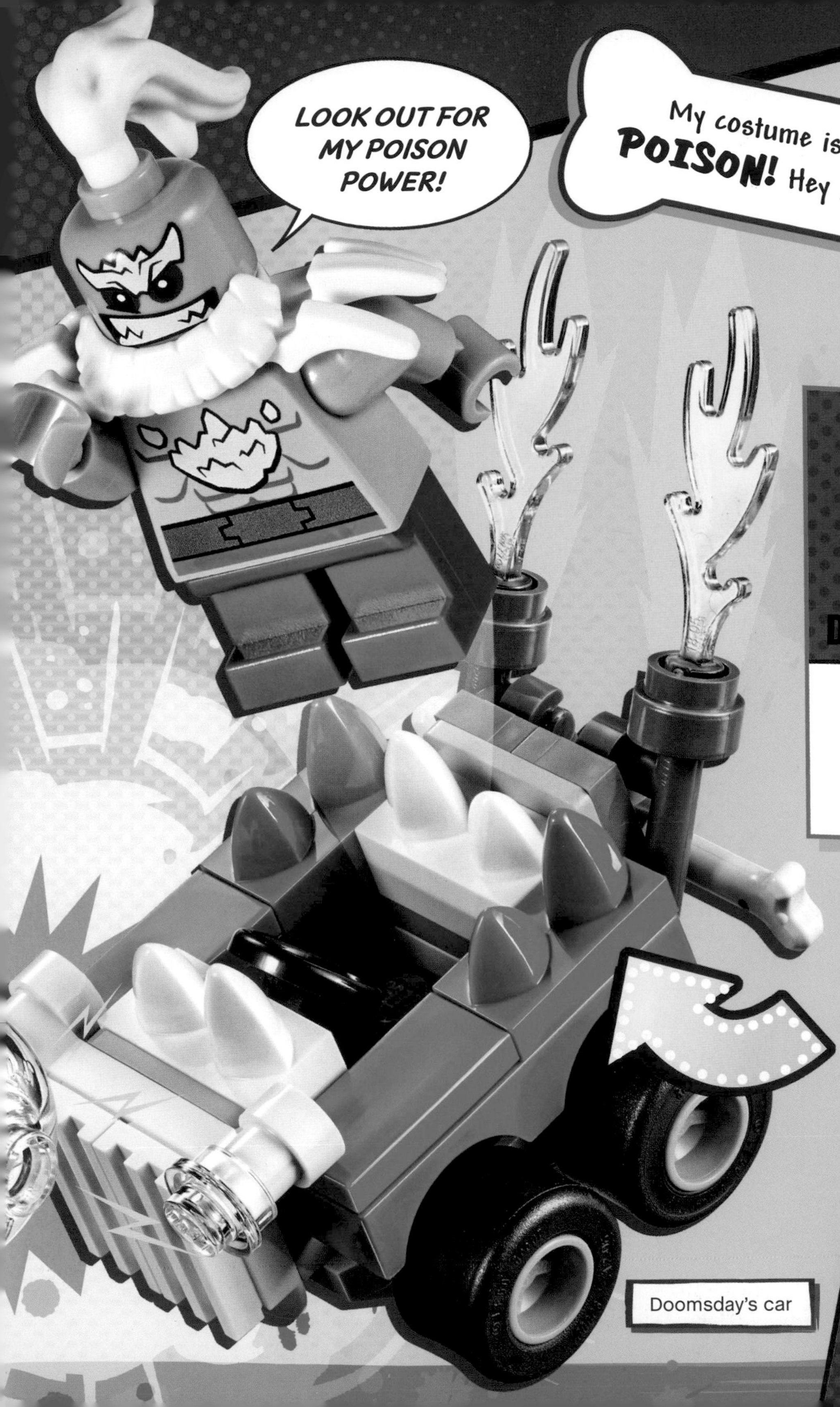
LOOK OUT FOR MY POISON POWER!
My costume is tipped with POISON! Hey ... want a hug?
My car is protected by JAGGED BONES

Doomsday's car

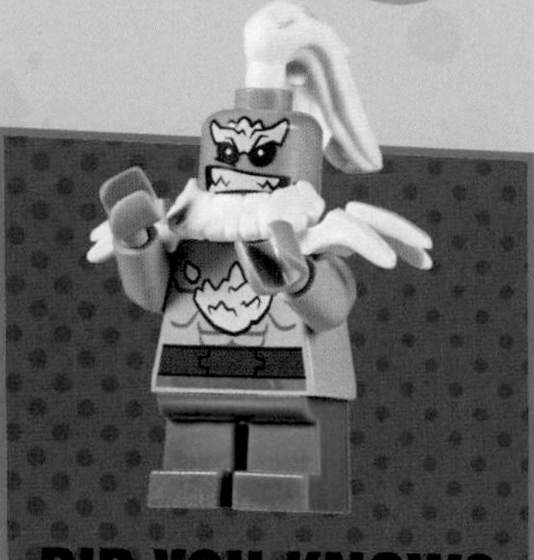

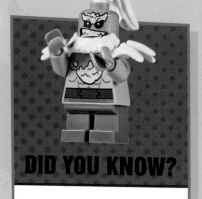

DID YOU KNOW?

Doomsday evolved on the planet Krypton. Unlike humans, he does not need to eat, sleep, or even breathe!

Which one will make their enemy disappear?

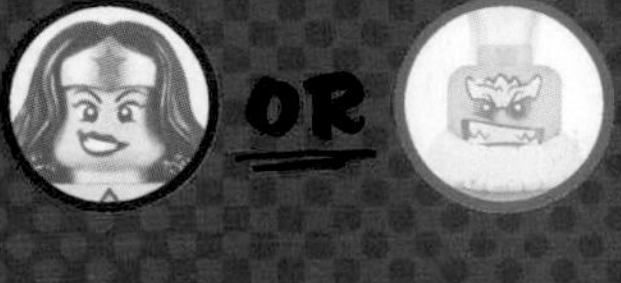
OR

BATMAN VS. THE RIDDLER

Batman has a puzzle to solve. How does he stop the Riddler from flying away with a stolen safe? Maybe his Bat-Tank will provide the answer!

You'll never hit me … not in this armored **COCKPIT**

My rotating **TURRET** fires missiles in all directions!

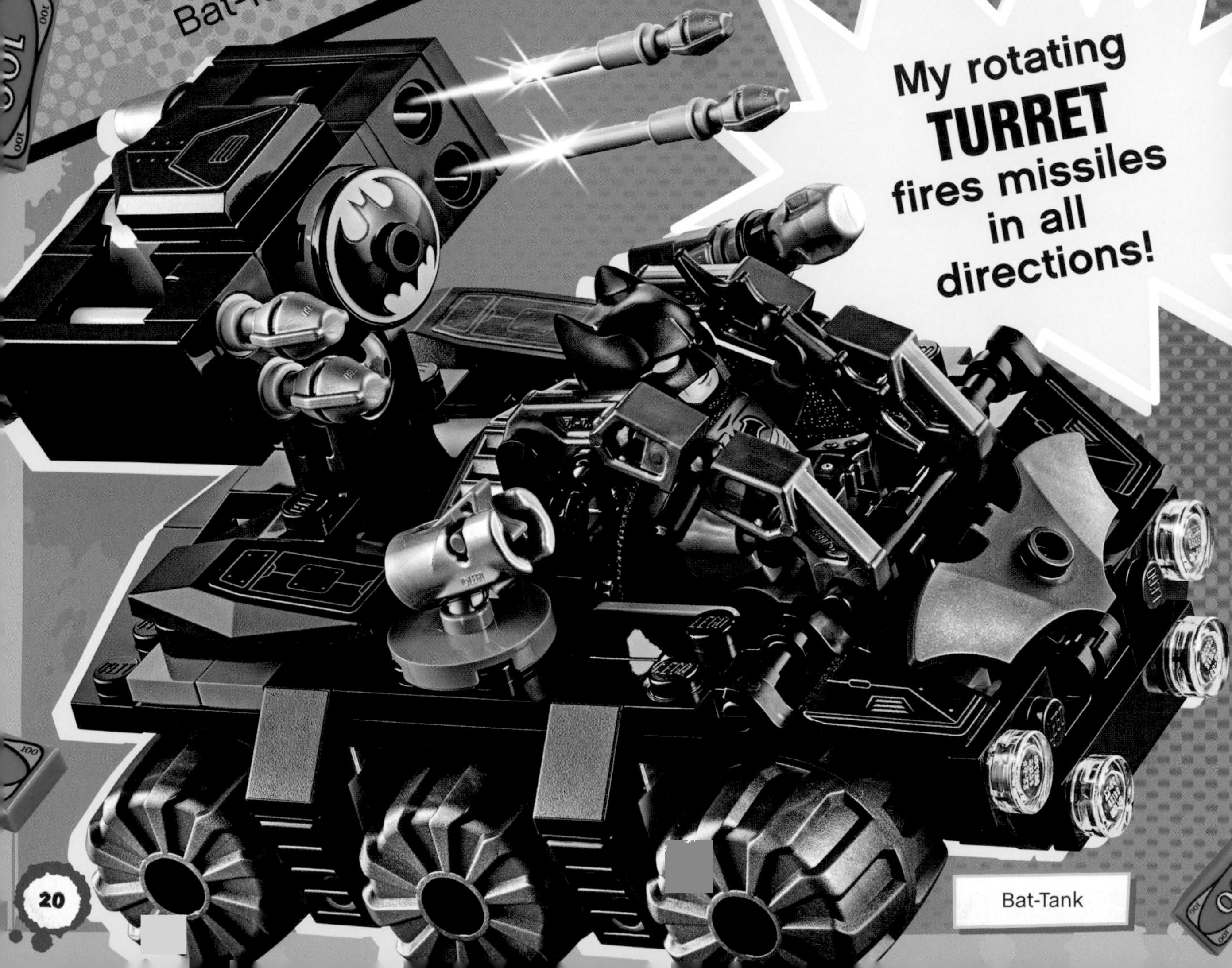

Bat-Tank

The Riddler landed his helicopter on the bank's roof. He then used the anchor and chain to hook a safe full of valuables!

Can you dodge the spinning shooters on **MY ROTOR?**

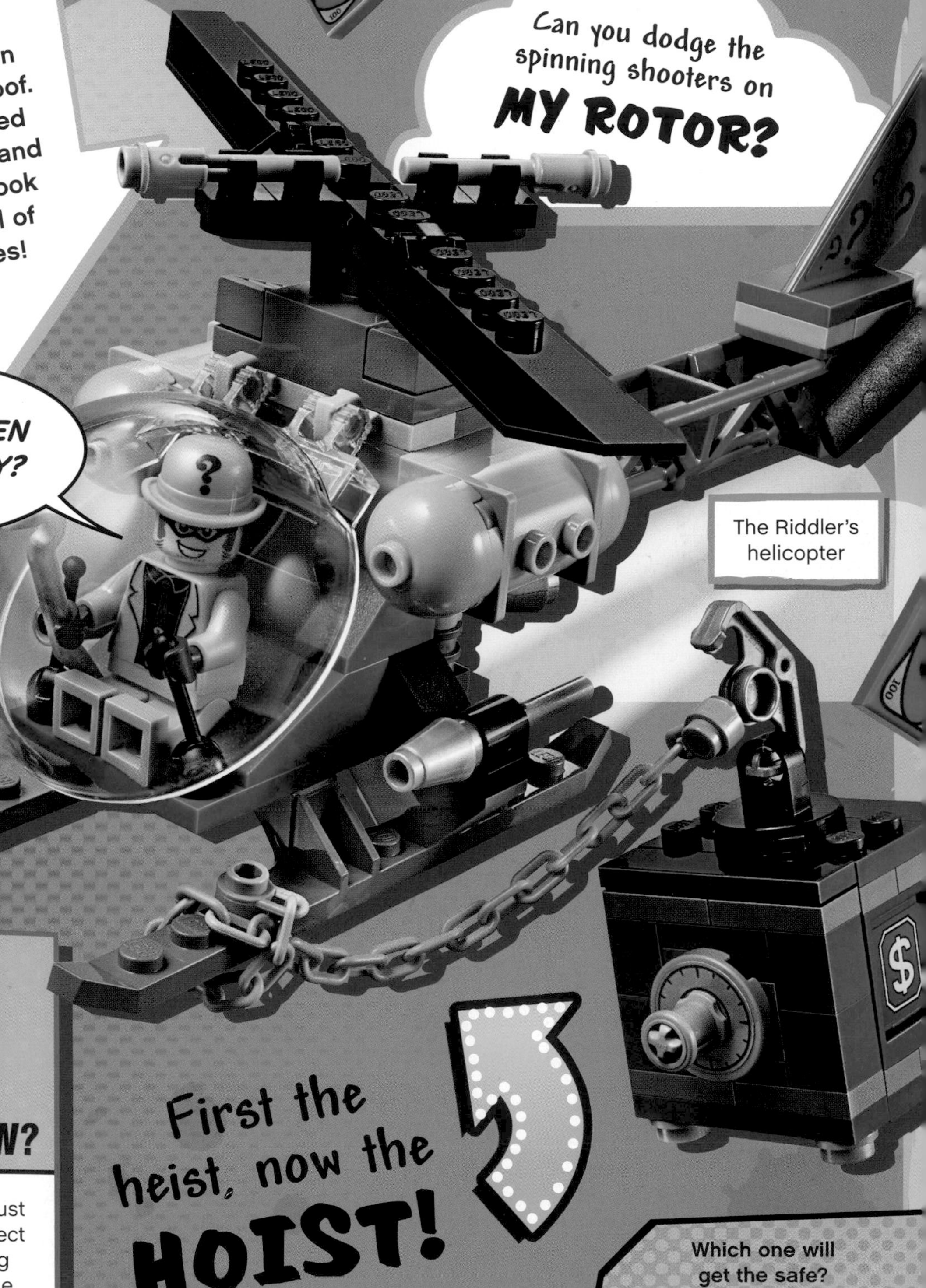

WHAT'S GREEN AND CAN FLY?

The Riddler's helicopter

First the heist, now the **HOIST!**

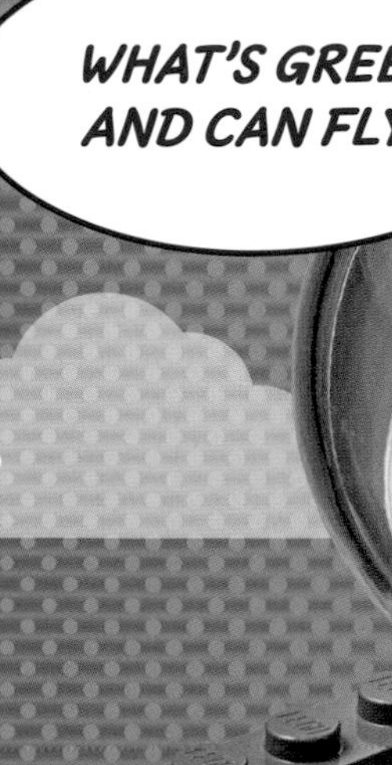

DID YOU KNOW?

To open a safe, you must turn the dial to the correct numbers. The cunning crook easily cracks the code to this one!

Which one will get the safe?

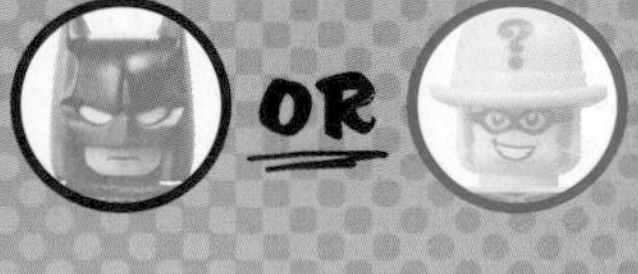

OR

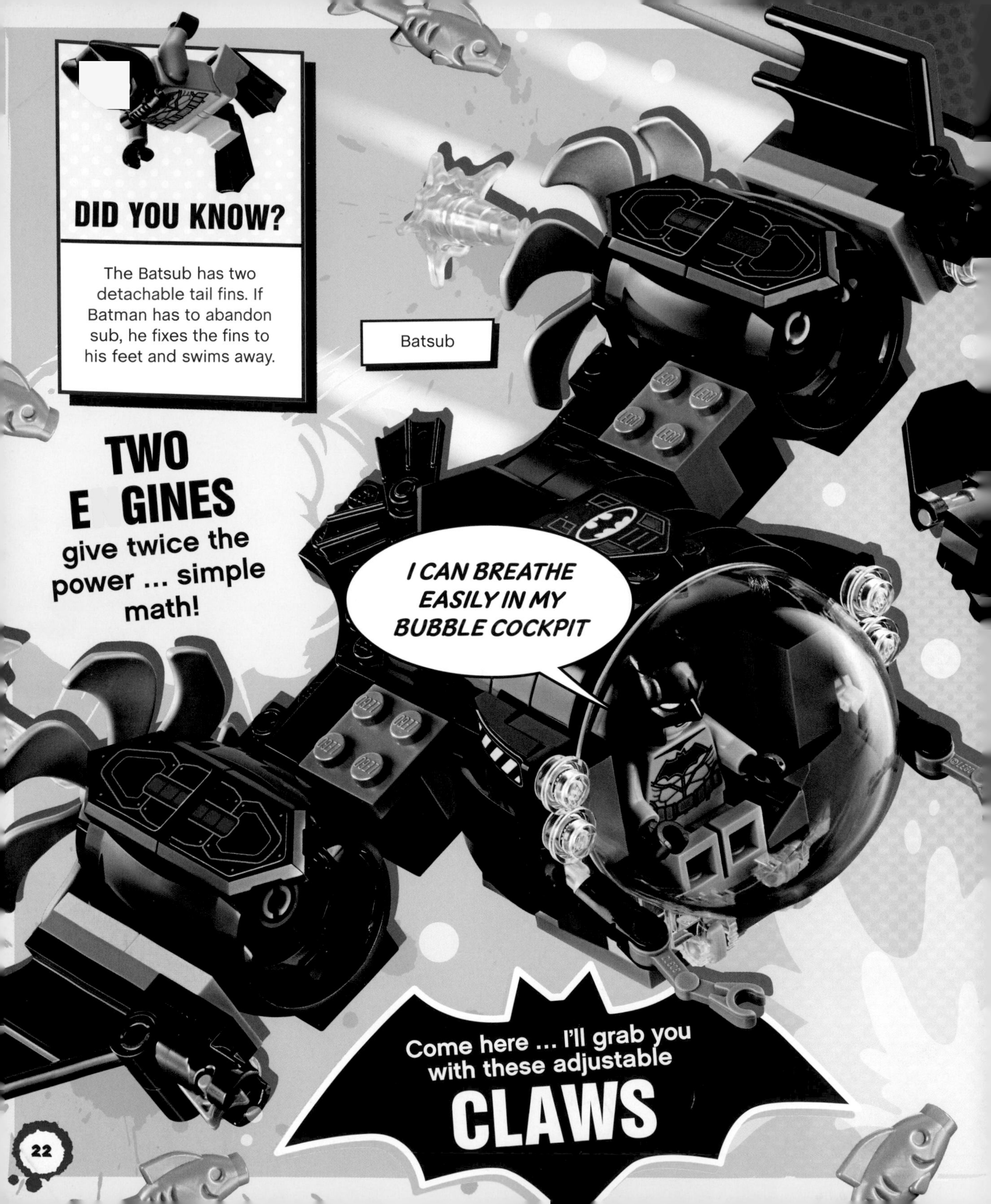
I CAN BREATHE EASILY IN MY BUBBLE COCKPIT

DID YOU KNOW?

The Batsub has two detachable tail fins. If Batman has to abandon sub, he fixes the fins to his feet and swims away.

Batsub

TWO E GINES give twice the power ... simple math!

Come here ... I'll grab you with these adjustable **CLAWS**

BATMAN VS. BLACK MANTA

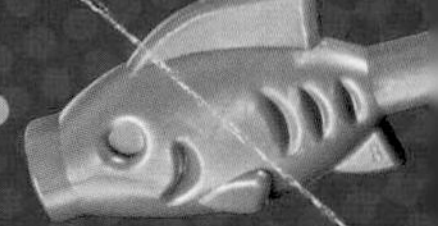

Black Manta is cruising the ocean in his submarine, looking for treasure to steal! Luckily, Batman is ready for him in a fin-tastic new sub of his own.

Black Manta's sub looks like a stingray, with wings and a tail. But unlike a ray—or any other fish—it boasts an array of shooters.

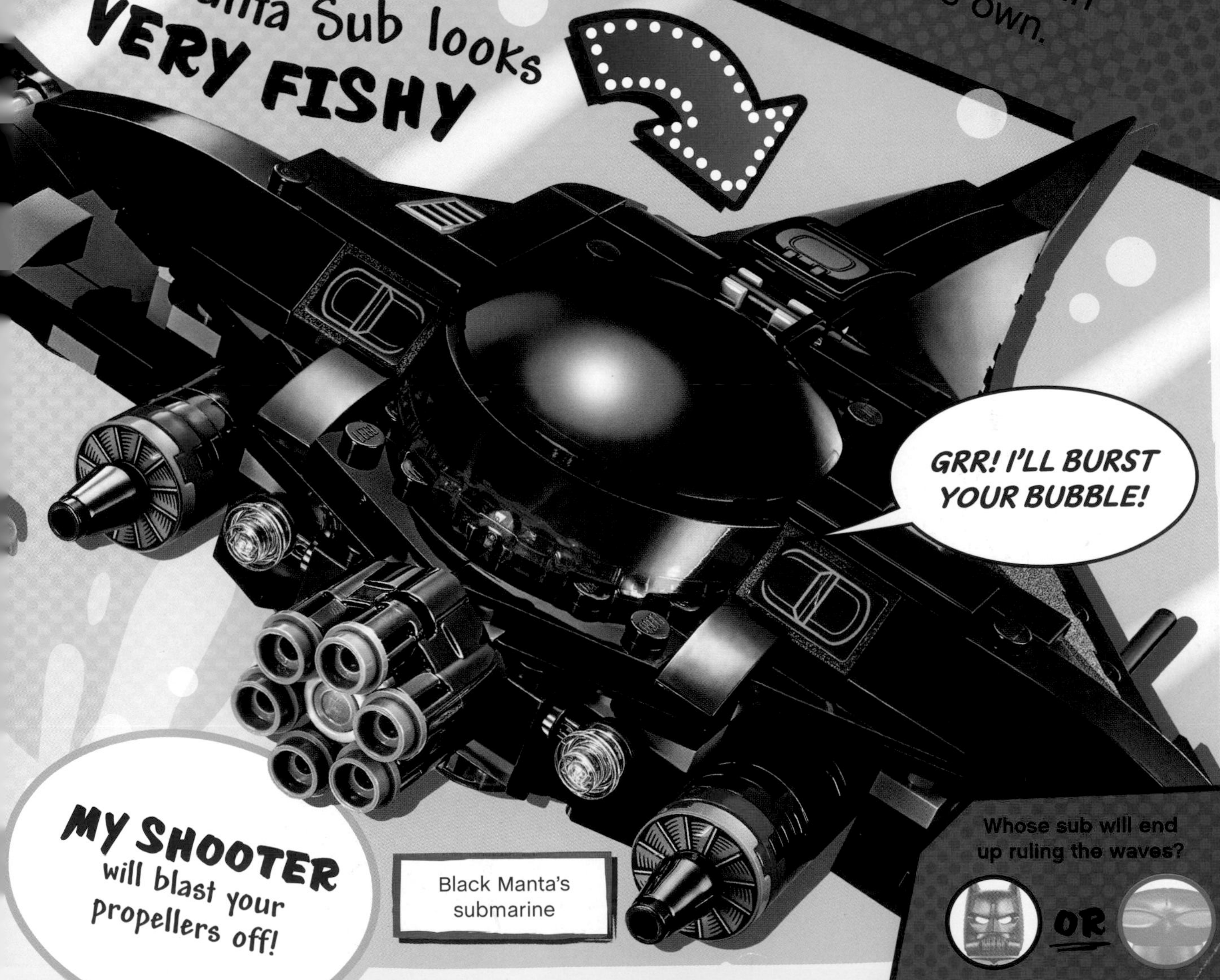

My Manta Sub looks VERY FISHY
GRR! I'LL BURST YOUR BUBBLE!
MY SHOOTER will blast your propellers off!

Black Manta's submarine

Whose sub will end up ruling the waves?

OR

SUPERMAN VS. BIZARRO

Bizarro is a backward version of Superman who wants to turn the world upside down. Can Superman put Bizarro's plans into reverse?

Superman has heat vision and freeze breath. That's the exact opposite of Bizarro's ice vision and flame breath!

Just call me the **MAN OF WHEEL!**

STOP YOUR BACK TALK, BIZARRO!

GIANT FISTS on my car pack a punch!

24

Superman's car

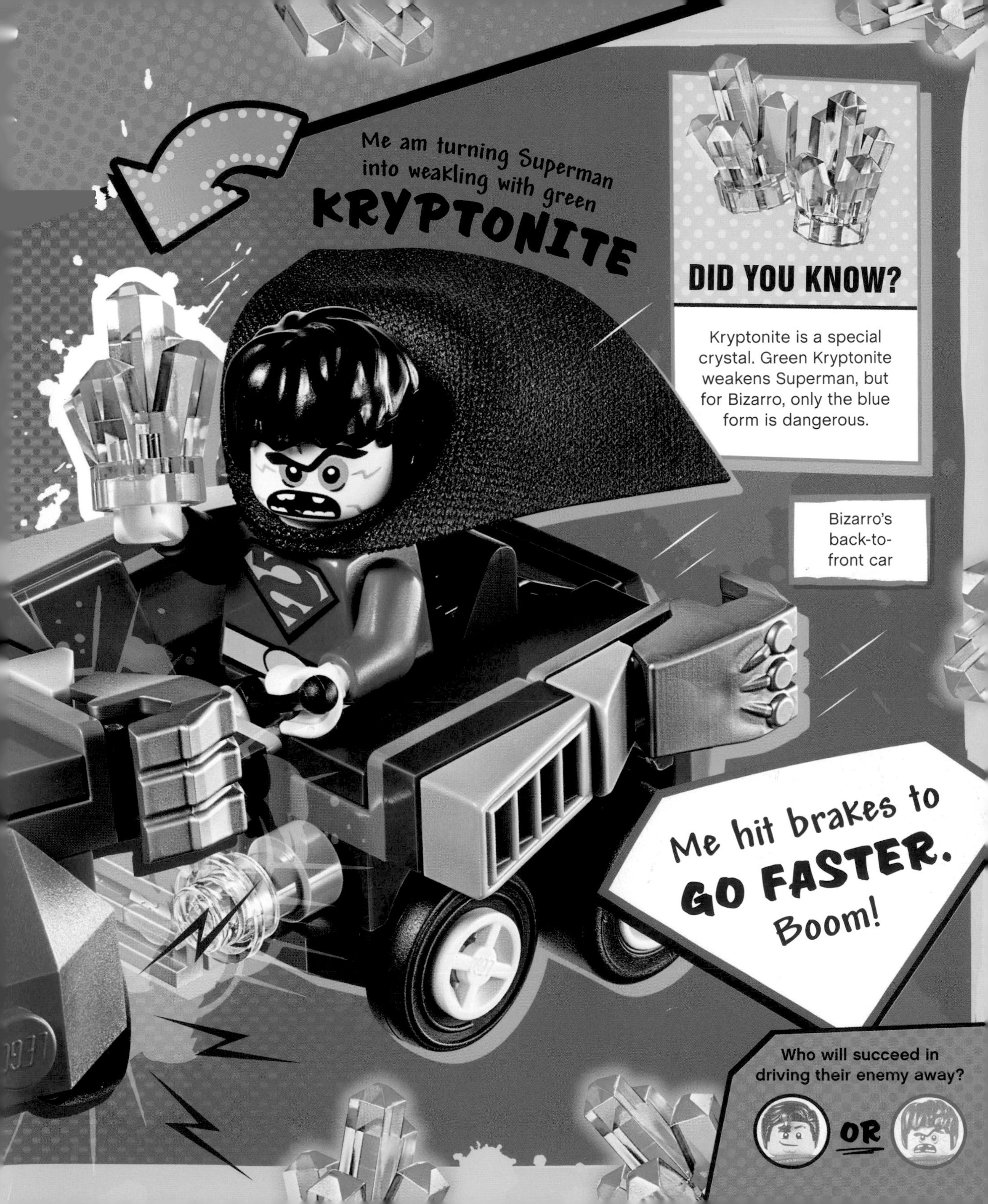
Me am turning Superman into weakling with green KRYPTONITE
Me hit brakes to GO FASTER. Boom!

Bizarro's back-to-front car

DID YOU KNOW?

Kryptonite is a special crystal. Green Kryptonite weakens Superman, but for Bizarro, only the blue form is dangerous.

Who will succeed in driving their enemy away?

OR

BATMAN VS. MR. FREEZE

What's that chill in the air? Mr. Freeze is zooming into town on his snow scooter, and he wants to freeze Batman! Things are about to heat up ...

The Batmobile has flaming exhausts. If it gets too close, it could put the snow scooter into meltdown!

You'll never be as **COOL** as me!

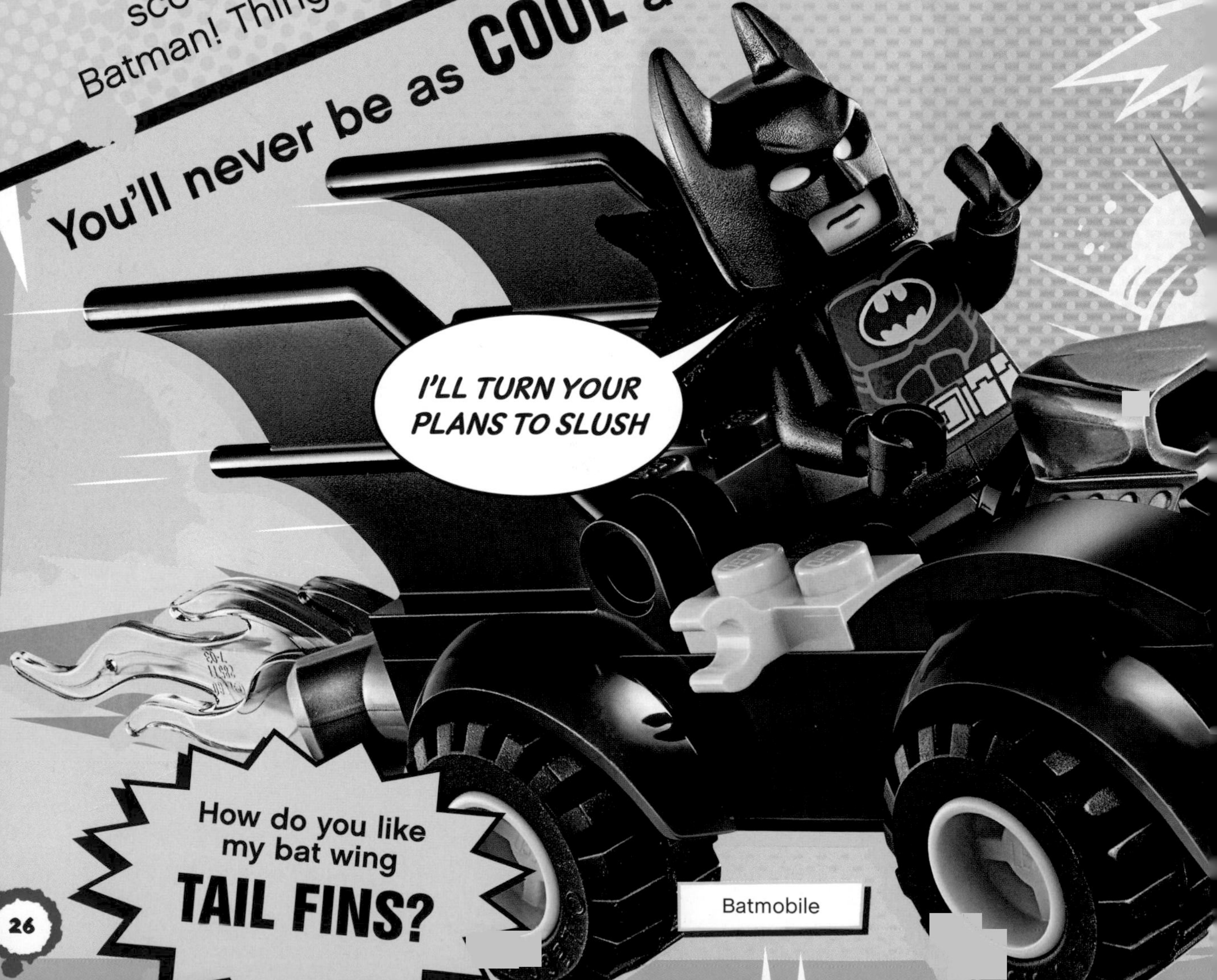
I'LL TURN YOUR PLANS TO SLUSH

Batmobile

How do you like my bat wing **TAIL FINS?**

Mr. Freeze's snow scooter

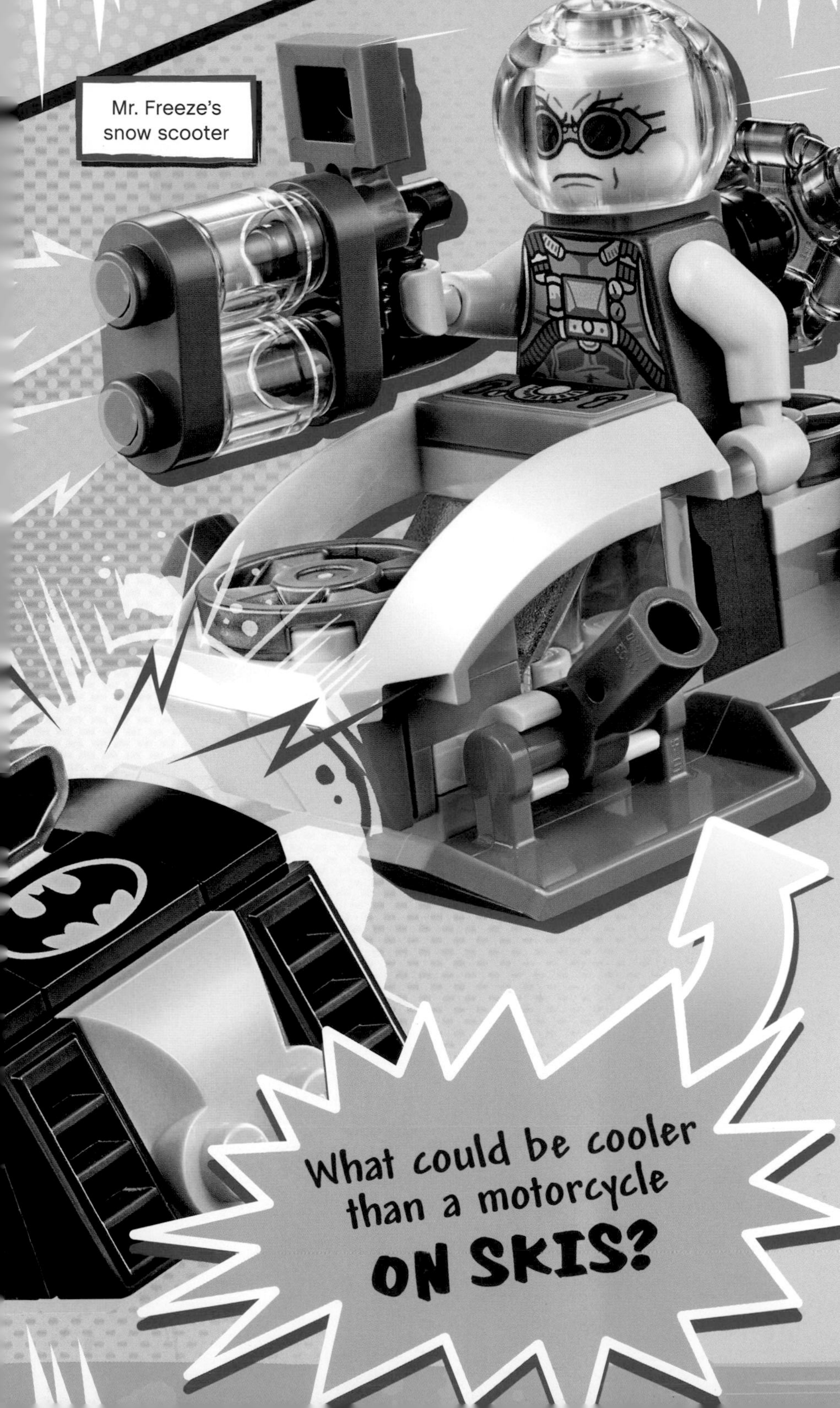
My red thermal GOGGLES scan for targets ... like you!
What could be cooler than a motorcycle ON SKIS?

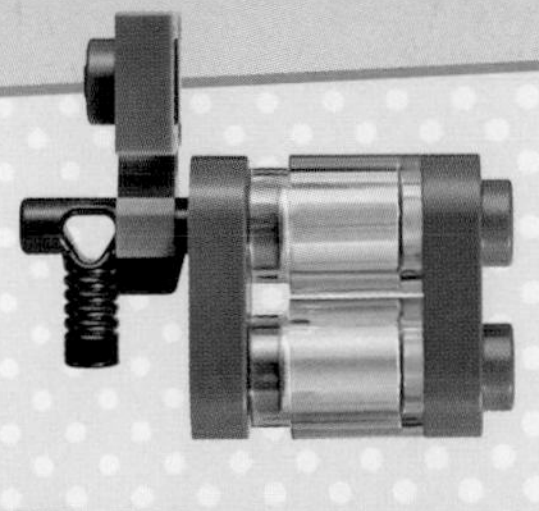

DID YOU KNOW?

Mr. Freeze is an expert in ice-cold technology. His favorite weapon is a twin-barreled freeze gun that turns enemies to ice.

Who will win this battle of heat vs. cold?

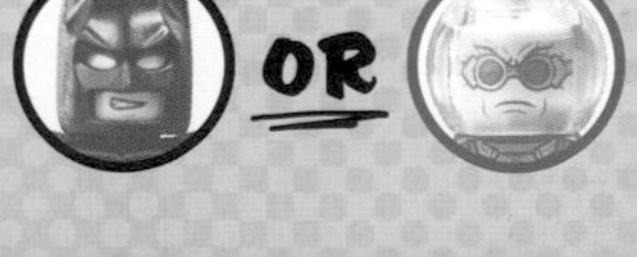
OR

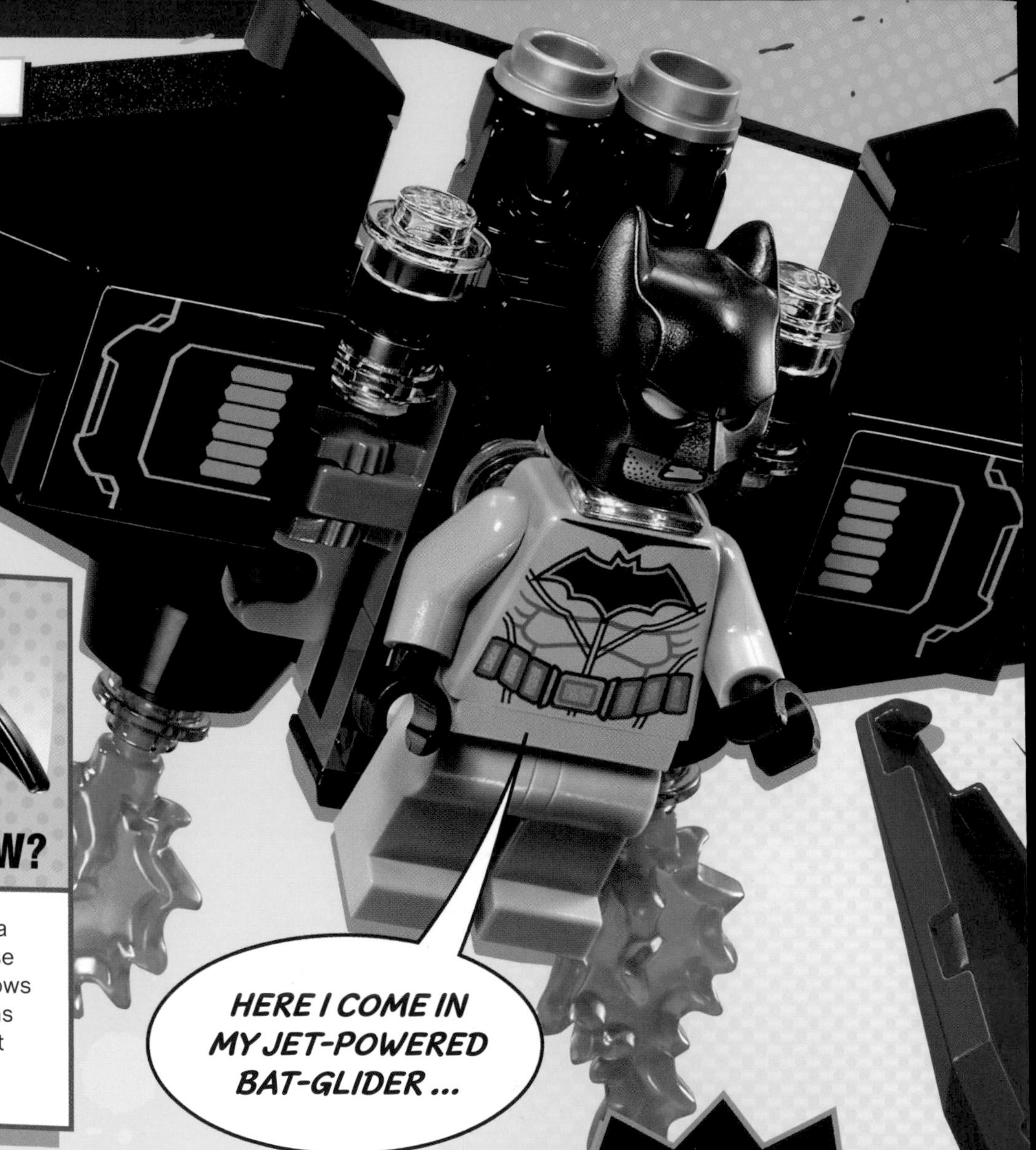

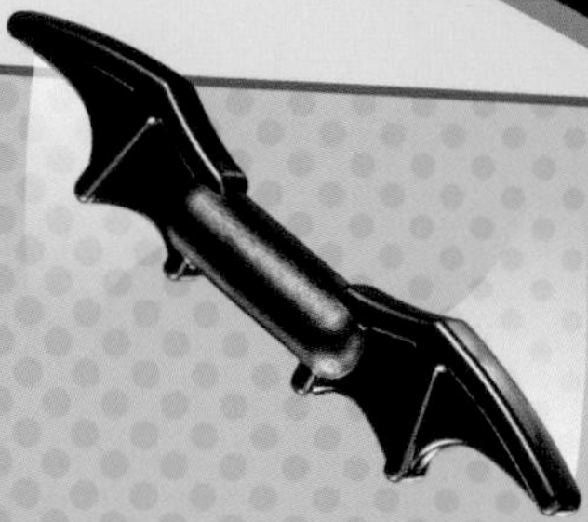

DID YOU KNOW?

Batman has made a promise never to use guns. Instead, he throws bat-shaped weapons called Batarangs at his enemies.

HERE I COME IN MY JET-POWERED BAT-GLIDER ...

I am a master of all the **MARTIAL ARTS** in the world. Beat that!

My **UTILITY BELT** is loaded with cool gadgets

BATMAN VS. LEX LUTHOR

Batman and Lex Luthor have no superpowers, so they rely on gadgets and skill. Who will win their air battle, and who will crash and burn?

Lex Luthor is a powerful businessman who can't stand Super Heroes. He's always trying to chase them out of Metropolis.

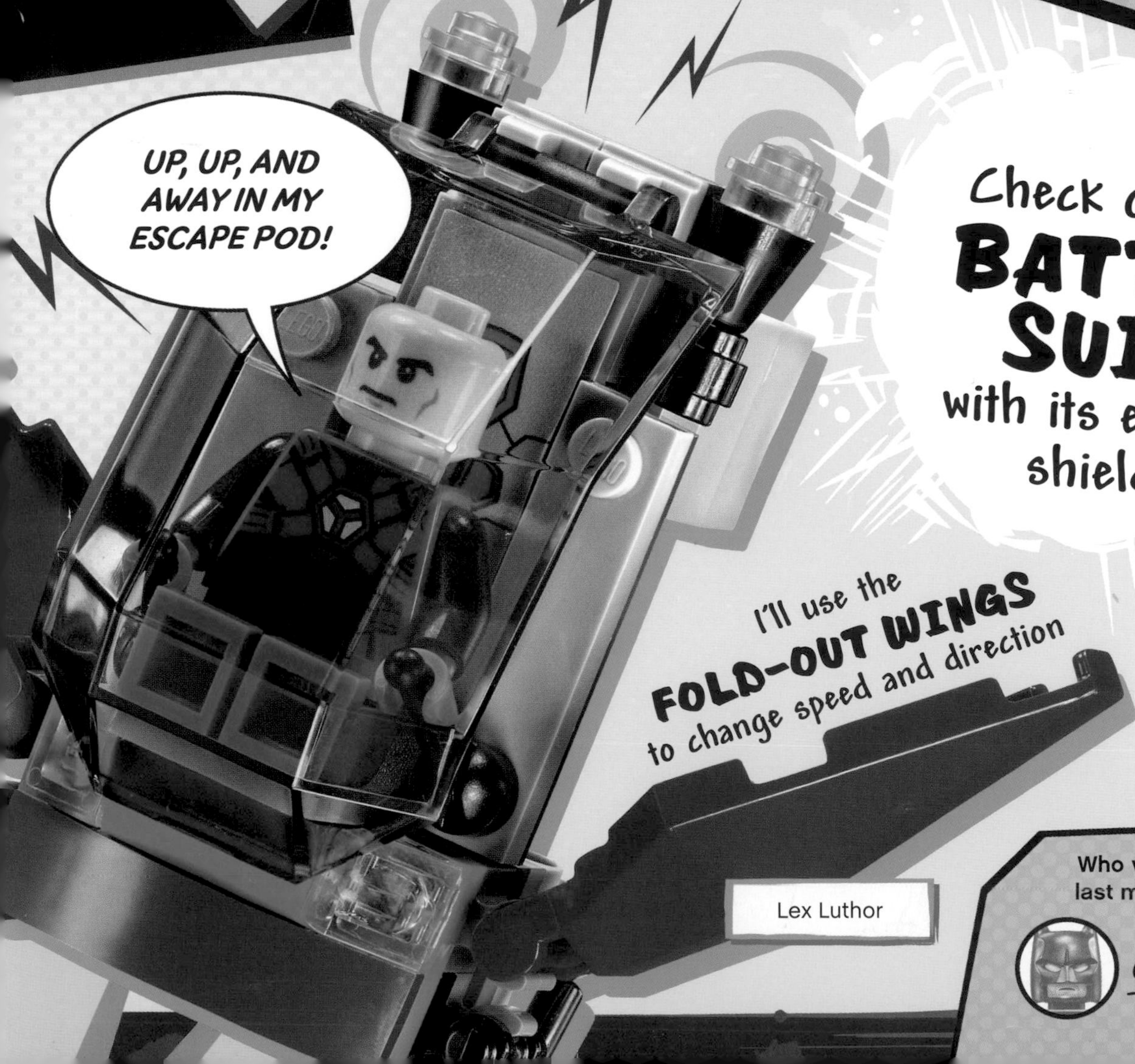

UP, UP, AND AWAY IN MY ESCAPE POD!
Check out my BATTLE SUIT with its energy shield!
I'll use the FOLD-OUT WINGS to change speed and direction
Lex Luthor

Who will be the last man flying?

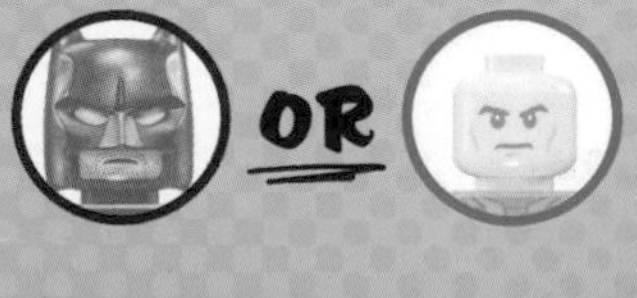

OR

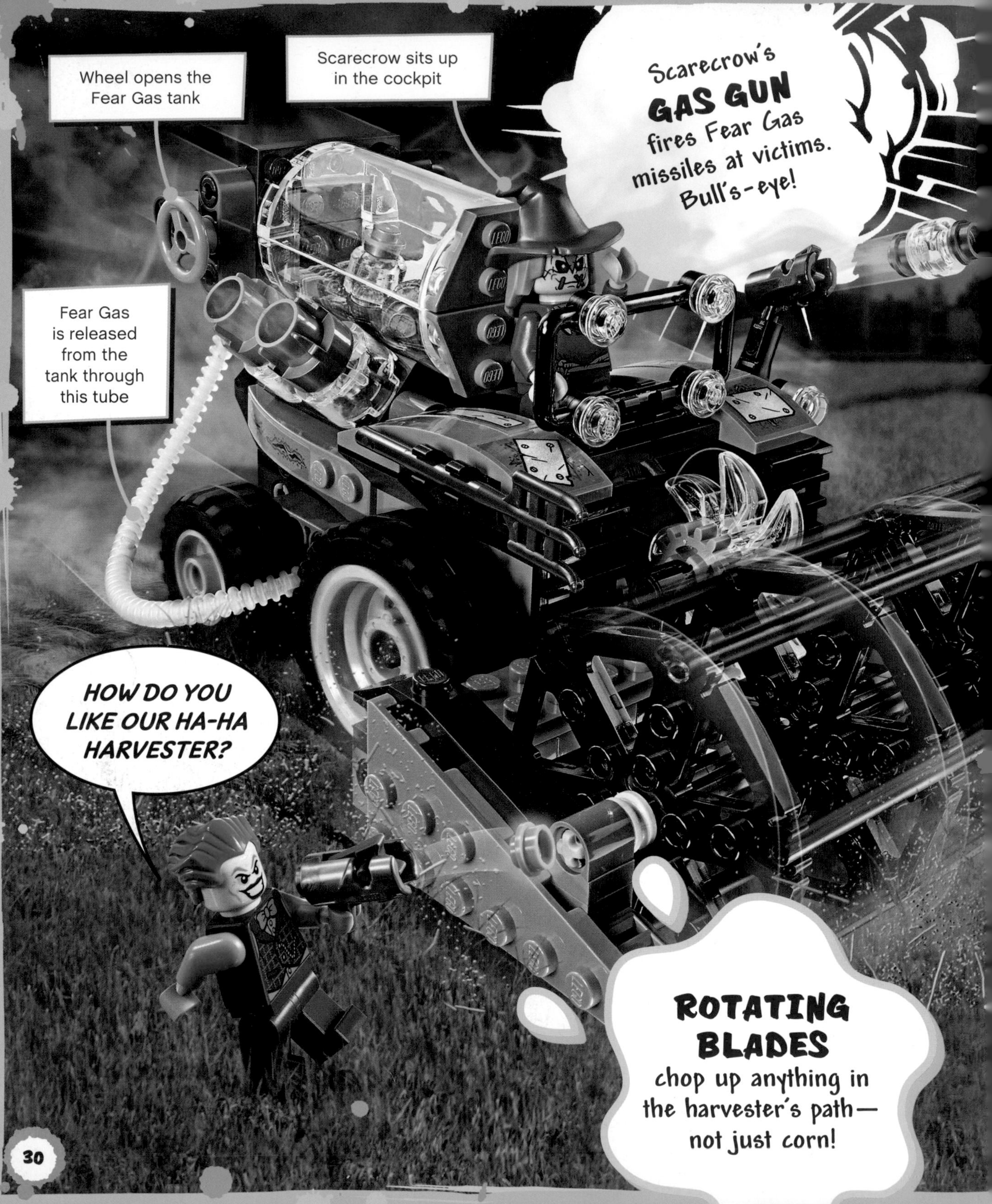
Wheel opens the Fear Gas tank
Scarecrow sits up in the cockpit
Scarecrow's GAS GUN fires Fear Gas missiles at victims. Bull's-eye!
Fear Gas is released from the tank through this tube
HOW DO YOU LIKE OUR HA-HA HARVESTER?
ROTATING BLADES chop up anything in the harvester's path—not just corn!

HARVEST OF FEAR

It's countryside chaos! The Joker and Scarecrow are menacing a poor farmer in their crazy harvester. Drive, farmer, drive ...

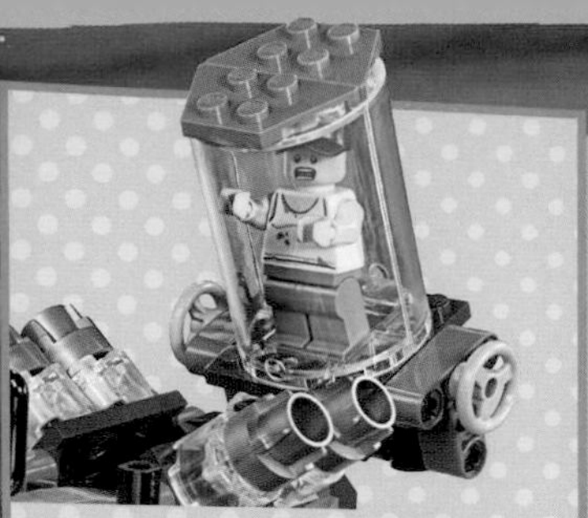

DID YOU KNOW?

The harvester's gas tank holds Fear Gas, ready to fire at victims! It is also big enough to trap the farmer inside!

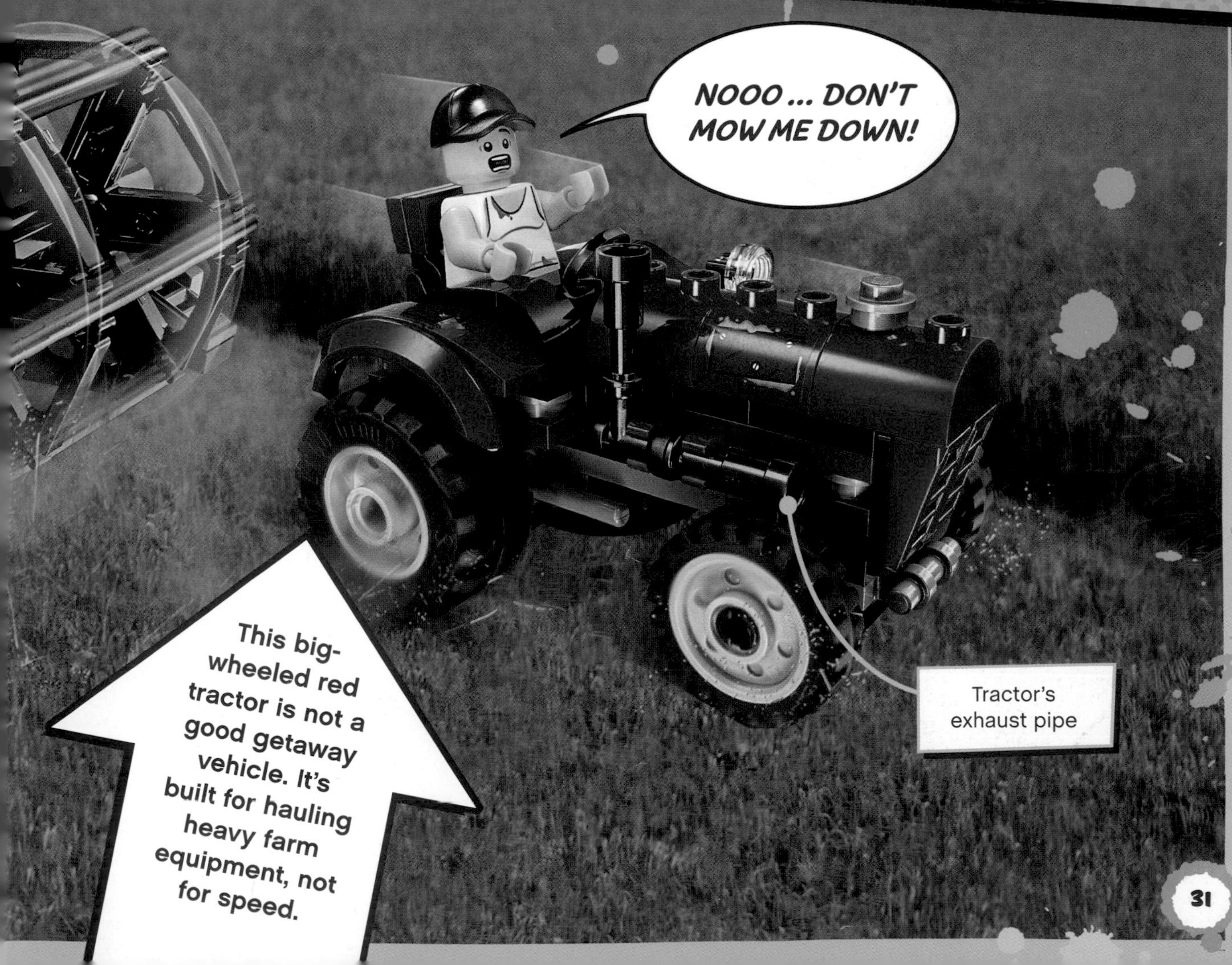
NOOO ... DON'T MOW ME DOWN!
Tractor's exhaust pipe

This big-wheeled red tractor is not a good getaway vehicle. It's built for hauling heavy farm equipment, not for speed.

THE FLASH VS. CAPTAIN COLD

Captain Cold hopes to push The Flash off the road, freeze him, and pelt him with snow cones! Can The Flash disarm him in time?

The Flash is often attacked by a team of super-villains called the Rogues. The team is led by The Flash's archenemy, Captain Cold!

The Flash's car

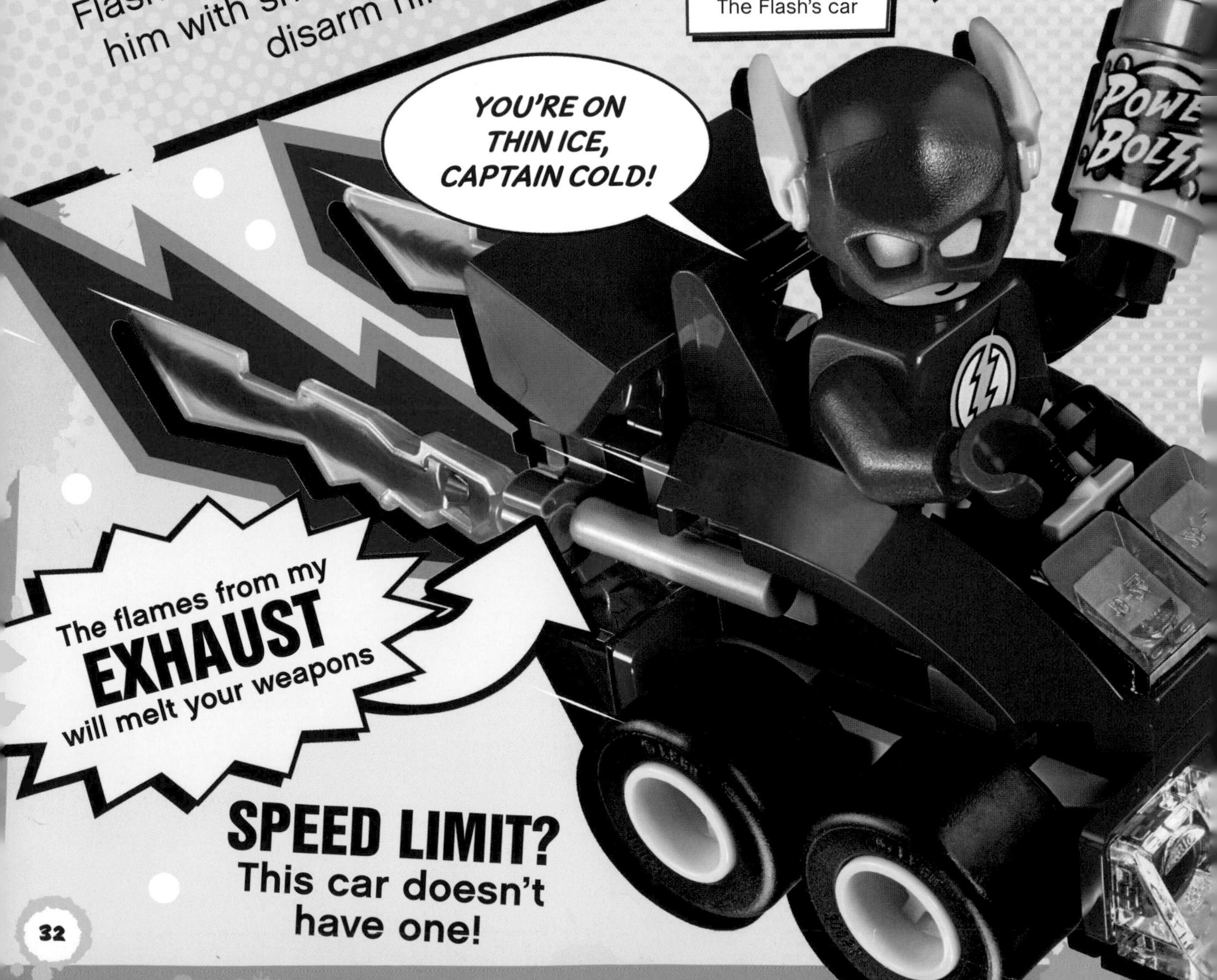

YOU'RE ON THIN ICE, CAPTAIN COLD!
The flames from my EXHAUST will melt your weapons

SPEED LIMIT? This car doesn't have one!

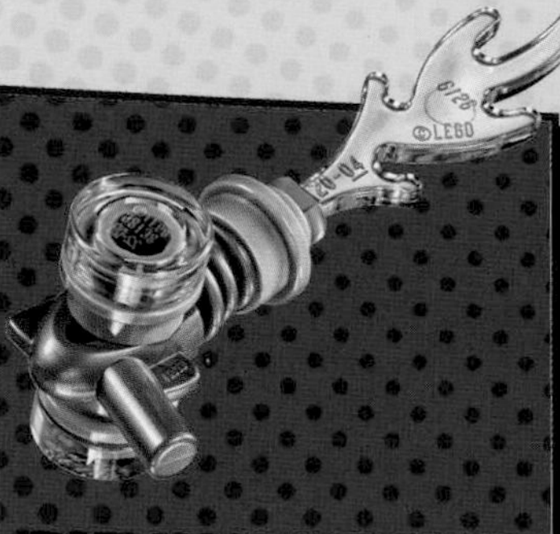

DID YOU KNOW?

Captain Cold's gun freezes people's atoms so they can't move. He once froze a whole city in its tracks!

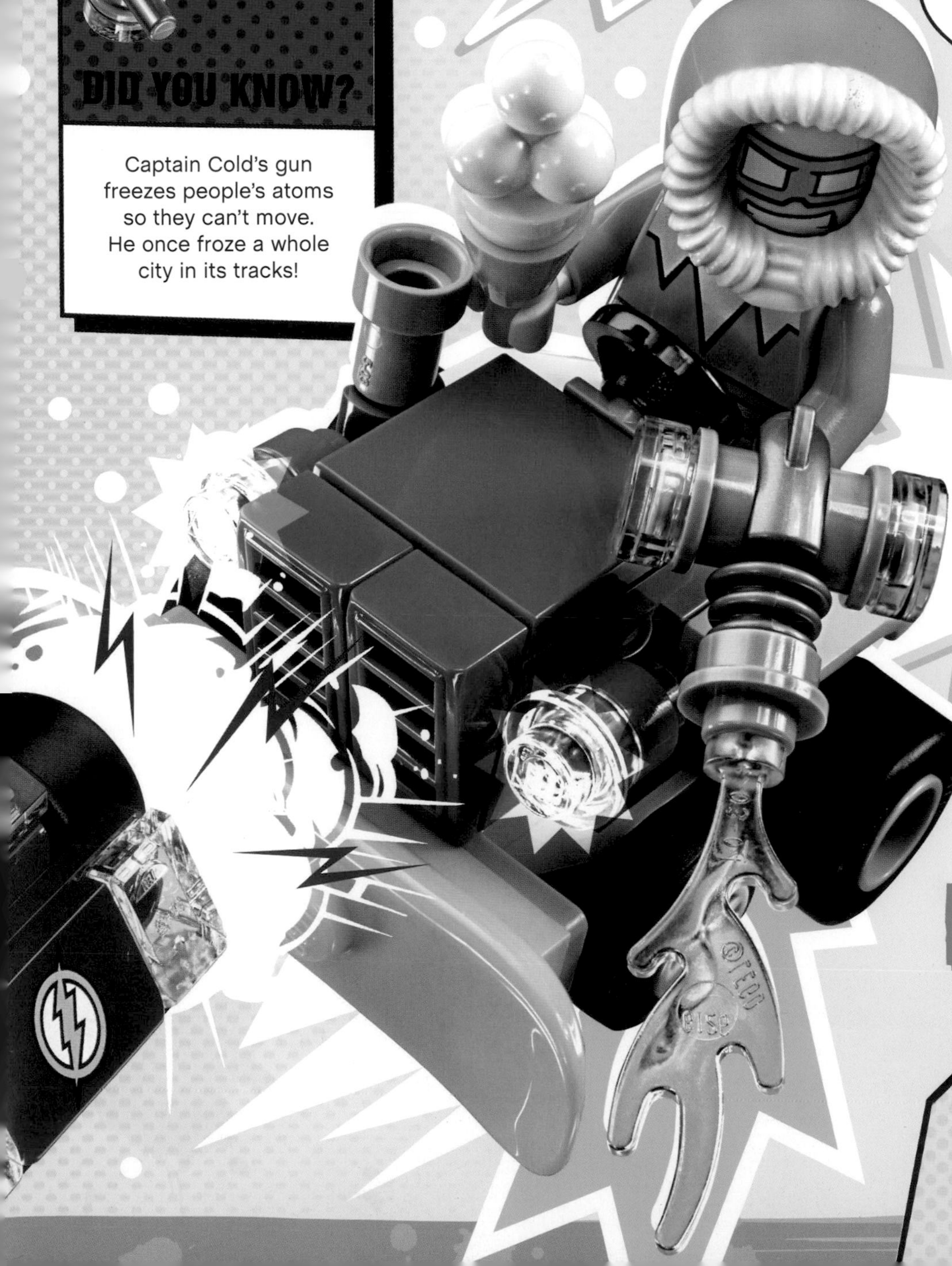

I feel so cool in my ICE-BLUE PARKA and snow visor
THIS SHOULD BE A PUSHOVER!
I'll shove you aside with my SNOWPLOW

Captain Cold's snowplow

Who will win? The speedster or the freezer?

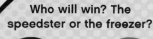

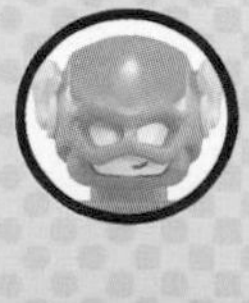
OR
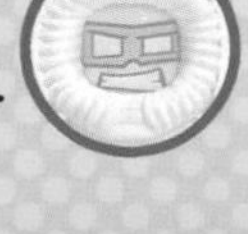

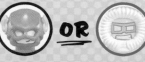

BATWOMAN VS. BROTHER EYE

Brother Eye is a satellite gone rogue. It spreads a virus that turns people into scary cyber-soldiers! Can Batwoman knock it out of the sky?

There's no doubt who owns this craft! It has bat wings, shooters, and places to attach bat weapons and elements.

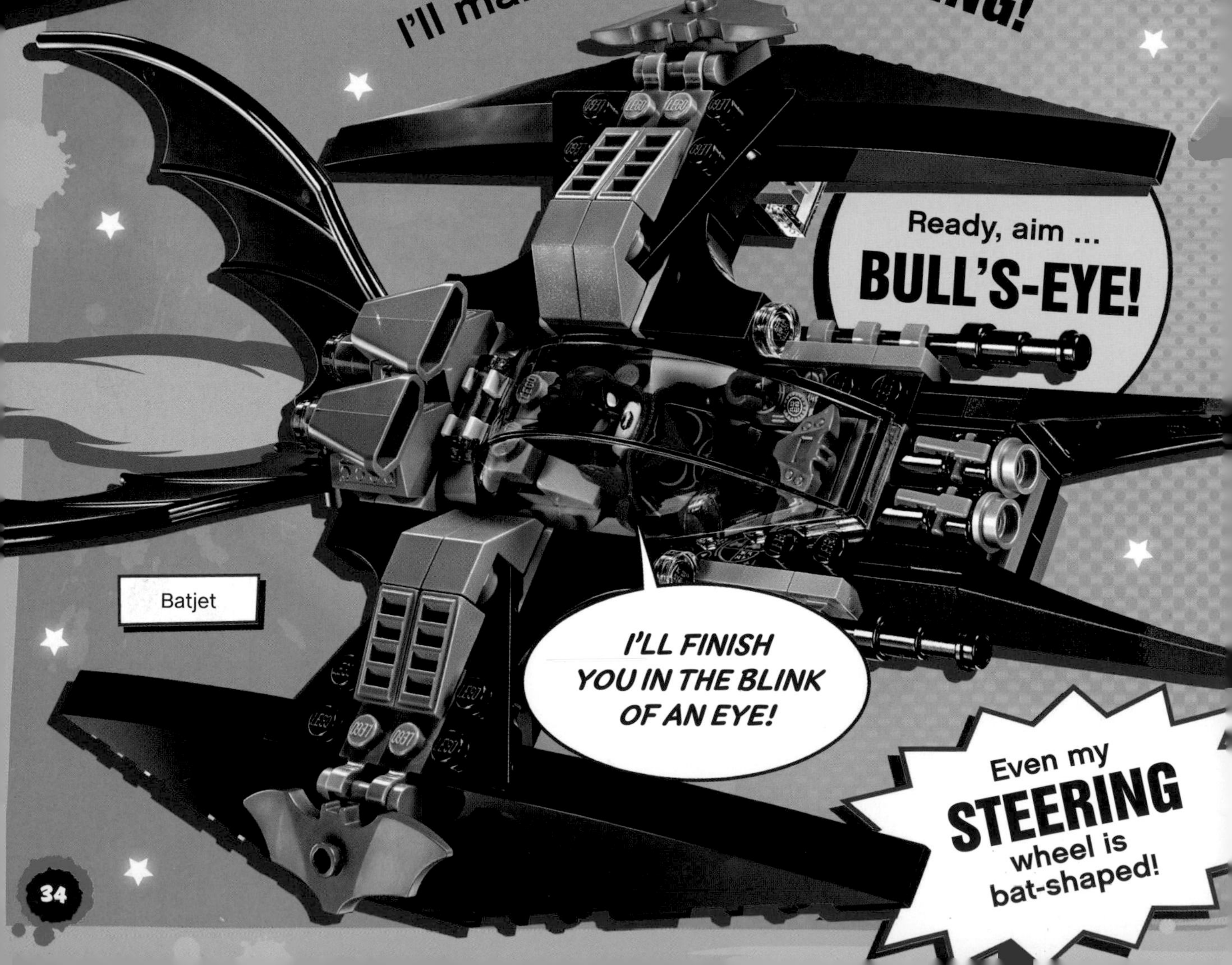

I'll make you STOP STARING!
Ready, aim ... BULL'S-EYE!
I'LL FINISH YOU IN THE BLINK OF AN EYE!
Even my STEERING wheel is bat-shaped!

Batjet

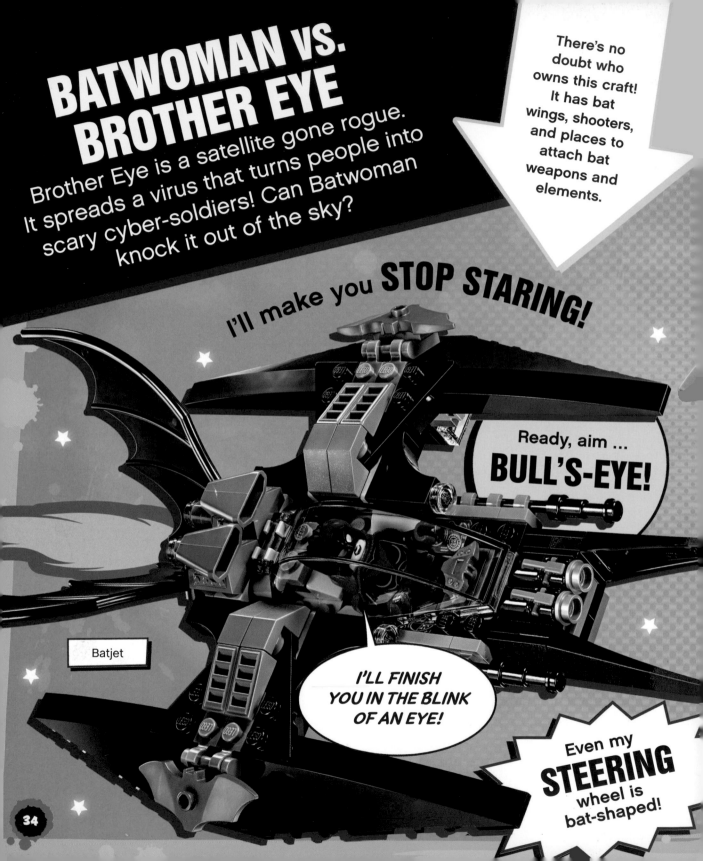

I'll befuddle you with **EYE-POPPING** energy beams!

DID YOU KNOW?

Brother Eye's soldiers are known as OMACs. OMAC stands for Observational Metahuman Activity Construct. Phew!

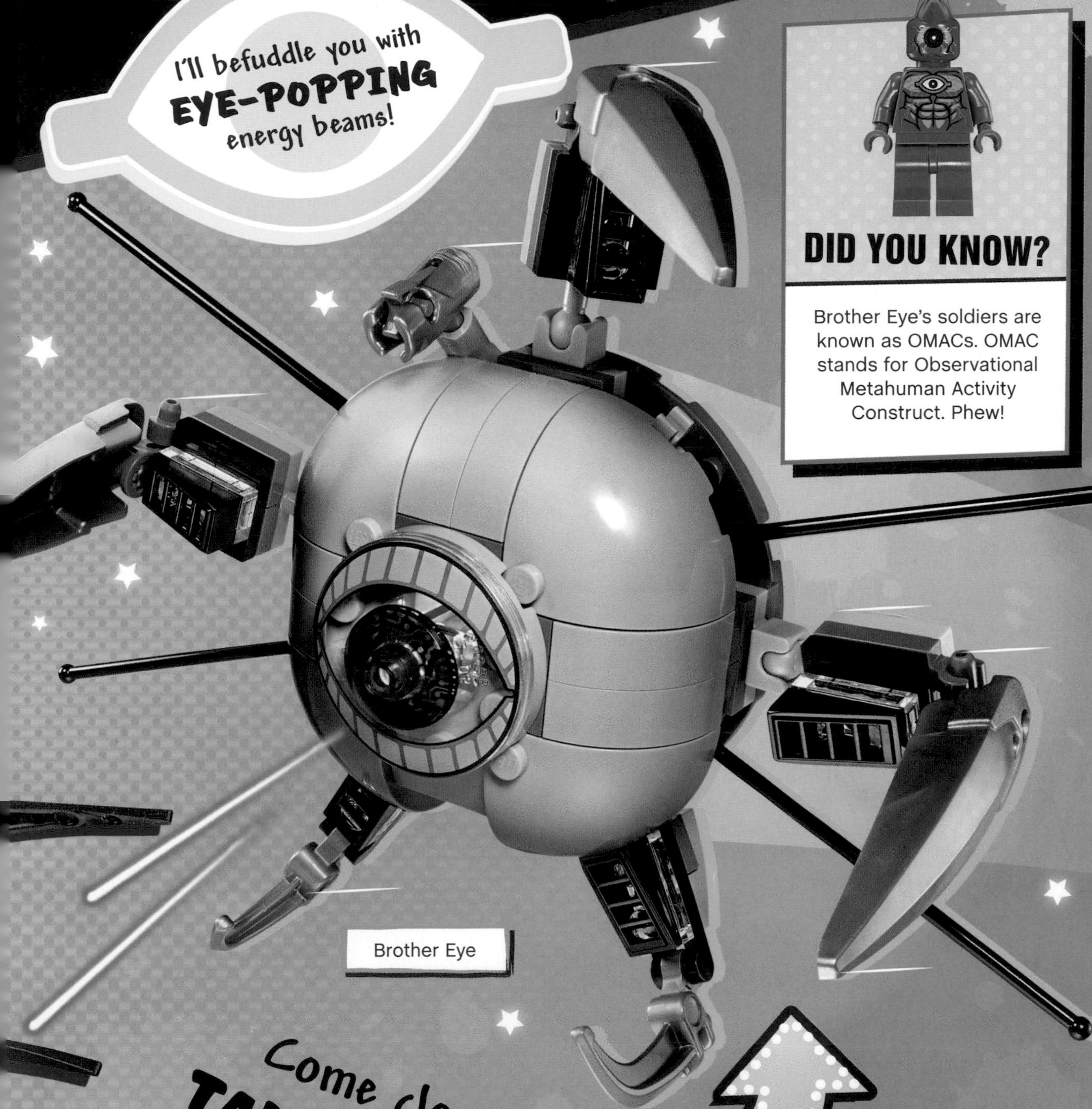

Brother Eye

Come closer ... my **TALONS AWAIT!**

Who will win this space struggle?

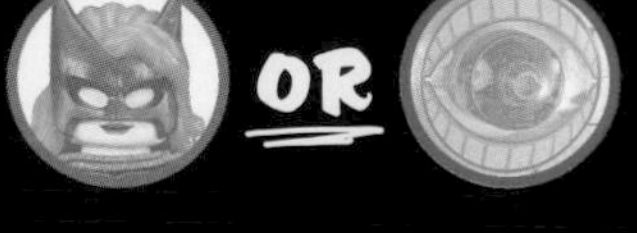
OR

BATMAN VS. KILLER MOTH

Killer Moth is buzzing in to face off with Batman. The Dark Knight is coming right back at him in his flame-red Batcopter. The fight is on!

Beware, moths! Batman's flame-red Batcopter has wings and a rotor. The cockpit gives Batman a great view for aiming Batarangs!

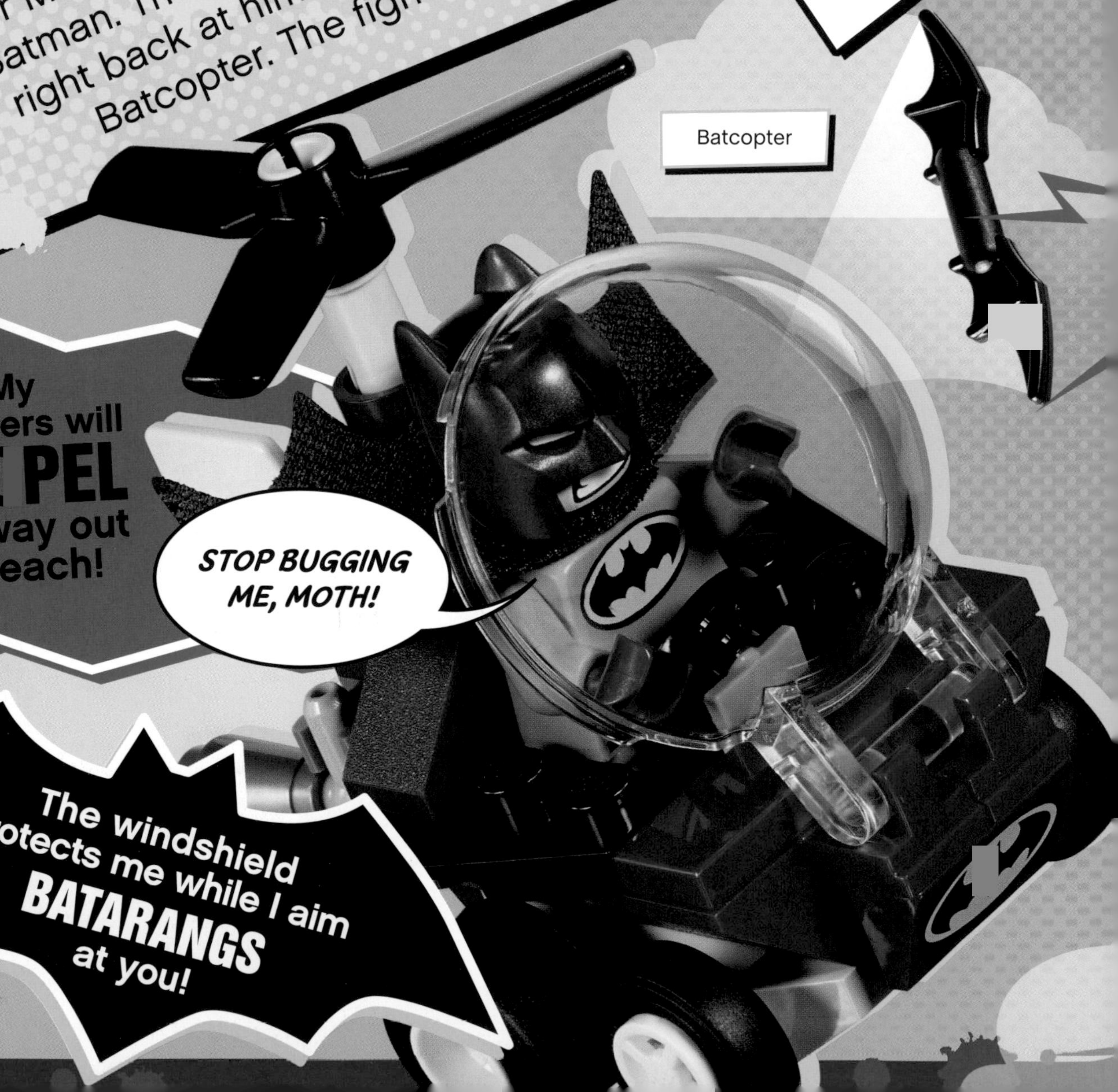

Batcopter
My boosters will PROPEL me way out of reach!
STOP BUGGING ME, MOTH!
The windshield protects me while I aim BATARANGS at you!

I'll squirt you with goo from my **COCOON GUN**

My agile flyer can **FLY CIRCLES AROUND YOU**

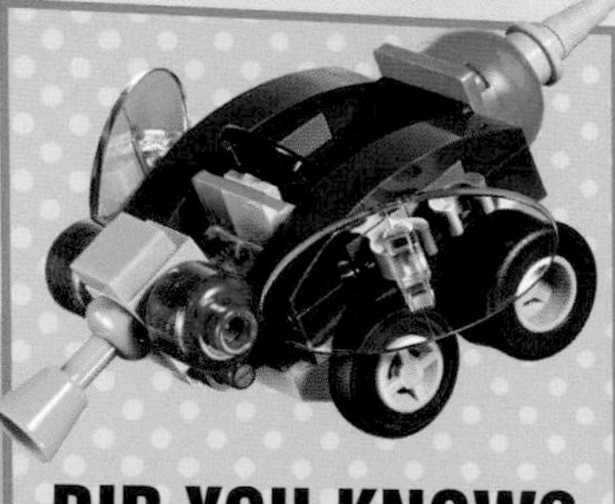

DID YOU KNOW?

Killer Moth's flyer looks like a big bug. It has a stinger in the tail and a gun in the nose that sprays sleeping gas at enemies!

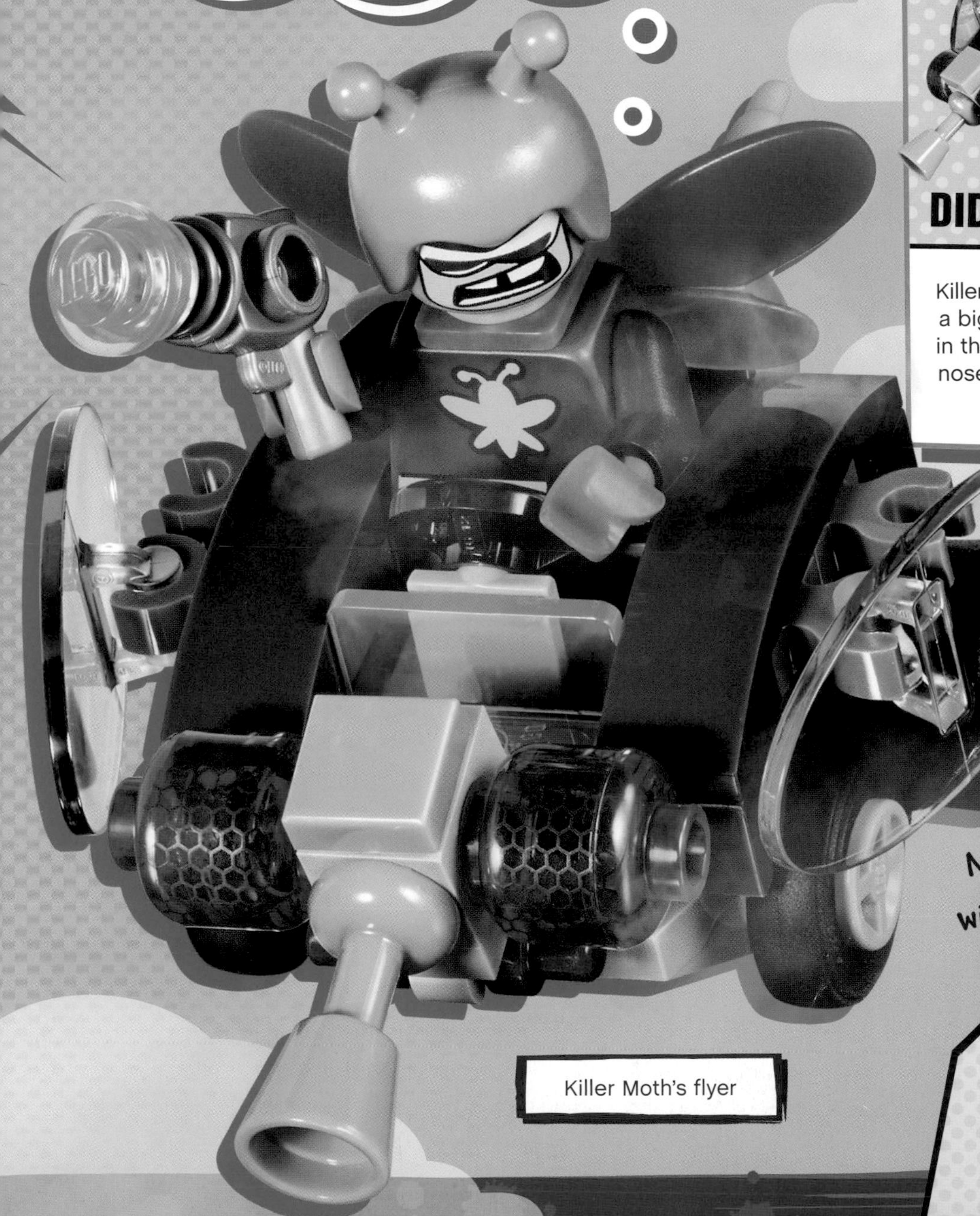

Killer Moth's flyer

My flyer's wings will **SWAT** your Batarang away!

Which one will bring his foe crashing down?

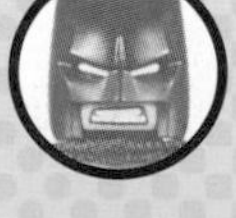 **OR** 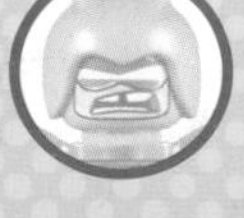

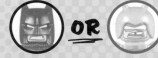

BATMAN VS. HARLEY QUINN

Batman's out on his Batcycle, but someone's chasing him! It's Harley Quinn, and she wants to race. Can her bike really beat Batman's?

The Batcycle is designed to be bulletproof … but it has never been tested against giant mallet attacks! Will it hold up?

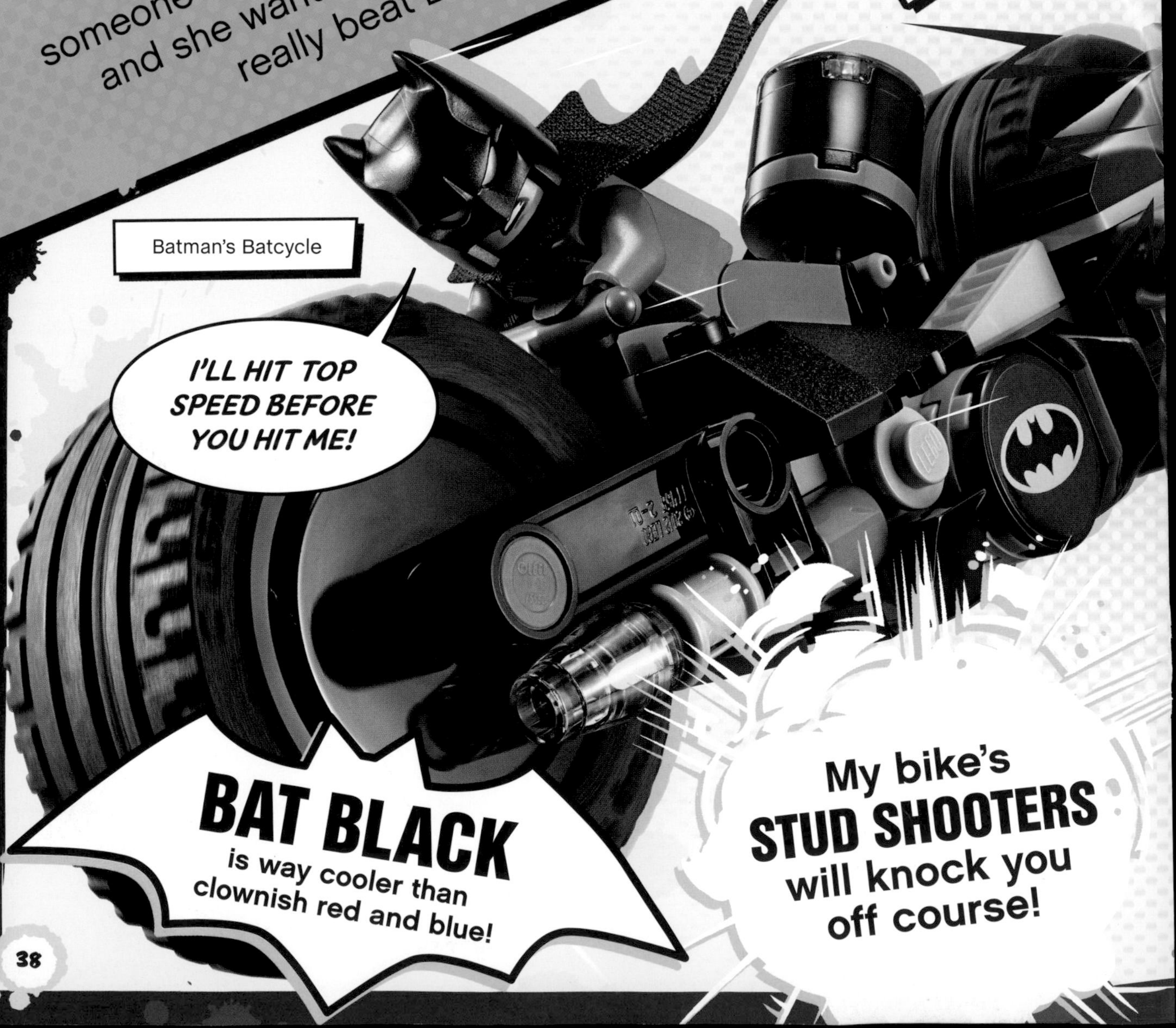
Batman's Batcycle
I'LL HIT TOP SPEED BEFORE YOU HIT ME!
BAT BLACK is way cooler than clownish red and blue!
My bike's STUD SHOOTERS will knock you off course!

You'll flip when my flip-out **MALLET** bops you!

YOU'RE DRIVING ME BATTY!

Harley Quinn's bike

That's not me squealing ... it's my **GIANT TIRES!**

I'm a **BIG WHEEL** in the world of crime, don't you know ...

DID YOU KNOW?

Harley is small but strong. Her favorite weapon is a giant mallet that's almost as big as she is!

Who will win the race into Gotham City?

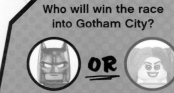

OR

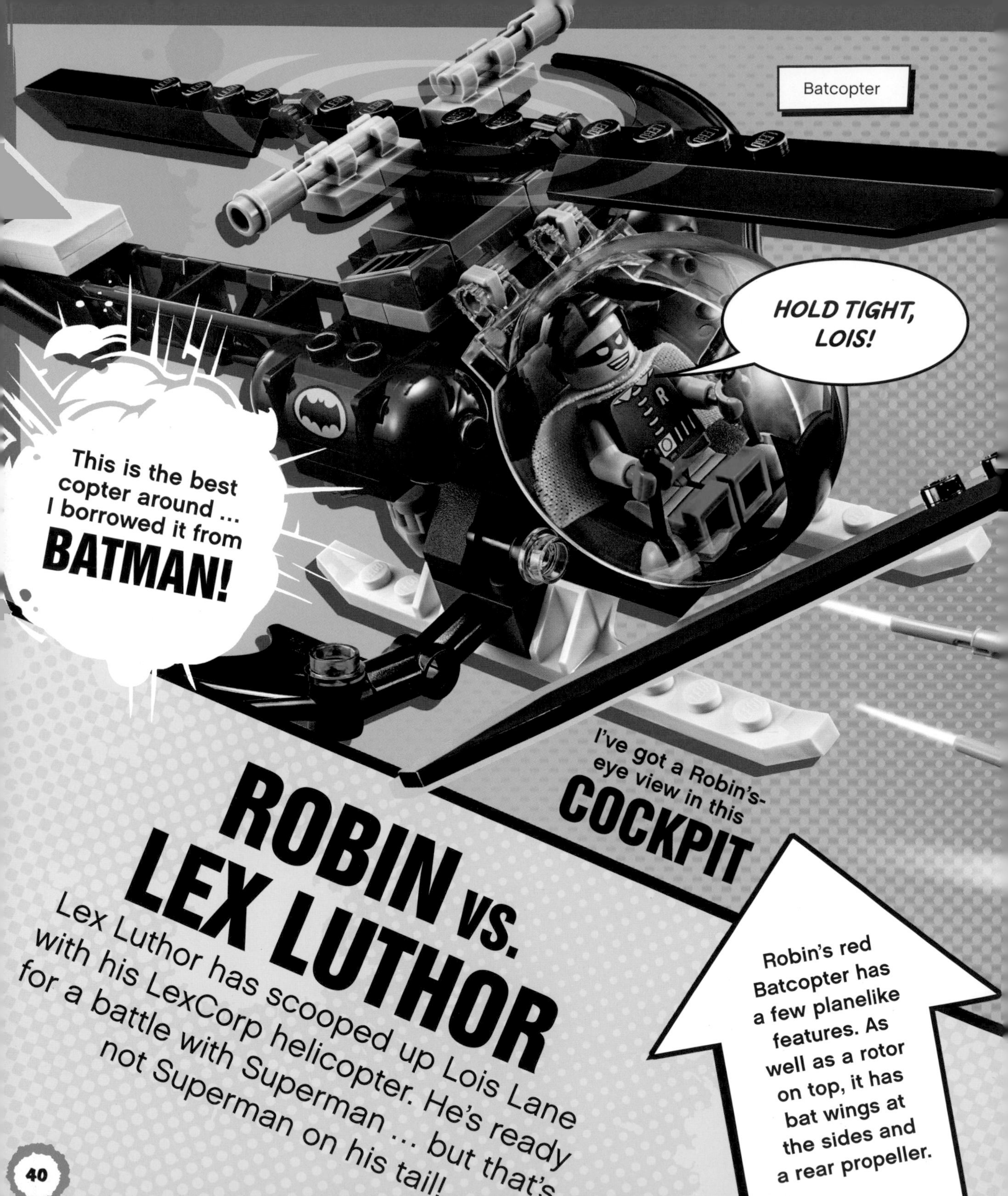
Batcopter
HOLD TIGHT, LOIS!
This is the best copter around … I borrowed it from BATMAN!

I've got a Robin's-eye view in this **COCKPIT**

ROBIN VS. LEX LUTHOR

Lex Luthor has scooped up Lois Lane with his LexCorp helicopter. He's ready for a battle with Superman … but that's not Superman on his tail!

Robin's red Batcopter has a few planelike features. As well as a rotor on top, it has bat wings at the sides and a rear propeller.

Y ROTOR is bigger than yours!

DID YOU KNOW?

As a young man, Lex Luthor had long, thick red hair. He later has a bald head.

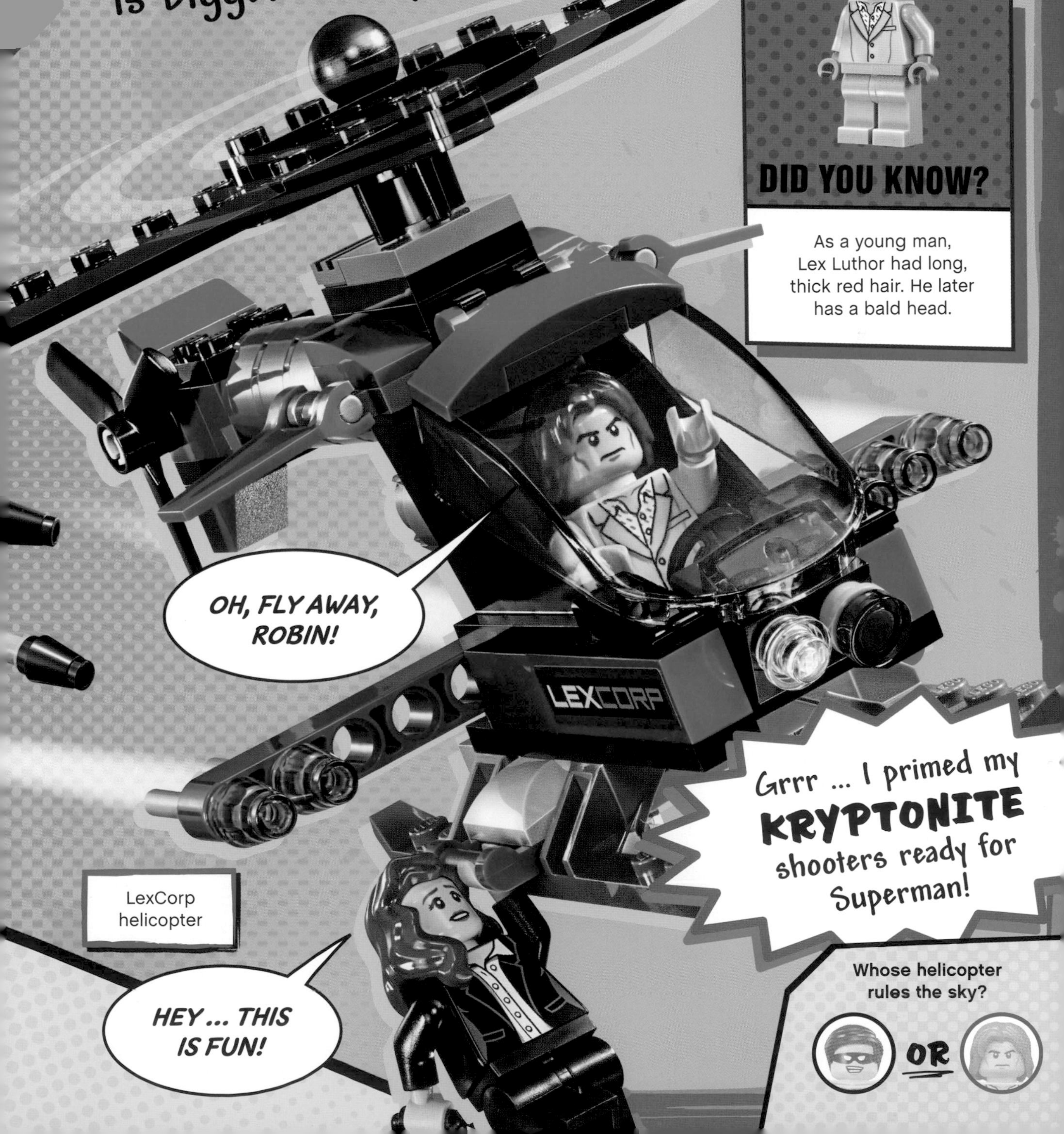
OH, FLY AWAY, ROBIN!
LEXCORP
Grrr ... I primed my KRYPTONITE shooters ready for Superman!
HEY ... THIS IS FUN!

LexCorp helicopter

Whose helicopter rules the sky?

OR

BATMAN VS. BANE

There's a driller on the road! It's big, bad Bane trying to prove he's stronger than Batman. But Batman just won't give way. It's driving Bane crazy!

Bane believes Batman is the toughest Super Hero of all. He has become obsessed with beating the Dark Knight!

Your drill is just **BORING!**

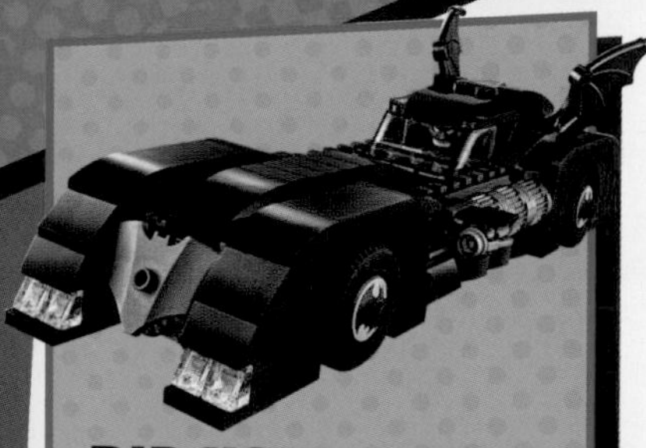

Batmobile

DID YOU KNOW?

Batman has lots of other Batmobiles. This one has a huge engine, bat wing tail fins, and bat-symbols on the hubcaps.

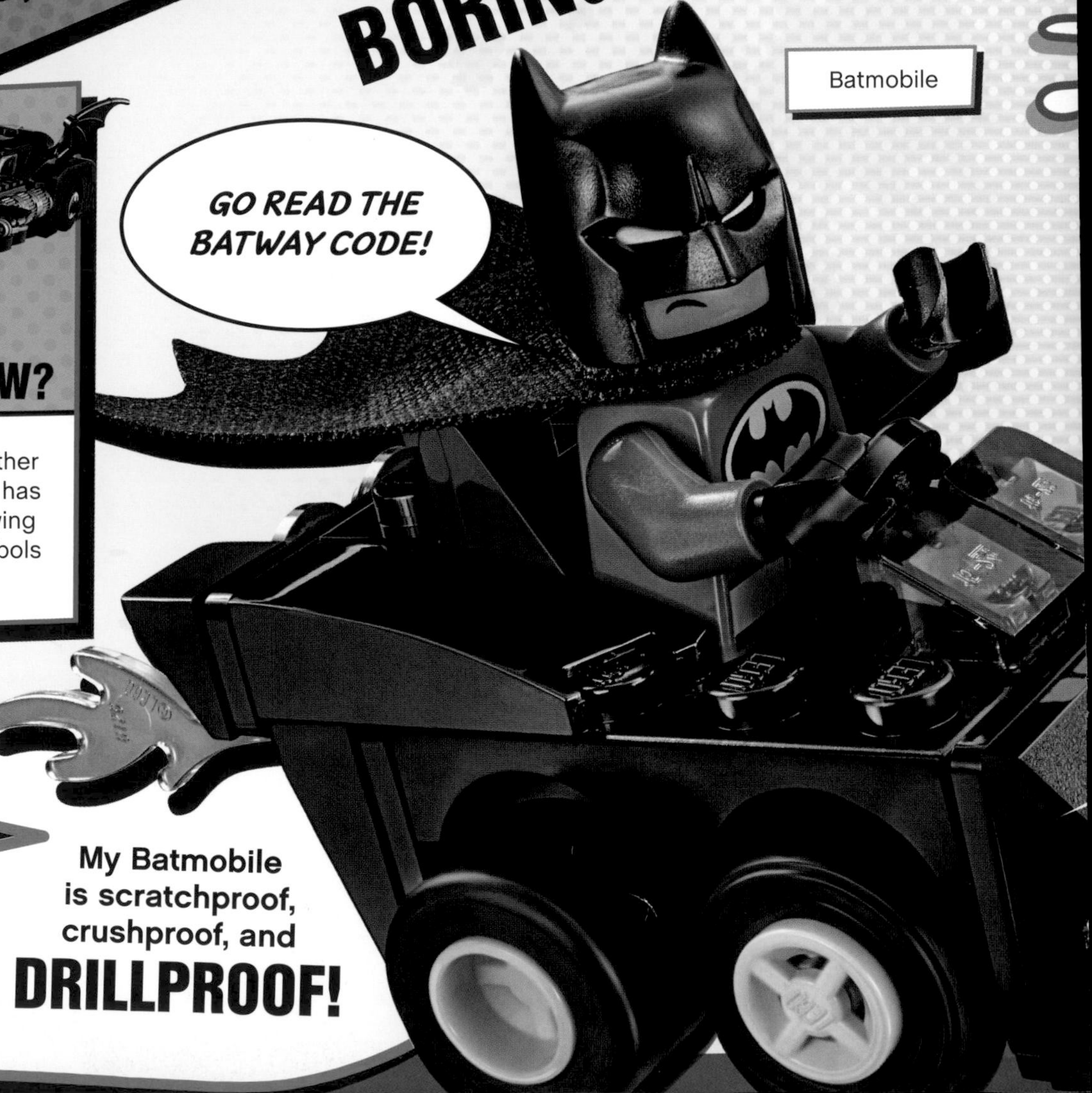
GO READ THE BATWAY CODE!

My Batmobile is scratchproof, crushproof, and **DRILLPROOF!**

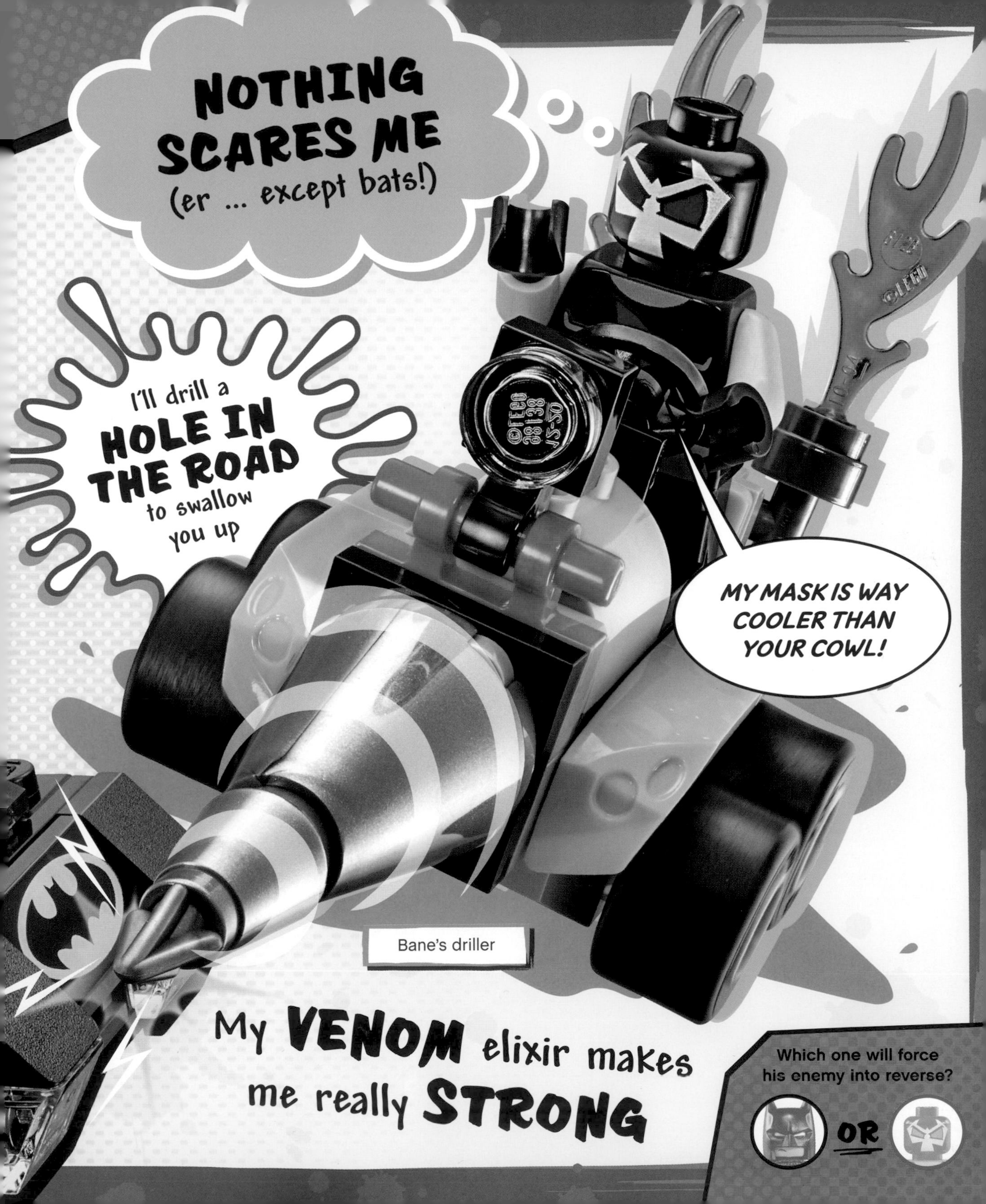
NOTHING SCARES ME
(er ... except bats!)
I'll drill a HOLE IN THE ROAD to swallow you up
MY MASK IS WAY COOLER THAN YOUR COWL!
My VENOM elixir makes me really STRONG
OR
Bane's driller

Which one will force his enemy into reverse?

RED HOOD VS. HARLEY

Red Hood is a very determined member of the Bat-Family. Maybe he's the one to stop Harley Quinn and her not-so-funny criminal capers!

Red Hood never takes his hood off in public. It hides the scars he got in an attack by the Joker, Harley Quinn's partner in crime.

CRIME MAKES ME SEE RED!

MY FAST MOTORCYCLE can catch up to any crook!

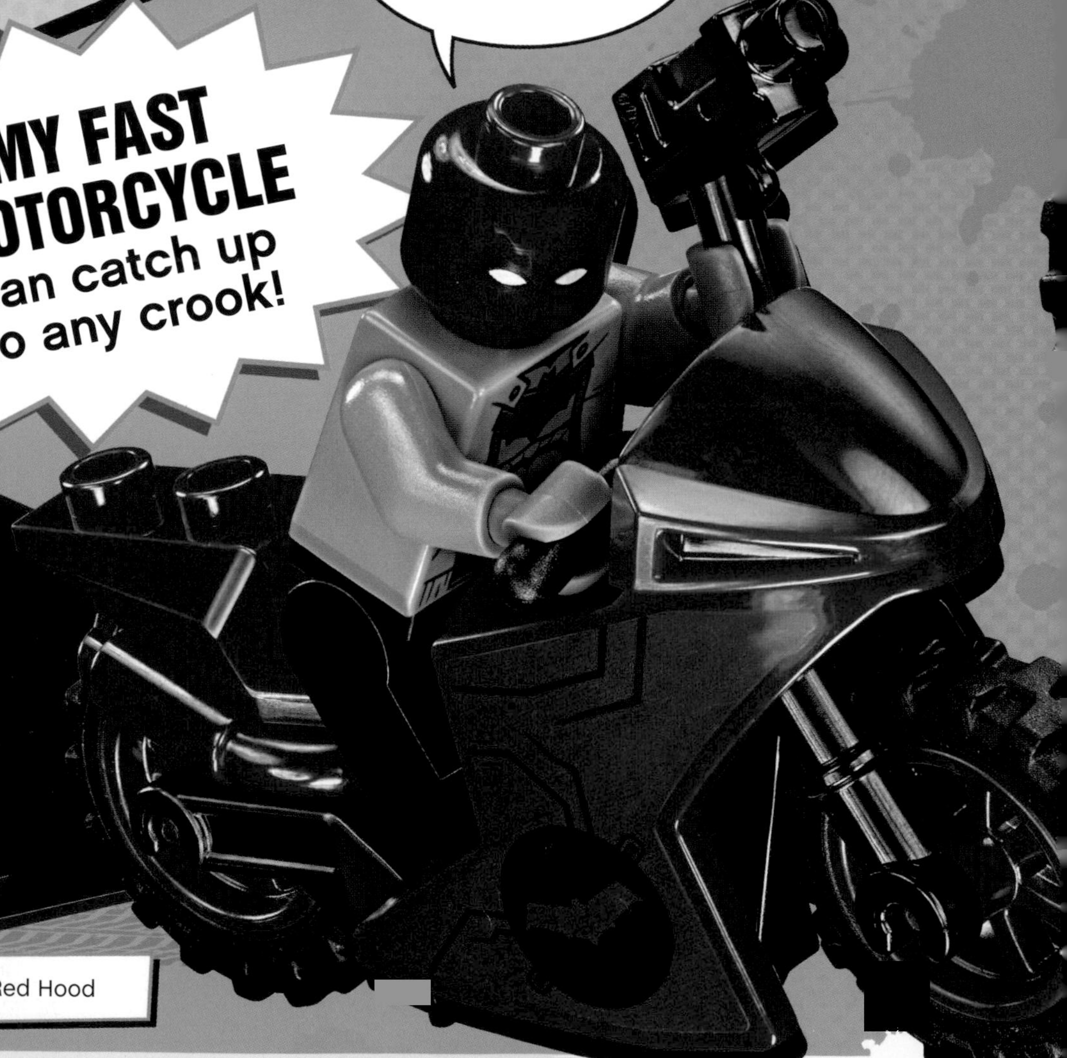

Check out the cool **SYMBOL** on my motorcycle

Red Hood

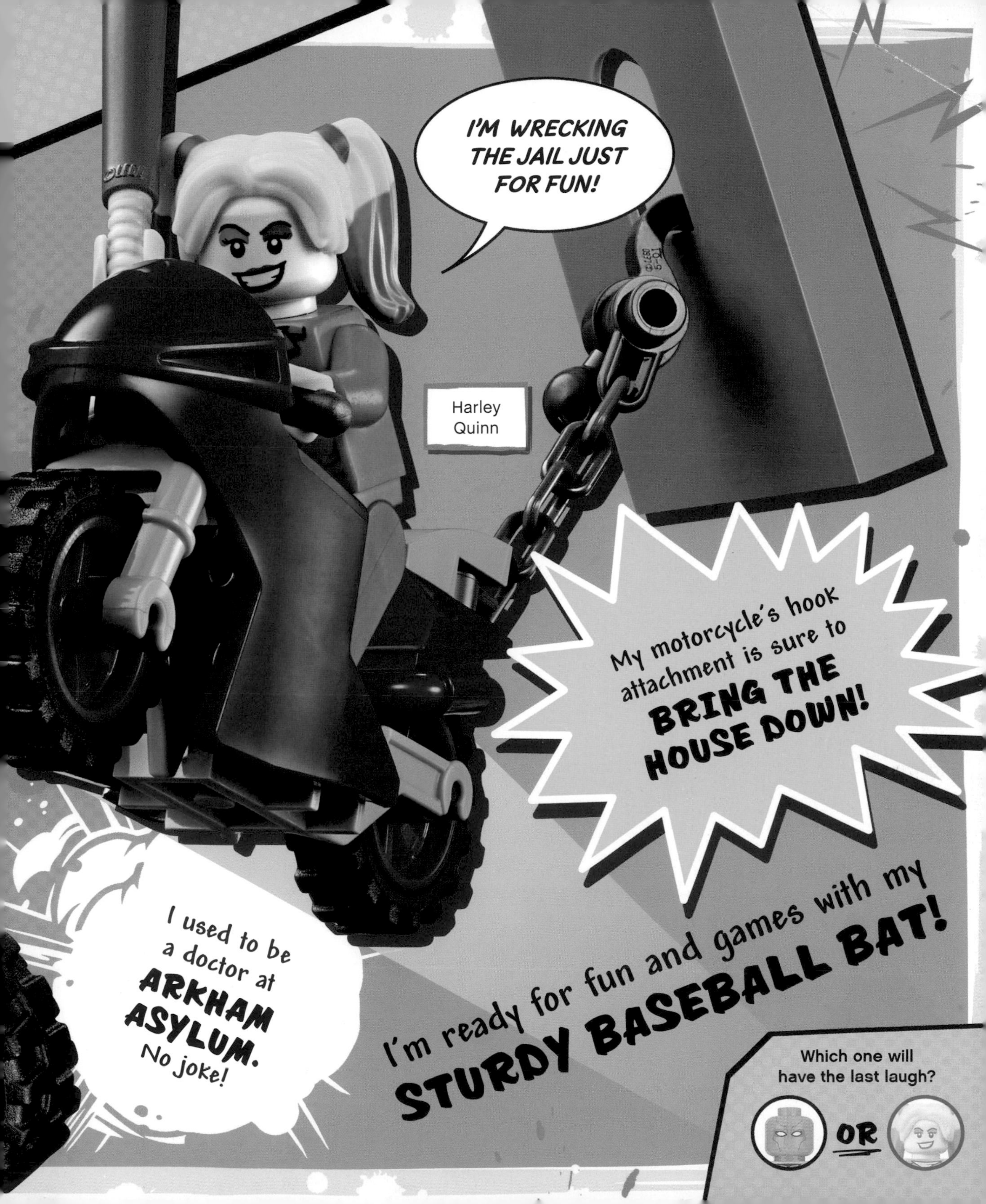
I'M WRECKING THE JAIL JUST FOR FUN!
Harley Quinn
My motorcycle's hook attachment is sure to BRING THE HOUSE DOWN!
I used to be a doctor at ARKHAM ASYLUM. No joke!
I'm ready for fun and games with my STURDY BASEBALL BAT!
Which one will have the last laugh?
OR

CHAPTER 2: GOTHAM CITY

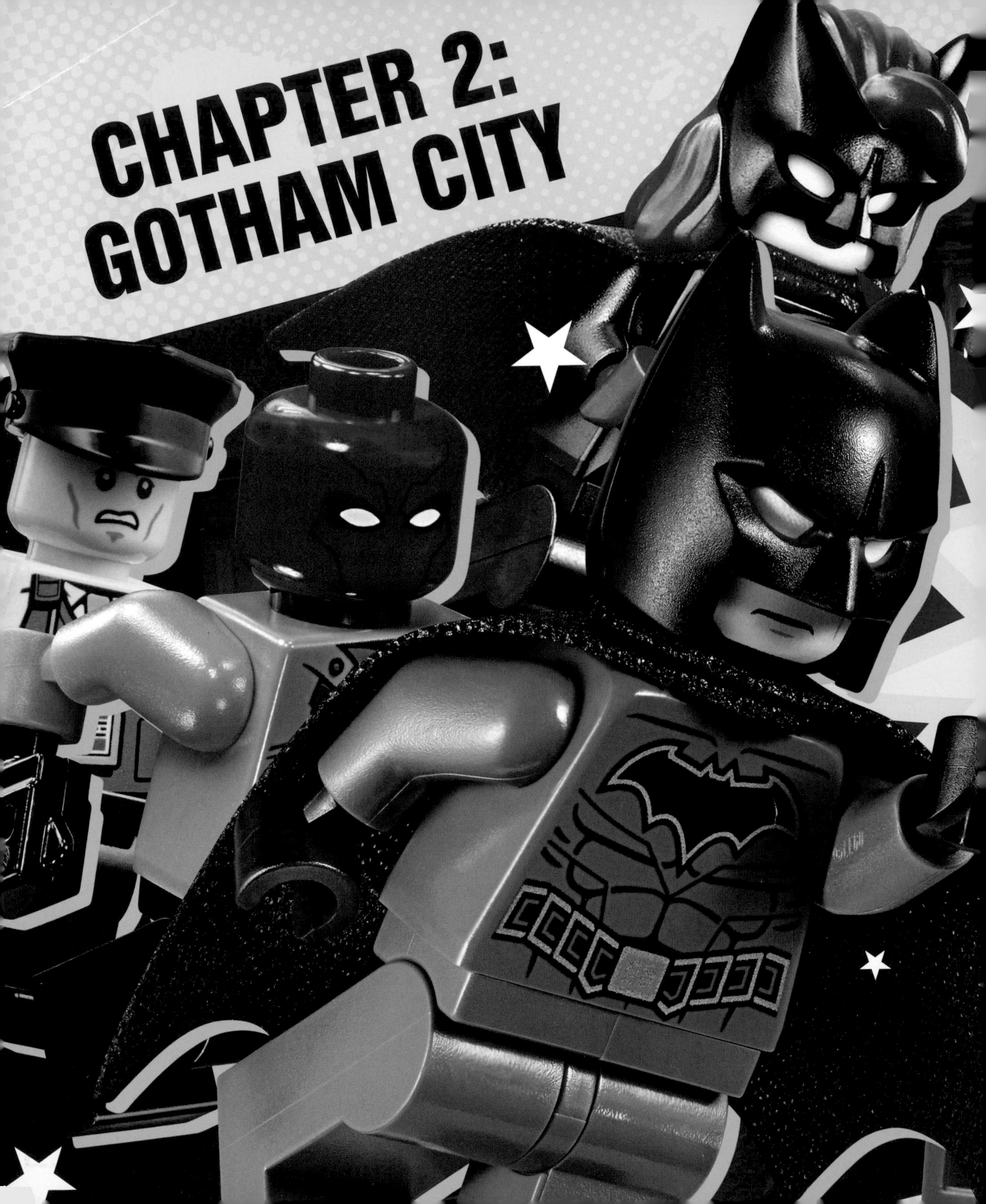

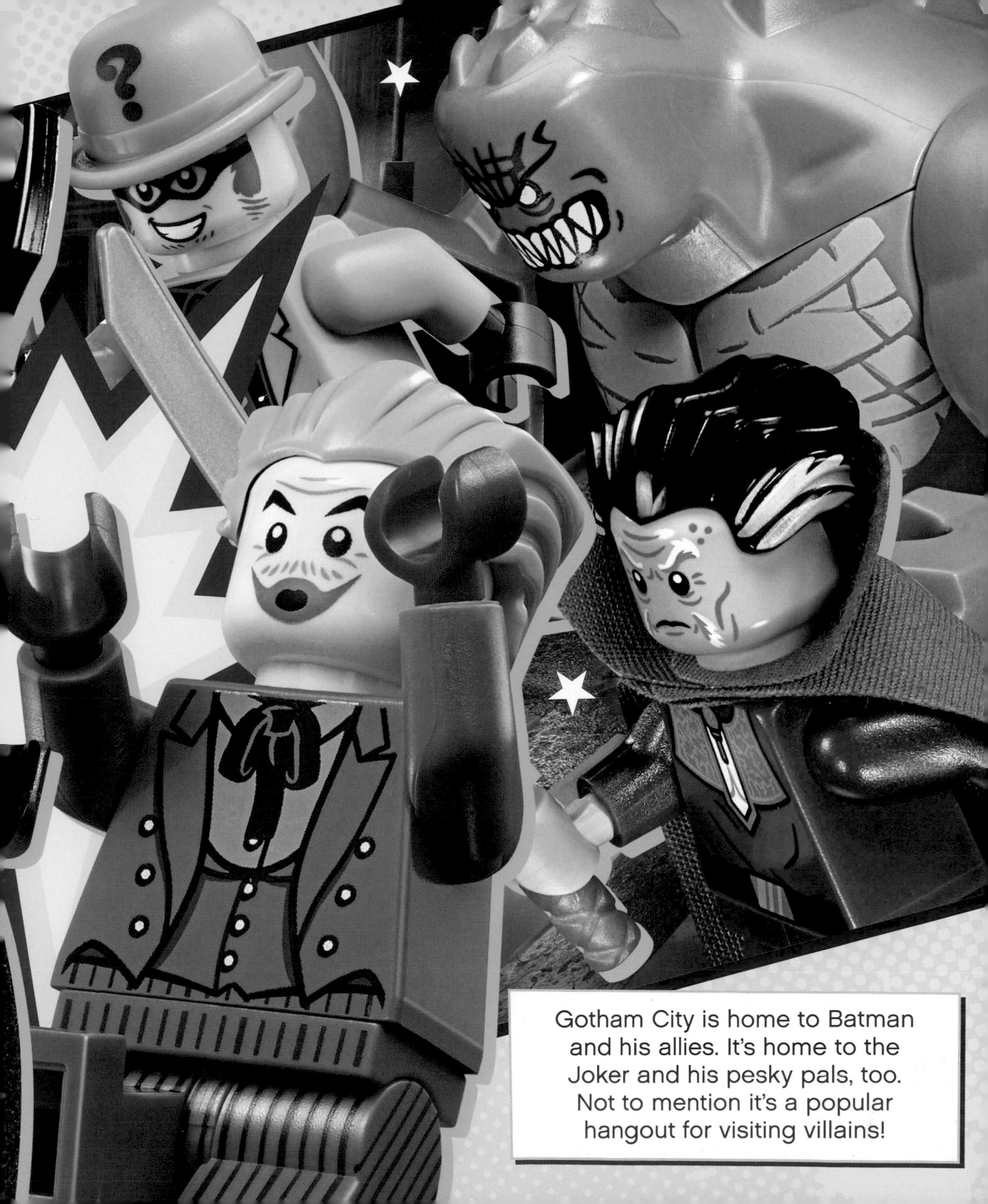

Gotham City is home to Batman and his allies. It's home to the Joker and his pesky pals, too. Not to mention it's a popular hangout for visiting villains!

I am a master of 14 different styles of **HAND-TO-HAND COMBAT**

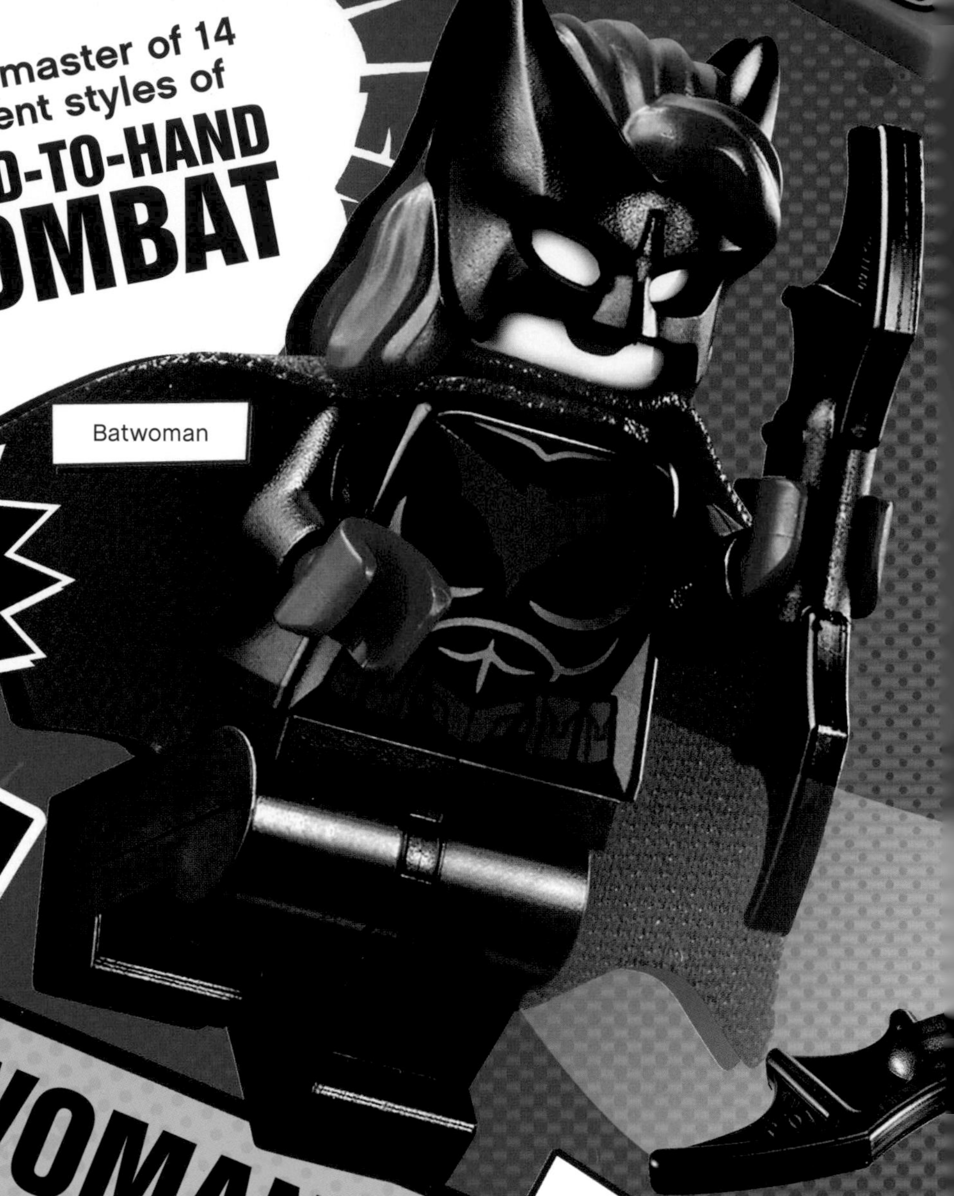

Batwoman

My high-flying **GYMNASTICS** skills give me the edge in battle!

BATWOMAN VS. THE RIDDLER

The Riddler has all kinds of tricks up his bright green sleeves. Is he a match for Batwoman's martial arts skills and high-tech gadgets?

Kate Kane is a master of stealth! She can sneak up on people undetected—very handy for catching crooks!

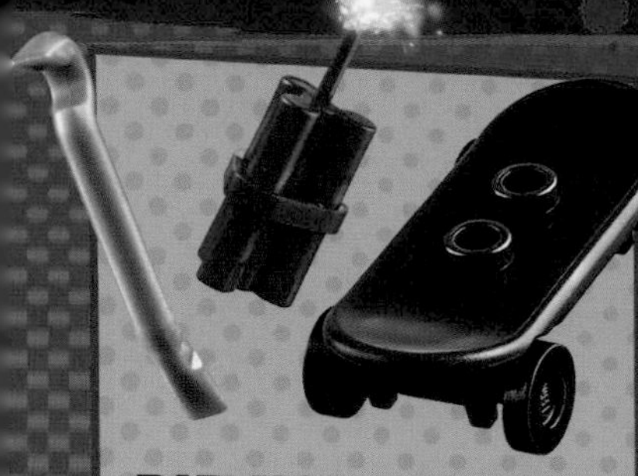

DID YOU KNOW?

The Riddler uses dynamite to break into banks. His cane doubles as a crowbar for prying open safes. His skateboard helps him make a speedy getaway!

I will outsmart you with **GENIUS LEVEL INTELLIGENCE**

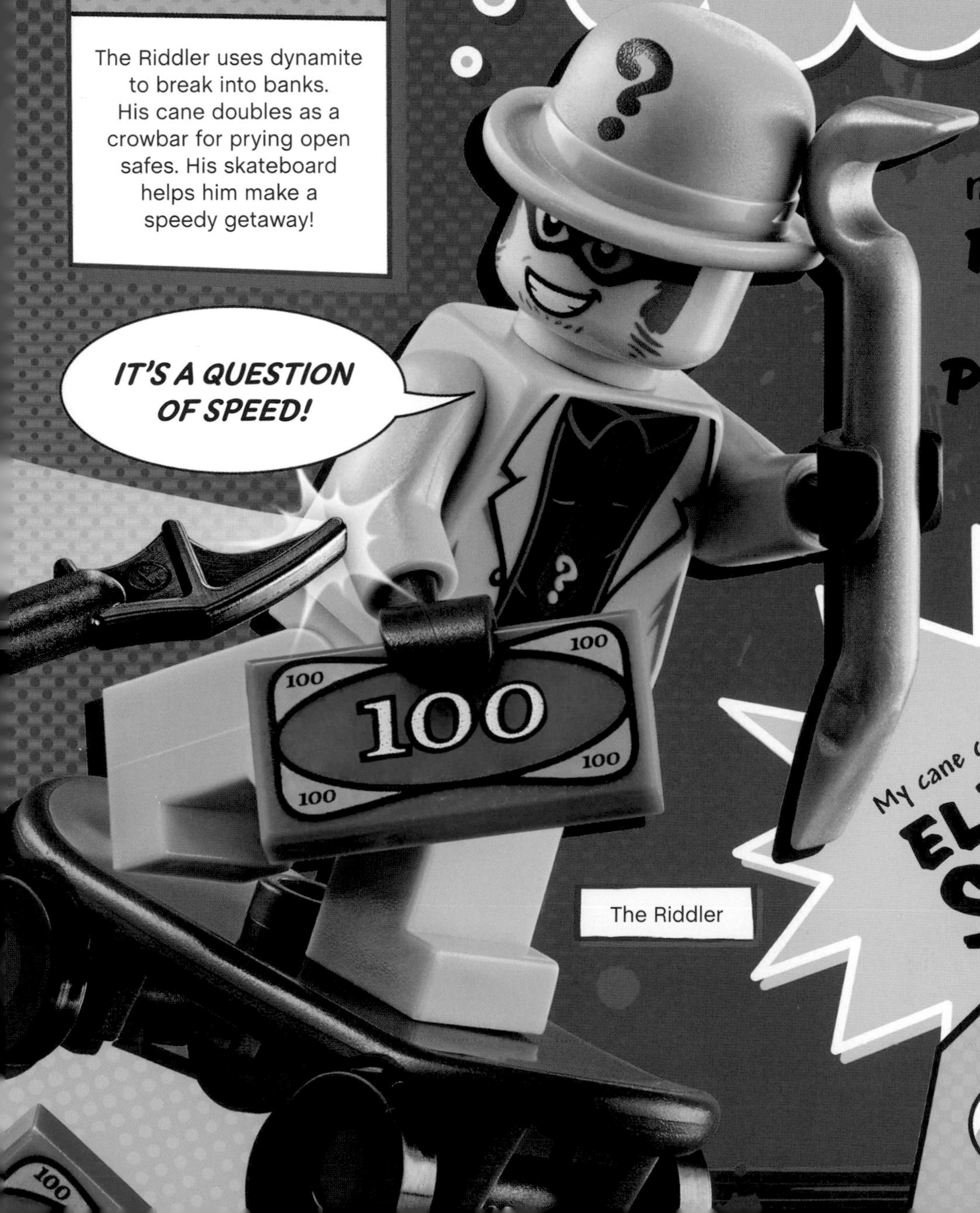
100
100
100
100
100

IT'S A QUESTION OF SPEED!

The Riddler

You will never solve my **RIDDLES AND PUZZLES!**

My cane can give you a nasty **ELECTRIC SHOCK**

Which character do you think is the coolest?

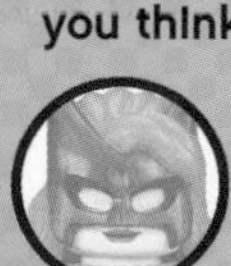

OR

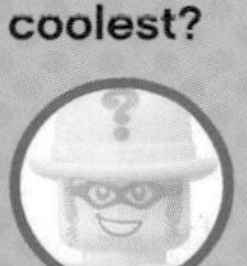

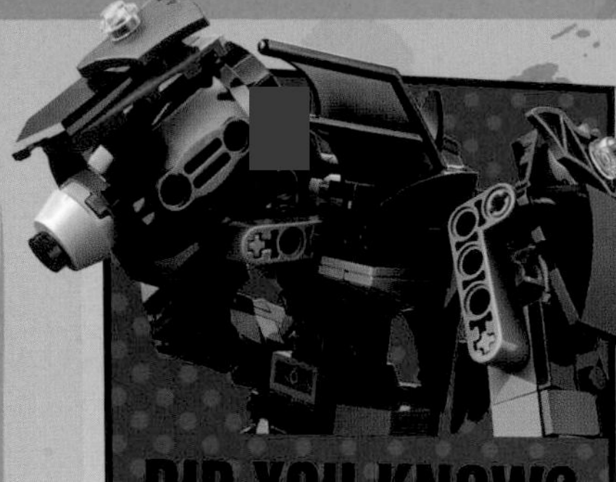

DID YOU KNOW?

Batman's mech is loaded with weapons. Some of them are hidden beneath bat-shaped details, like the shoulder epaulets.

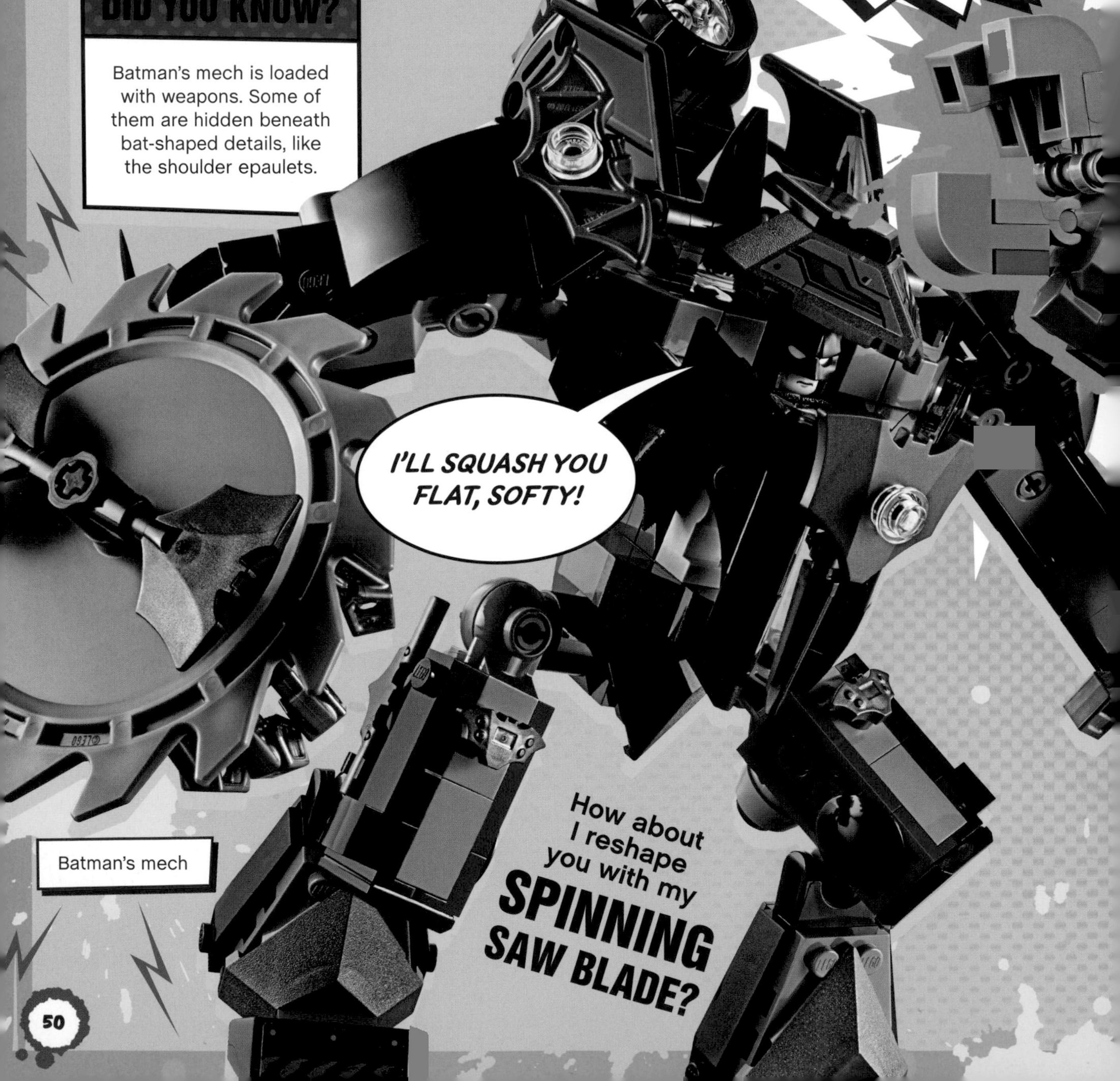

Time to fire my NET LAUNCHER
Five, four, three ...
I'LL SQUASH YOU FLAT, SOFTY!
How about I reshape you with my SPINNING SAW BLADE?

Batman's mech

BATMAN VS. CLAYFACE

Batman's mech is hard to beat, but Clayface is no soft touch. When mech meets mud man, one of them will come to a sticky end. But which?

Clayface is a versatile villain. He can reshape his clay body into anything he wants—even another person. Shifty!

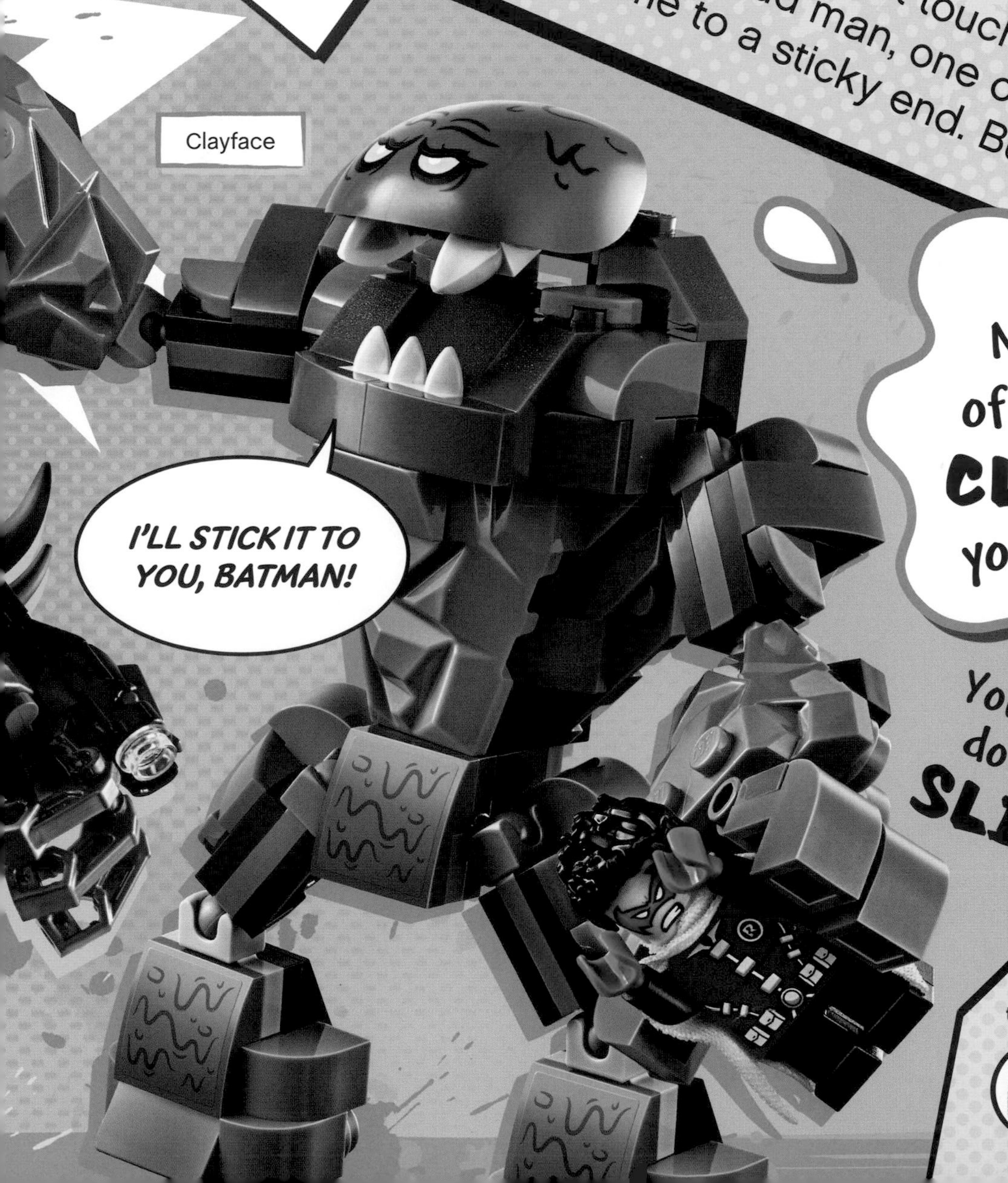
Clayface
I'LL STICK IT TO YOU, BATMAN!
My mitts of mud will CLOG UP your mech!
You can't pin me down—I'm too SLIPPERY

Who will triumph in this battle of opposites?

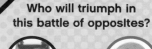

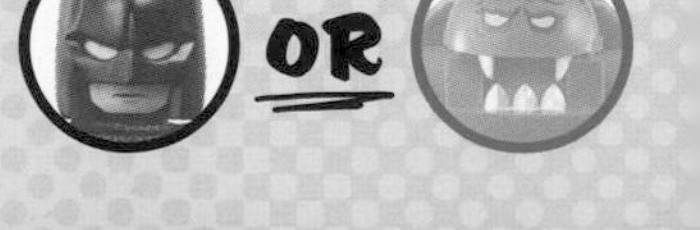
OR

I've radioed for **BACKUP,** and it's on the way

Getting **HANDCUFFS** on tricky convicts is my specialty

Prison guard

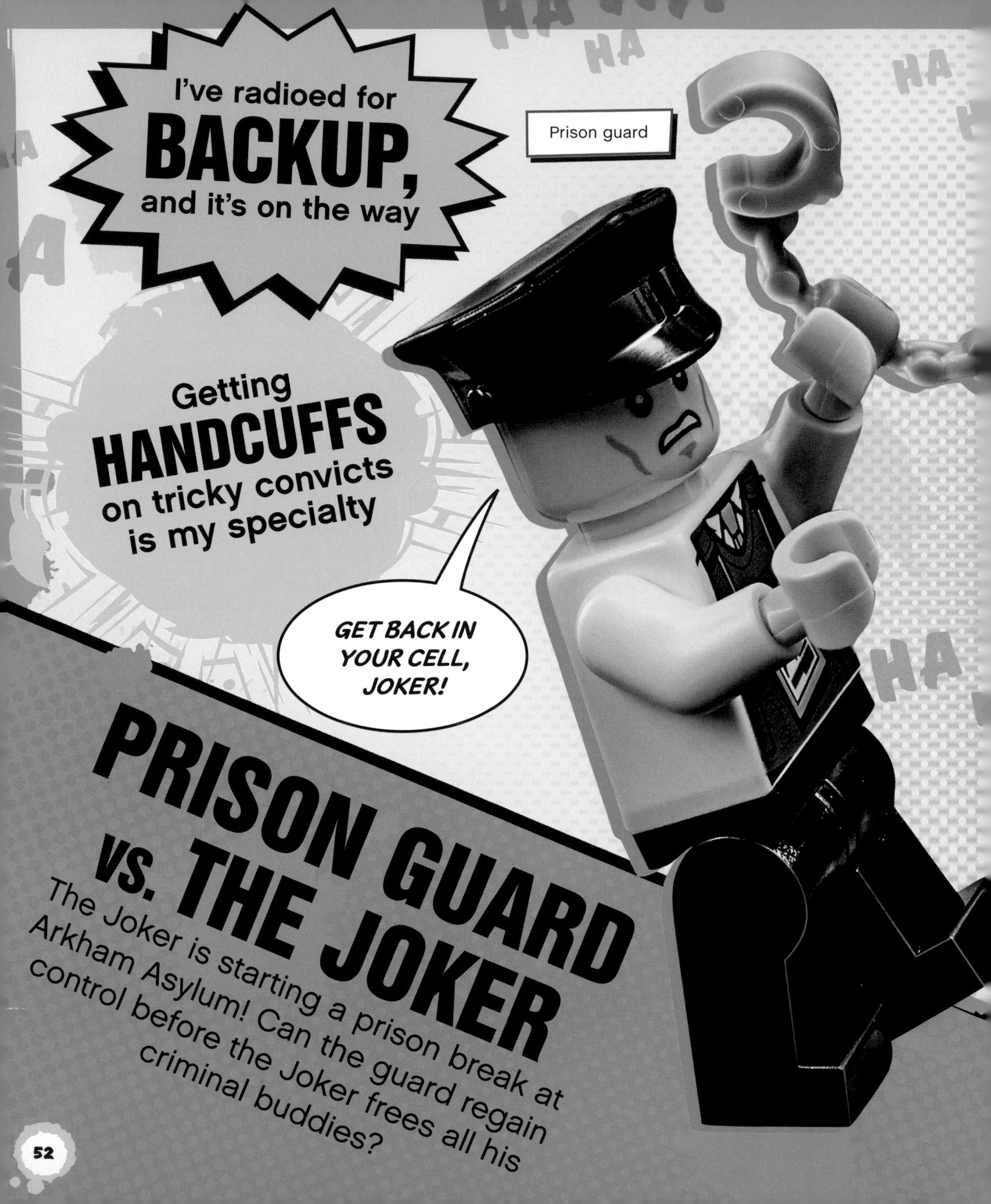

GET BACK IN YOUR CELL, JOKER!

PRISON GUARD VS. THE JOKER

The Joker is starting a prison break at Arkham Asylum! Can the guard regain control before the Joker frees all his criminal buddies?

The Joker does not like the orange prison suit he has to wear in Arkham Asylum. It clashes with his green hair!

One whiff of my **LAUGHING GAS** will have you rolling on the floor!

I'll shout jokes through this **MEGAPHONE** to drown out the sirens

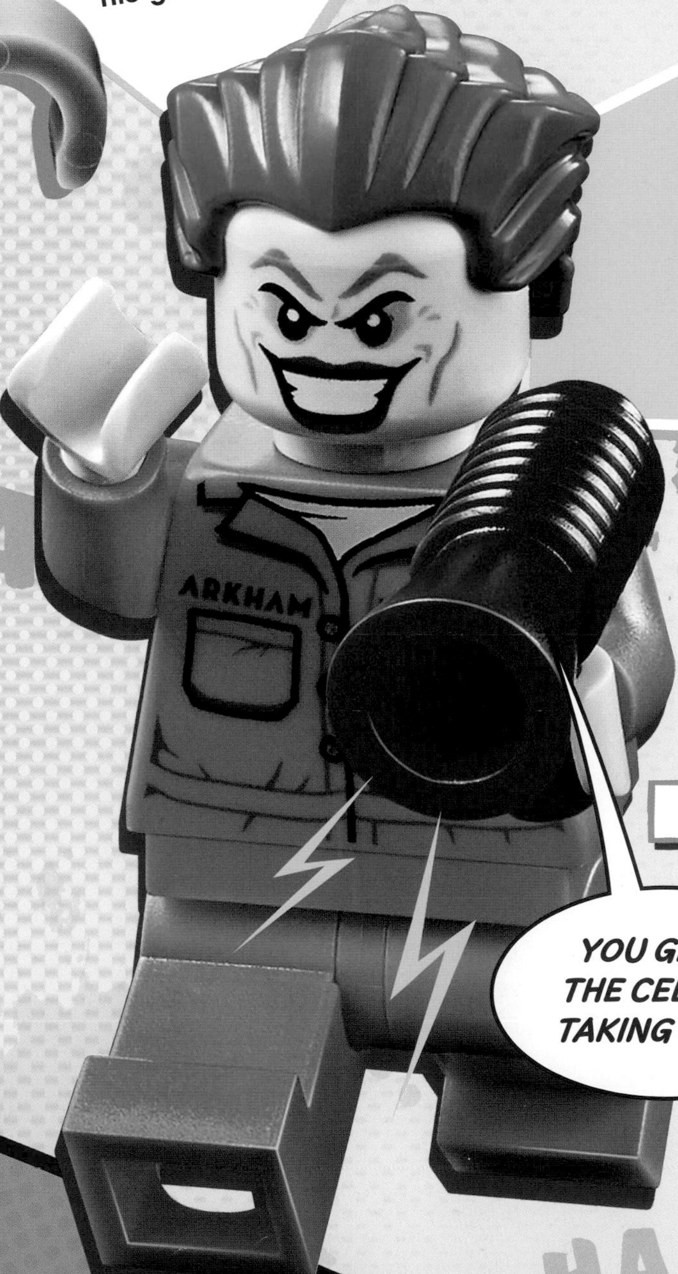
ARKHAM

The Joker

YOU GET IN THE CELL! I'M TAKING OVER!

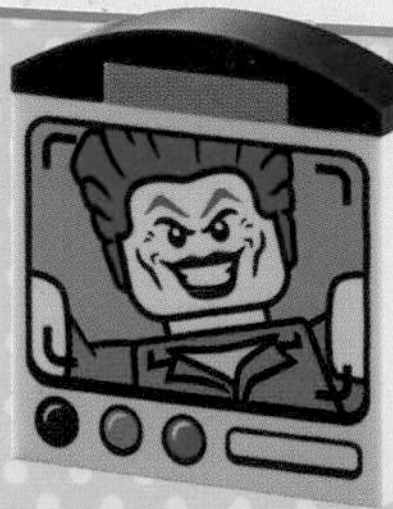

DID YOU KNOW?

To let everyone know he's on the loose, the Joker takes over the prison's TV system. There's only one channel: the Joker Channel!

Who will take control of Arkham Asylum?

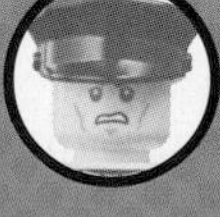 **OR** 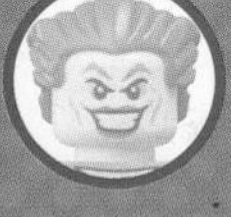

BATMAN VS. POISON IVY

Poison Ivy is attacking Gotham City in her plantlike mech, spreading seeds and pollen. Batman must stop her or the city will become a jungle!

Poison Ivy uses her toxic touch to take over people's minds. Batman can resist her toxins because he is incredibly strong-minded.

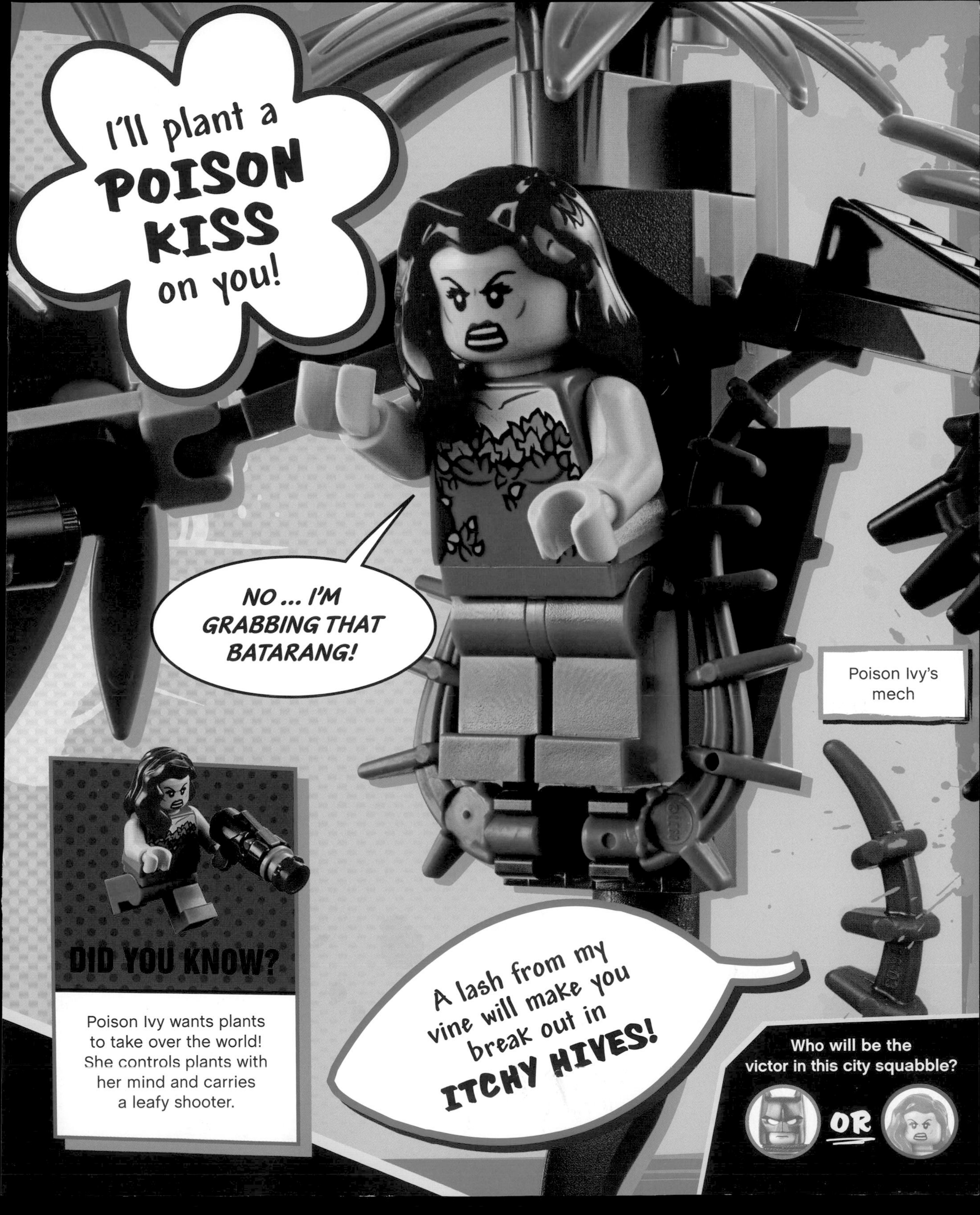
I'll plant a POISON KISS on you!
NO ... I'M GRABBING THAT BATARANG!
A lash from my vine will make you break out in ITCHY HIVES!
OR

Poison Ivy's mech

DID YOU KNOW?

Poison Ivy wants plants to take over the world! She controls plants with her mind and carries a leafy shooter.

Who will be the victor in this city squabble?

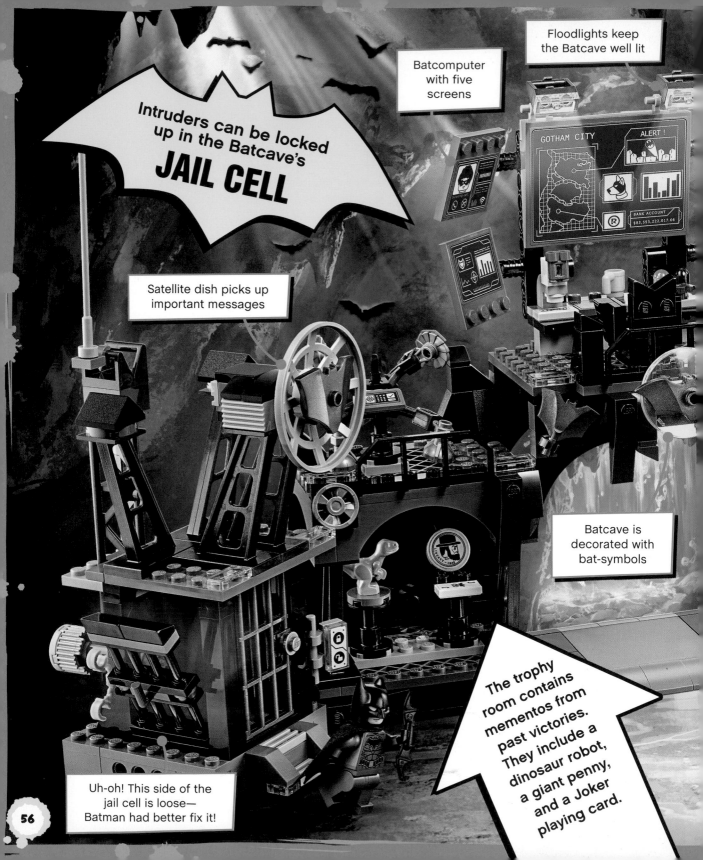

Floodlights keep the Batcave well lit

Batcomputer with five screens

Intruders can be locked up in the Batcave's **JAIL CELL**

Satellite dish picks up important messages

GOTHAM CITY   ALERT !

BANK ACCOUNT
$83,553,222,017.66

Batcave is decorated with bat-symbols

The trophy room contains mementos from past victories. They include a dinosaur robot, a giant penny, and a Joker playing card.

Uh-oh! This side of the jail cell is loose— Batman had better fix it!

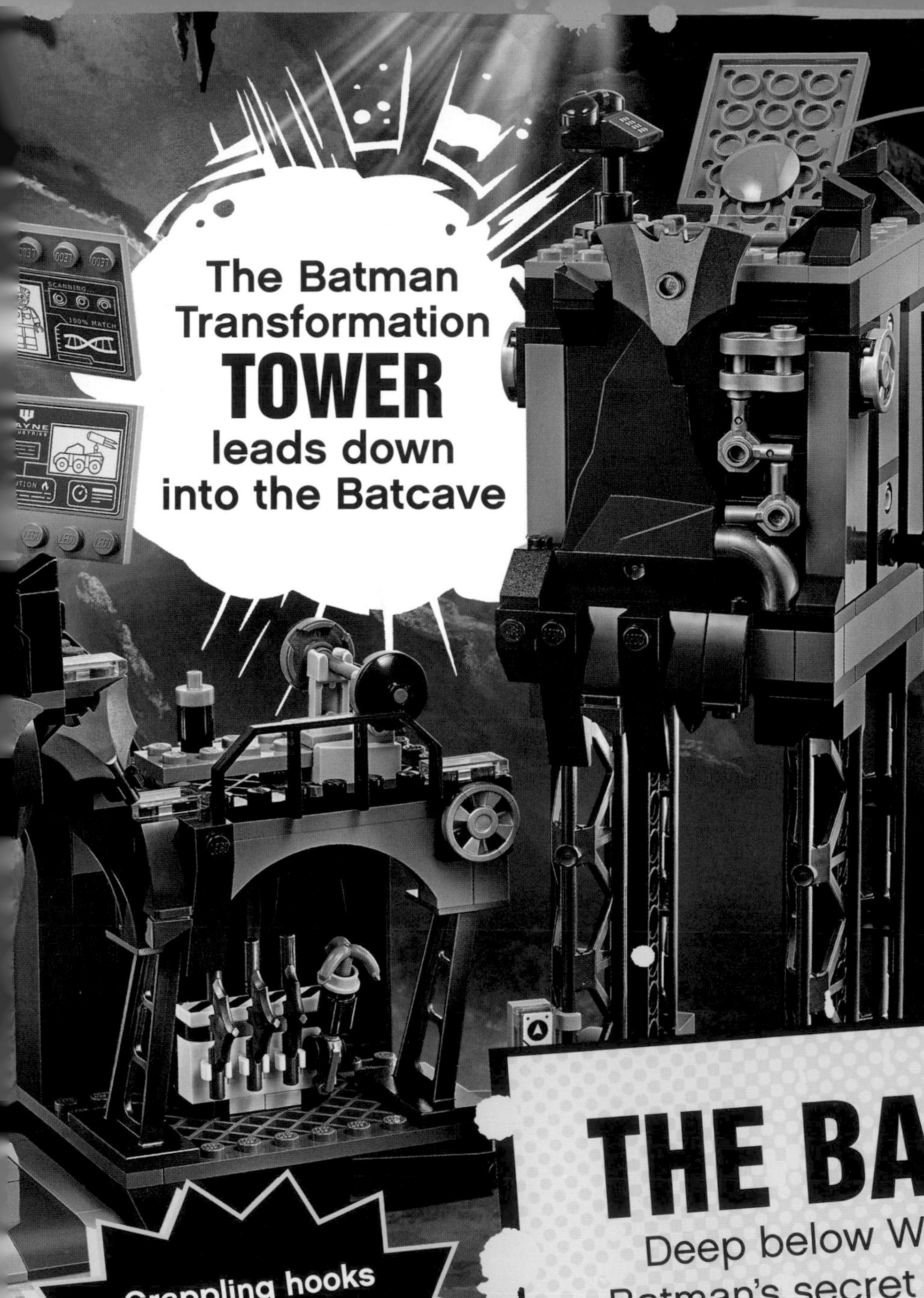

Batman enters the Batcave through this hatch

The Batman Transformation **TOWER** leads down into the Batcave

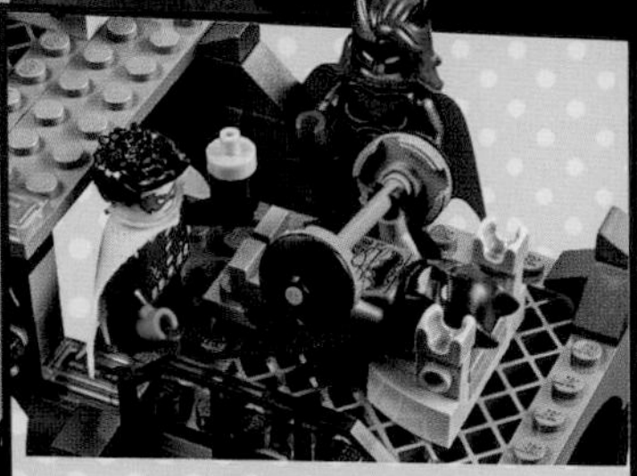

DID YOU KNOW?

All the Bat-Family make regular use of the Batcave's workout zone. Super Heroes need to stay in top condition!

Grappling hooks and gas-pellet guns fill the **WEAPONS ROOM**

THE BATCAVE

Deep below Wayne Manor is Batman's secret headquarters … the Batcave! This amazing place includes a Batcomputer zone, a trophy room, a weapons room, a workout room, and much more.

RED HOOD VS. CAPTAIN BOOMERANG

Red Hood is the angriest member of the Bat-Family. He believes in being tough on crime. That could be bad news for Captain Boomerang!

Mysterious Red Hood keeps his face hidden. His real name is Jason Todd, and he once acted as Batman's sidekick, Robin!

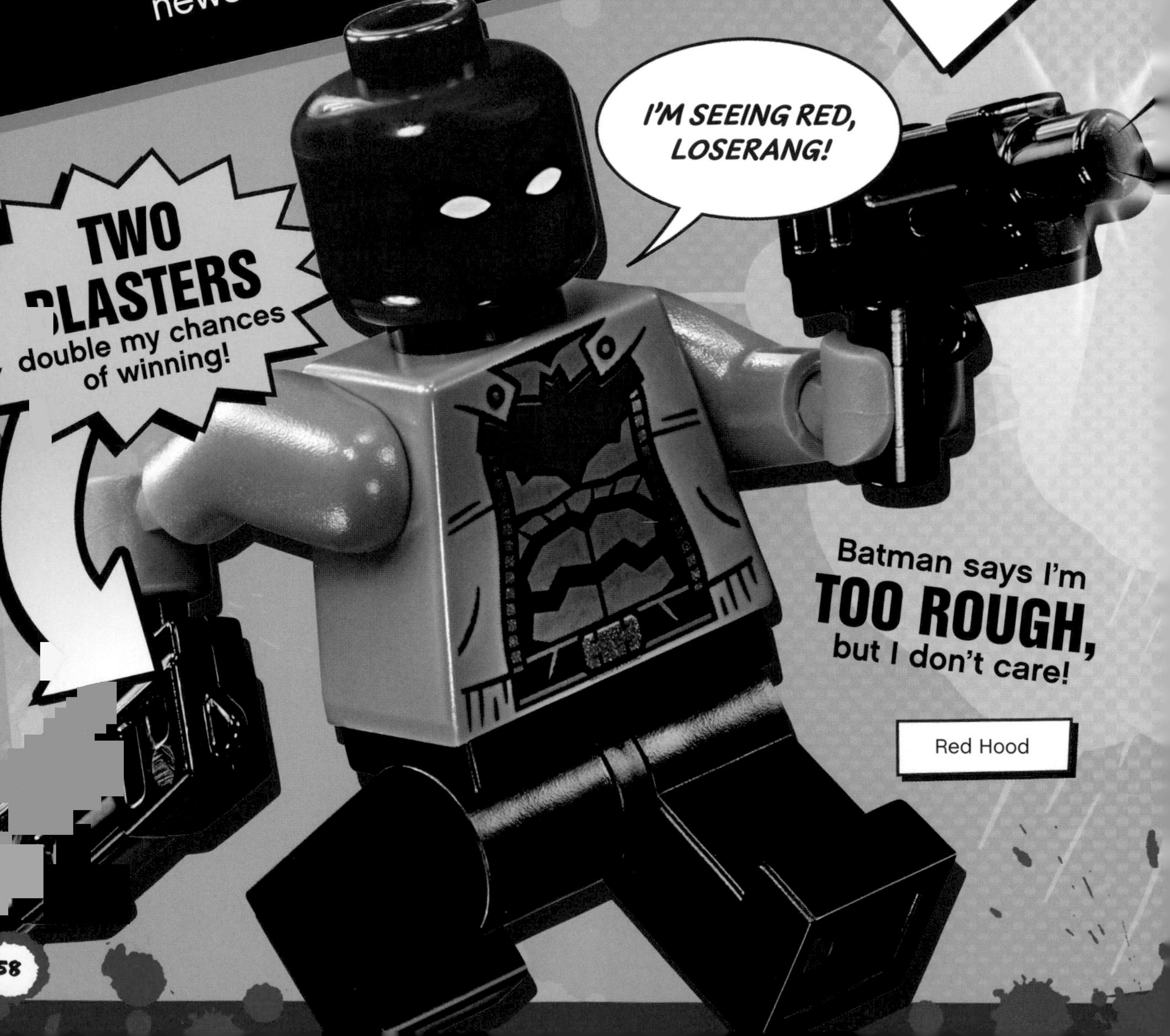
I'M SEEING RED, LOSERANG!
TWO BLASTERS double my chances of winning!
Batman says I'm TOO ROUGH, but I don't care!

Red Hood

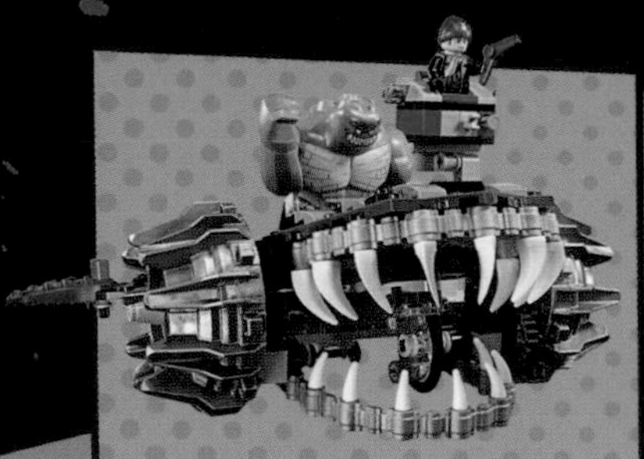

DID YOU KNOW?

Captain Boomerang once joined Killer Croc on his Battle Chomper. They had fun firing boomerangs at terrified citizens!

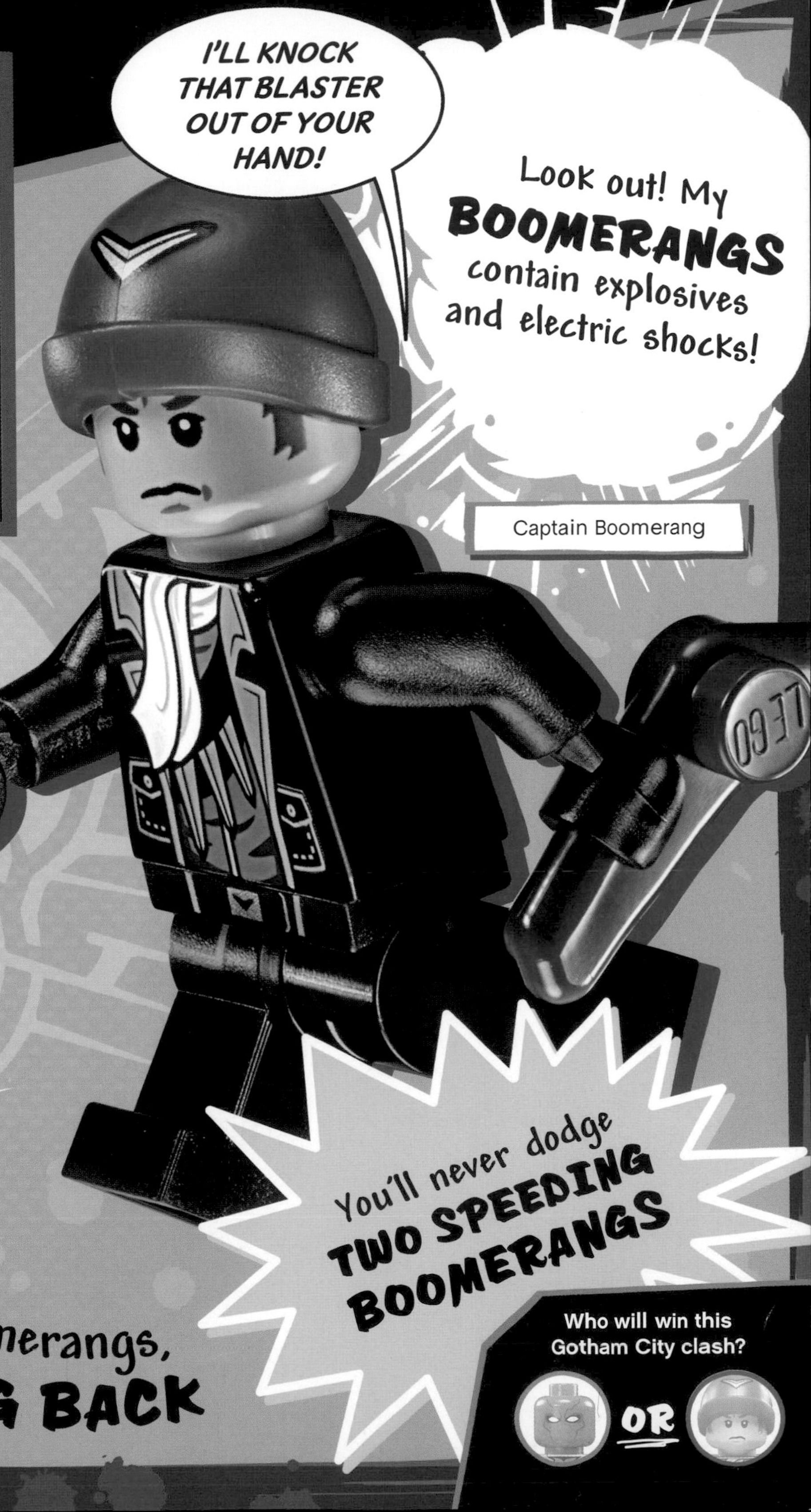
I'LL KNOCK THAT BLASTER OUT OF YOUR HAND!
Look out! My BOOMERANGS contain explosives and electric shocks!
Captain Boomerang
LEGO
LEGO
Just like my boomerangs, I KEEP COMING BACK
You'll never dodge TWO SPEEDING BOOMERANGS
Who will win this Gotham City clash?
OR

BATMAN VS. TWO-FACE

Two-Face is double trouble. He has a half-scarred face and a dual personality. Batman needs to stop this bank robber—on the double.

I'M DYNAMITE AT PUTTING OUT EXPLOSIVES.

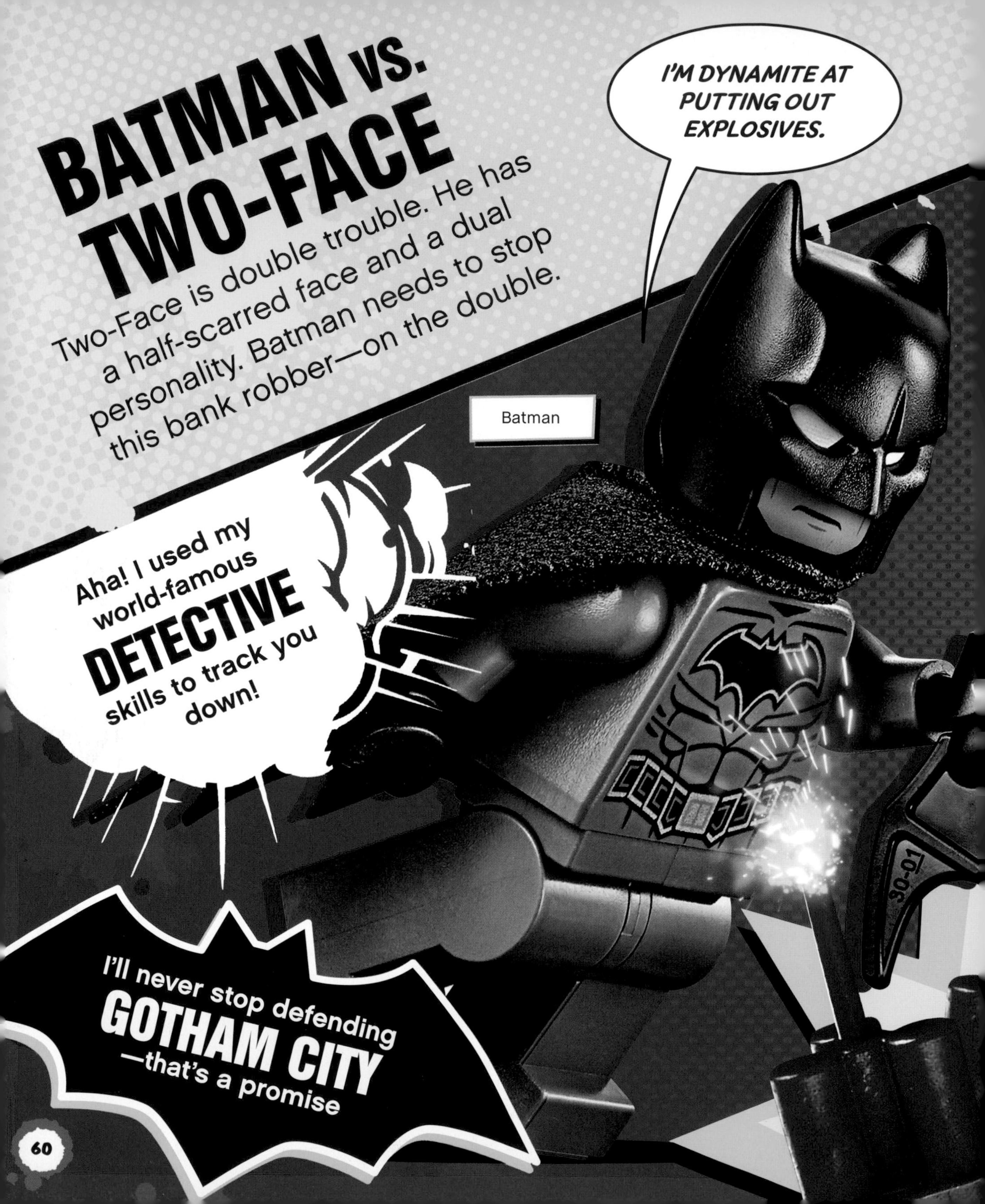
30-01

Batman

Aha! I used my world-famous **DETECTIVE** skills to track you down!

I'll never stop defending **GOTHAM CITY** —that's a promise

When he has a choice of doing good things or bad things, Two-Face flips his "lucky" coin to decide.

I'm not afraid of the law—I'm an **EX-LAWYER**

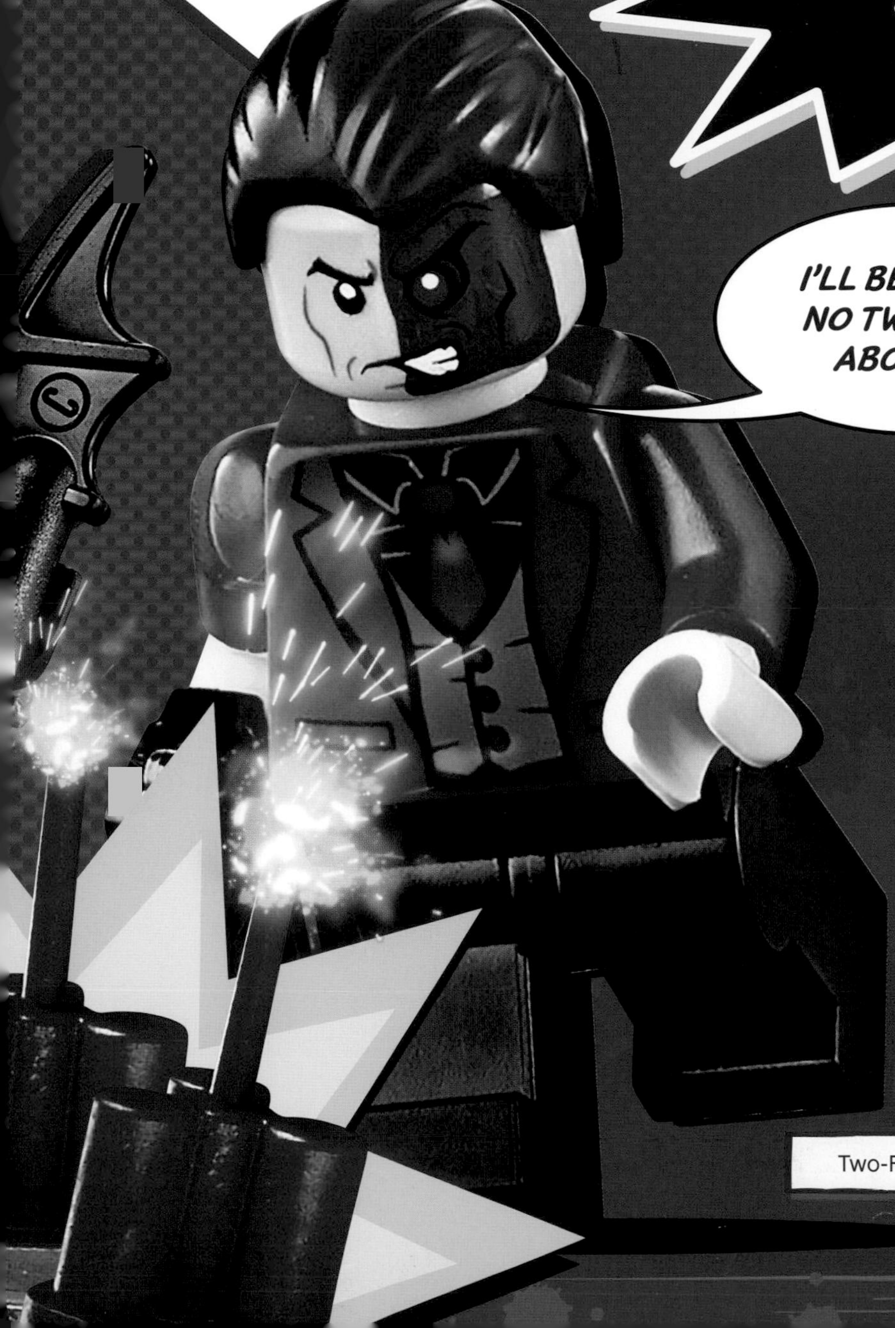

I'LL BEAT YOU, NO TWO WAYS ABOUT IT!

Two-Face

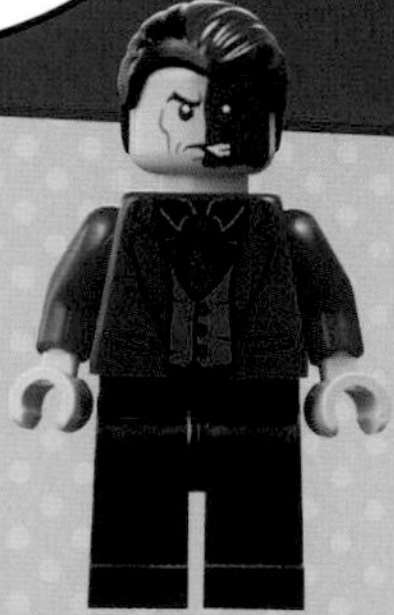

DID YOU KNOW?

Two-Face is one of Gotham City's greatest criminal crack shots. If he can't blast his way into a bank, he can usually shoot the locks off.

Who will win in the battle of the bank?

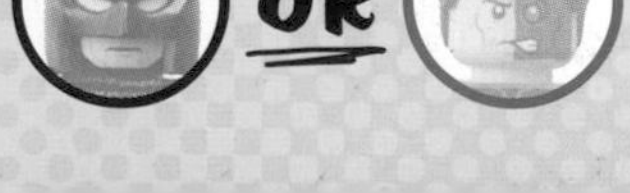

OR

BATMAN VS. RĀ'S AL GHŪL

Rā's al Ghūl is in his hideout, creating a virus to attack humans. Batman can stop the villain's evil plan, but only if he beats him in an epic duel.

Rā's al Ghūl respects Batman so much, he often tries to win him over to evil. Batman always says NO!

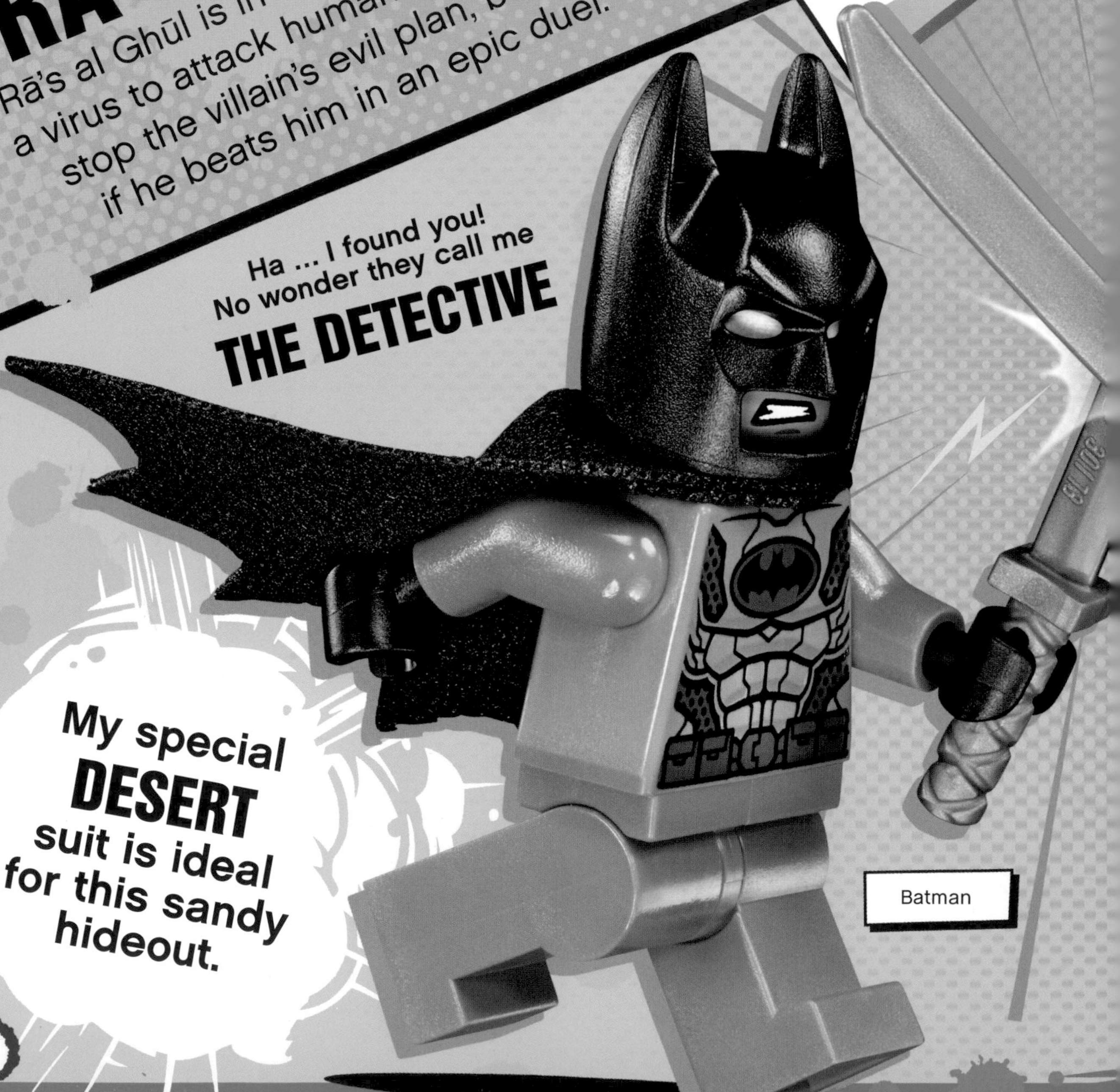
Ha ... I found you! No wonder they call me THE DETECTIVE
My special DESERT suit is ideal for this sandy hideout.

Batman

What if I reveal your true identity, **MR. WAYNE?**

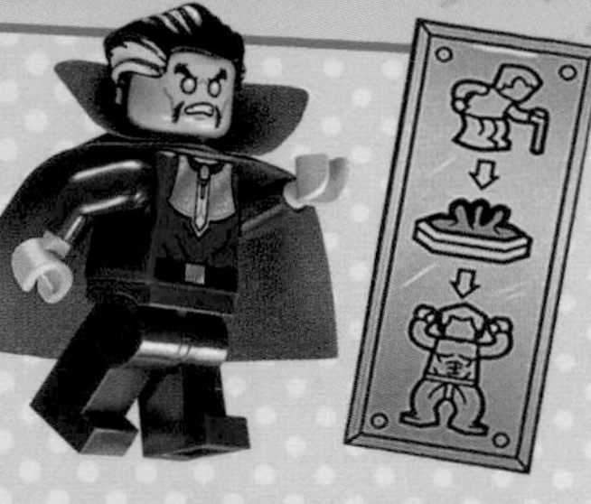

DID YOU KNOW?

Rā's al Ghūl has no fear of aging. He has control of the Lazarus Pits. These goo-filled baths restore old or sick people to youth and health.

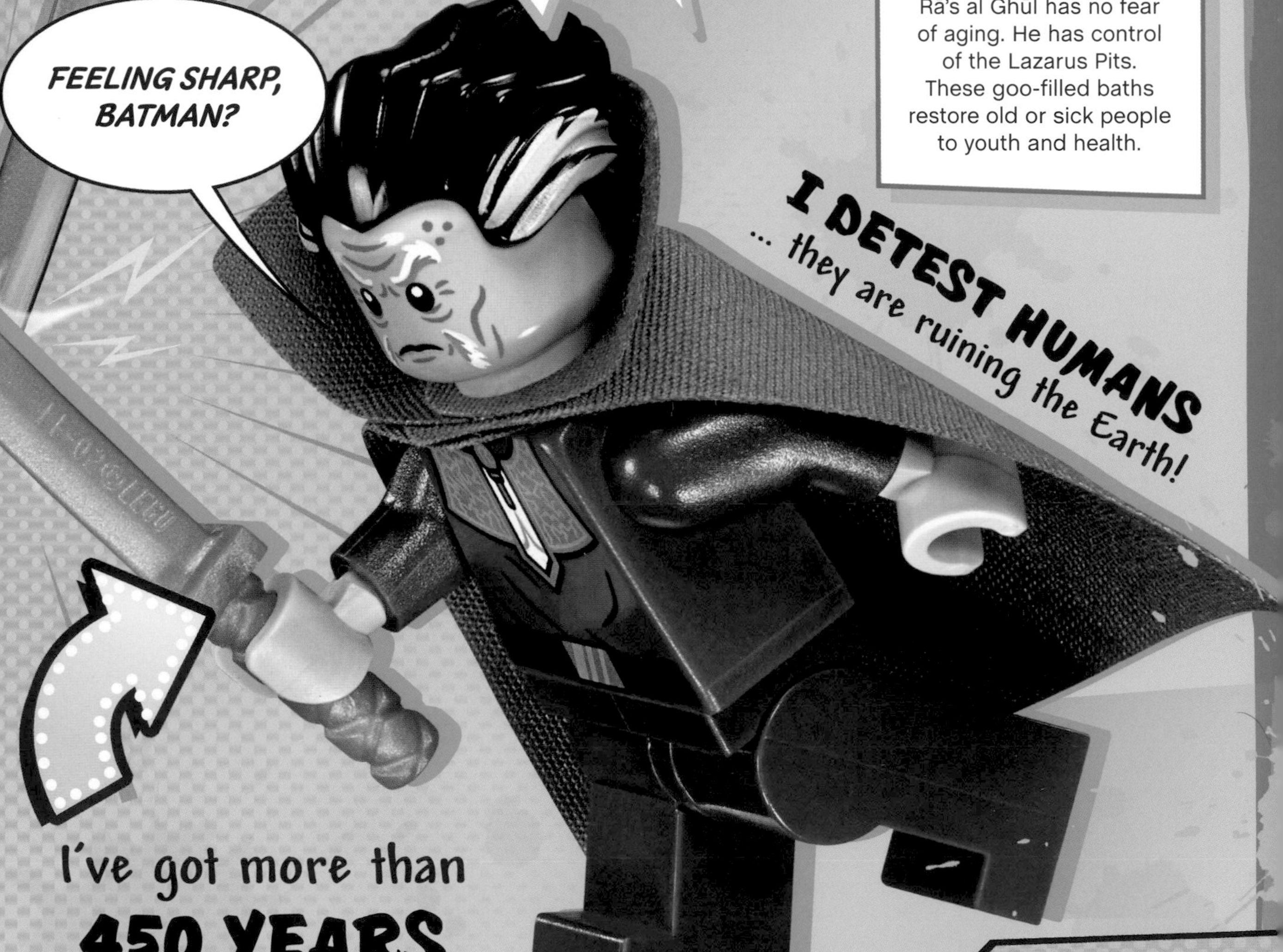

FEELING SHARP, BATMAN?

I DETEST HUMANS ... they are ruining the Earth!

I've got more than **450 YEARS** of experience as a master swordsman!

Rā's al Ghūl

Which swordsman will prove his mettle?

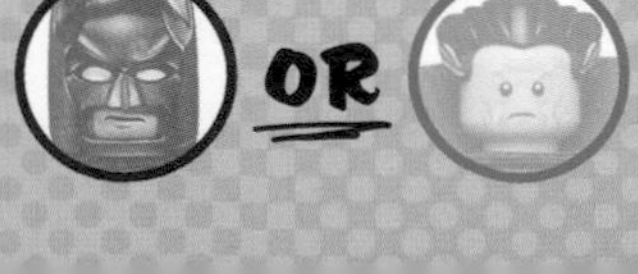

OR

THE FLASH VS. KILLER CROC

Killer Croc has taken a hostage. It's Red Hood! Can The Flash save him, or will the Bat-Family have to pay the rotten reptilian a ransom?

Even a huge ex-wrestler like Killer Croc can't endure The Flash's lightning bolts forever. The Flash's energy is limitless!

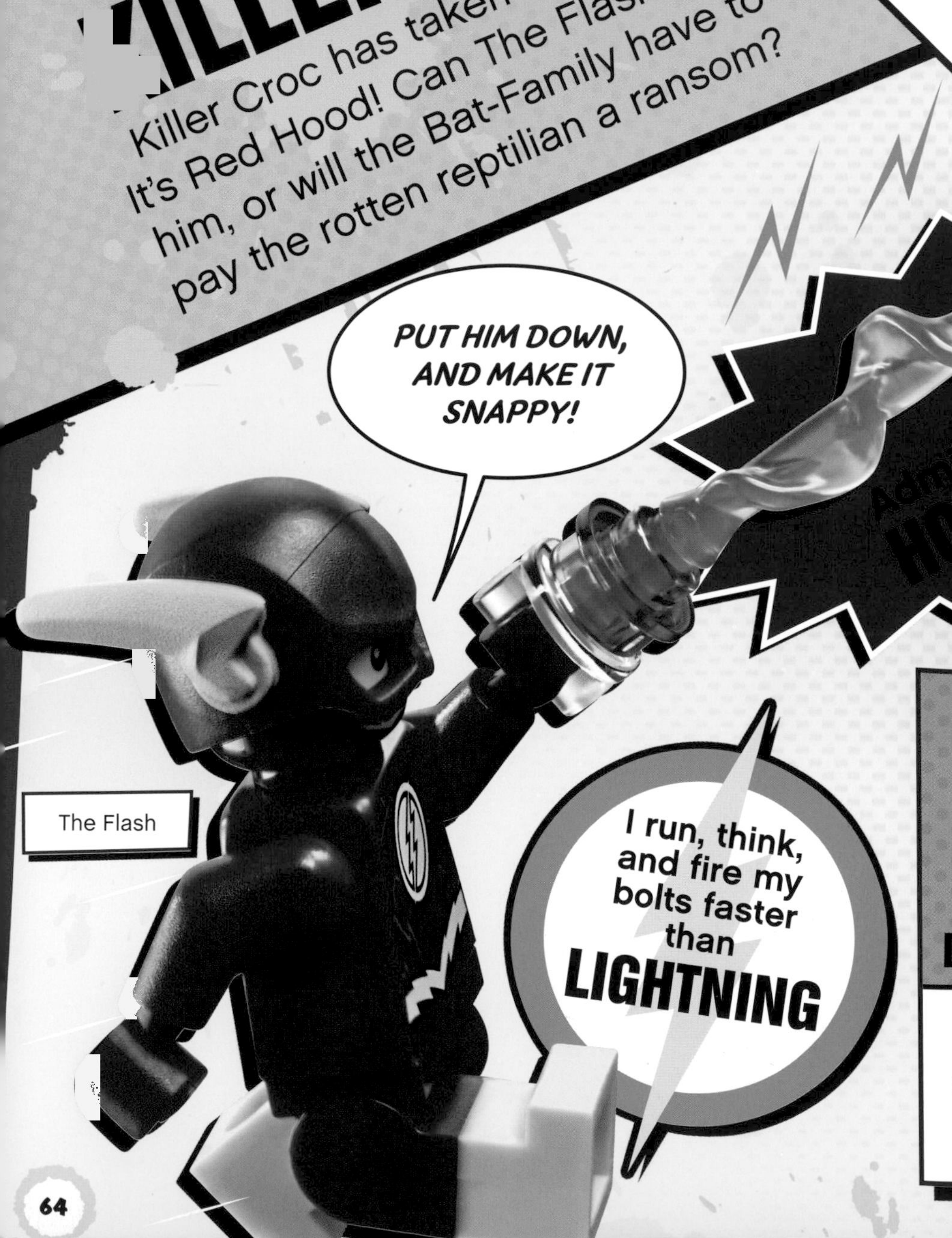
PUT HIM DOWN, AND MAKE IT SNAPPY!
Admit it, I'm a HOTSHOT!
I run, think, and fire my bolts faster than LIGHTNING

The Flash

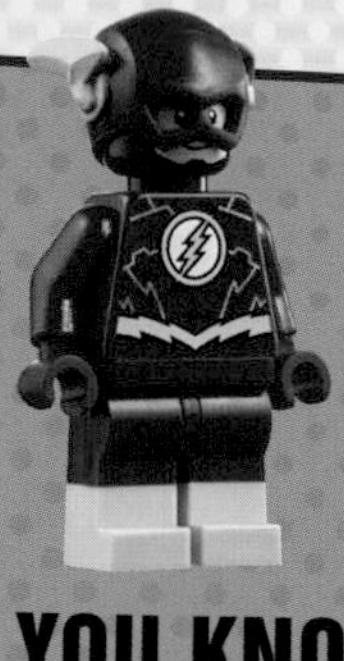

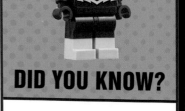

DID YOU KNOW?

The Flash gets his swiftness from the Speed Force. This cosmic energy field even helps him run through time!

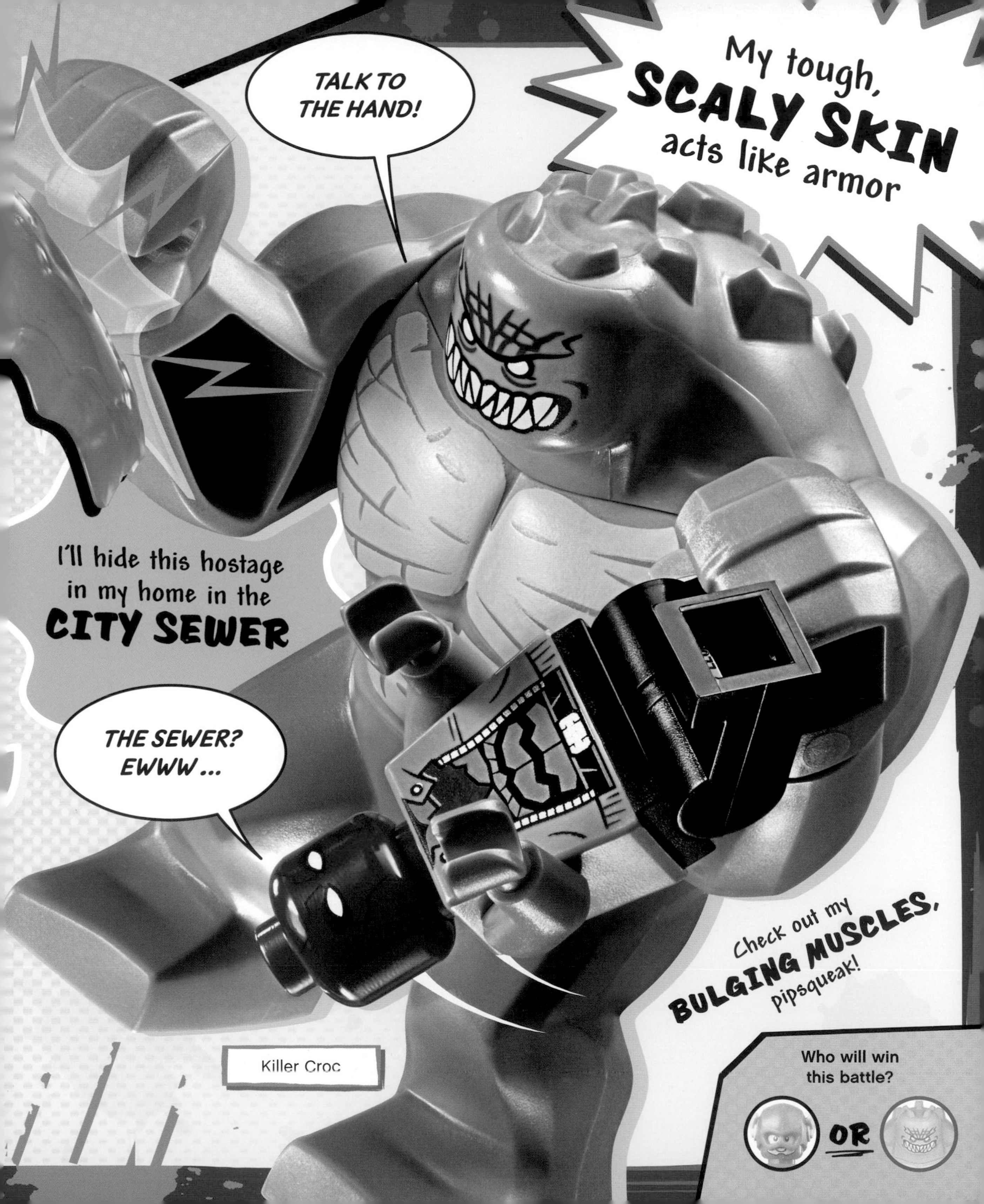
TALK TO THE HAND!
My tough, SCALY SKIN acts like armor
I'll hide this hostage in my home in the CITY SEWER
THE SEWER? EWWW...
Check out my BULGING MUSCLES, pipsqueak!
Killer Croc
Who will win this battle?
OR

I'll knock the stuffing out of you with a **KARATE CHOP**

Batman

My trusty **GAS MASK** is filtering out your toxic gas

STAND DOWN, SACKHEAD!

BATMAN VS. SCARECROW

Scarecrow is aiming his Fear Gas gun at Batman, but Batman is wearing a gas mask! Maybe only hand-to-hand combat can settle this fight.

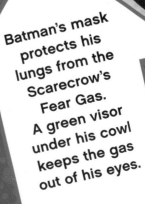

Batman's mask protects his lungs from the Scarecrow's Fear Gas. A green visor under his cowl keeps the gas out of his eyes.

I'll fire **FEAR GAS** to scare you away!

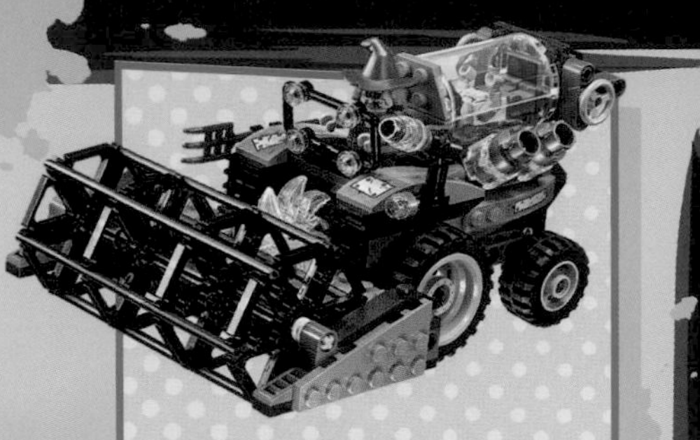

DID YOU KNOW?

Scarecrow drives a horrible harvester. Its tank holds enough Fear Gas to scare everyone for miles around!

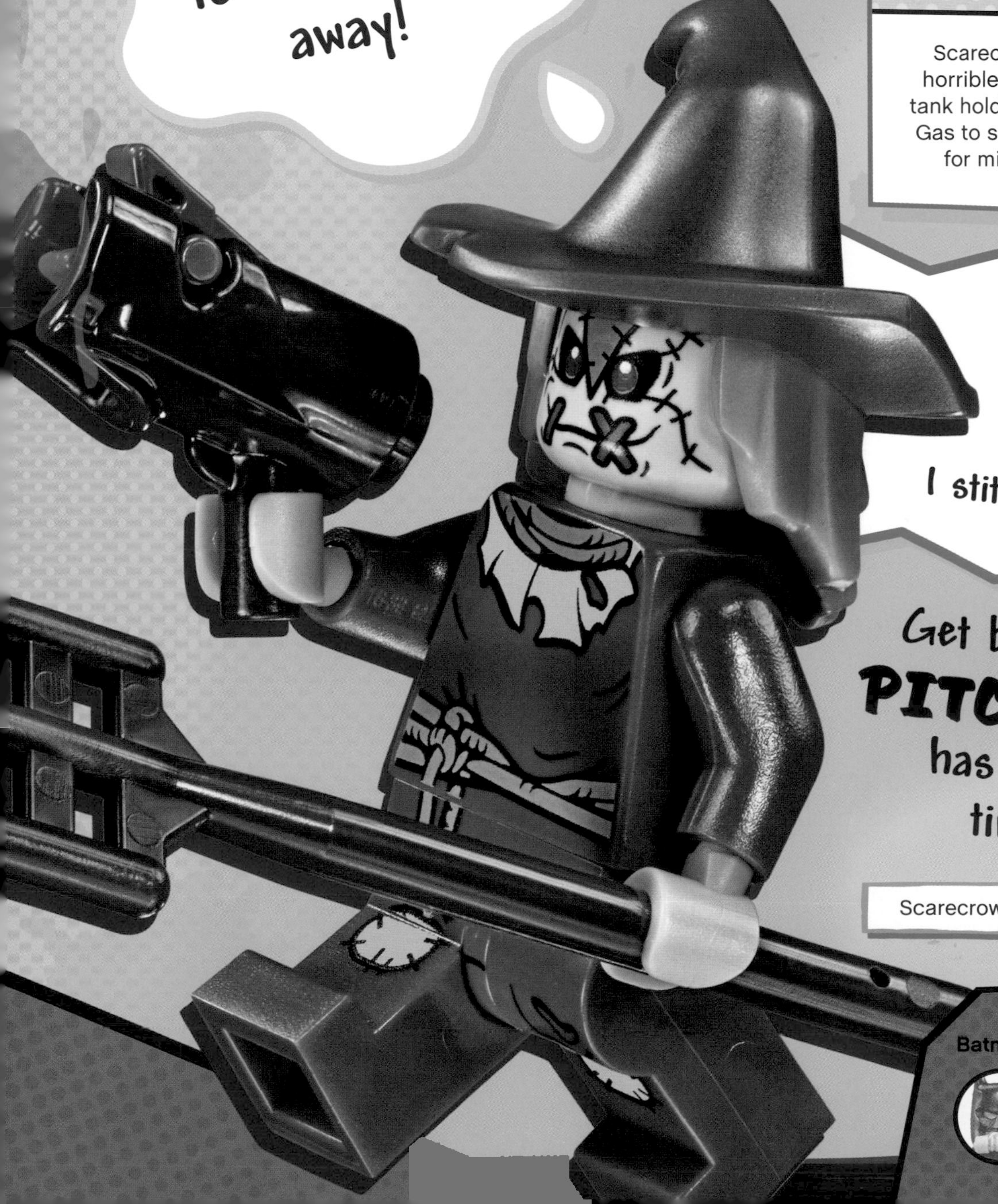

Like my **SCARY GRIN?** I stitched it myself!

Get back—my **PITCHFORK** has pointy tines!

Scarecrow

Who will win, the Batman or the straw man?

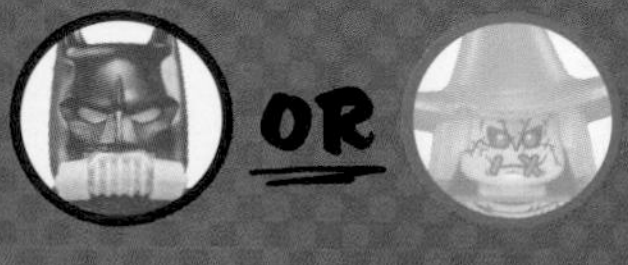
OR

BATMAN VS. THE JOKER

Oh no! Batman has caught the Joker in the Batcave planting explosives. The Batcave and all its precious equipment could soon be blown sky high!

Batman has a wardrobe full of Batsuits. Most of them are tasteful shades of blue and gray—perfect for keeping a low profile.

No flashy colors for me! Deep blue is **MUCH CLASSIER!**

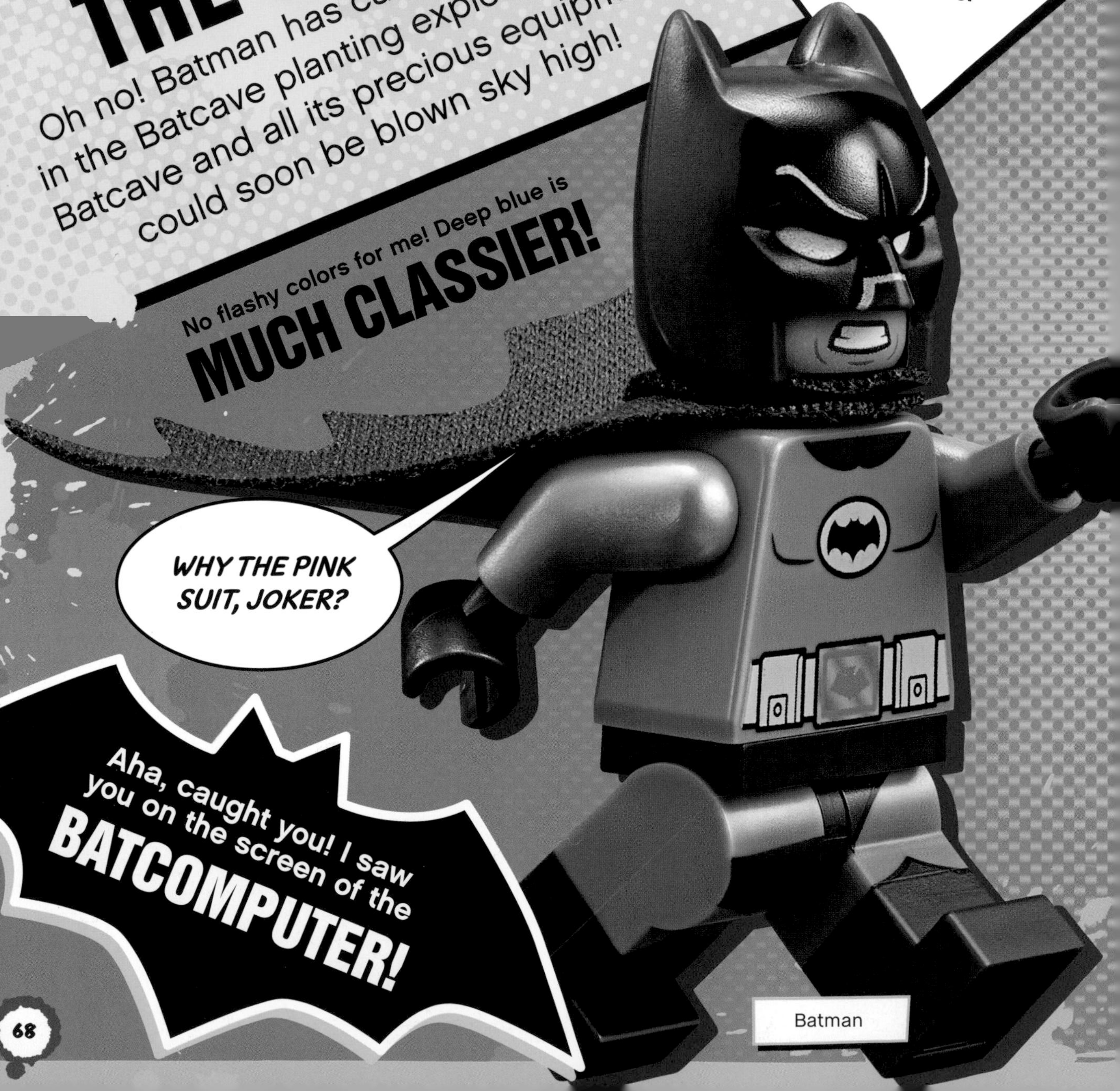

WHY THE PINK SUIT, JOKER?

Aha, caught you! I saw you on the screen of the **BATCOMPUTER!**

Batman

MY POISON can harm you ... but not me!

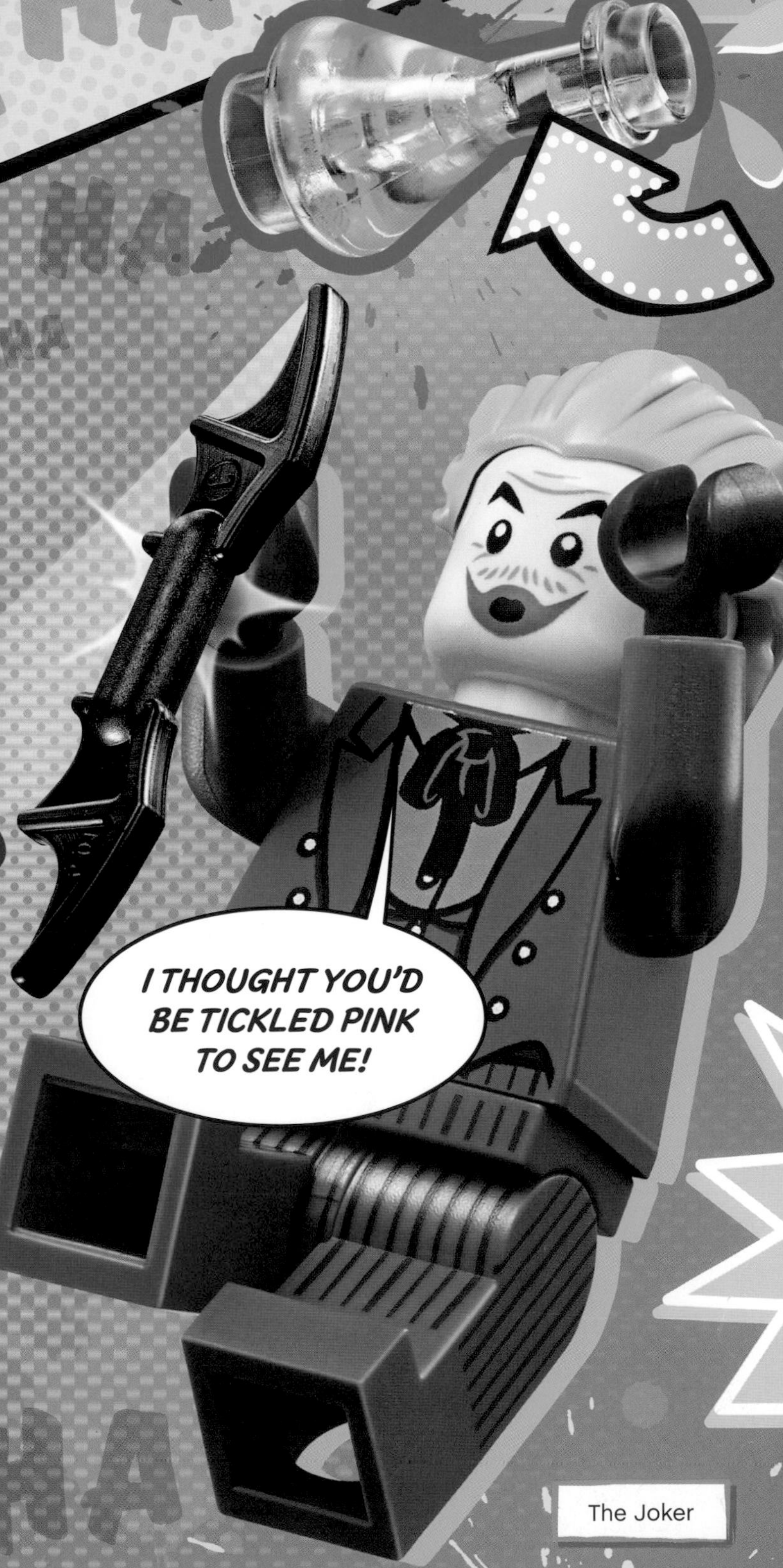
I THOUGHT YOU'D BE TICKLED PINK TO SEE ME!

The Joker

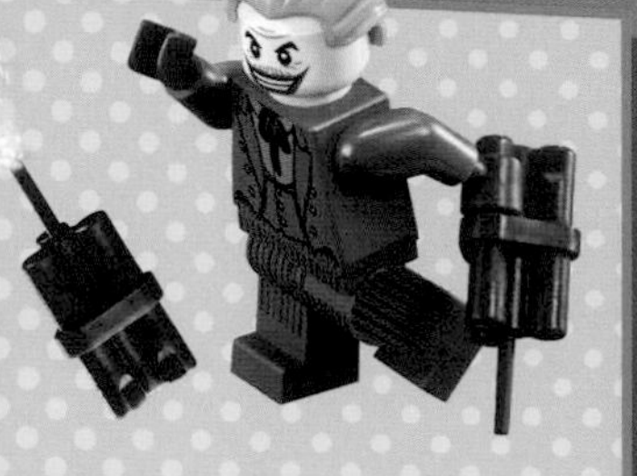

DID YOU KNOW?

The Joker loves comedy weapons like squirting flowers, but he also uses dynamite. His crimes are truly a blast!

I'll catch this **BATARANG,** no sweat!

Who will win the battle of the Batcave?

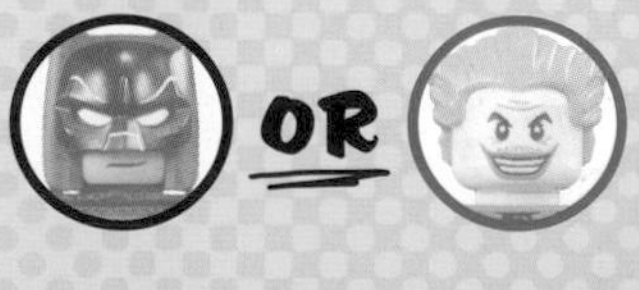
OR

CHAPTER 3: WIDER WORLD

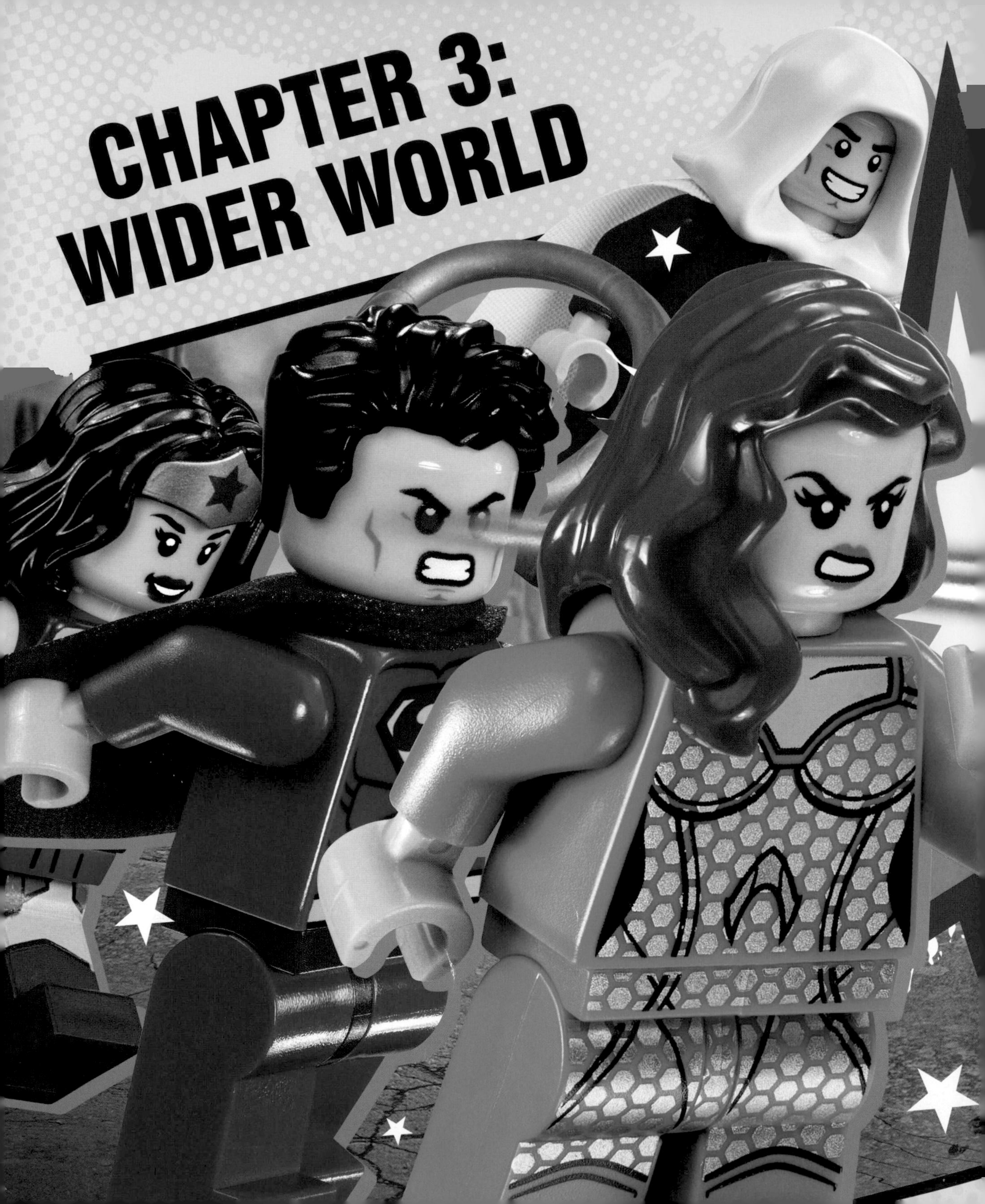

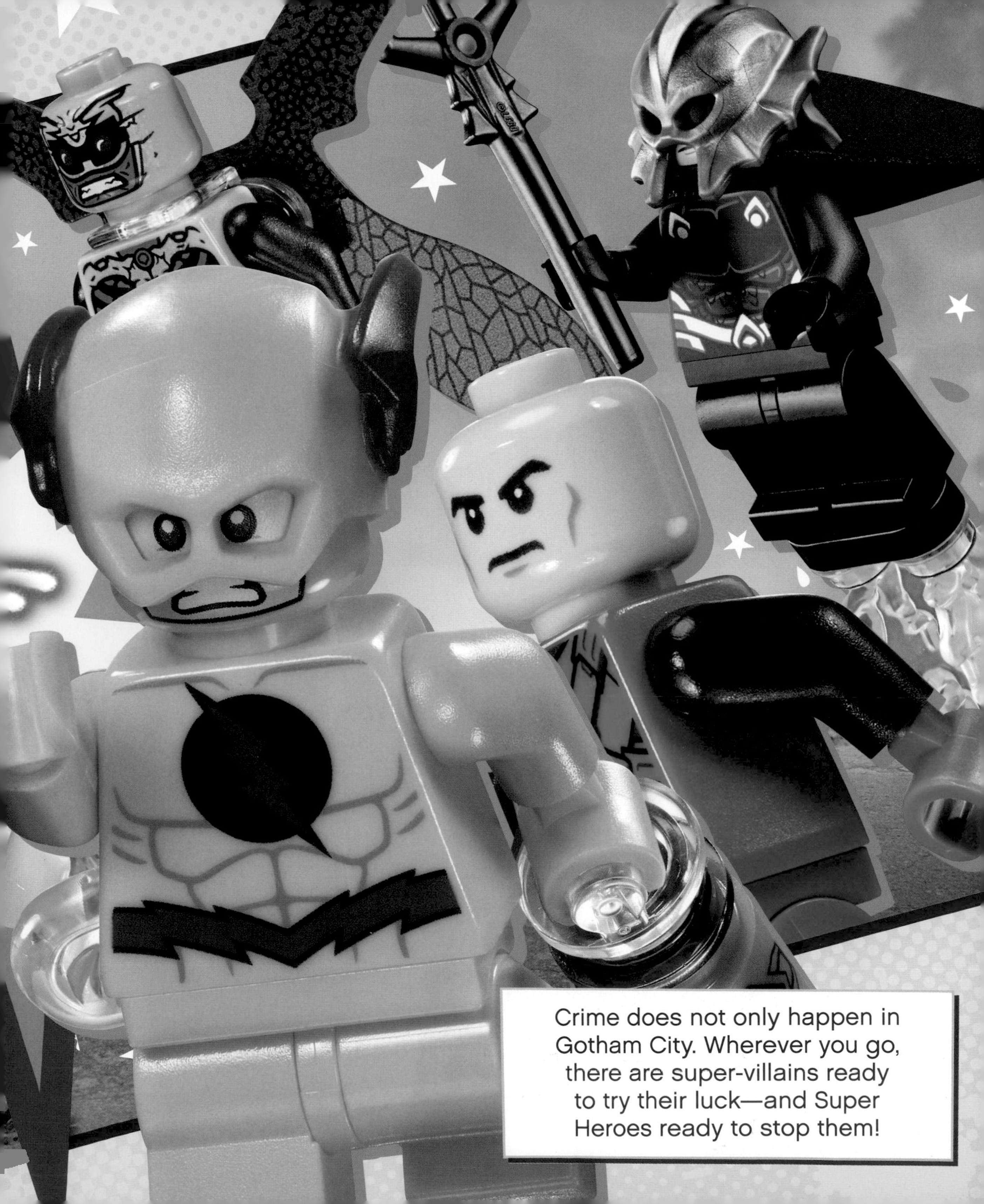

Crime does not only happen in Gotham City. Wherever you go, there are super-villains ready to try their luck—and Super Heroes ready to stop them!

GREEN LANTERN VS LEX LUTHOR

Is that [illegible] The suit is right, but the face [illegible] Lex Luthor! Is he up to no good? Maybe Green Lantern can zap a confession out of him.

Jessica Cruz uses a special power ring to make weapons out of light. She was trained by Hal Jordan, the first ever Green Lantern.

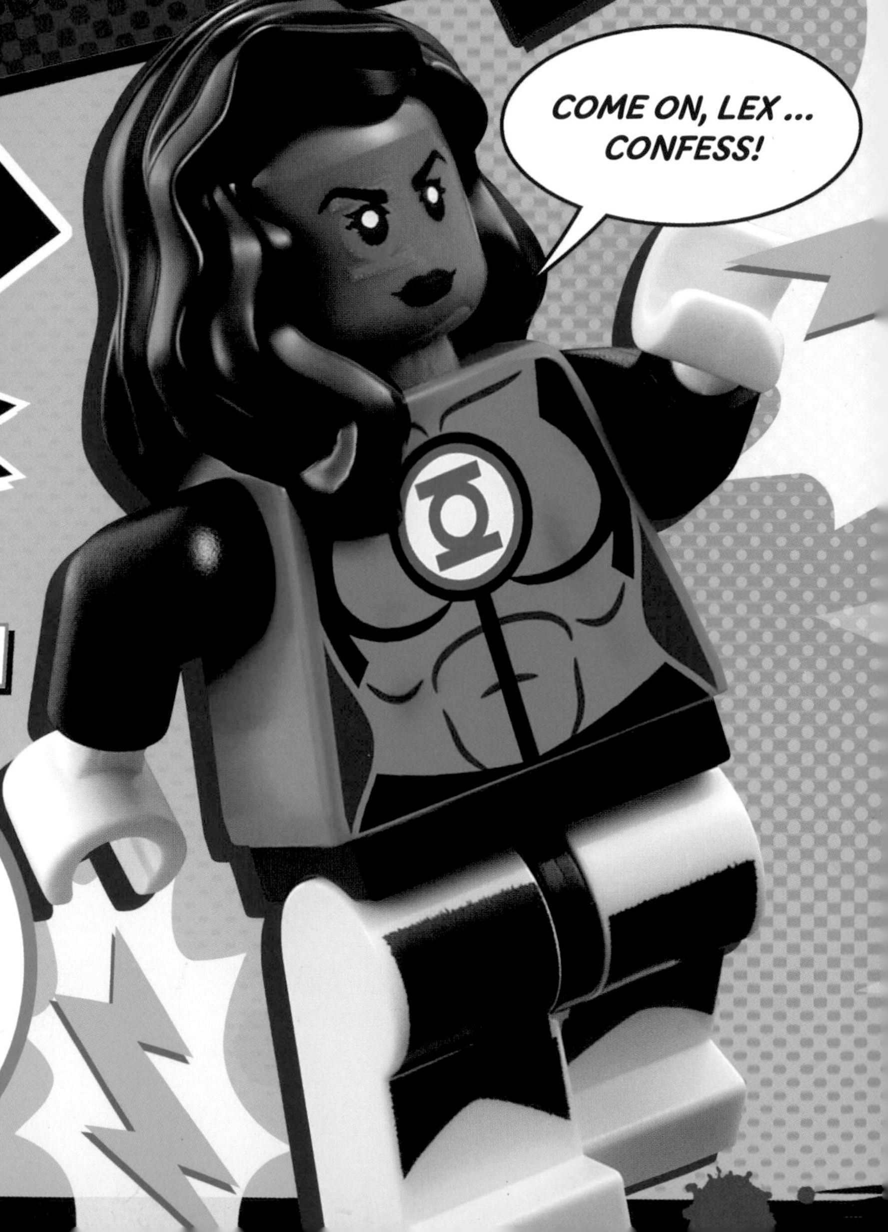

COME ON, LEX ... CONFESS!

Green Lantern

I wear the Green Lantern Corps **SYMBOL** on my chest

I'm not nervous ... I know how to **CONQUER MY FEARS!**

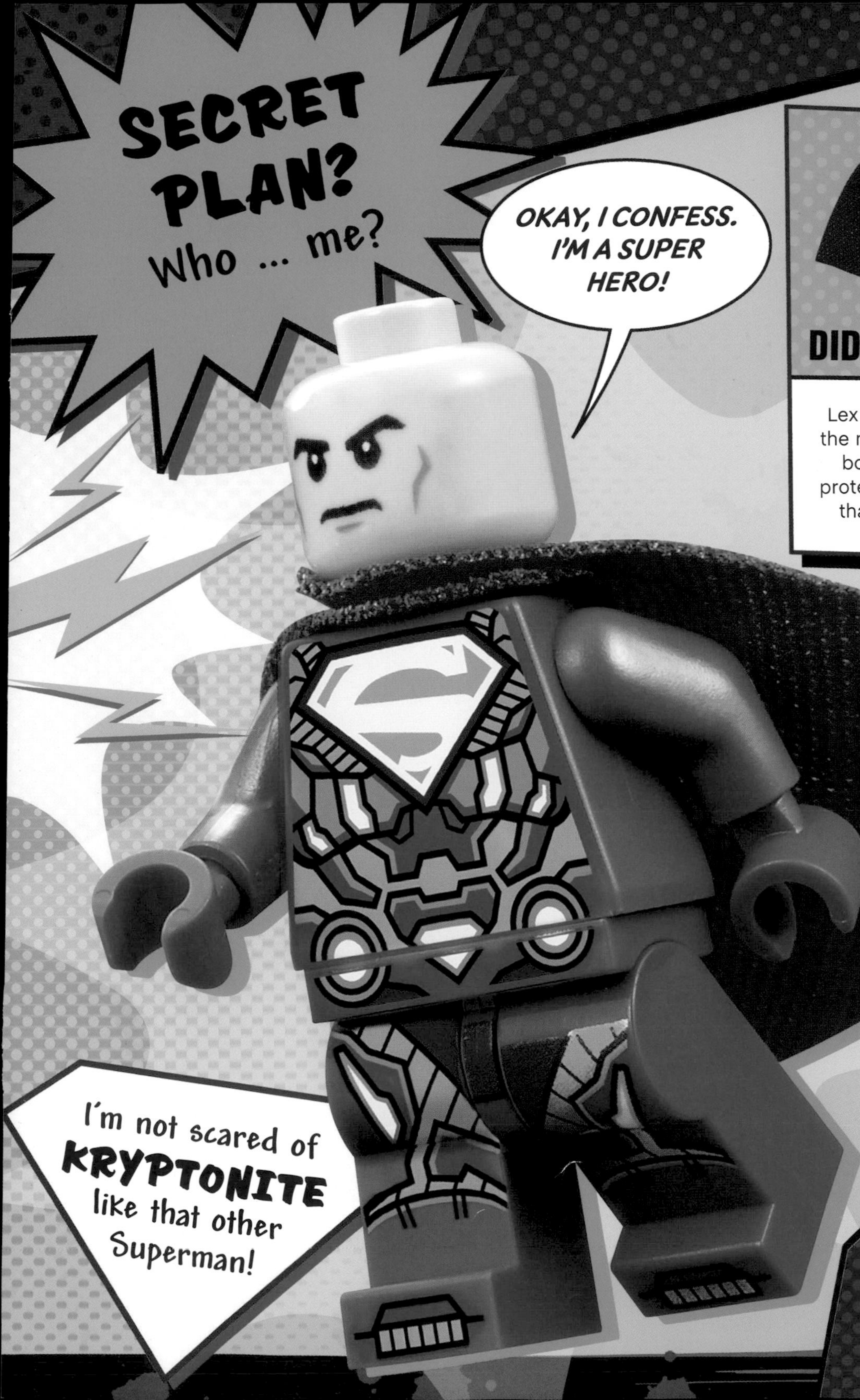
SECRET PLAN? Who ... me?
OKAY, I CONFESS. I'M A SUPER HERO!
I'm not scared of KRYPTONITE like that other Superman!

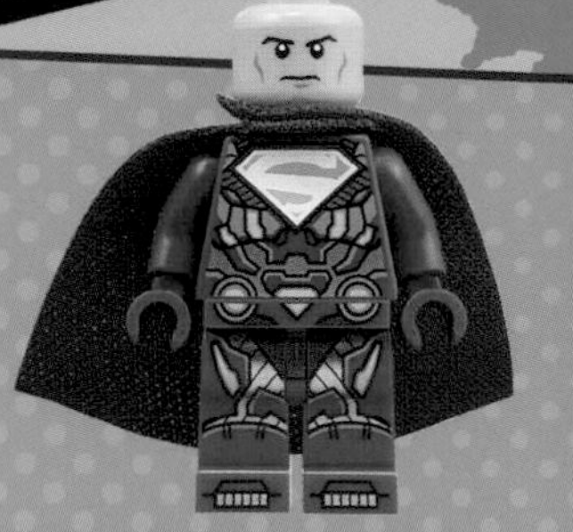

DID YOU KNOW?

Lex Luthor claims to be the new Superman. He is boasting that he will protect Metropolis better than the old one did!

Lex Luthor Superman

Which one will win this fierce face-off?

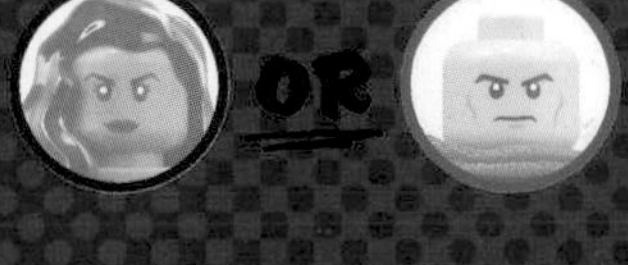
OR

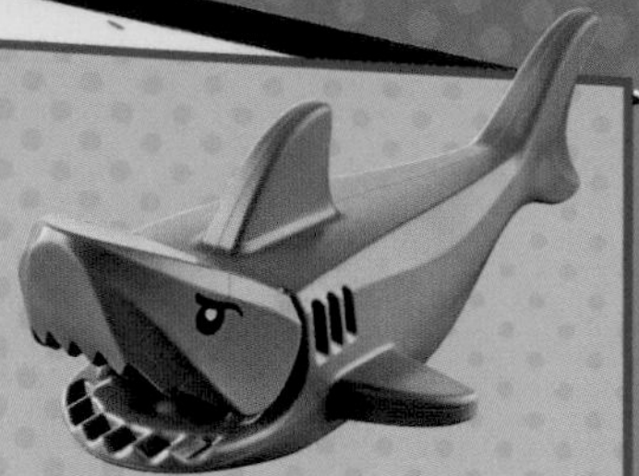

DID YOU KNOW?

Aquaman can communicate with sea animals. When he brings his snapping shark friend to the battle, it's crunch time for Ocean Master!

Ha! Your **HELMET** just looks silly ...

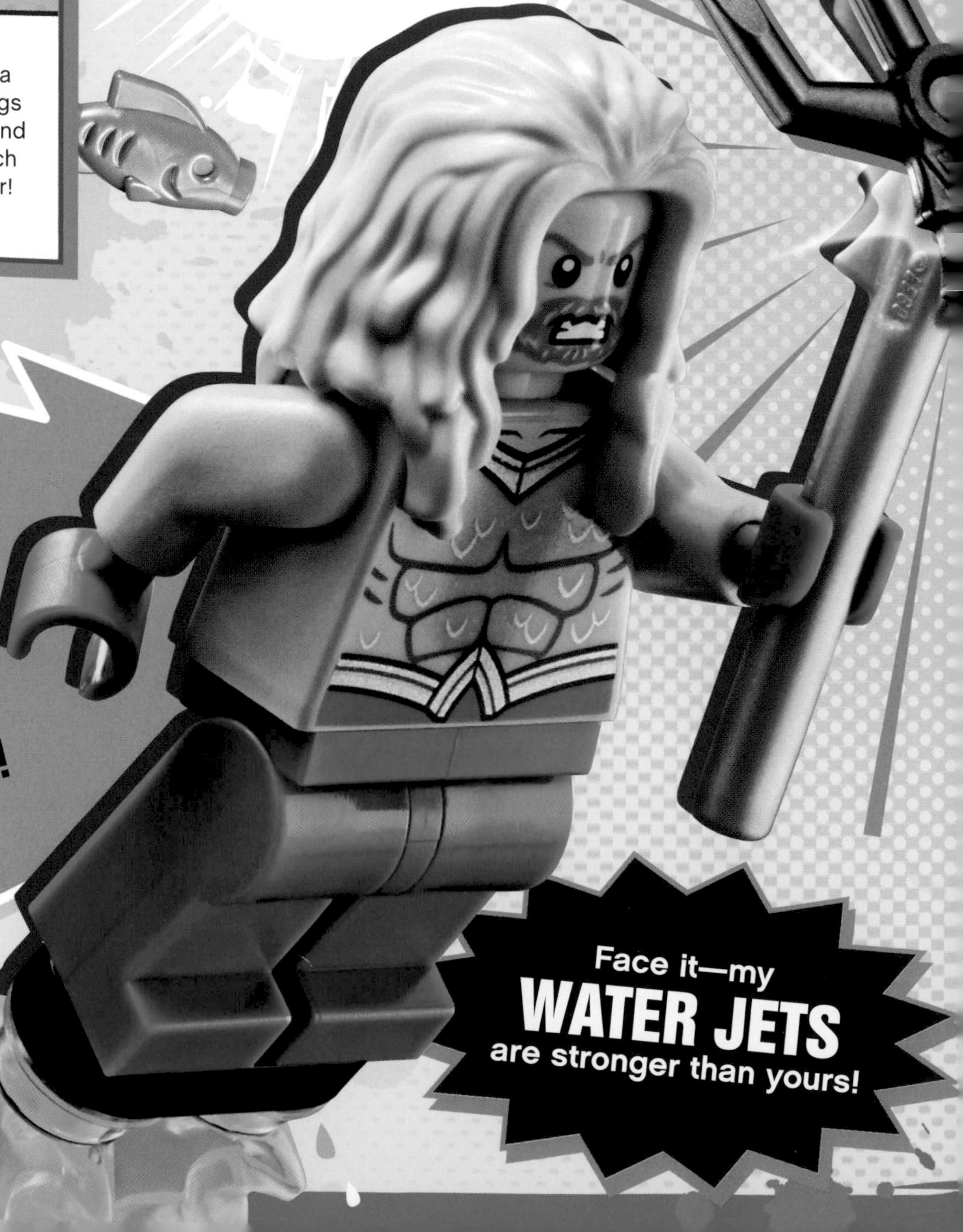

Only the **TRUE KING** of Atlantis can use this gold trident!

Face it—my **WATER JETS** are stronger than yours!

Aquaman

AQUAMAN VS. OCEAN MASTER

Aquaman and Ocean Master are battling beneath the waves. Which of them will win the throne of Atlantis? Tridents at the ready ...

Aquaman's trident controls the sea, and Ocean Master's trident controls lightning. It's a close contest!

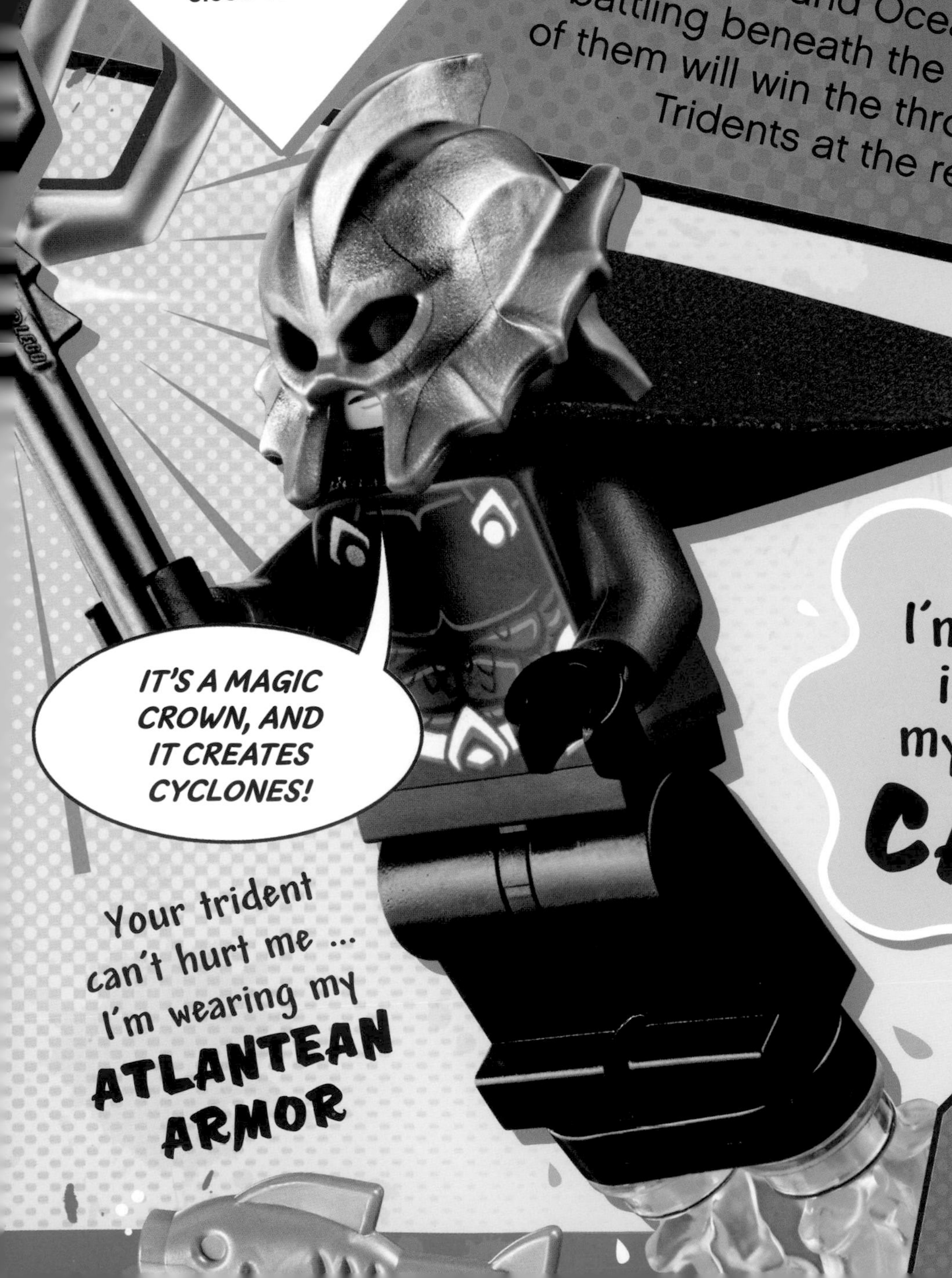

IT'S A MAGIC CROWN, AND IT CREATES CYCLONES!
Your trident can't hurt me ... I'm wearing my ATLANTEAN ARMOR
I'm a style icon in my bright CAPE

Ocean Master

Who would you like to see as King of Atlantis?

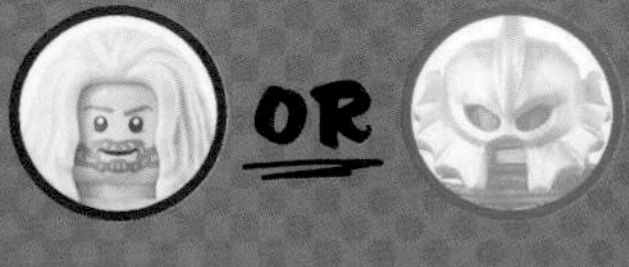

OR

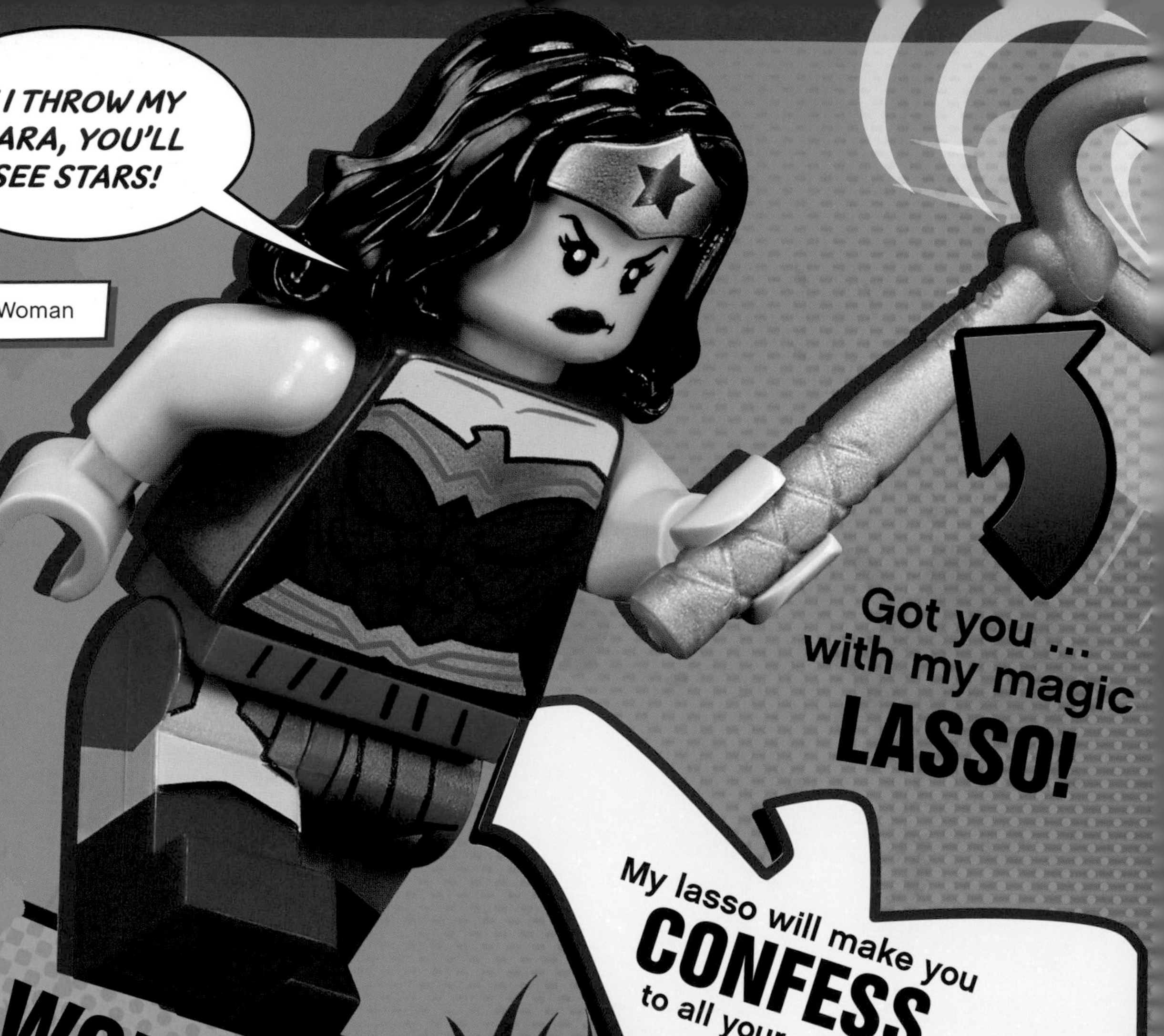
IF I THROW MY TIARA, YOU'LL SEE STARS!

Wonder Woman

Got you ... with my magic **LASSO!**

My lasso will make you **CONFESS** to all your crimes!

WONDER WOMAN VS. THE CHEETAH

The Cheetah is racing to attack Wonder Woman. Yikes ... she's fast! Can the Amazon princess capture the fast felon before she swipes her tiara?

Wonder Woman's royal tiara is like a boomerang ... it always returns to her. It might not stay in The Cheetah's claws for long!

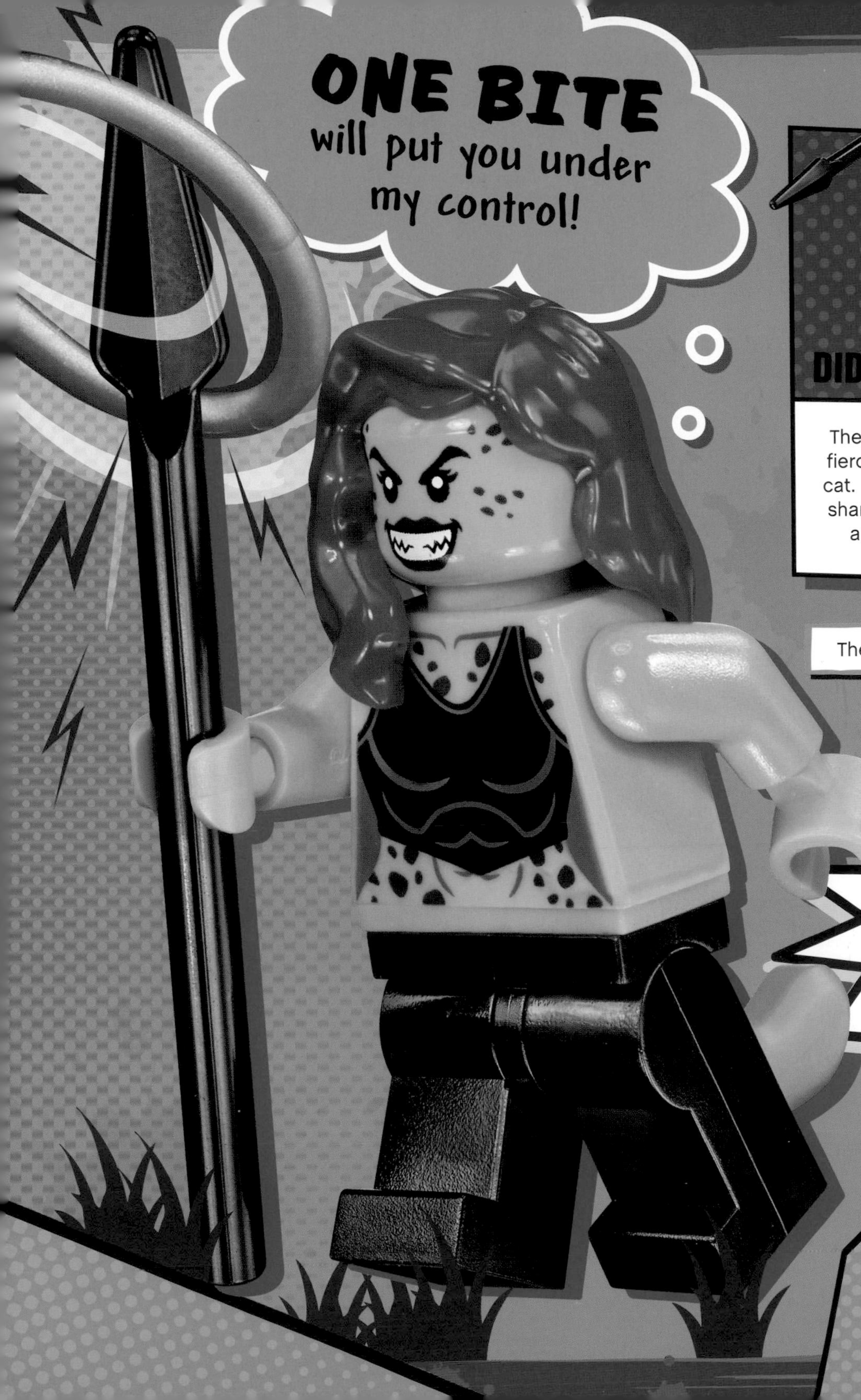
ONE BITE
will put you under my control!
I've got strong senses, and
I SENSE VICTORY!

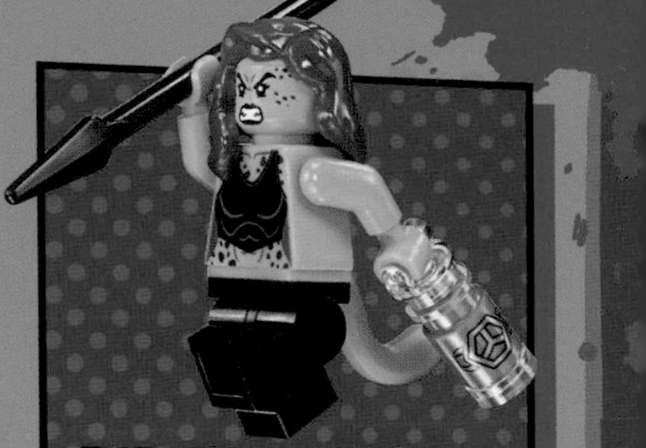

DID YOU KNOW?

The Cheetah is fast and fierce, just like a real big cat. She has sharp claws, sharp fangs, and carries a very sharp spear!

The Cheetah

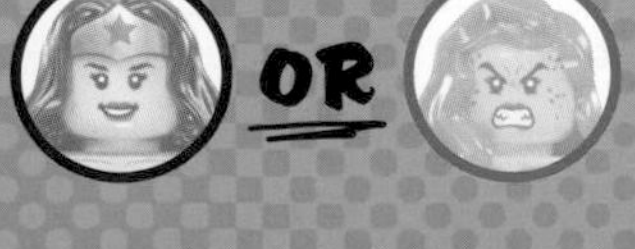
Which one will knock spots off their opponent?
OR

So what if I get hurt? I have rapid **HEALING** powers!

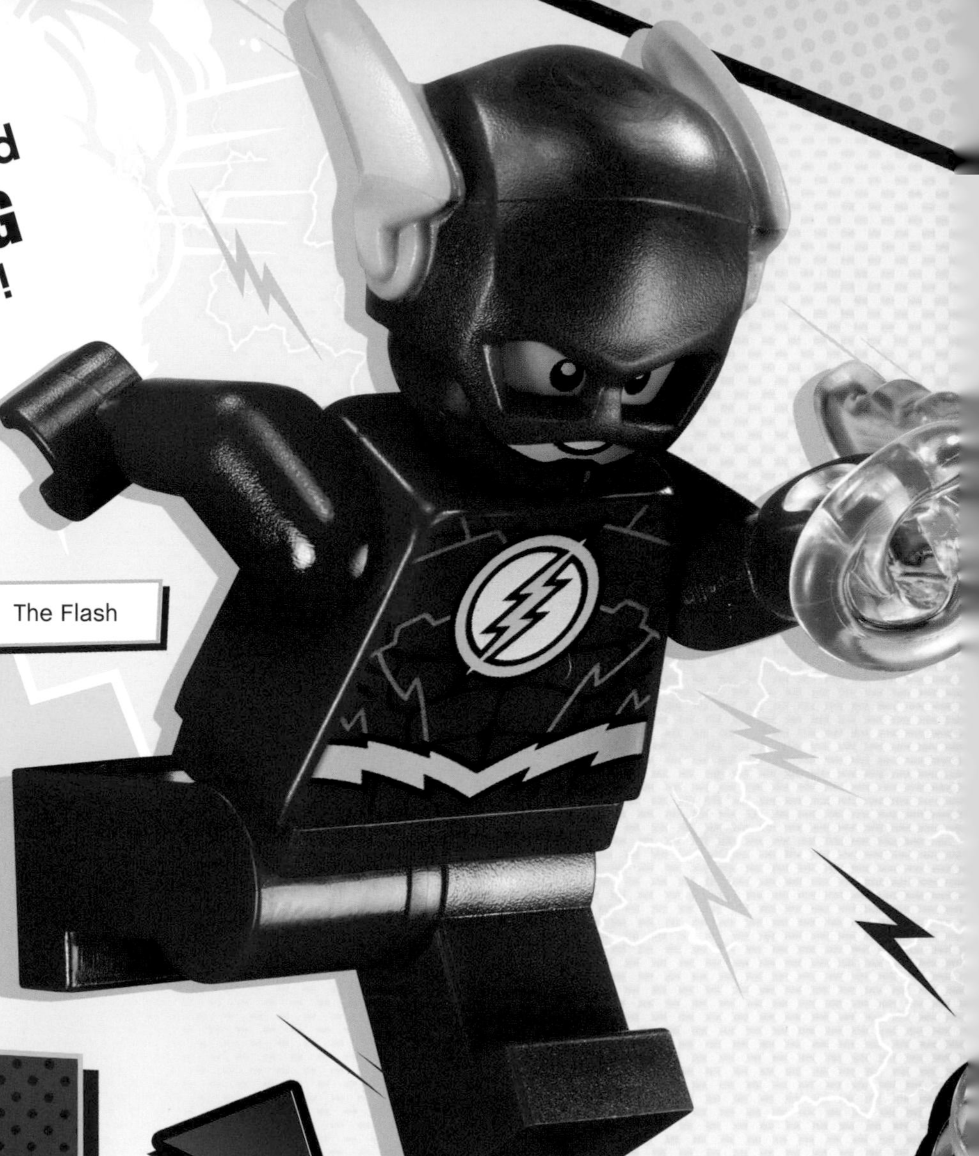

The Flash

When I whirl my arms, I create **CYCLONES** that put crooks in a spin!

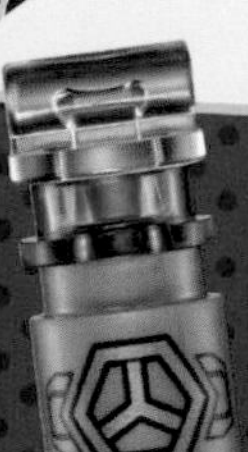

DID YOU KNOW?

This Blue Energy Infuser holds energy that can greatly enhance strength. Reverse-Flash didn't miss his chance to steal it!

You're fast ... but **NOT FASTER** than me!

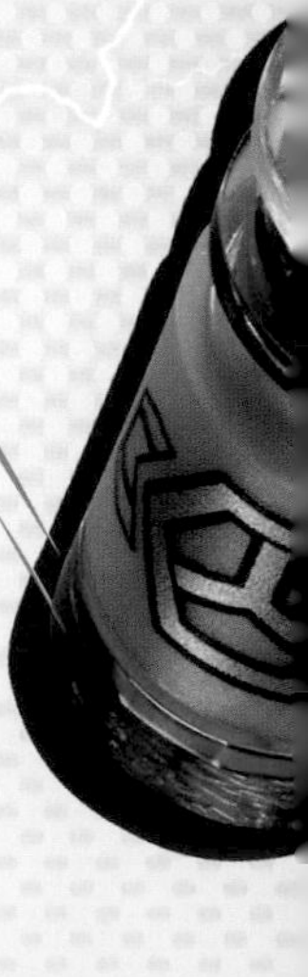

THE FLASH VS. REVERSE-FLASH

The Flash taps into the Speed Force to fight crime. Reverse-Flash taps into the negative Speed Force to commit crime. No wonder they are enemies!

The Flash and Reverse-Flash can run at speeds faster than light. When they go by, all you see is a blur.

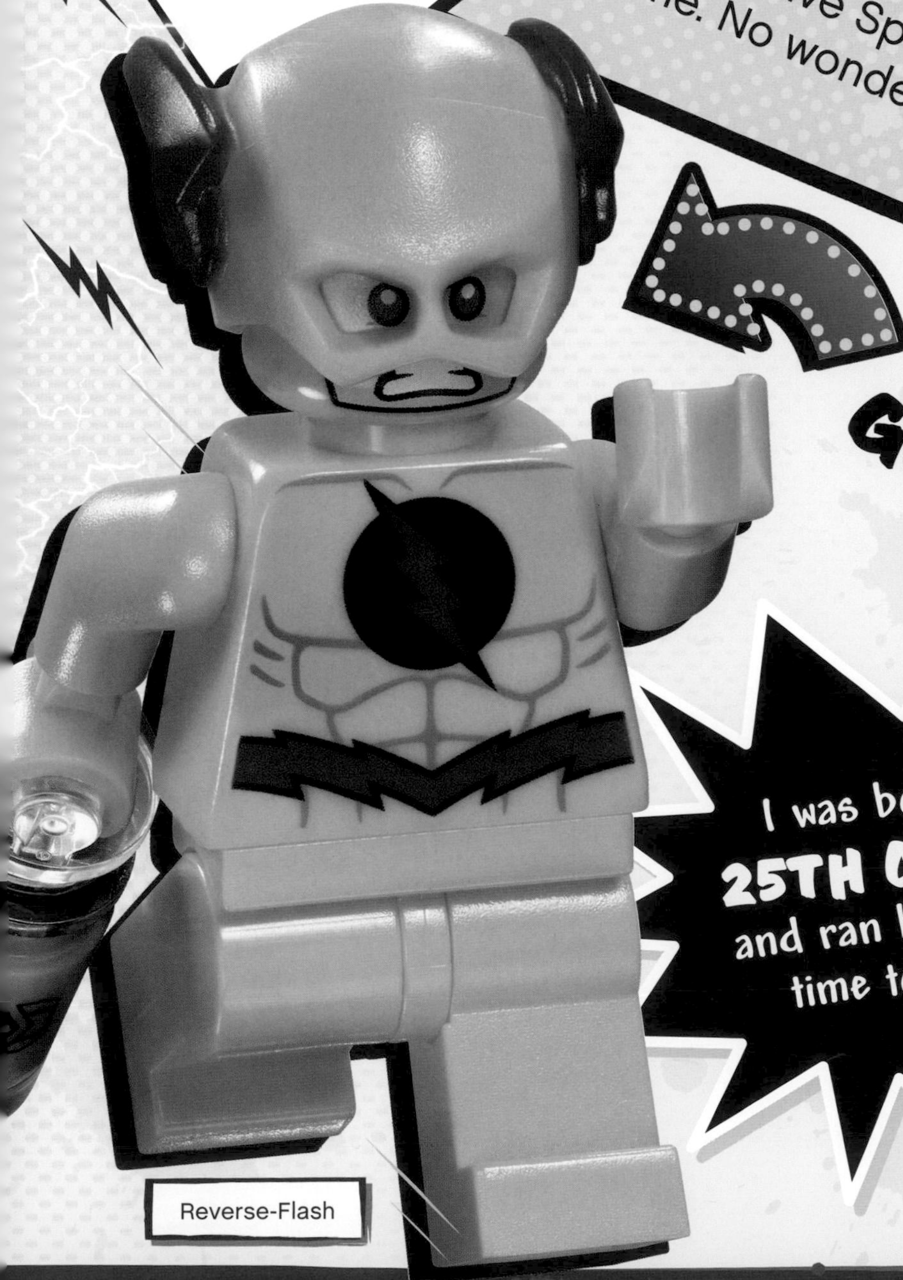

Reverse-Flash

I can focus electricity to make my eyes **GLOW RED!** Scary, huh?

I was born in the **25TH CENTURY** and ran back through time to get here.

Which Flash will outrun his archenemy?

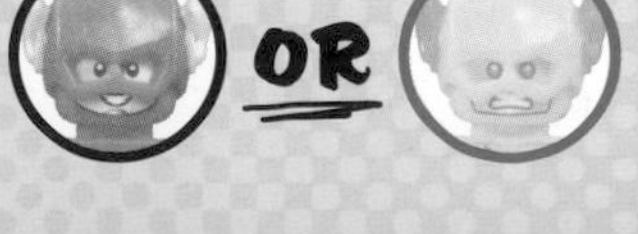
OR

SUPERMAN VS. LEX LUTHOR

Lex Luthor is a rich businessman who tries to control Metropolis. Superman knows Lex isn't the good guy he claims to be. He has to take Lex down—fast!

The "S" symbol on Superman's chest is not just his initial. It is also the crest of his Kryptonian family, the House of El.

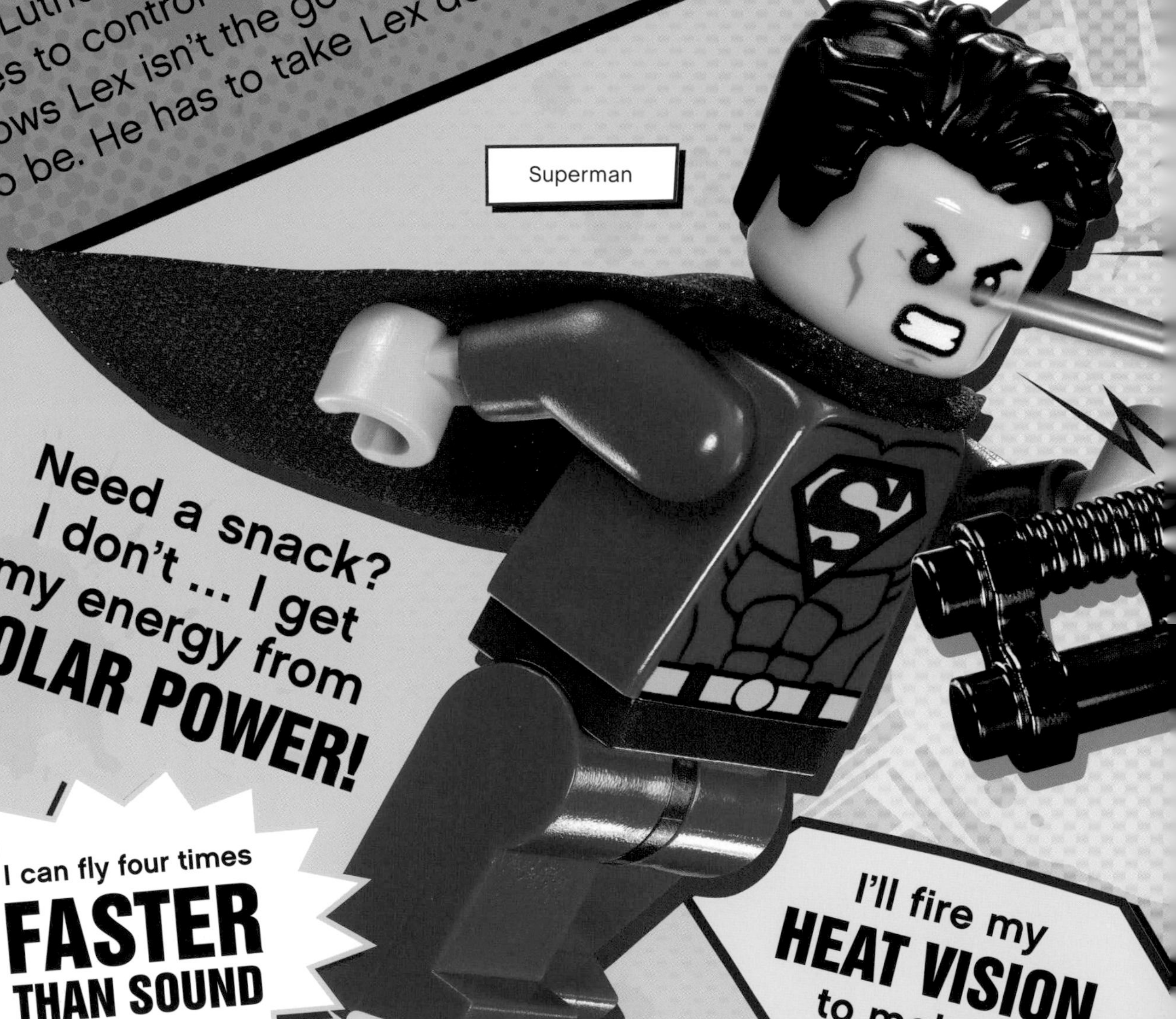

Superman

Need a snack? I don't ... I get my energy from **SOLAR POWER!**

I can fly four times **FASTER THAN SOUND**

I'll fire my **HEAT VISION** to melt your suit, Lex!

I've got Metropolis in the palm of my hand. My charity donations make me **MEGA POPULAR!**

Admit it, my **BALD HEAD** makes me look cool and streamlined!

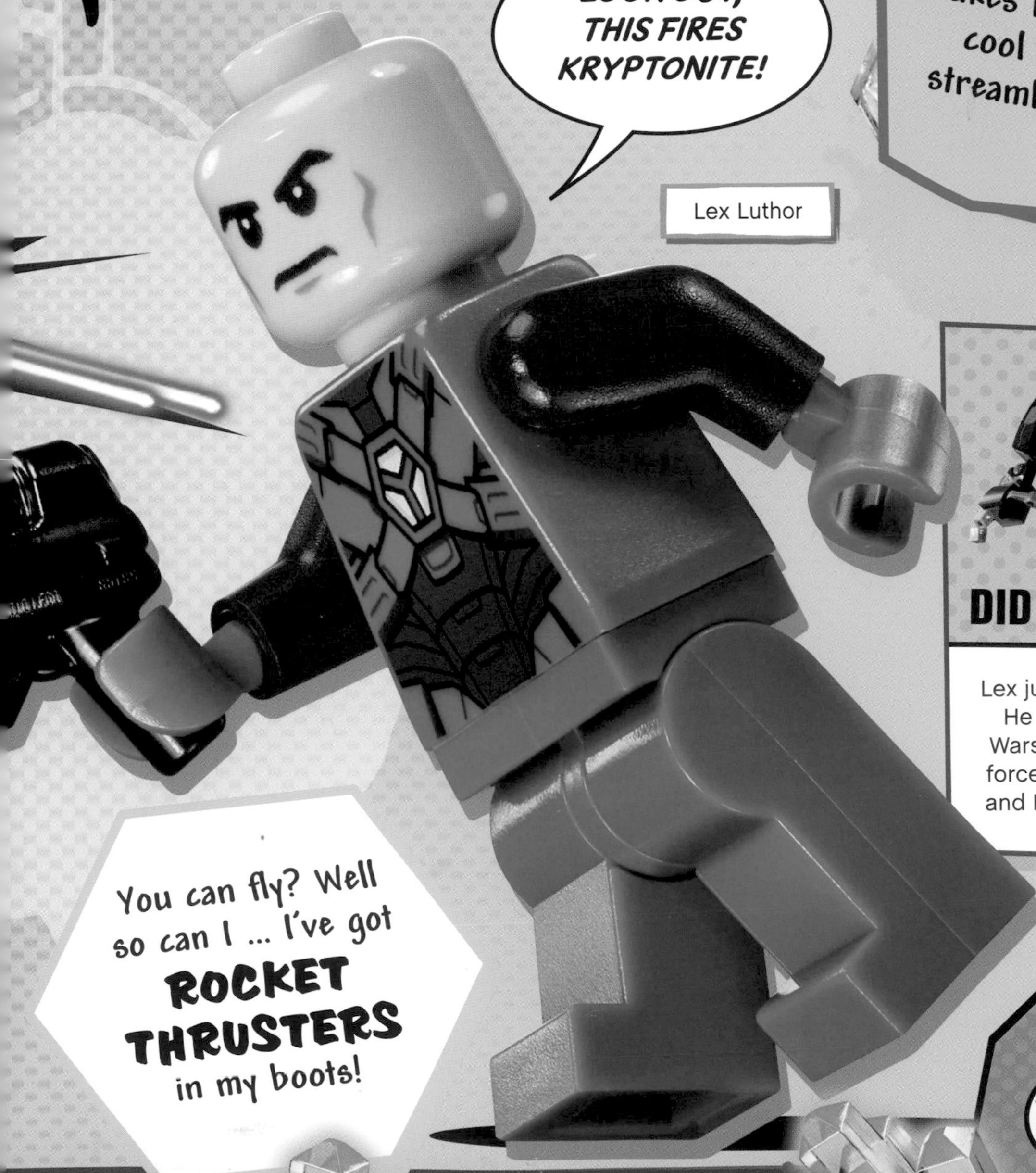
LOOK OUT, THIS FIRES KRYPTONITE!

Lex Luthor

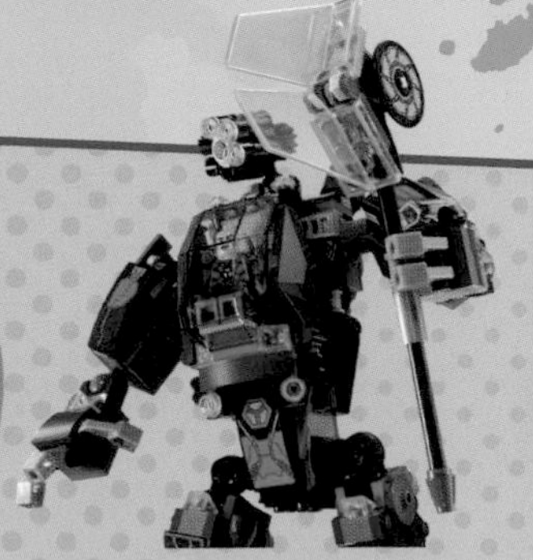

DID YOU KNOW?

Lex just loves technology. He owns a number of Warsuits with protective force fields, flight power, and Kryptonite weapons.

You can fly? Well so can I ... I've got **ROCKET THRUSTERS** in my boots!

Who will end up as the champion of Metropolis?

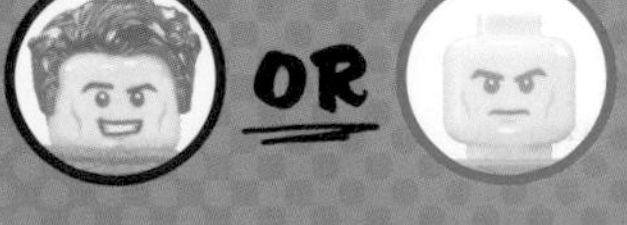
OR

FIRESTORM VS. FIREFLY

That pesky Firefly is starting fires everywhere just for fun. But Firestorm, the nuclear hero, is in hot pursuit. This battle could be explosive!

Firestorm can manipulate nuclear energy. He uses it to fly, transform objects, and fire explosive energy blasts!

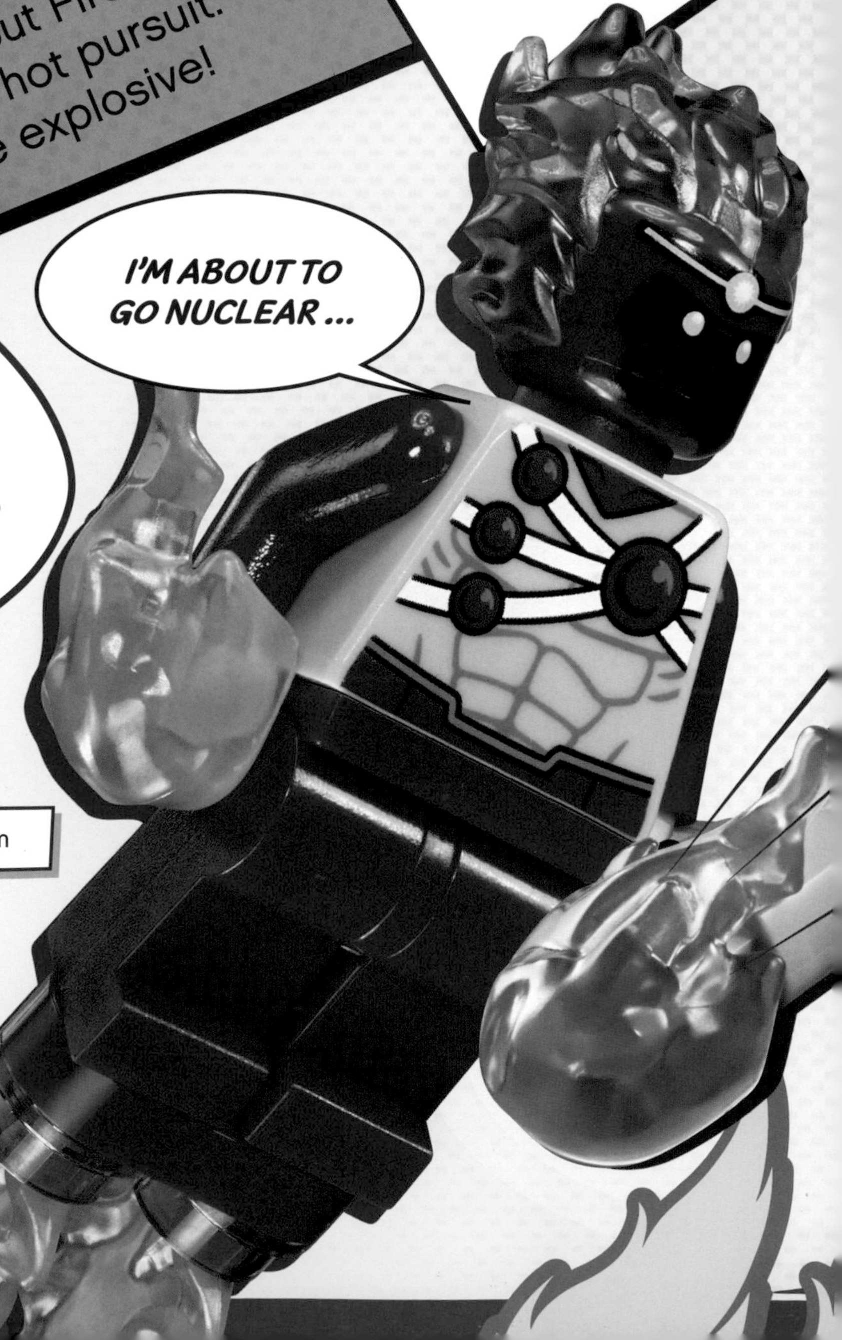

I'M ABOUT TO GO NUCLEAR ...
I'll tweak the **ATOMS** in your blaster and turn it into a sticky bun!

Firestorm

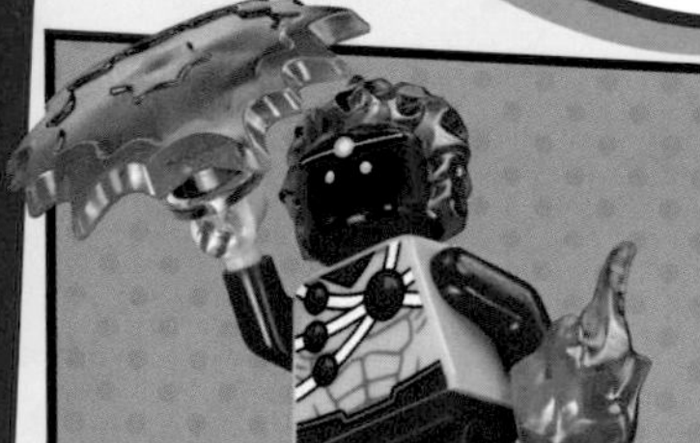

DID YOU KNOW?

Firestorm is two people in one! Scientist Jason Rusch and sporty Ronnie Raymond were joined together by the "Firestorm Matrix."

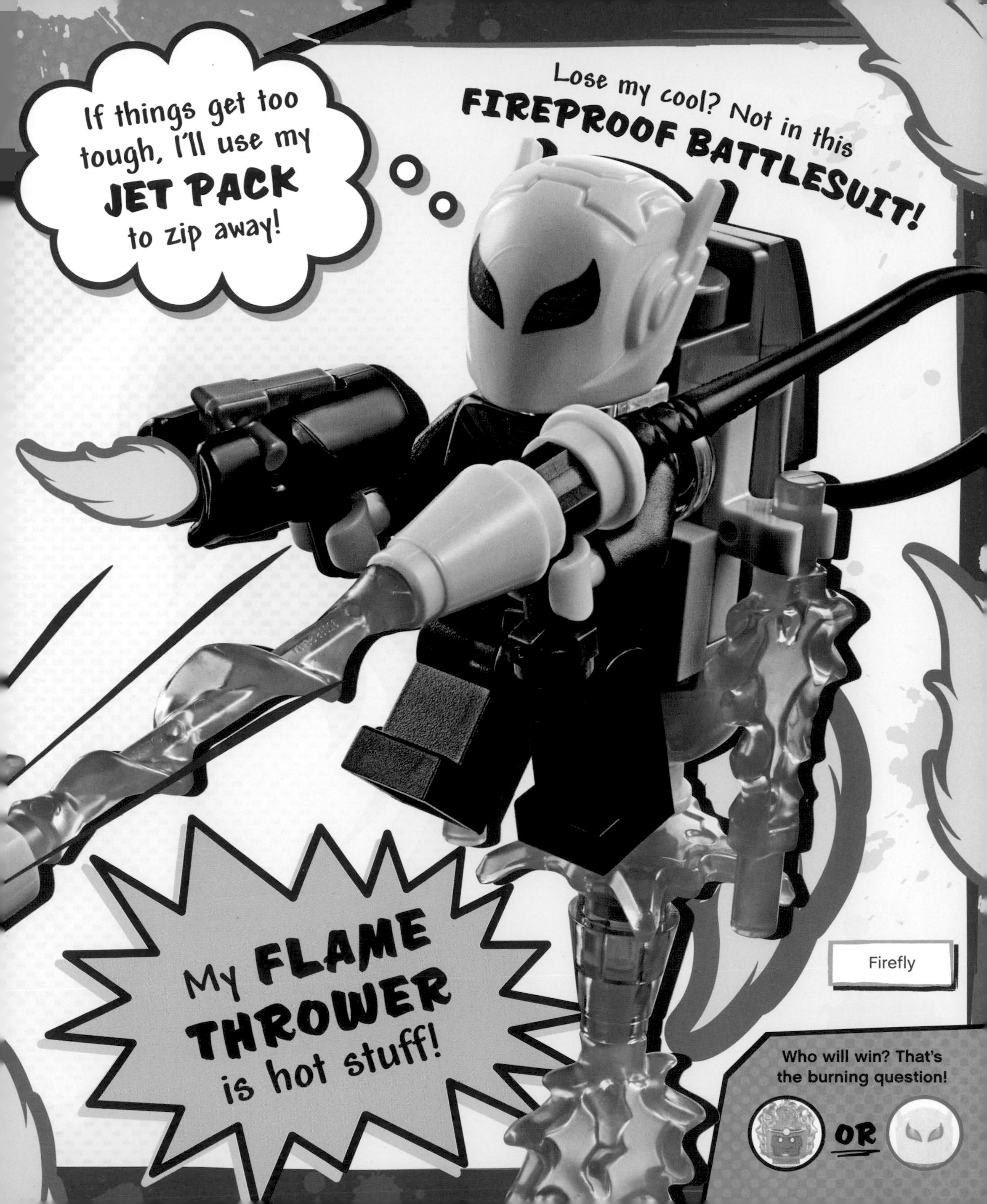
If things get too tough, I'll use my JET PACK to zip away!
Lose my cool? Not in this FIREPROOF BATTLESUIT!
My FLAME THROWER is hot stuff!
Firefly
Who will win? That's the burning question!
OR

MERA VS. BLACK MANTA

A shark is chasing Black Manta and Mera! Who is most likely to escape: Black Manta with his technology or Mera with her Atlantean powers?

Queen Mera of Atlantis is a super-fast swimmer. She often travels at 300,000 miles an hour—and that's just her cruising speed!

I'M NOBODY'S FAST FOOD!

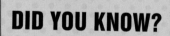

Mera

DID YOU KNOW?

Mera controls water with just her thoughts. She can build solid objects out of water or use it to create powerful blasts.

Back off, or I'll **BLAST** you both out of the water!

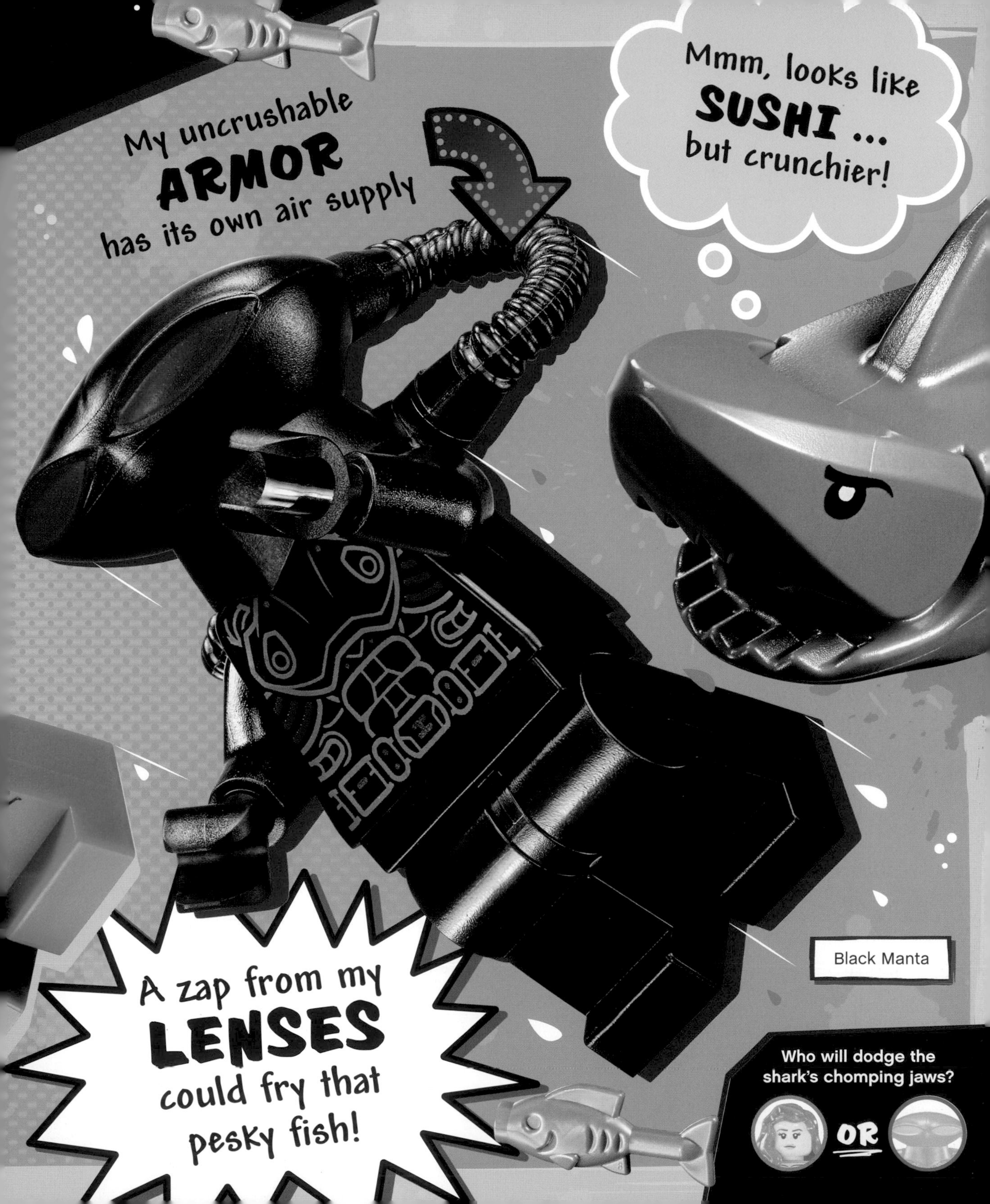

My uncrushable ARMOR has its own air supply
Mmm, looks like SUSHI ... but crunchier!
Black Manta
A zap from my LENSES could fry that pesky fish!
Who will dodge the shark's chomping jaws?
OR

LEX ON THE LOOSE

Billionaire Lex Luthor is stomping in his mech while The Cheetah steals the Energy Infuser. The Super Heroes must stop them!

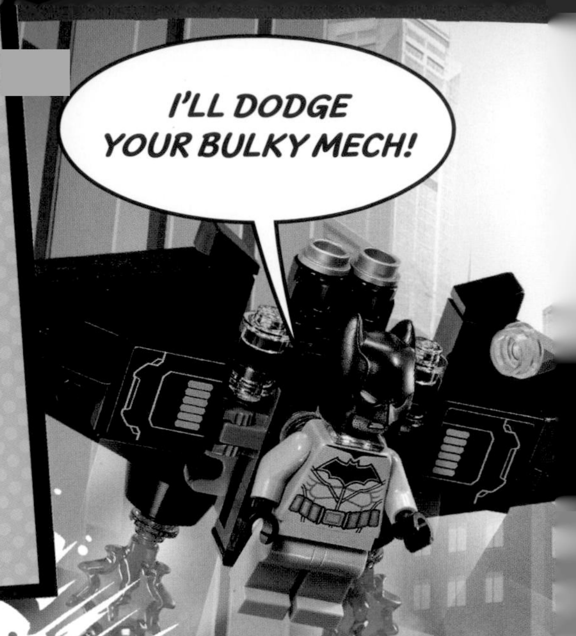
I'LL DODGE YOUR BULKY MECH!

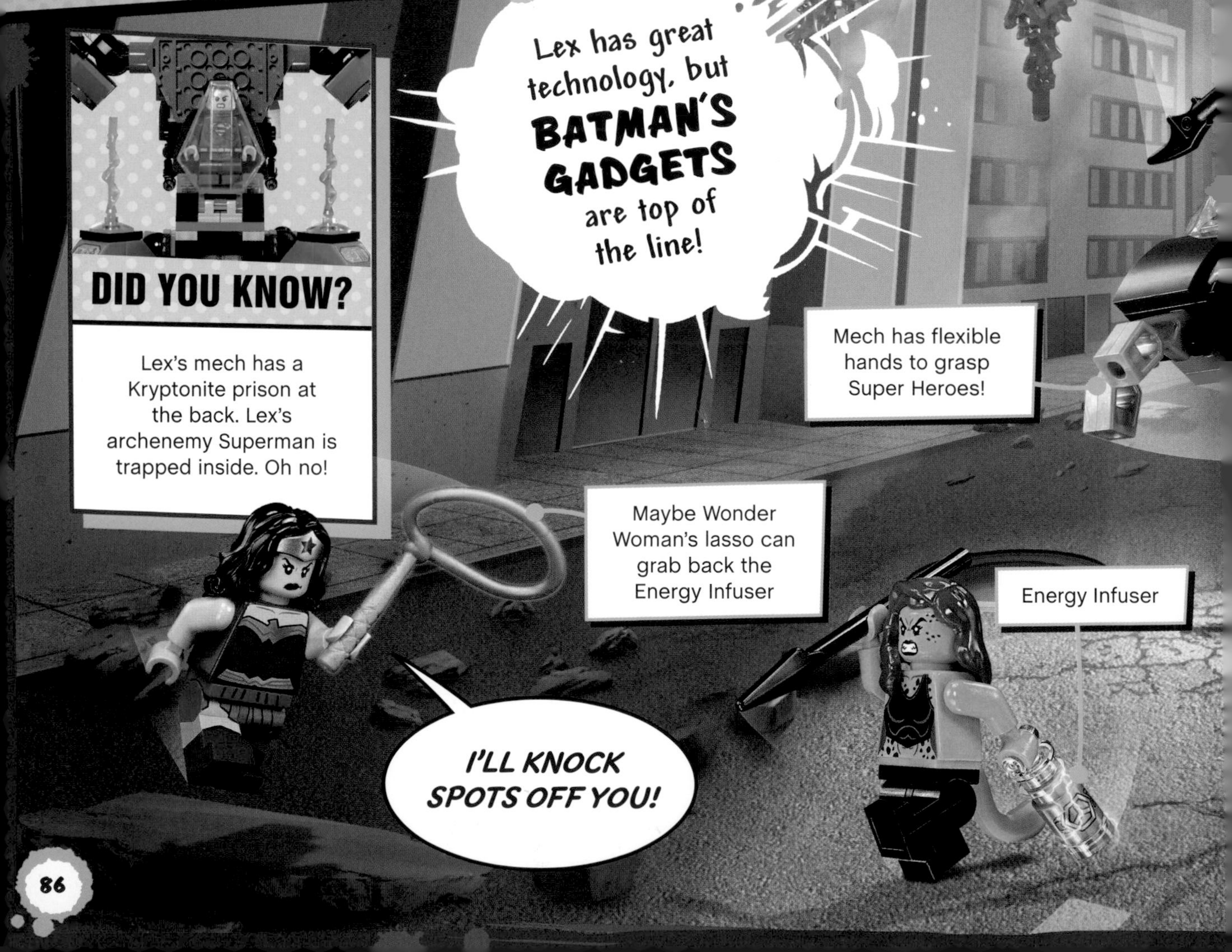
Lex has great technology, but BATMAN'S GADGETS are top of the line!
Mech has flexible hands to grasp Super Heroes!
Maybe Wonder Woman's lasso can grab back the Energy Infuser
Energy Infuser
I'LL KNOCK SPOTS OFF YOU!

DID YOU KNOW?

Lex's mech has a Kryptonite prison at the back. Lex's archenemy Superman is trapped inside. Oh no!

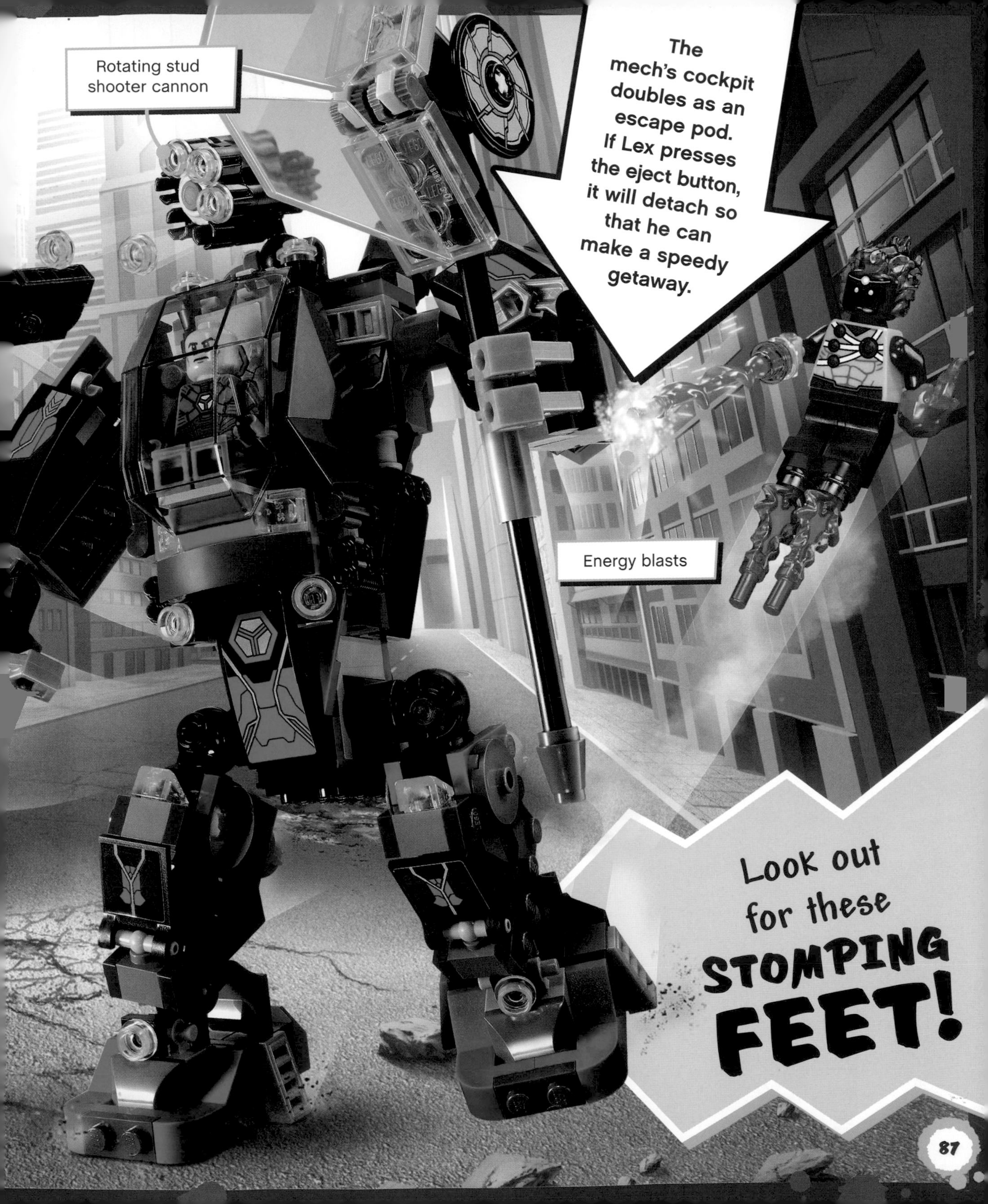
Rotating stud shooter cannon
The mech's cockpit doubles as an escape pod. If Lex presses the eject button, it will detach so that he can make a speedy getaway.
Energy blasts
Look out for these STOMPING FEET!

SHAZAM VS. PARADEMON

Argh! The tyrant Darkseid has sent one of his Parademons to ravage the Earth. Can Shazam send the invader packing—without his stolen loot?

Billy Batson is a teenage boy, but if he says "Shazam!", he becomes a superpowered hero. A wizard gave him his amazing abilities.

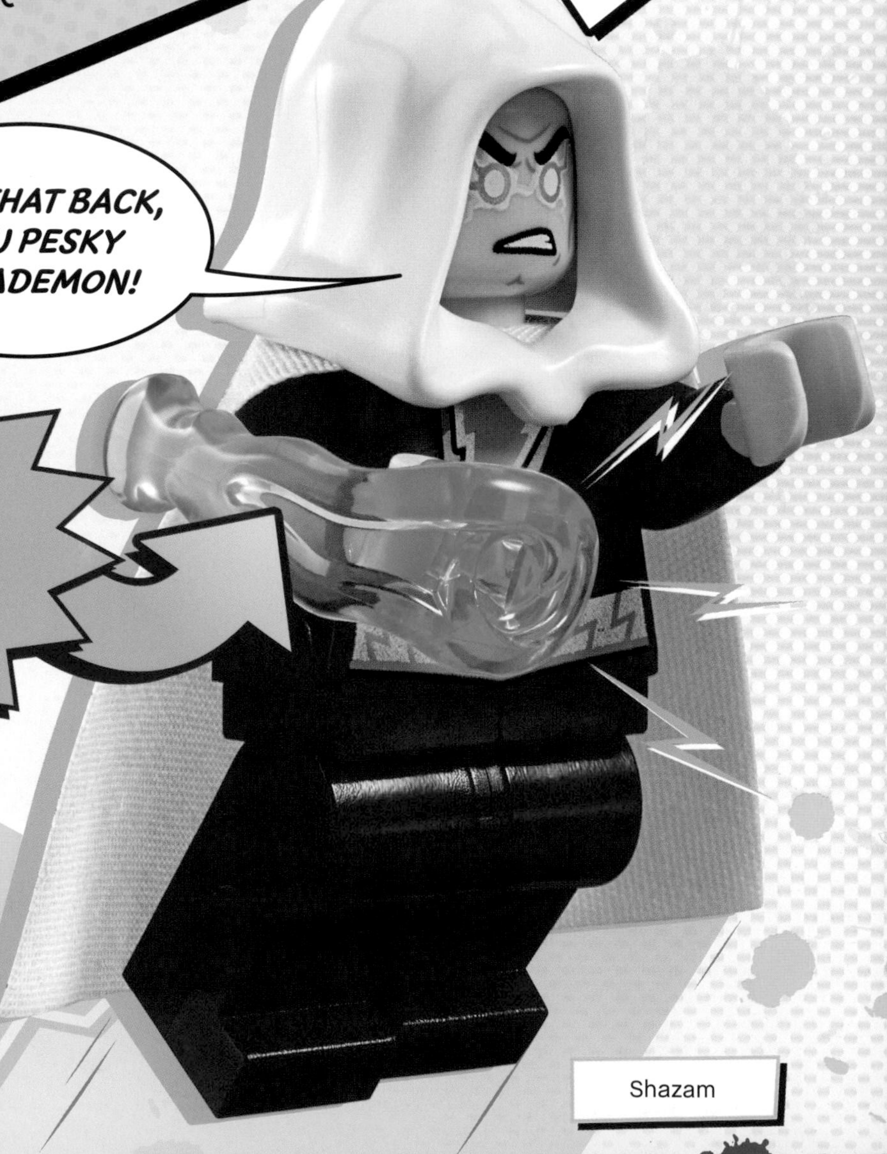
GIVE THAT BACK, YOU PESKY PARADEMON!

Shazam

Stand back! This blue bolt of **ENERGY** means I'm powering up ...

I have the powers of the legendary **GREEK GODS**

You can chase me home **TO APOKOLIPS,** but I'll be back ... with a Parademon posse!

Parademon

I am protected by my strong **ARMOR**

DID YOU KNOW?

A Mother Box is a living computer that is loyal to its owner. This means if it gets stolen, it won't work for the thief!

Don't underestimate me—I have **SUPERHUMAN** strength!

Which one will get the better of his opponent?

 **OR** 

DID YOU KNOW?

Blue Beetle is allowed to borrow the Batcopter to chase after Killer Moth. Batman trusts his beetle buddy to fly carefully!

YOU'RE JUST A PEST. ADIOS!

Blue Beetle

My armor is **ROBOTIC** and loaded with weapons

If things get tight, I'll call my teammates: THE TEEN TITANS

I'll open a WORMHOLE in space ... and send you through it!

BLUE BEETLE VS. KILLER MOTH

Killer Moth is a villain for hire. For a fee, he will assist other villains in their evil deeds. If Blue Beetle can stop him in full flight, many crimes will be avoided!

Killer Moth has a blaster that shoots sticky threads. Enemies who get too close find themselves wrapped up in a tight cocoon!

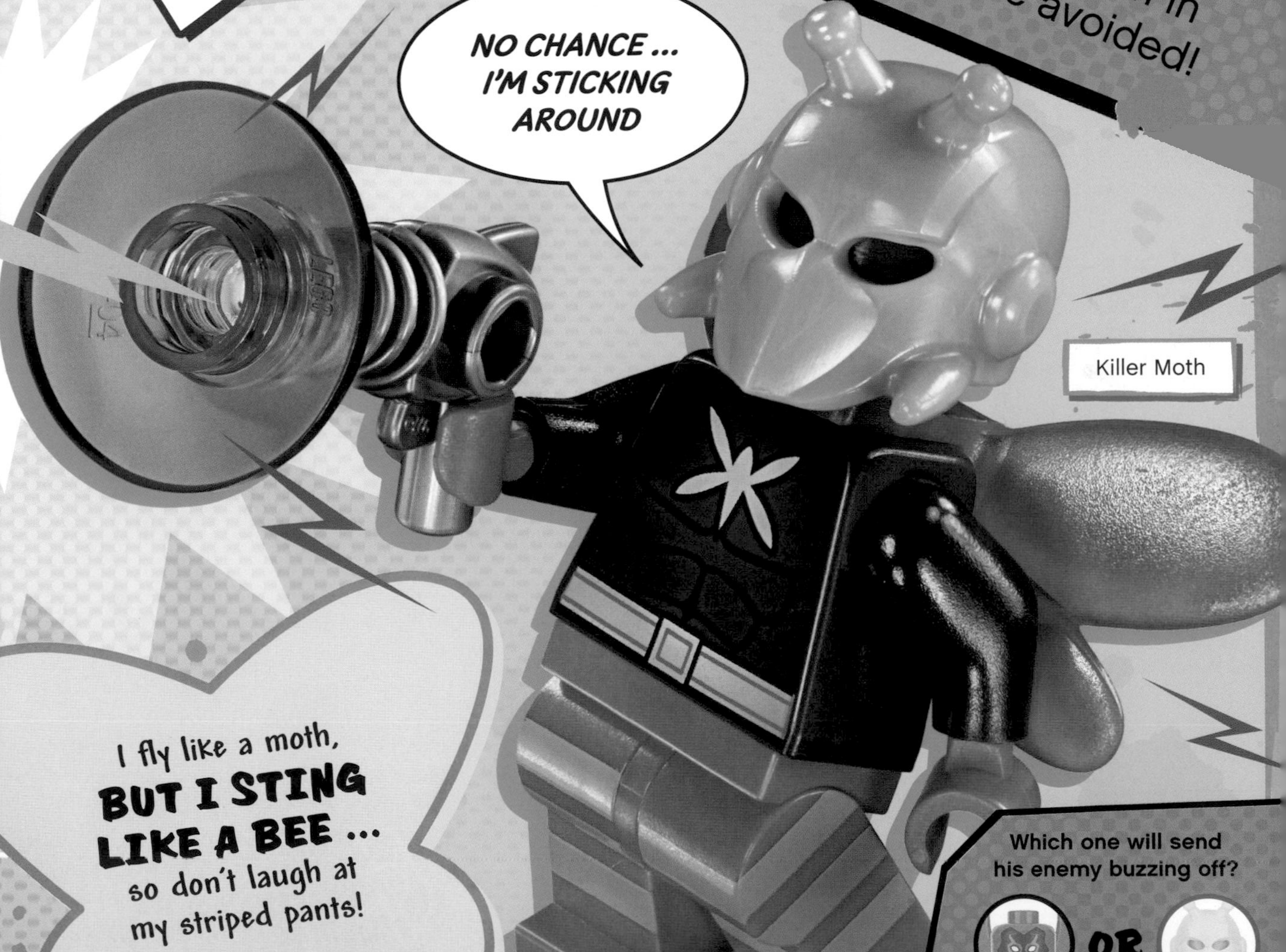
NO CHANCE ... I'M STICKING AROUND
Killer Moth
I fly like a moth, BUT I STING LIKE A BEE ... so don't laugh at my striped pants!

Which one will send his enemy buzzing off?

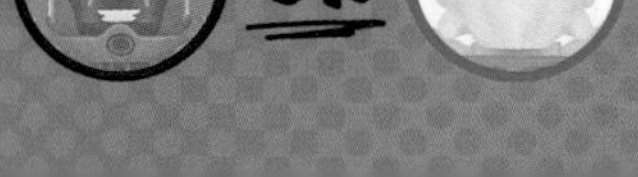
OR

CYBORG VS. DEADSHOT

That mean sniper-for-hire Deadshot is coming for Cyborg, but he's got his work cut out for him. Cyborg is ready to put up a metal-mashing fight!

Deadshot will hunt down anyone for the right fee. Many villains would happily pay to get rid of the crime-busting Cyborg!

I have an **IQ OF 170:** that's genius level!

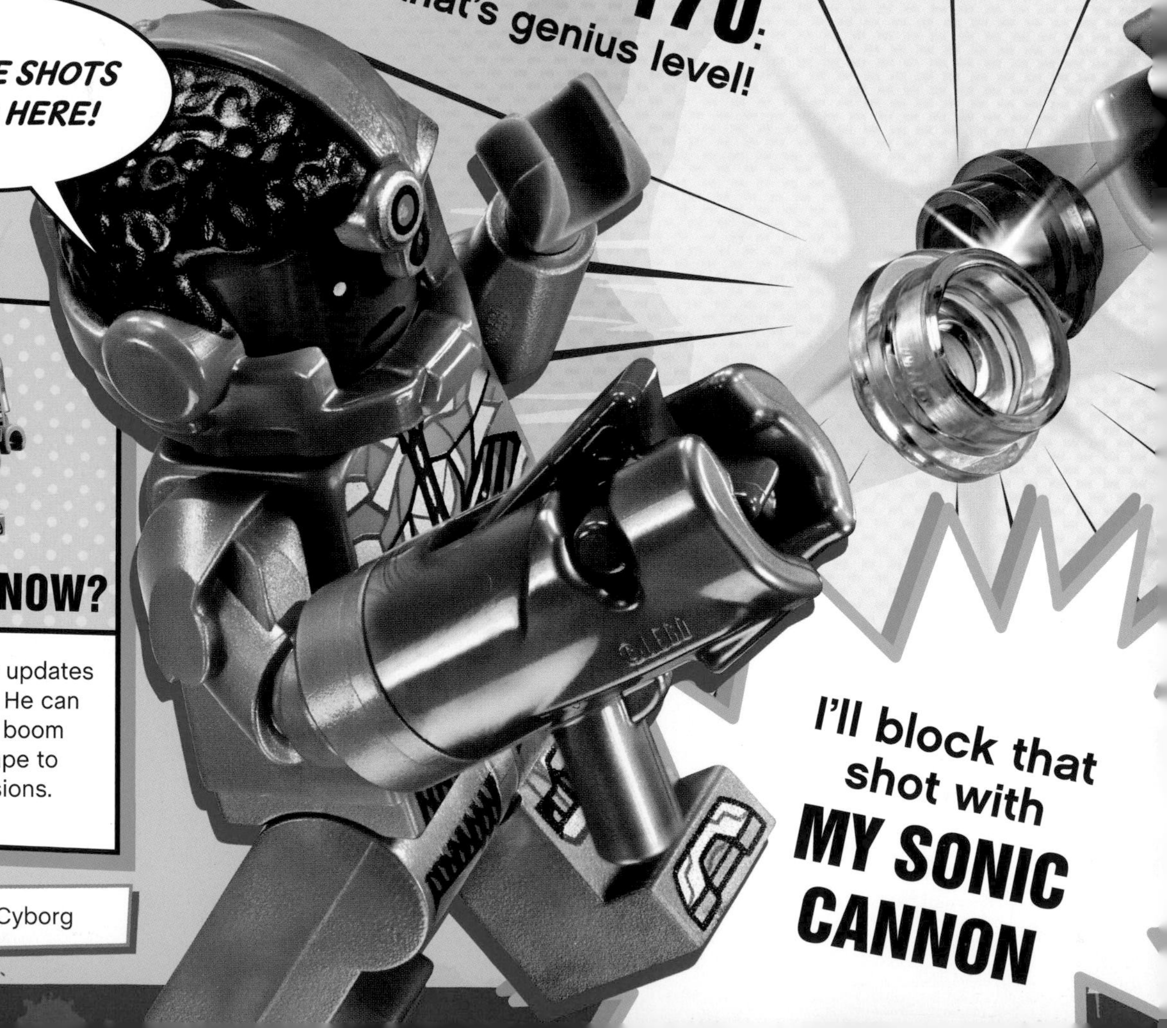
I CALL THE SHOTS AROUND HERE!

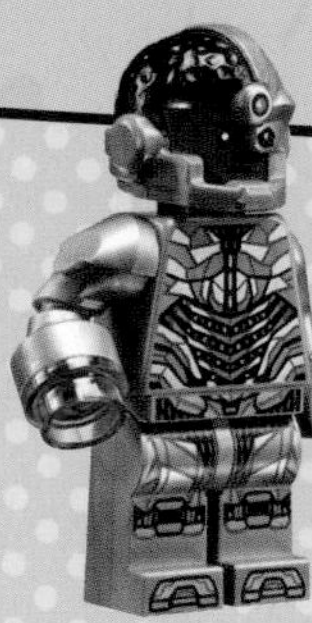

DID YOU KNOW?

Cyborg regularly updates his robot parts. He can also generate boom tubes to escape to other dimensions.

Cyborg

I'll block that shot with **MY SONIC CANNON**

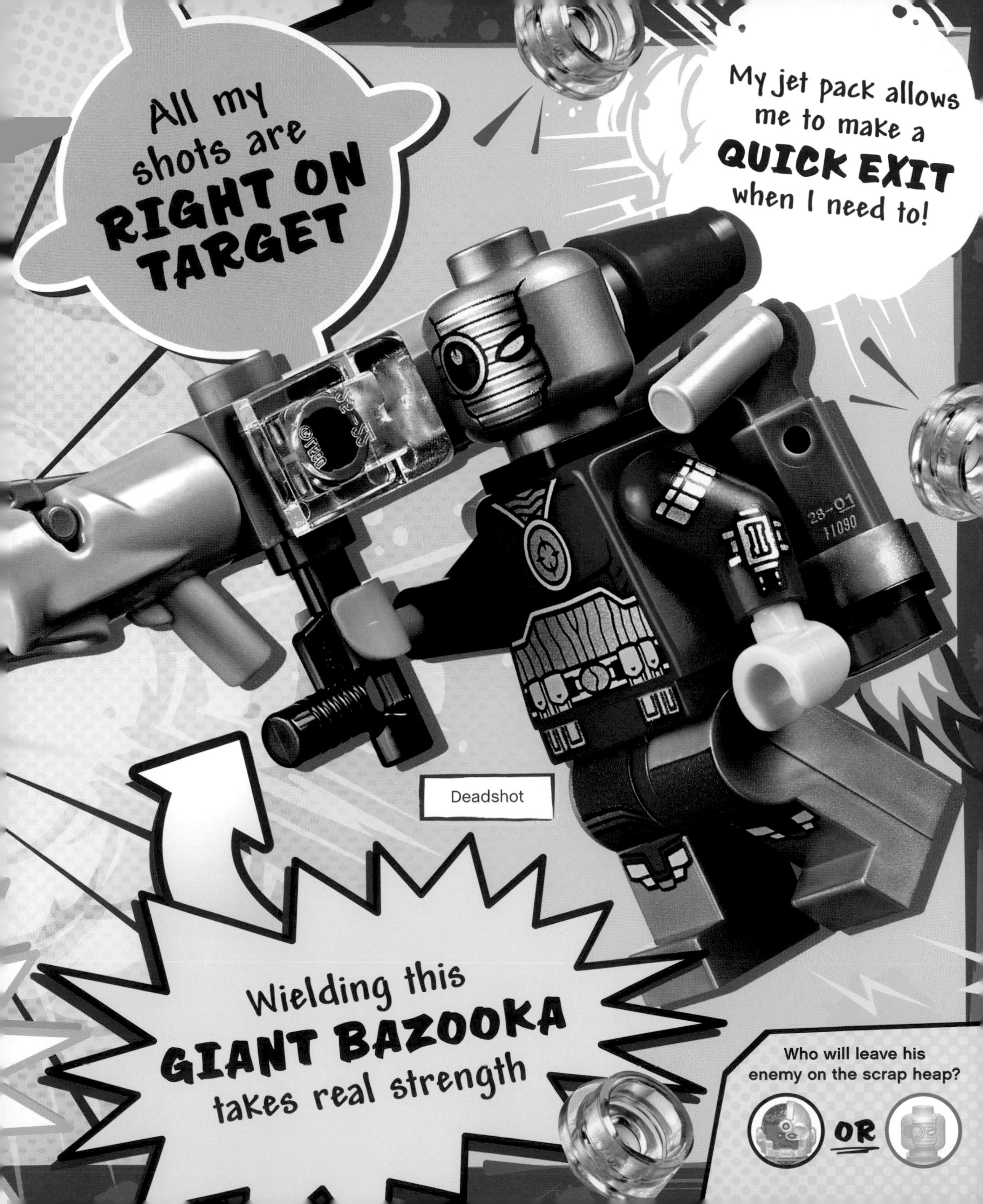
All my shots are RIGHT ON TARGET
My jet pack allows me to make a QUICK EXIT when I need to!
Deadshot
Wielding this GIANT BAZOOKA takes real strength
Who will leave his enemy on the scrap heap?
OR

KATANA VS. TALON

Who is the finest ninja fighter? Heroic Katana and a villainous Talon plan to settle the matter. Expect amazing swordplay and sneaky skills!

STEALTH is my game ... I just appear out of nowhere!

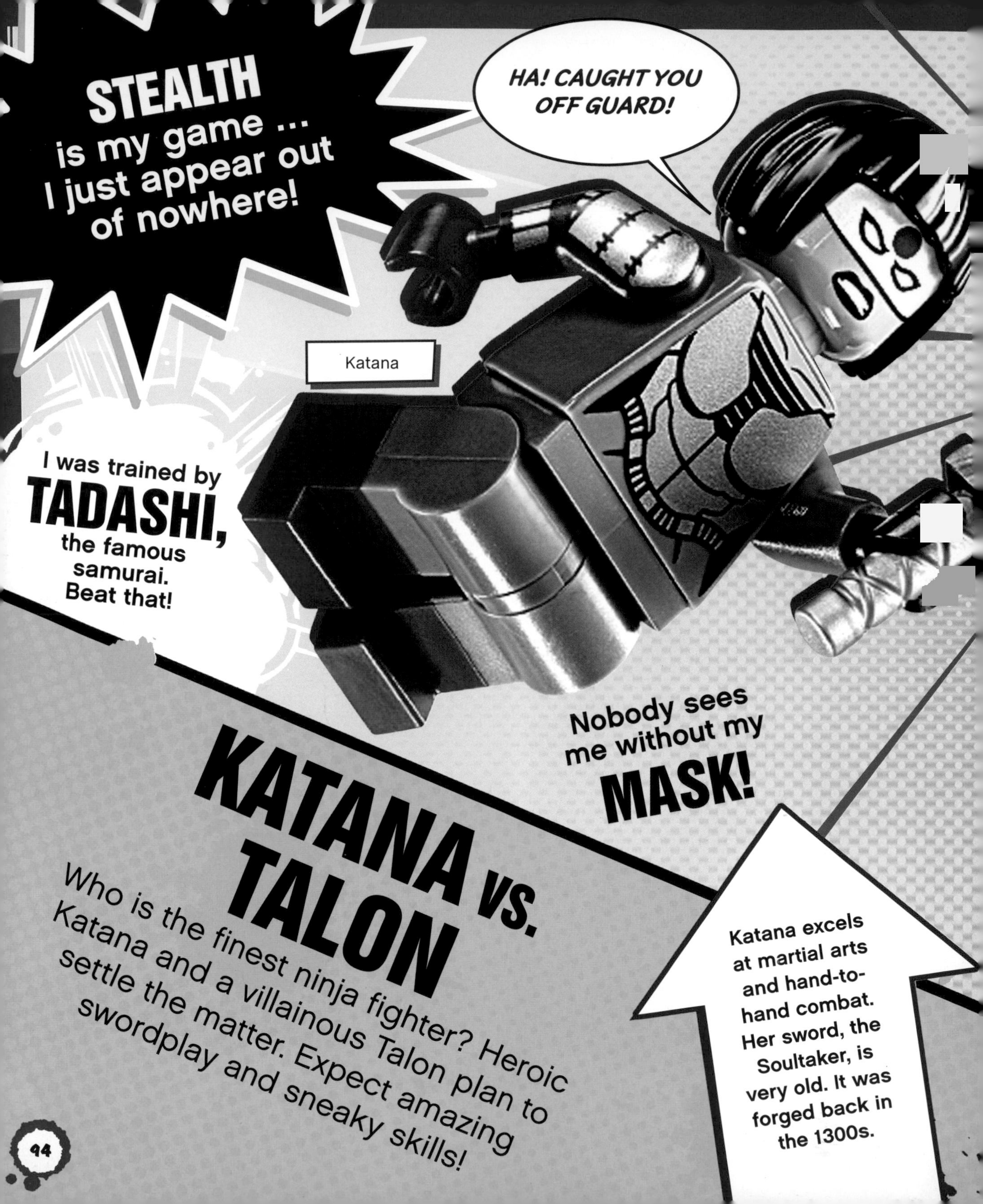

HA! CAUGHT YOU OFF GUARD!
Katana

I was trained by **TADASHI,** the famous samurai. Beat that!

Nobody sees me without my **MASK!**

Katana excels at martial arts and hand-to-hand combat. Her sword, the Soultaker, is very old. It was forged back in the 1300s.

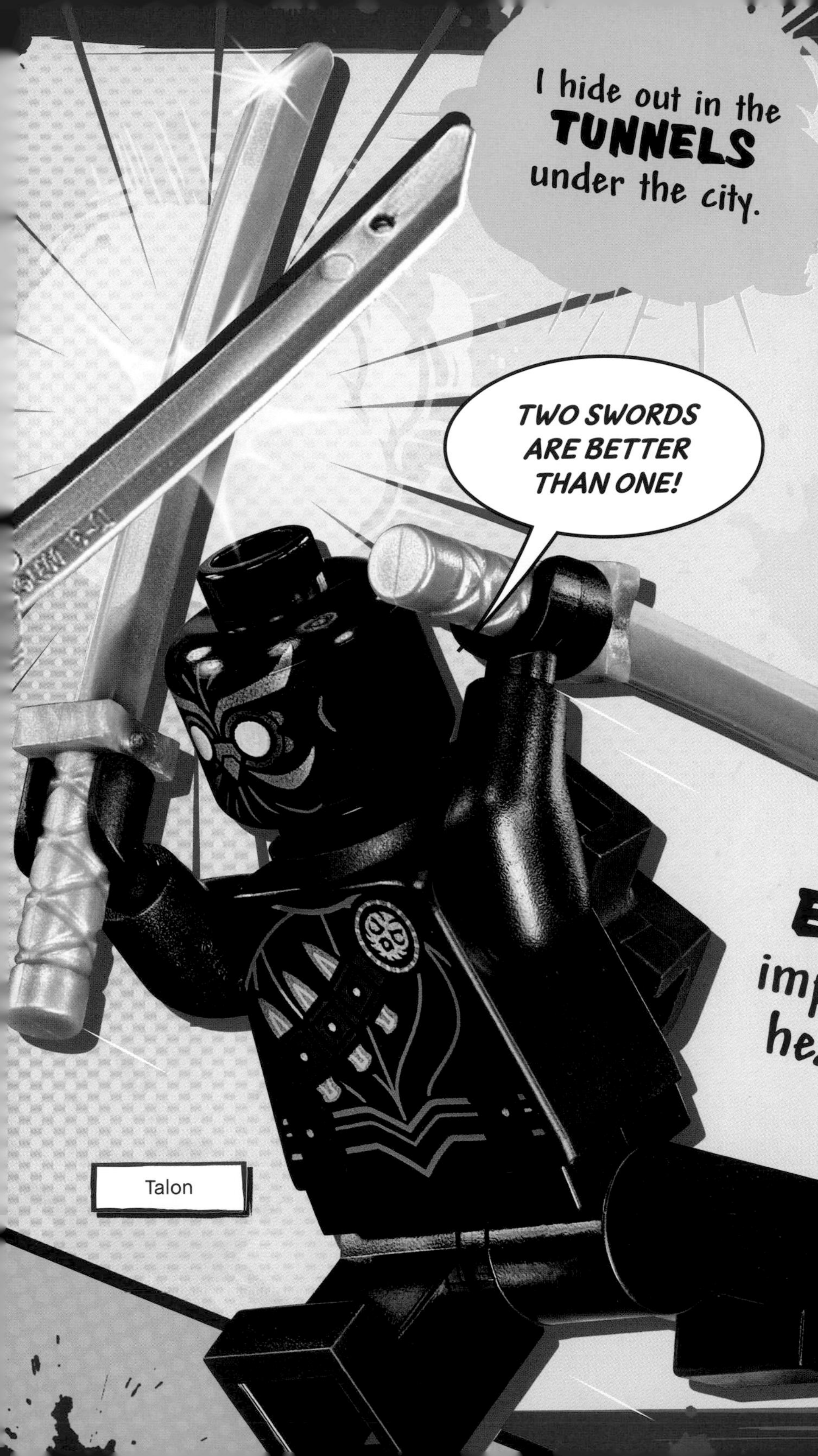
I hide out in the TUNNELS under the city.
TWO SWORDS ARE BETTER THAN ONE!
ELECTRUM implants give me healing powers
Talon

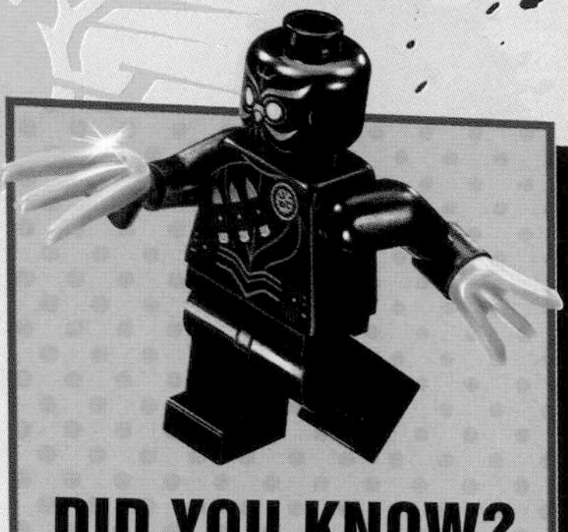

DID YOU KNOW?

The Talons are trained assassins who work for criminals called the Court of Owls. They are known as Talons because of their bladed claws.

Who is the nimblest ninja in Gotham City?

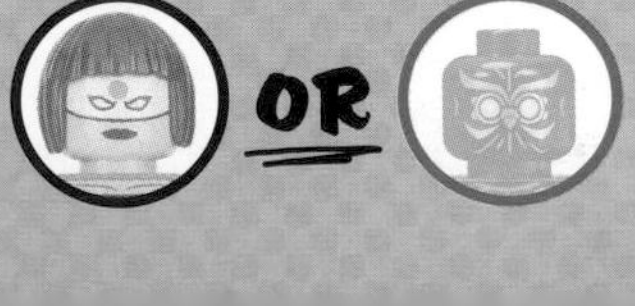
OR

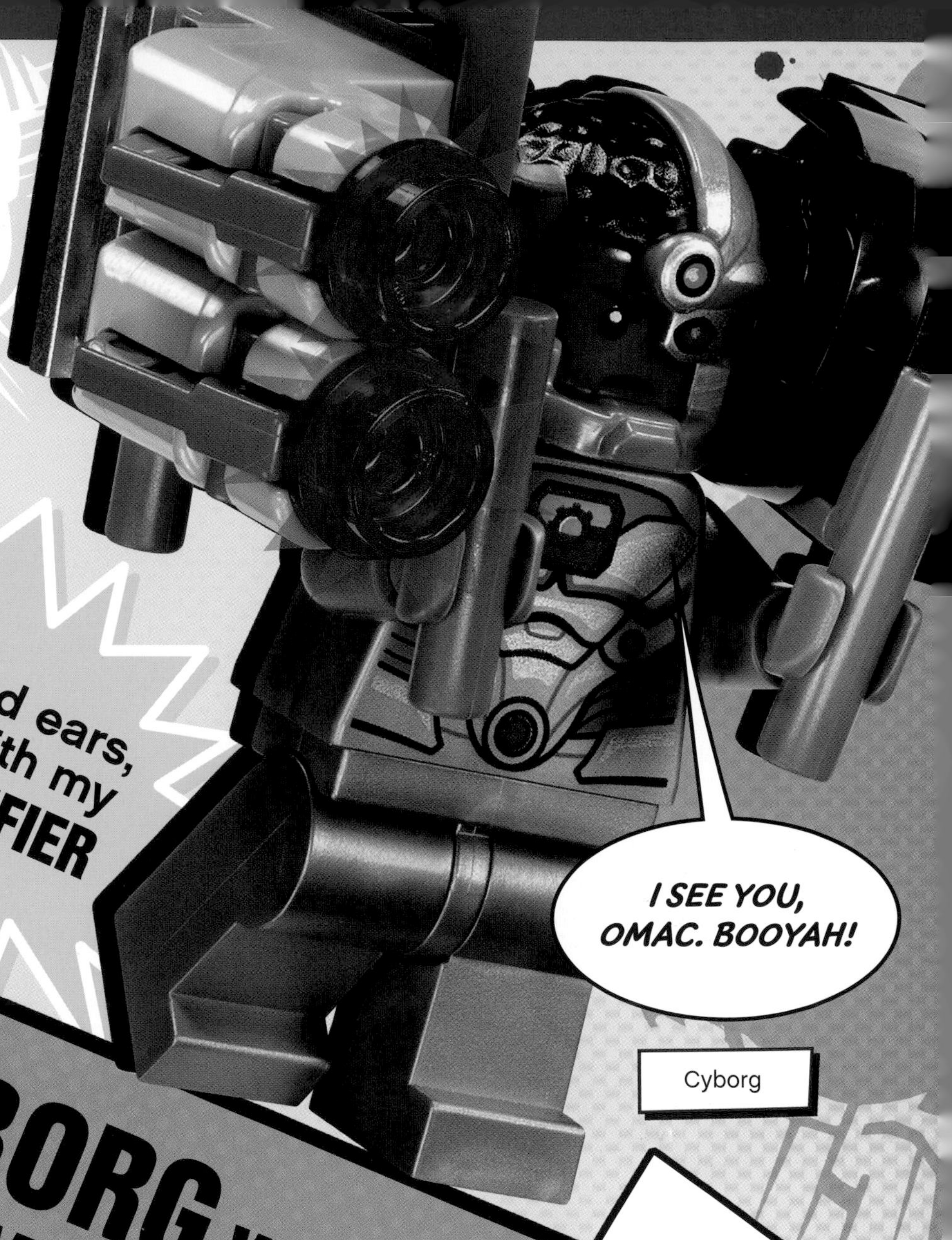
My amazing ELECTRONIC EYE gives me superhuman vision
If only you had ears, I'd stun you with my SOUND AMPLIFIER
I SEE YOU, OMAC. BOOYAH!
Cyborg

CYBORG VS. OMAC

When machines don't see eye-to-eye, expect a serious clash! Cyborg must stop OMAC from leading a cyber army invasion. Can he do it?

After a bad accident, half of Cyborg's body was rebuilt with robotic parts. Now he is half man, half machine—and all hero!

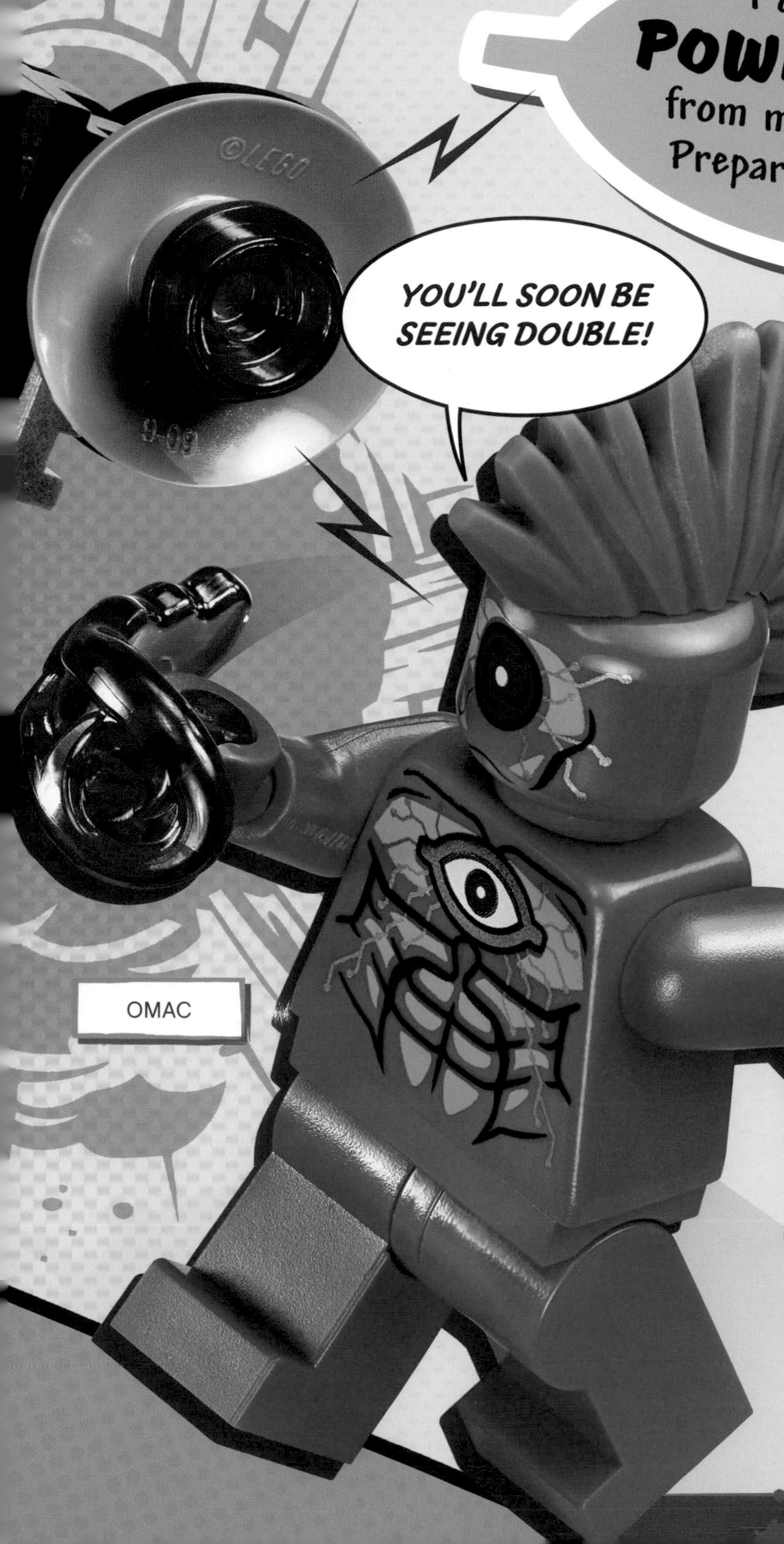
I can fire mighty POWER BLASTS from my eye and hands. Prepare to be dazzled!
YOU'LL SOON BE SEEING DOUBLE!
OMAC
I'm infected with a HIGH-TECH VIRUS... I couldn't stop if I wanted to!

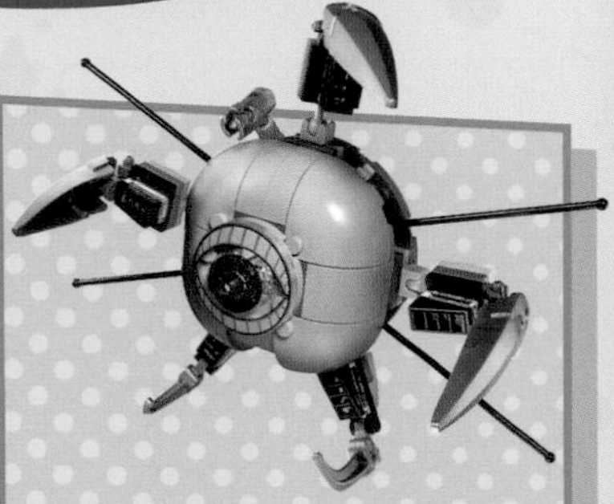

DID YOU KNOW?

OMAC is a member of a large cybernetic army controlled by a sinister satellite orbiting the Earth. The satellite's name is Brother Eye.

Which machine will overpower his foe?

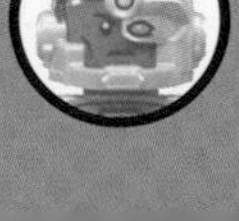 OR 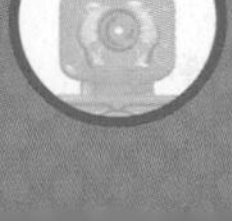

I've protected METROPOLIS from bigger threats than you!
Superman's everyday name is Clark Kent. Even that isn't his real one! He was born Kal-El on the planet Krypton.
Superman
COME FLY WITH ME ... TO JAIL!
With my X-RAY VISION, I can see your hidden weapons!
Hey, Joker ... you dropped your venom SHOOTER! Now that's funny!

SUPERMAN VS. THE JOKER

The Joker is in a new city—Metropolis. He thinks he will get away with his crimes because Batman is not there to fight him. Fortunately, Superman is!

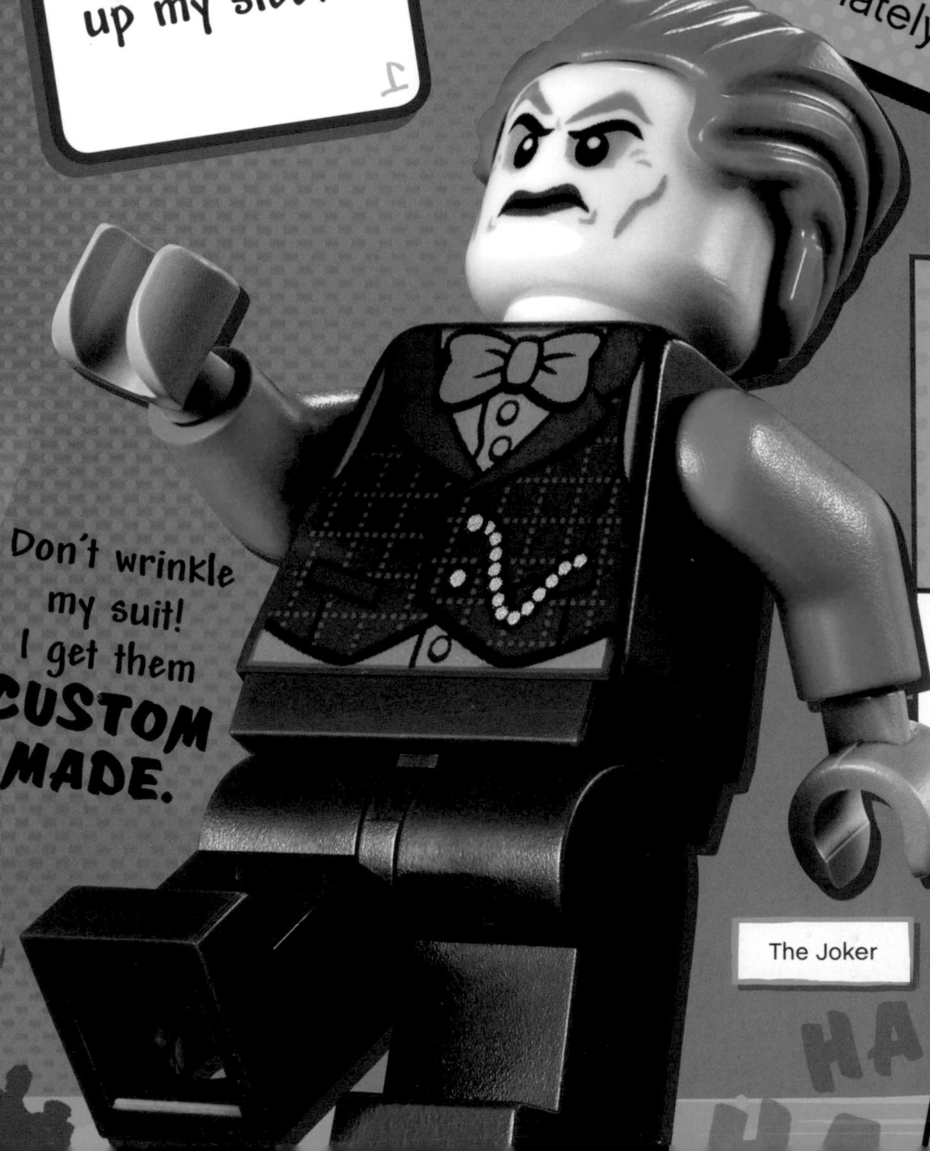
HA HA HA
I've got plenty of TRICKS up my sleeve!
Don't wrinkle my suit! I get them CUSTOM MADE.
HA

The Joker

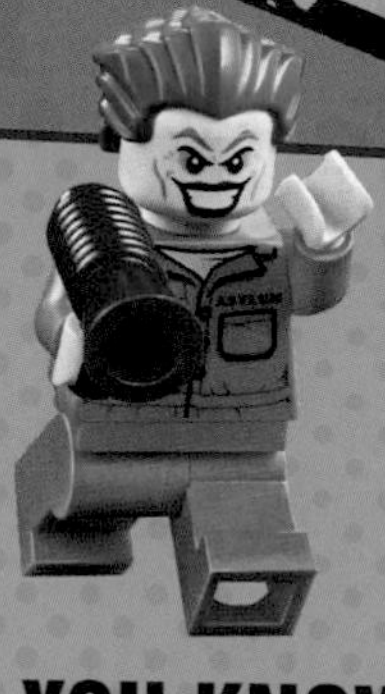

DID YOU KNOW?

The Joker has been to Arkham Asylum several times. He always manages to escape!

Who will triumph in this Metropolis showdown?

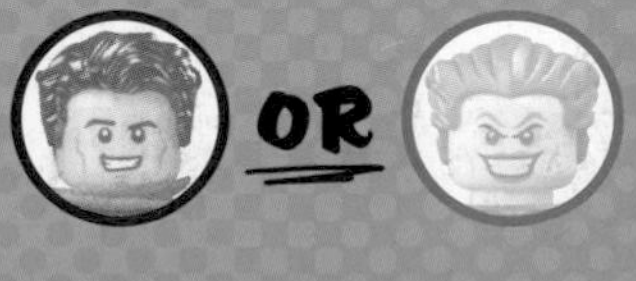
OR

My dad was a US Army general ... he taught me to **FIGHT!**

What a scoop! My **CAMERA** has captured Lex's nasty threats!

I'll write an **ARTICLE** about your dirty deeds!

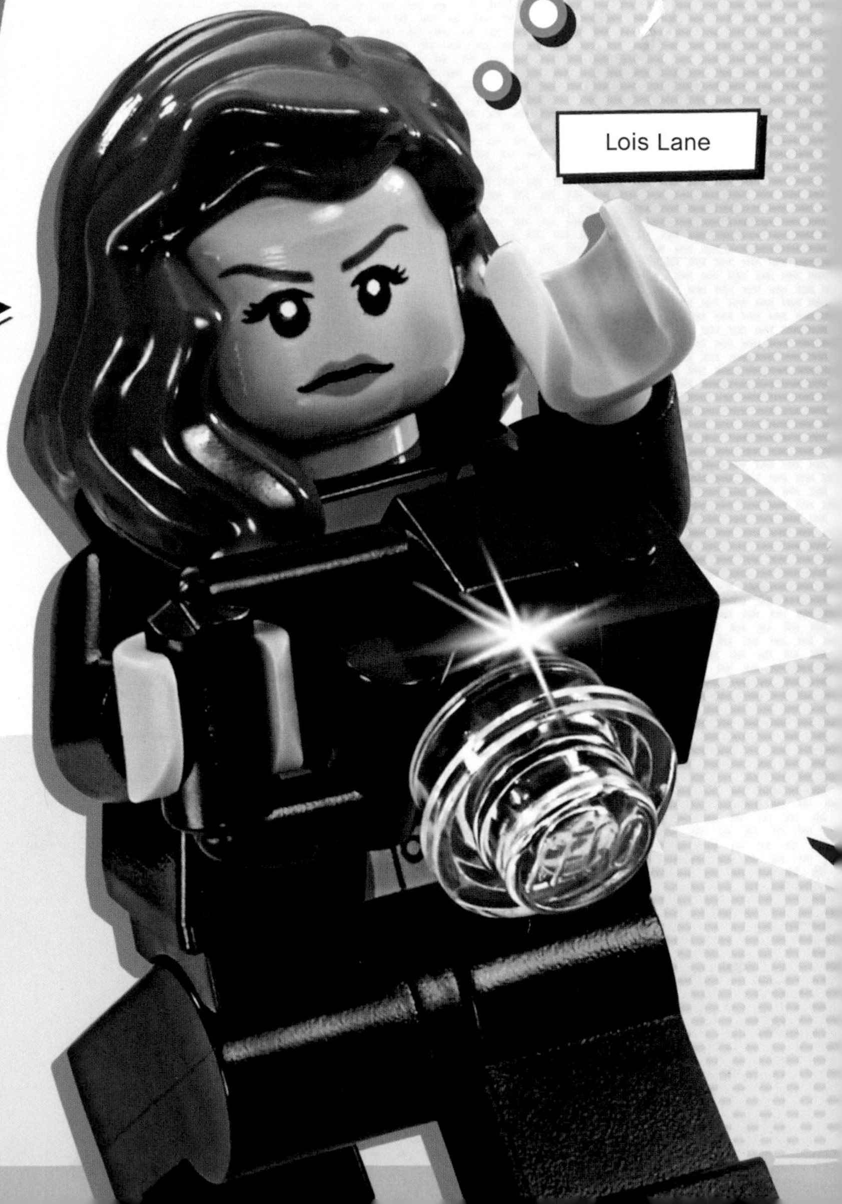

Lois Lane

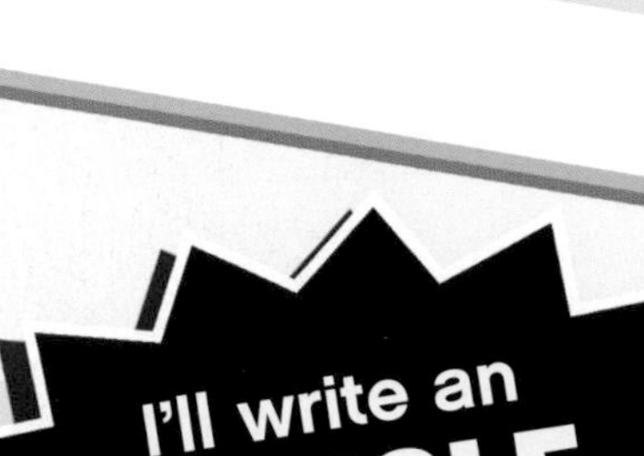

DID YOU KNOW?

Lois is a reporter for the *Daily Planet* newspaper. She knows Superman is really her co-worker Clark Kent—but she won't tell!

LOIS LANE VS. LEX LUTHOR

Lex Luthor has been desperately trying to extract information out of reporter Lois Lane. He's tried bribery, tricks, and bugging. Now it's time to battle!

Lex Luthor is a rich, corrupt businessman in Metropolis. He loathes the *Daily Planet*, as it supports his archenemy, Superman.

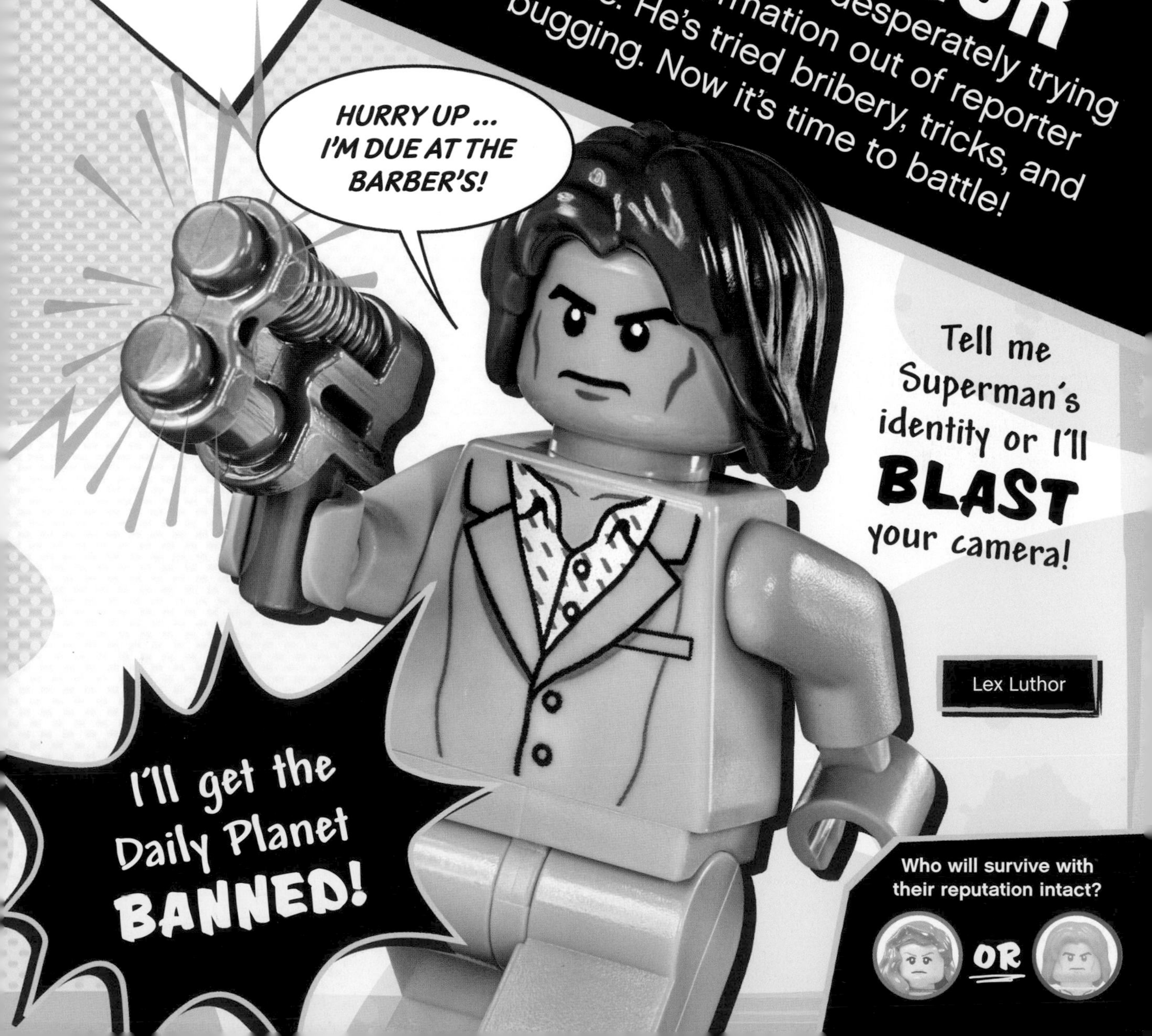
HURRY UP ... I'M DUE AT THE BARBER'S!
Tell me Superman's identity or I'll BLAST your camera!
I'll get the Daily Planet BANNED!

Lex Luthor

Who will survive with their reputation intact?

WONDER WOMAN VS. KILLER FROST

Killer Frost wants to turn the Amazons' homeland, Themyscira, into an icy waste. Wonder Woman won't have that. She's about to bring the heat of battle!

Wonder Woman has a bird design on her shield. It's the symbol of her people, warrior women called the Amazons.

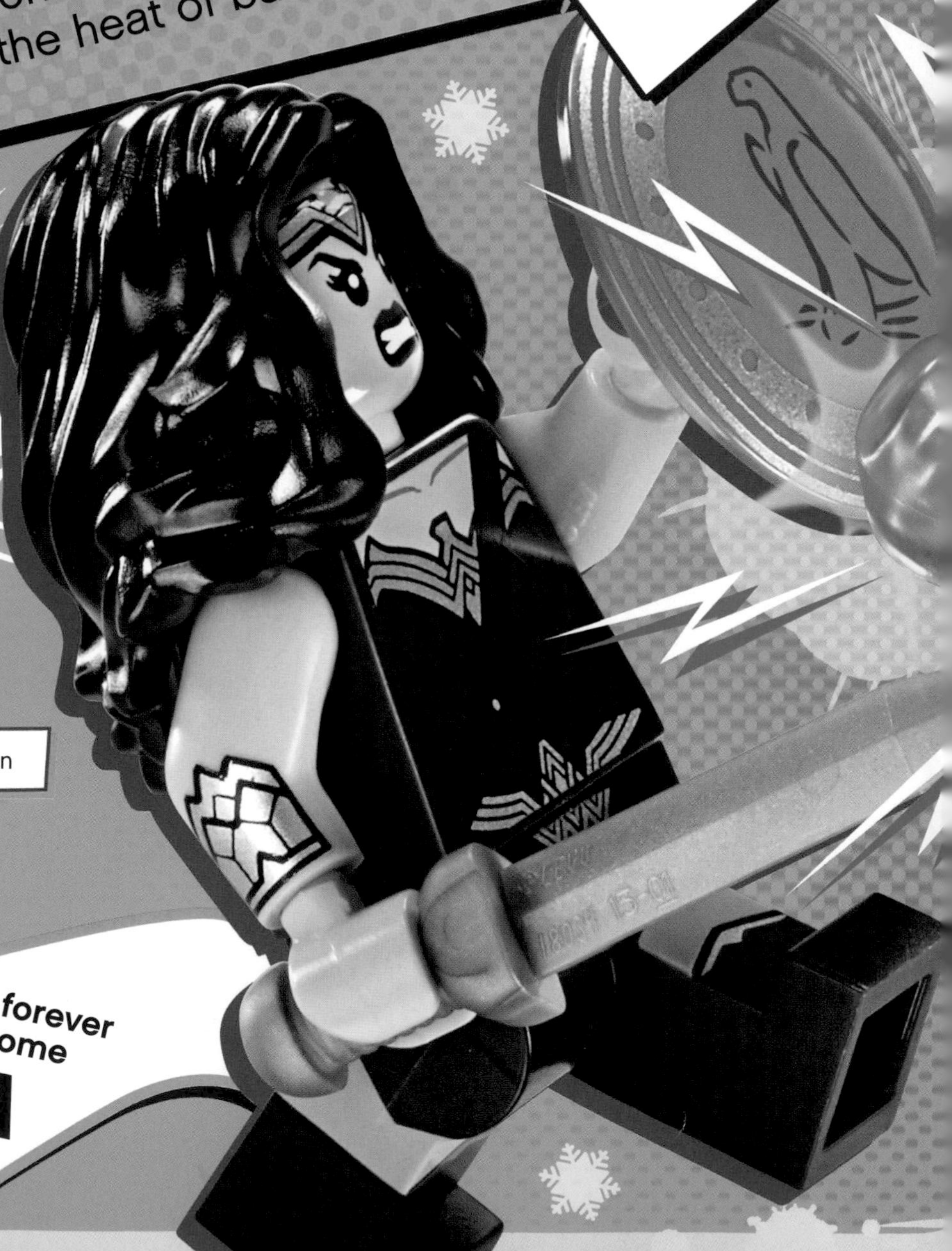

My magic **BRACELETS** stop missiles (even icy ones)!

Wonder Woman

I could keep fighting forever thanks to my awesome **STAMINA**

Fly? I ride the **ARCTIC WIND** ... it's easier!

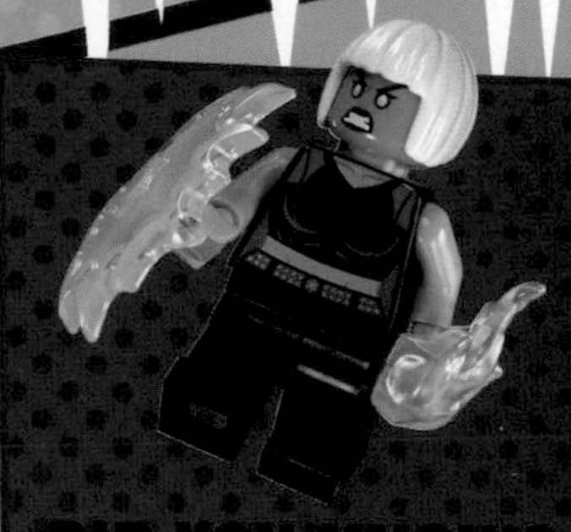

DID YOU KNOW?

Killer Frost's body was merged with ice. Now she is a heat vampire, feeding off the body heat of others.

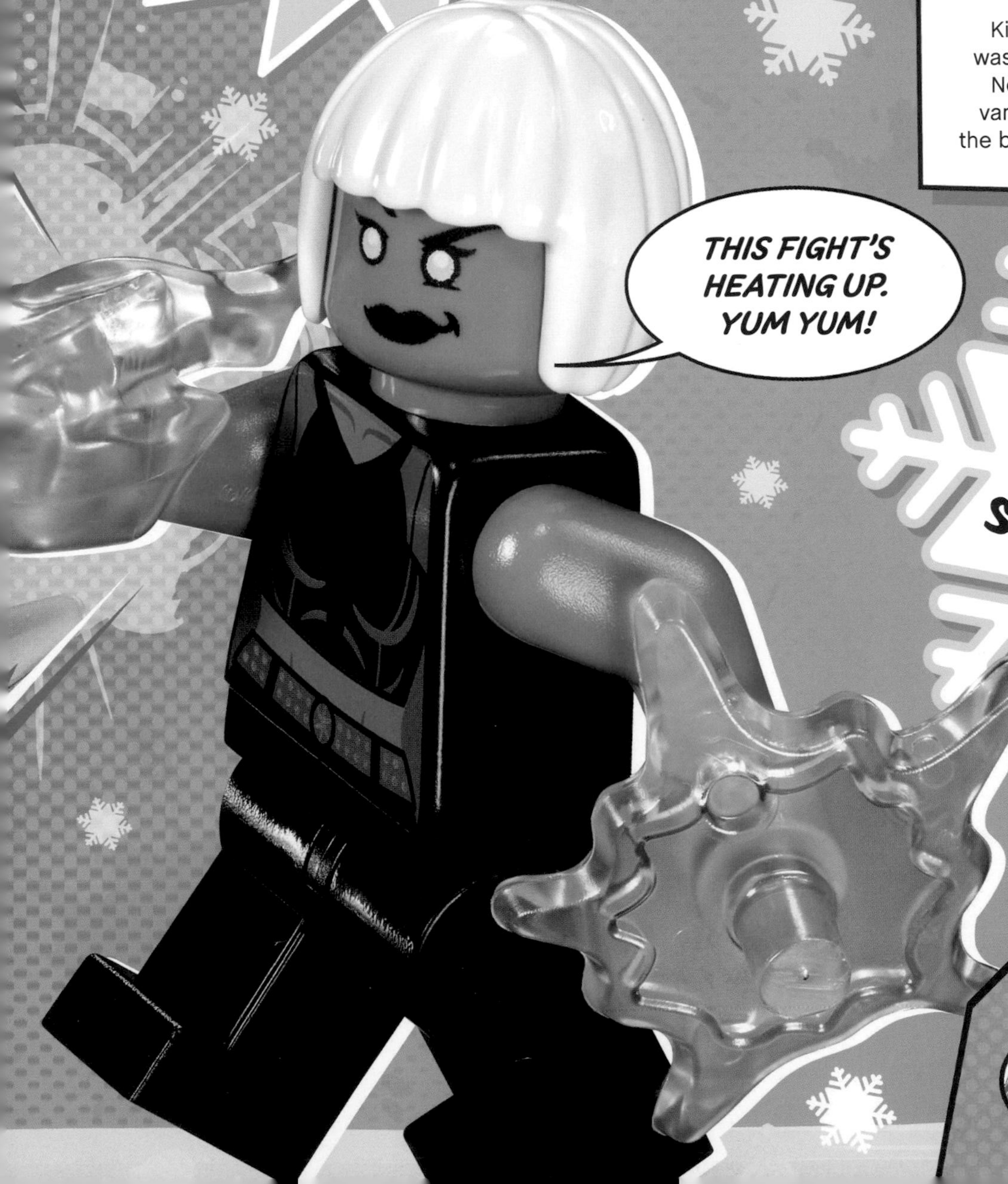
THIS FIGHT'S HEATING UP. YUM YUM!

Did I tell you about the time **I FROZE SUPERMAN?**

Killer Frost

Who will send her enemy packing?

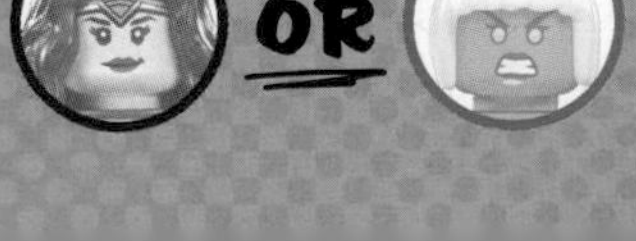
OR

CHAPTER 4: LOYAL FRIENDS

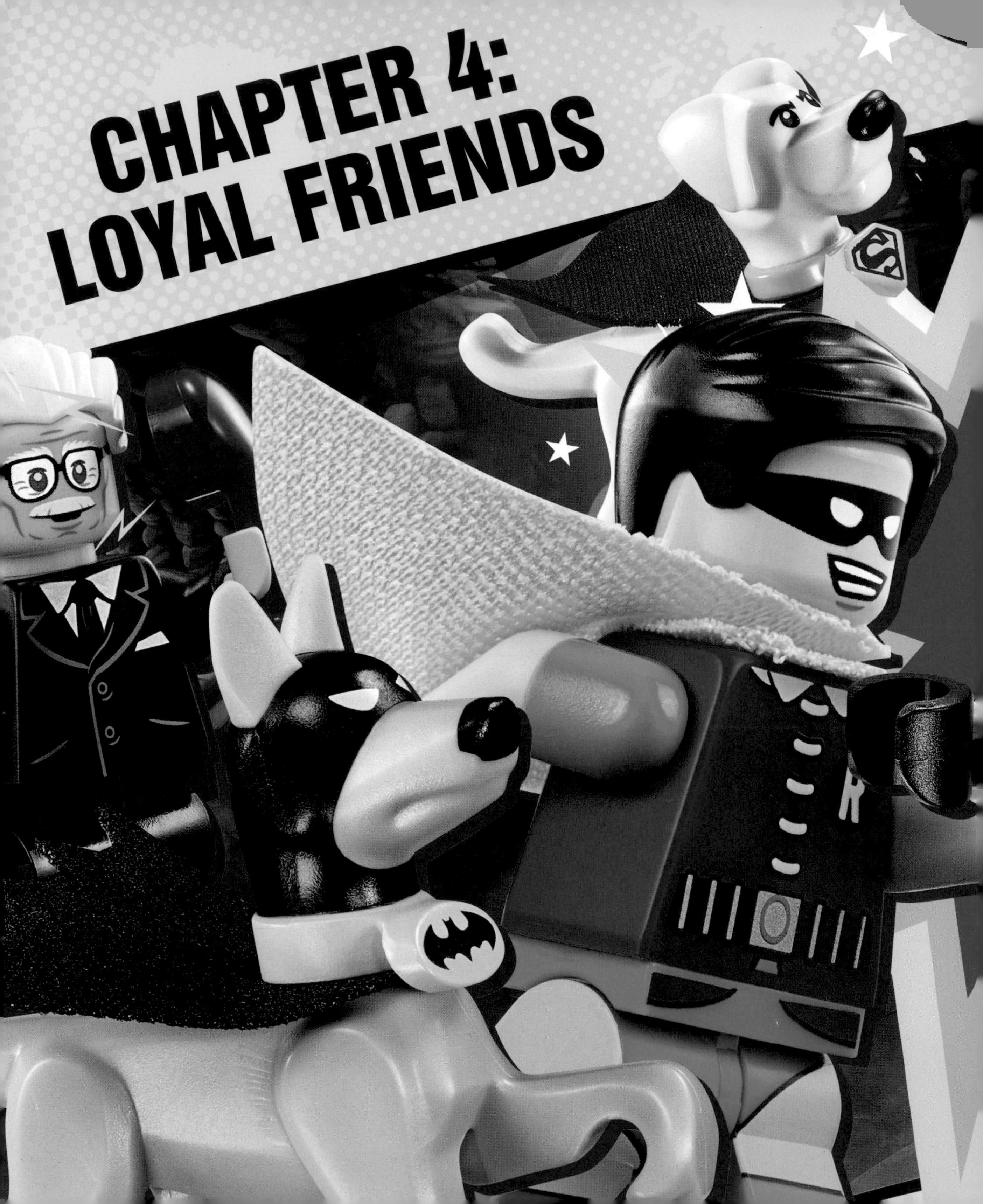
S
R

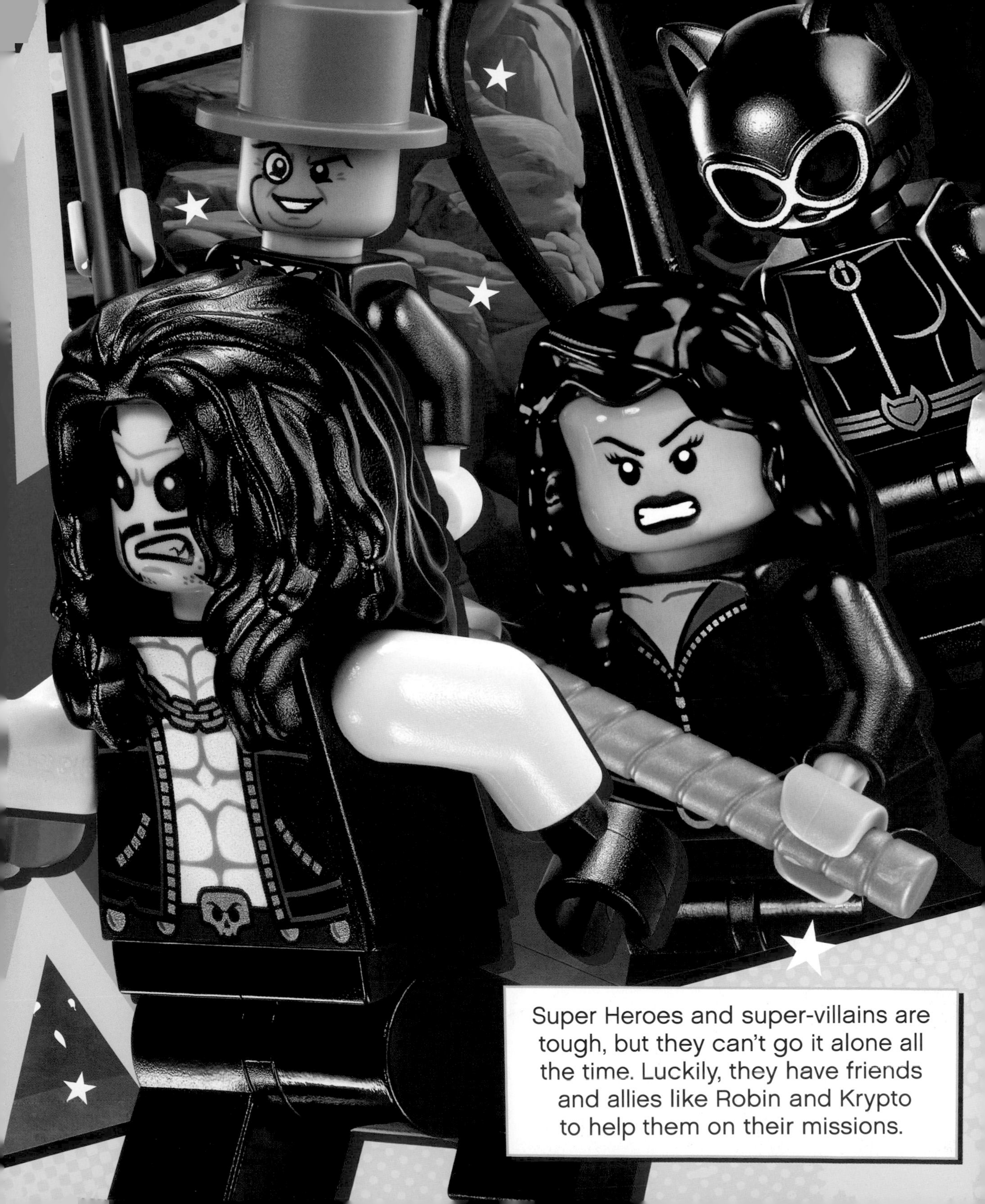

Super Heroes and super-villains are tough, but they can't go it alone all the time. Luckily, they have friends and allies like Robin and Krypto to help them on their missions.

GORDON VS. HENCHMEN

Some LexCorp workers are loading illegal Kryptonite at the docks. Commissioner Gordon is chasing them down—but will they come quietly?

Commissioner Gordon can handle most crimes alone, but if things get dicey, he uses the Bat-Signal to call Batman.

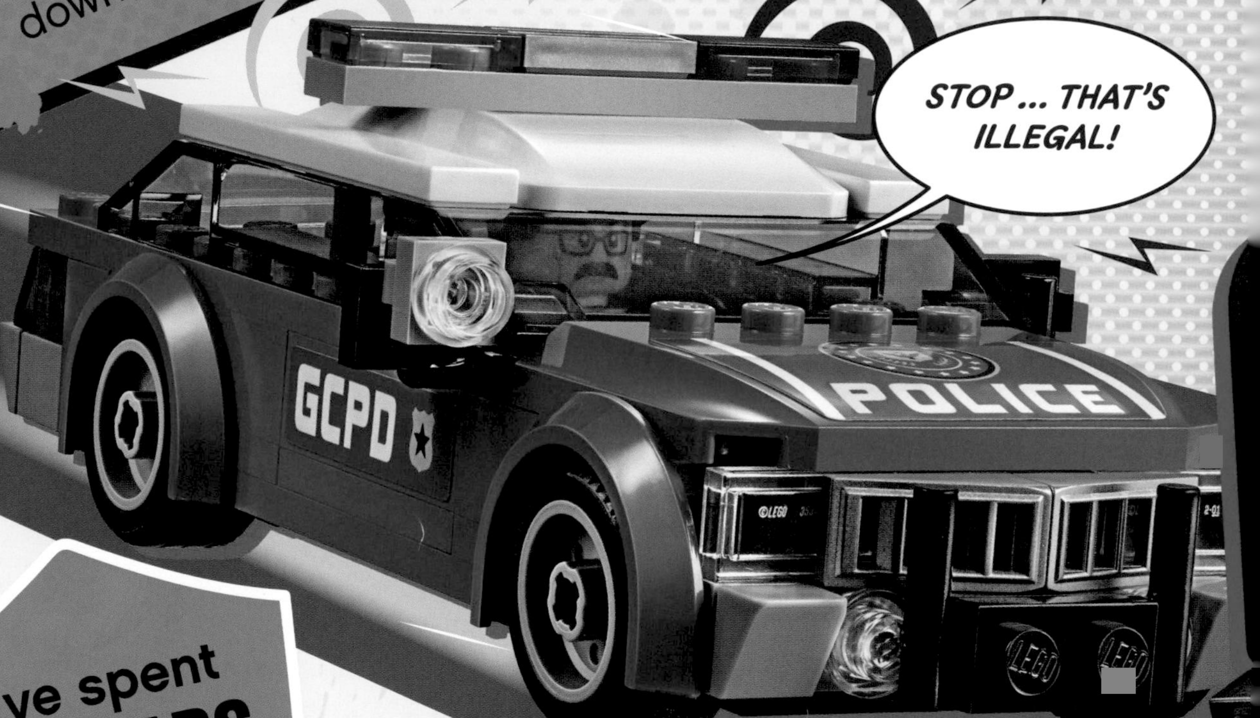

STOP ... THAT'S ILLEGAL!
GCPD
POLICE

Police car

I've spent **20 YEARS** fighting crime!

I'm used to combat ... I was in the **US MILITARY**

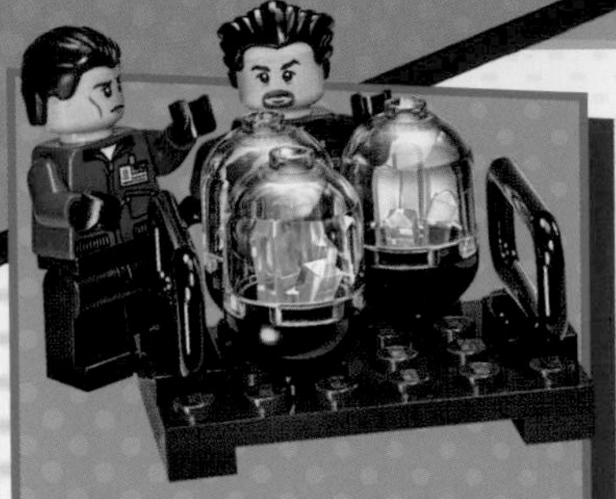

DID YOU KNOW?

The LexCorp goons know their jobs involve breaking the law. But Lex pays them well, so they don't ask questions!

There's enough **KRYPTONITE** here to knock out Superman!

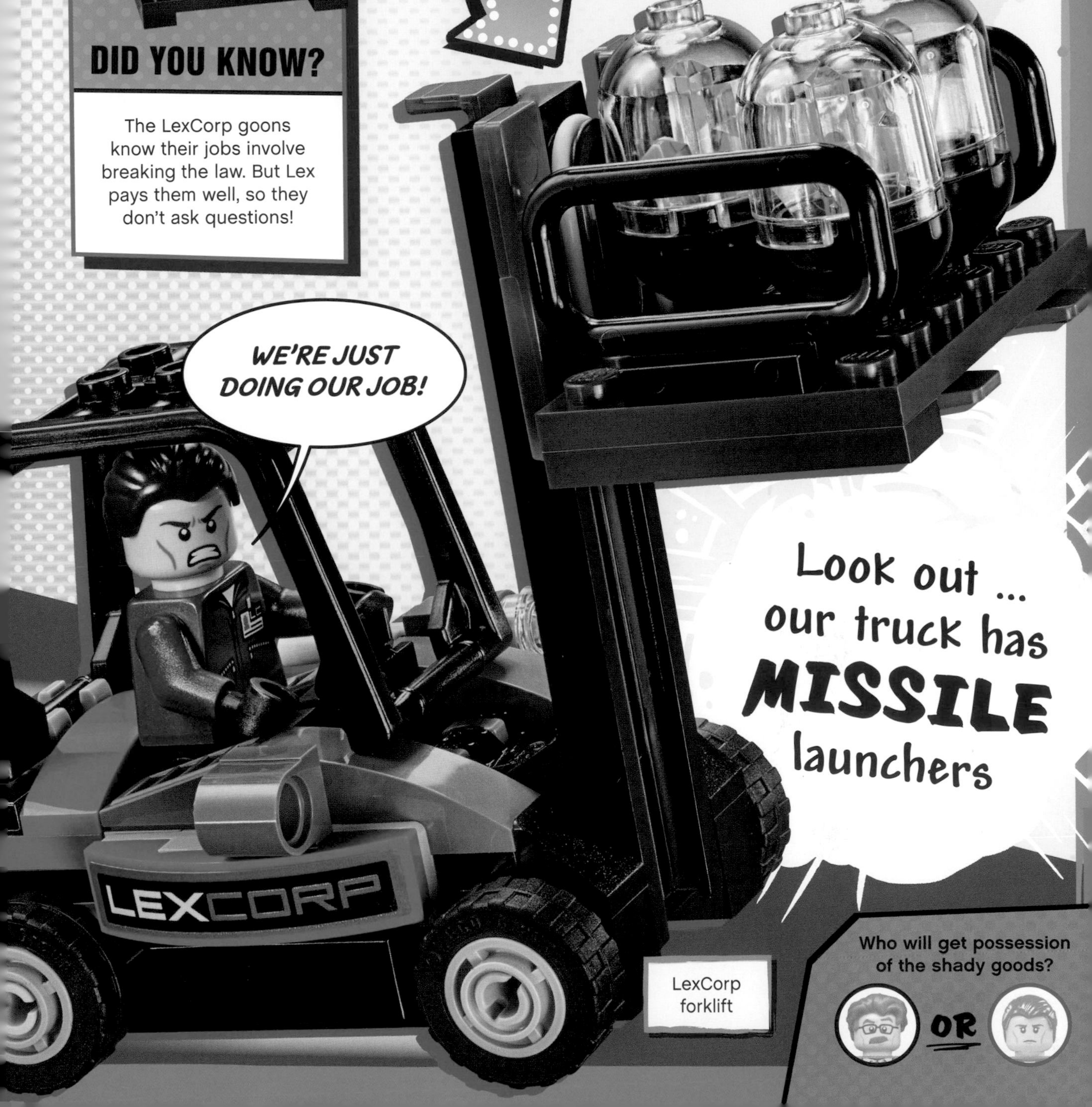
WE'RE JUST DOING OUR JOB!
LEXCORP

LexCorp forklift

Look out ... our truck has **MISSILE** launchers

Who will get possession of the shady goods?

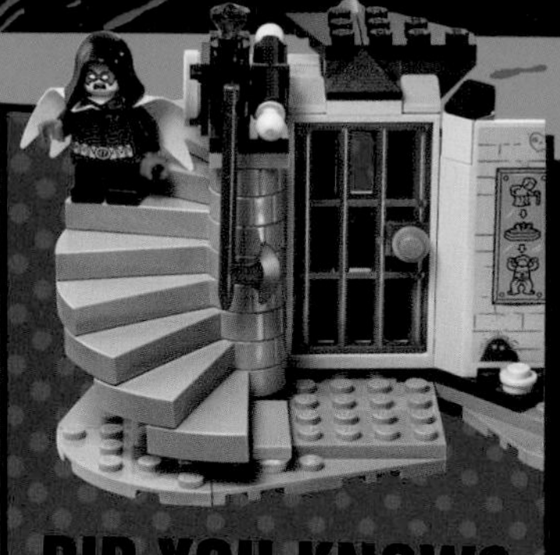

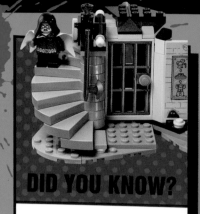

DID YOU KNOW?

Rā's al Ghūl's hideout contains sneaky traps, like the swinging axe at the bottom of these stairs. Look out, Robin!

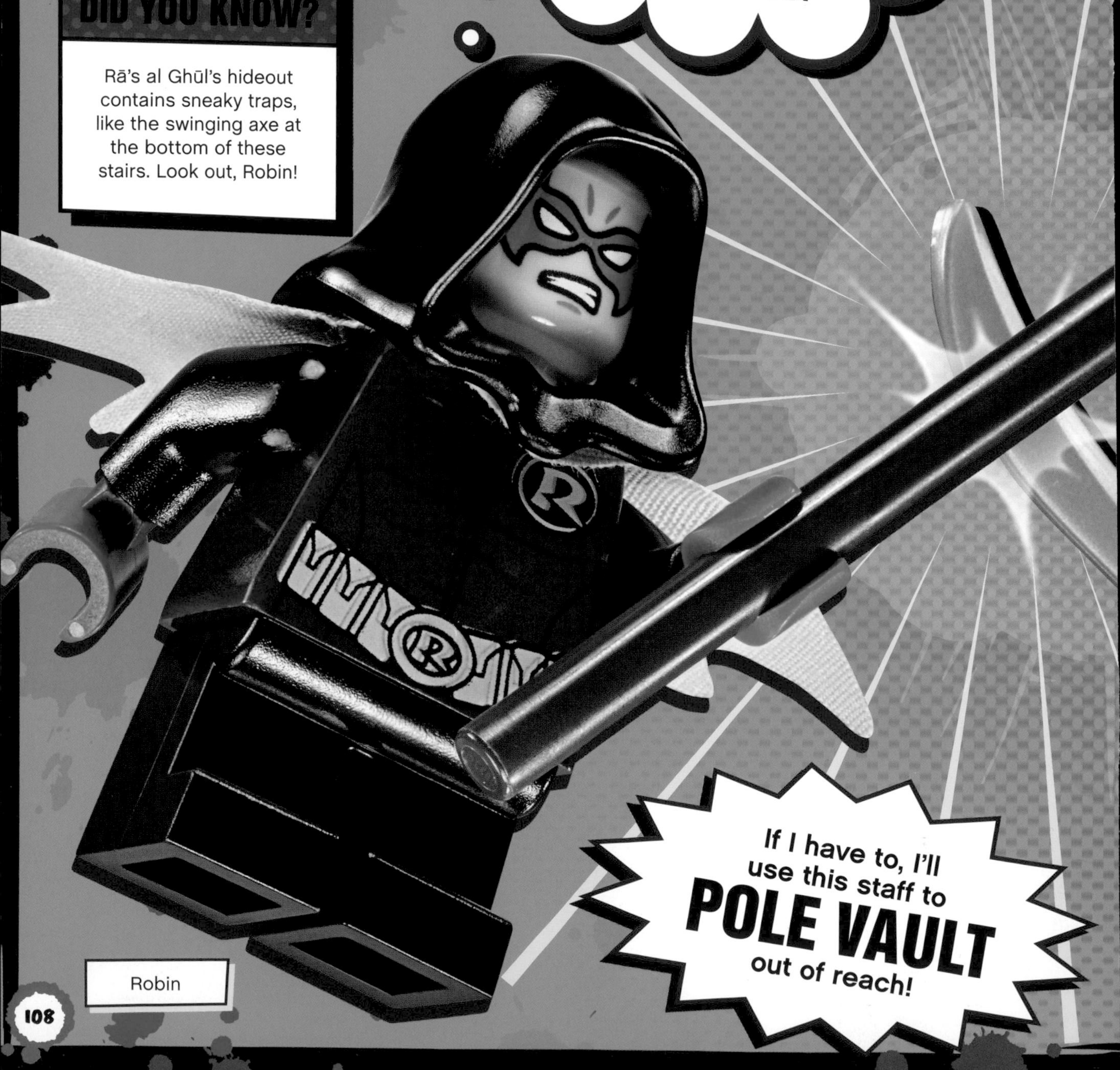
MY HOOD shields my ears from sand ... and from your screeches!
If I have to, I'll use this staff to POLE VAULT out of reach!

Robin

Talia is loyal to her dad but also admires his enemy, Batman. She is a bit jealous of Robin because he is Batman's sidekick!

ROBIN VS. TALIA AL GHŪL

Rā's al Ghūl has asked his daughter, Talia, to capture Robin. She's really going for it! It's the Bat-Family against the al Ghūl family, but who will win?

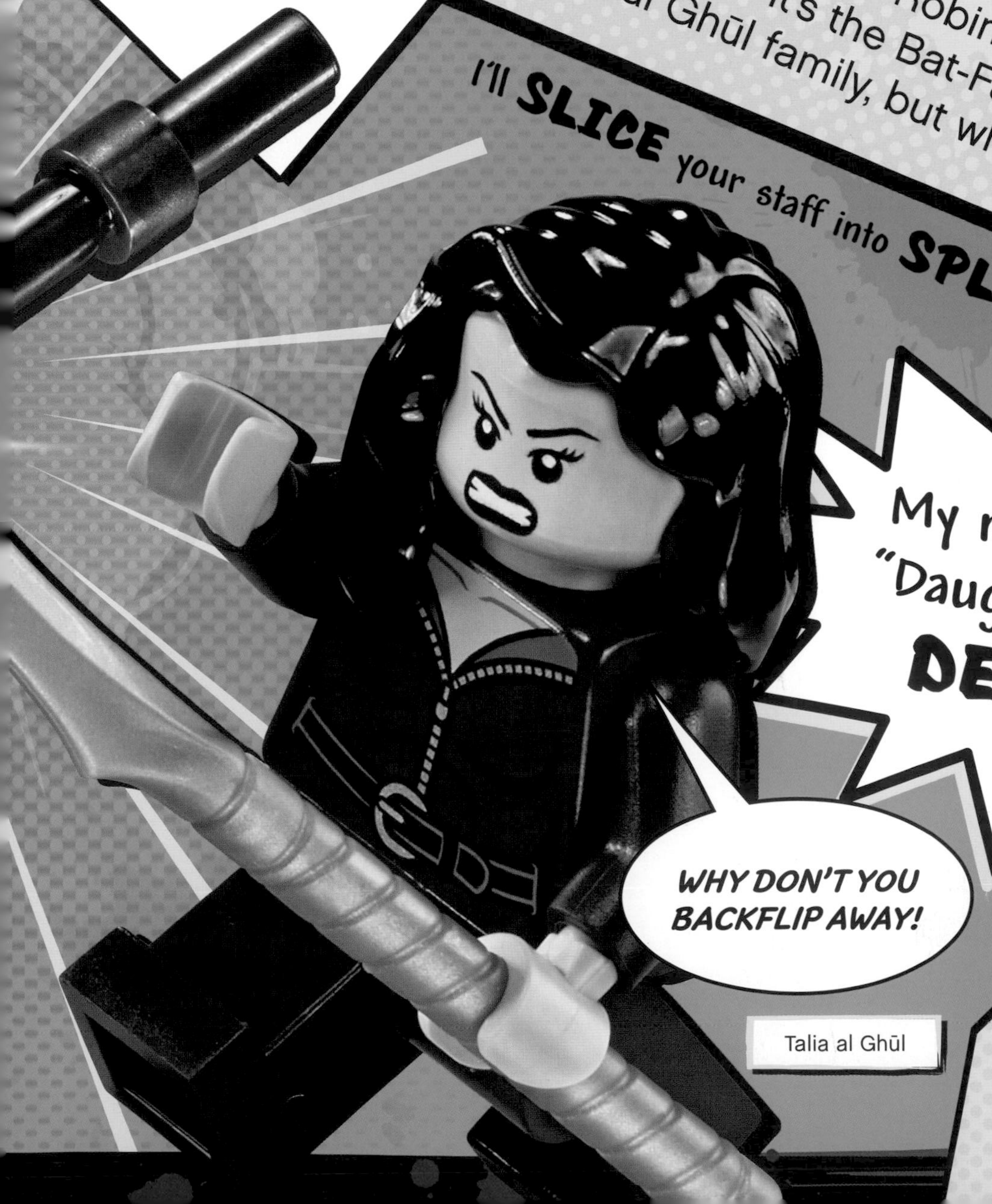
I'll SLICE your staff into SPLINTERS!
My name means "Daughter of the DEMON"
WHY DON'T YOU BACKFLIP AWAY!

Talia al Ghūl

Which dueler will defeat their opponent?

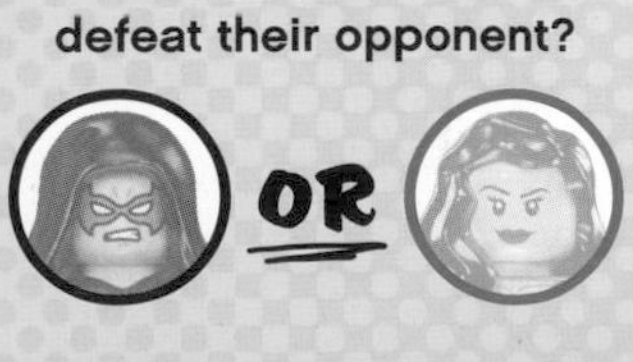
OR

ACE VS. CATWOMAN

Ace the Bat-Hound has cornered Catwoman in the middle of a jewel heist. Better step back—the fur is about to fly!

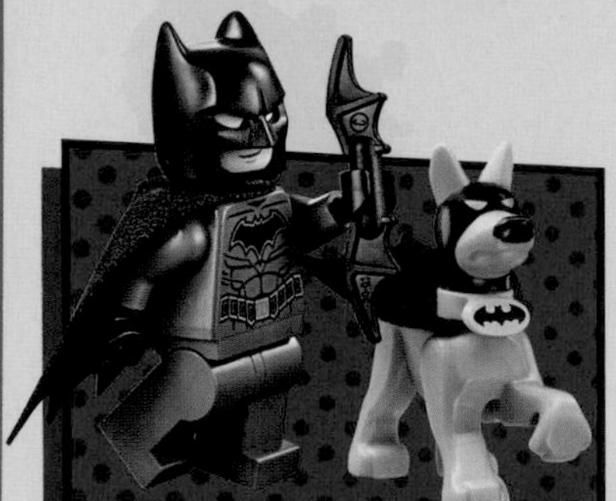

DID YOU KNOW?

Batman rescued Ace from the dog pound. He trained his new friend to fight crime and gave him his hood and collar.

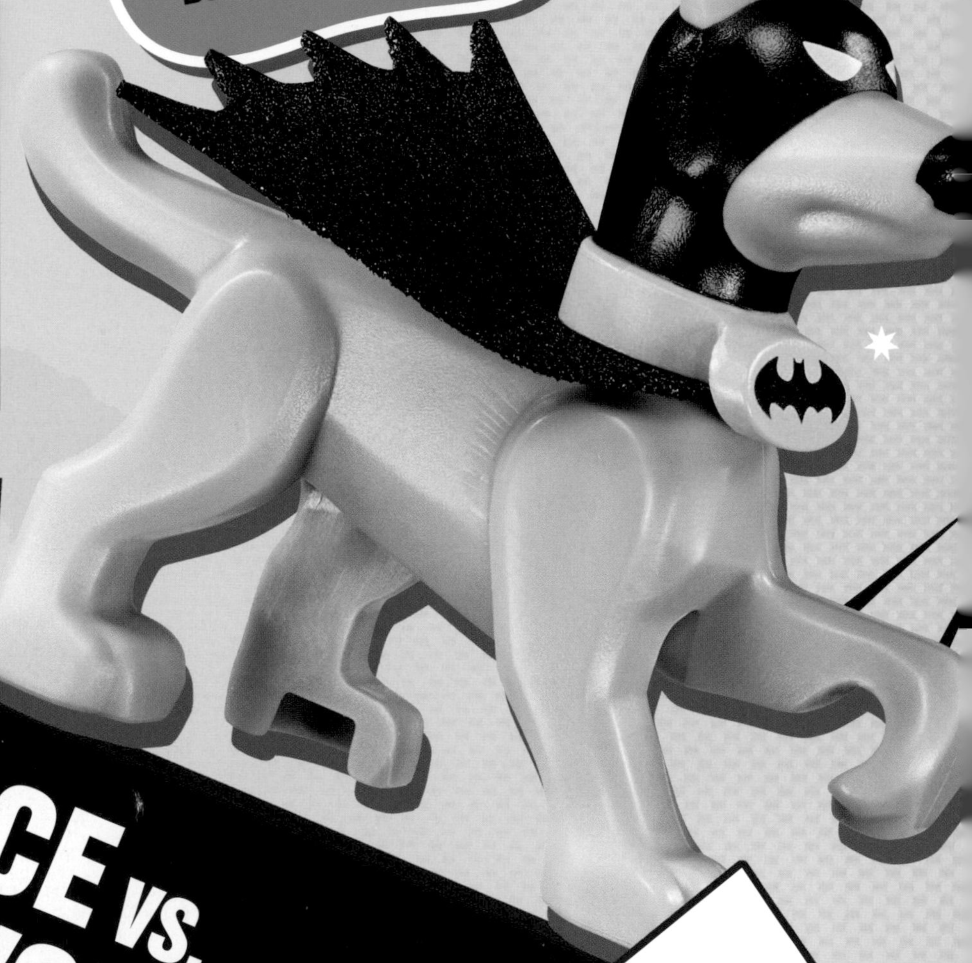

A receiver in MY COLLAR lets me know when Batman needs me
TIME TO GET RUFF!

Ace the Bat-Hound

Ace has sharp teeth and a keen sense of smell. Like Batman, he wears a cape and cowl to hide his identity.

By night, I'm a cat burglar; by day, I'm the rich and popular **SELINA KYLE**

ROLL OVER, ACE ... YOU'RE BEATEN!

Catwoman

It took one expert **SNAP OF MY WHIP** to steal this gem

I'll use my gymnastic skills to make a **ROOFTOP GETAWAY!**

Which adversary will defeat the other?

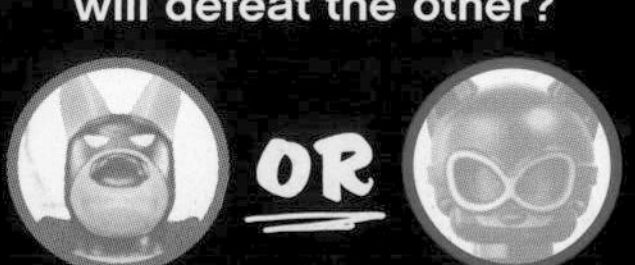

OR

AIRLIFT ATTACK

Big, bad Steppenwolf and the Parademons are attacking! The Super Heroes arrive in their Flying Fox to stop him.

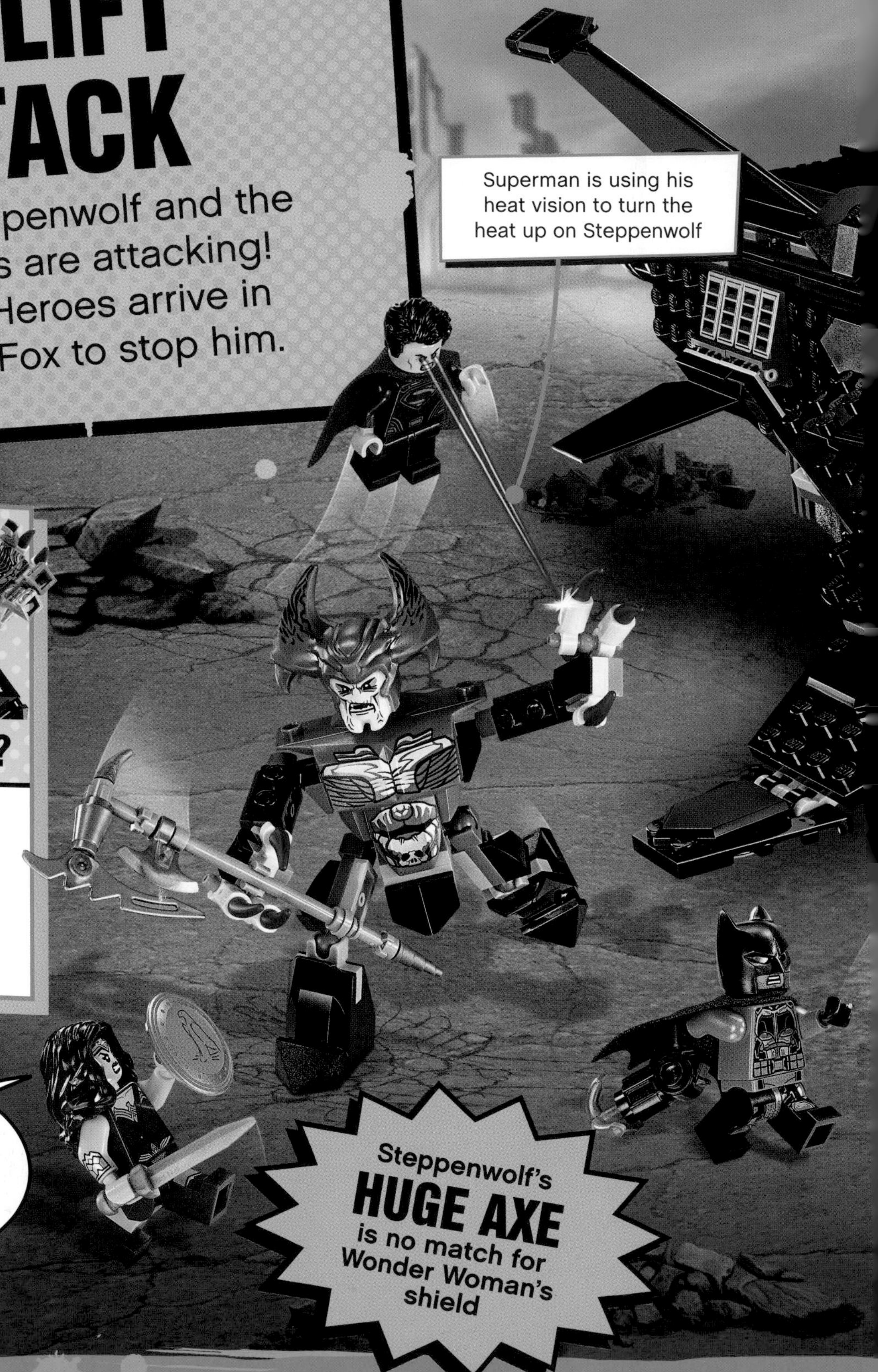
WHY DON'T YOU PICK ON SOMEONE YOUR OWN SIZE?

Superman is using his heat vision to turn the heat up on Steppenwolf

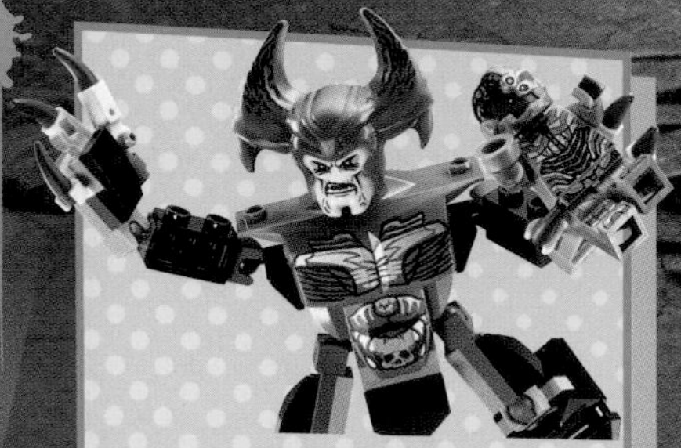

DID YOU KNOW?

This giant villain is from the planet Apokolips. Big bones must run in the family—he is the uncle of enormous bad guy Darkseid.

Steppenwolf's **HUGE AXE** is no match for Wonder Woman's shield

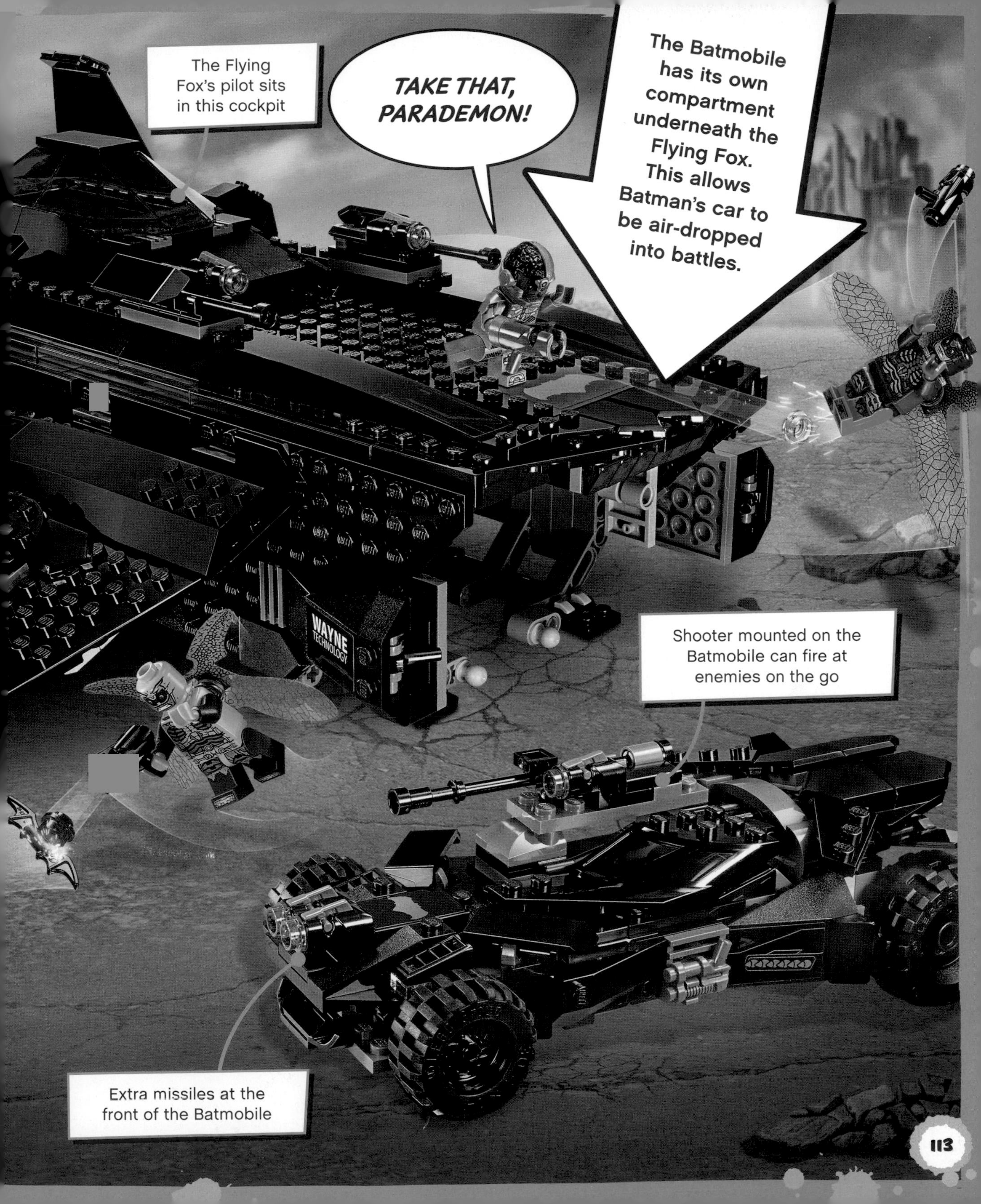
The Flying Fox's pilot sits in this cockpit
TAKE THAT, PARADEMON!
The Batmobile has its own compartment underneath the Flying Fox. This allows Batman's car to be air-dropped into battles.
WAYNE TECHNOLOGY
Shooter mounted on the Batmobile can fire at enemies on the go
Extra missiles at the front of the Batmobile

ROBIN VS. THE PENGUIN

Batman is away, so the Penguin has decided to attack his sidekick, Robin. The Boy Wonder must try to defeat the sneaky, beaky villain all on his own!

Robin has been training with Batman since the age of 8. He is now an expert in martial arts and cunning disguises.

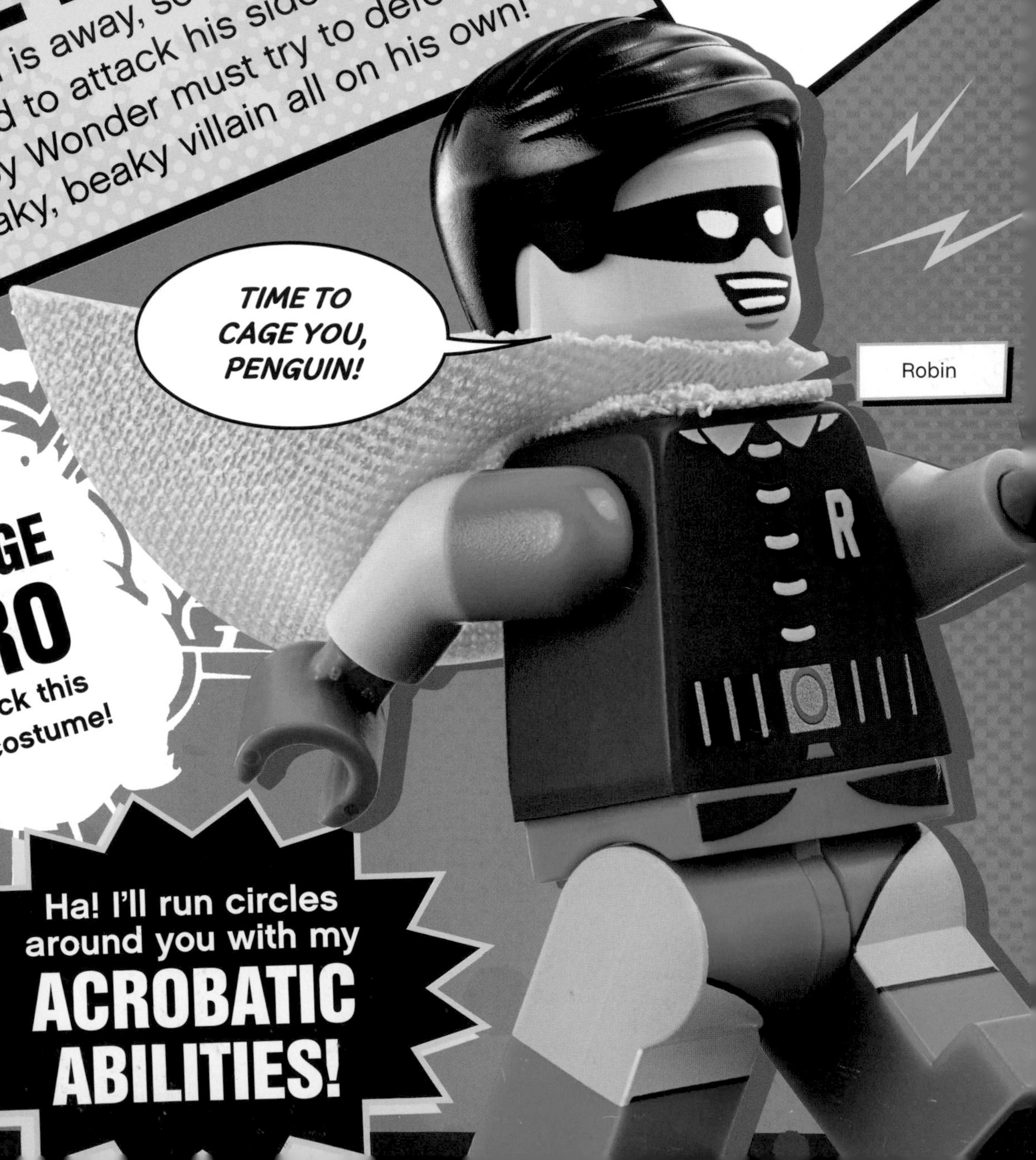
TIME TO CAGE YOU, PENGUIN!

Robin

Only a **TEENAGE HERO** could rock this classic costume!

Ha! I'll run circles around you with my **ACROBATIC ABILITIES!**

I've got weapons hidden **IN MY UMBRELLA!**

The Penguin

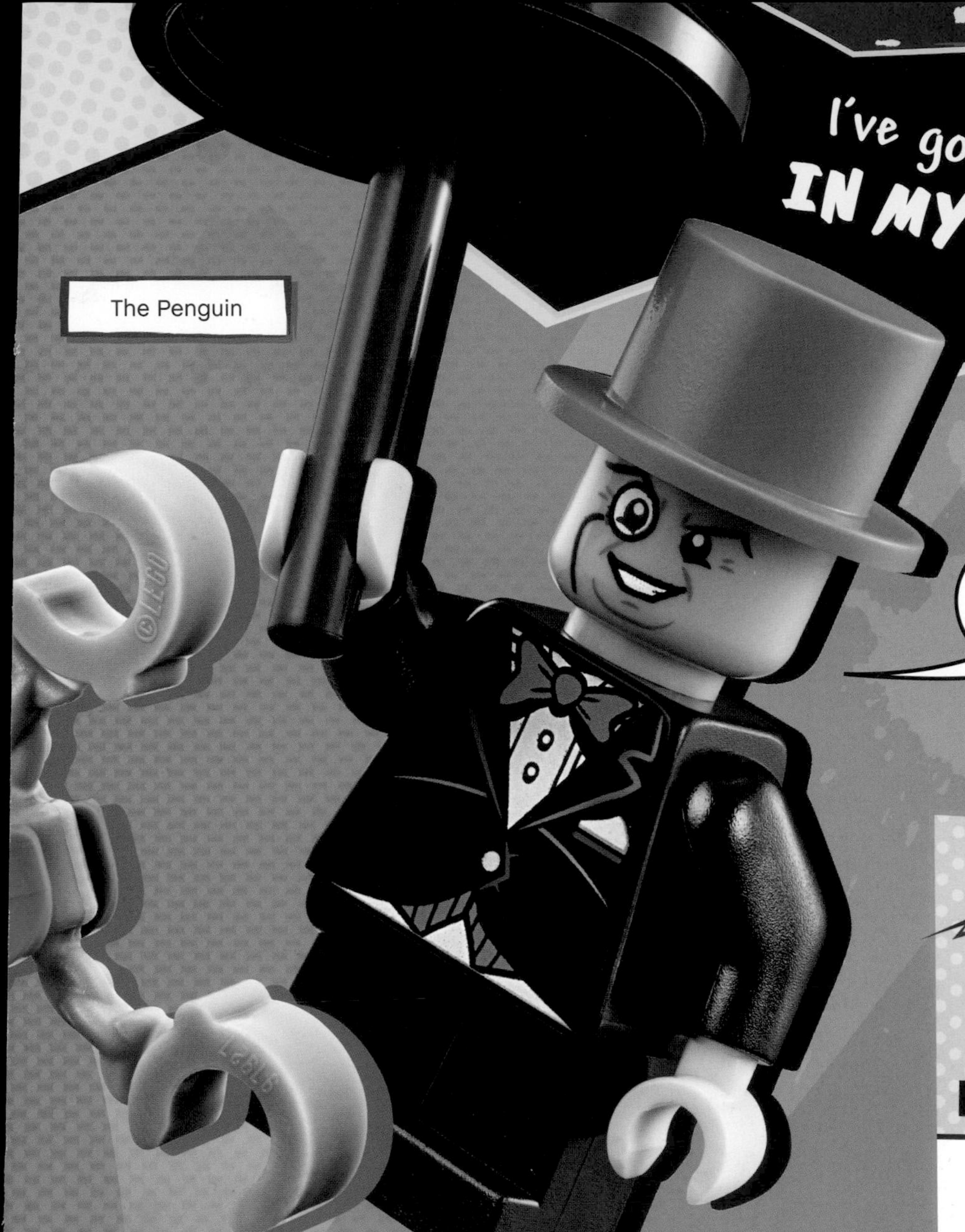

I'M TOO CLEVER FOR YOU, BIRDBRAIN!

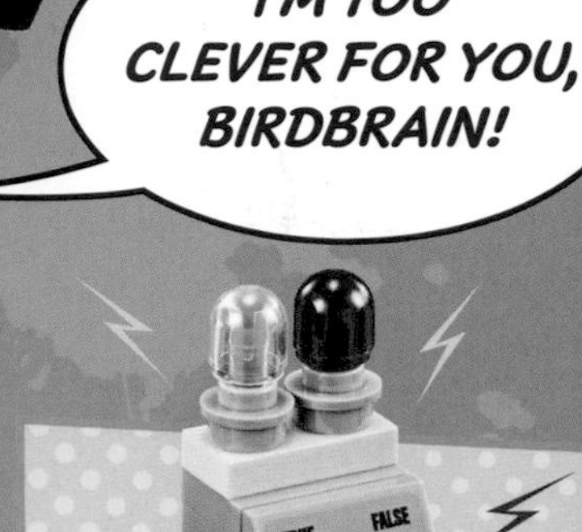

TRUE
FALSE

DID YOU KNOW?

There is a lie detector in the Batcave. The Penguin plans to wire Robin up to it and ask him where Batman is. A fib will make the red light glow!

Money squawks! This expensive **TUXEDO AND TOP HAT** turn my waddle into a swagger!

Who will win this battle of the birds?

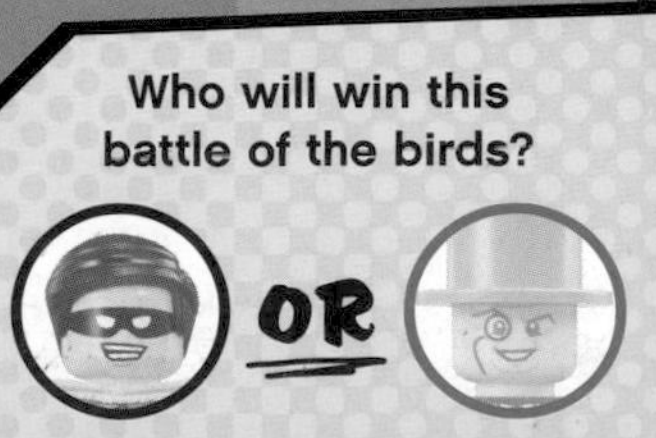

OR

KRYPTO VS LOBO

That mean old bounty hunter Lobo has come after Krypto, Superman's dog. Fur will fly and snarls will echo through space. Who will end up as top dog?

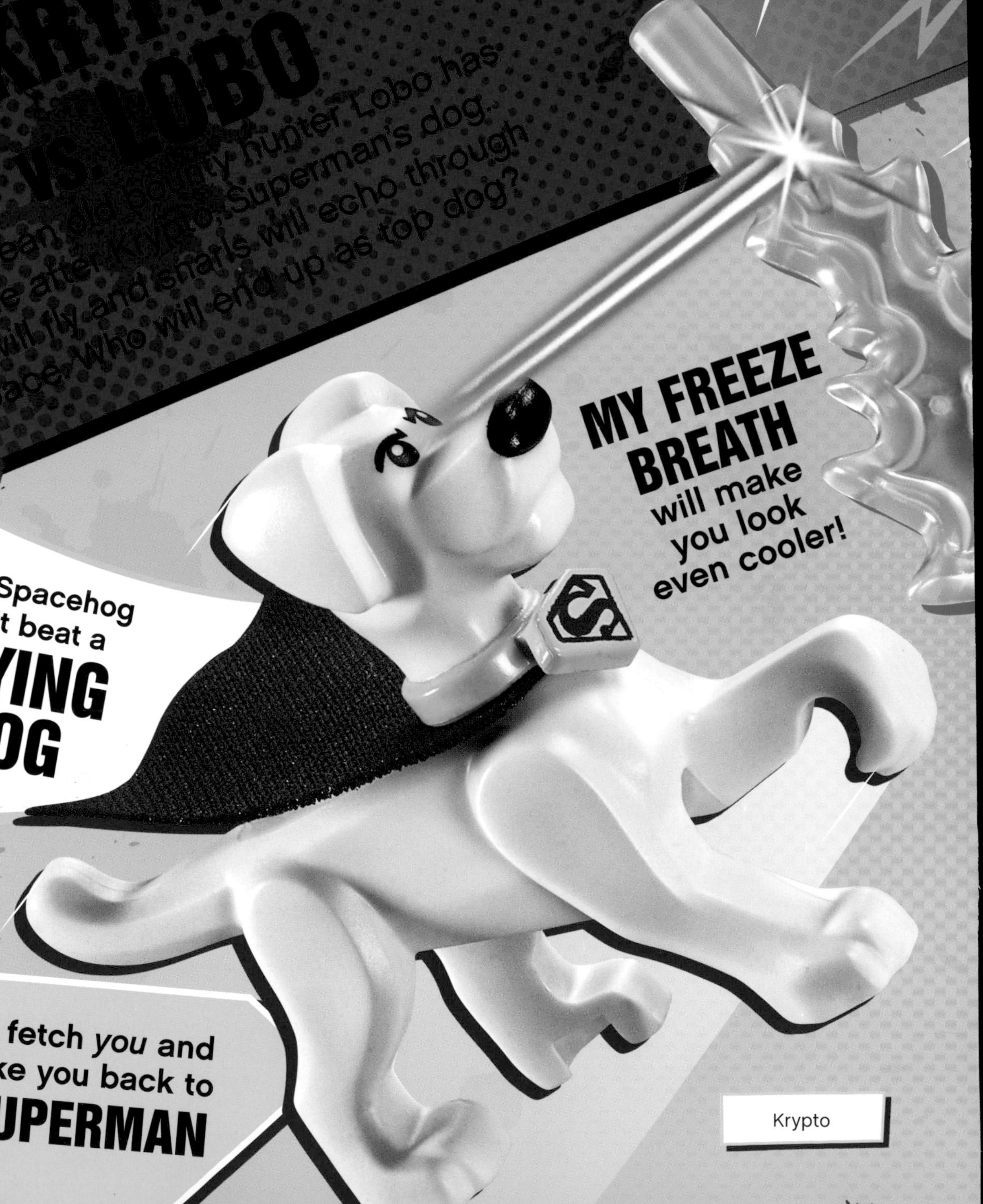

MY FREEZE BREATH will make you look even cooler!

Your Spacehog can't beat a **FLYING DOG**

I'll fetch *you* and take you back to **SUPERMAN**

Krypto

Lobo is from the planet Czarnia. He likes to look cool and tough! He wears black leather biker gear with chains and scary skulls.

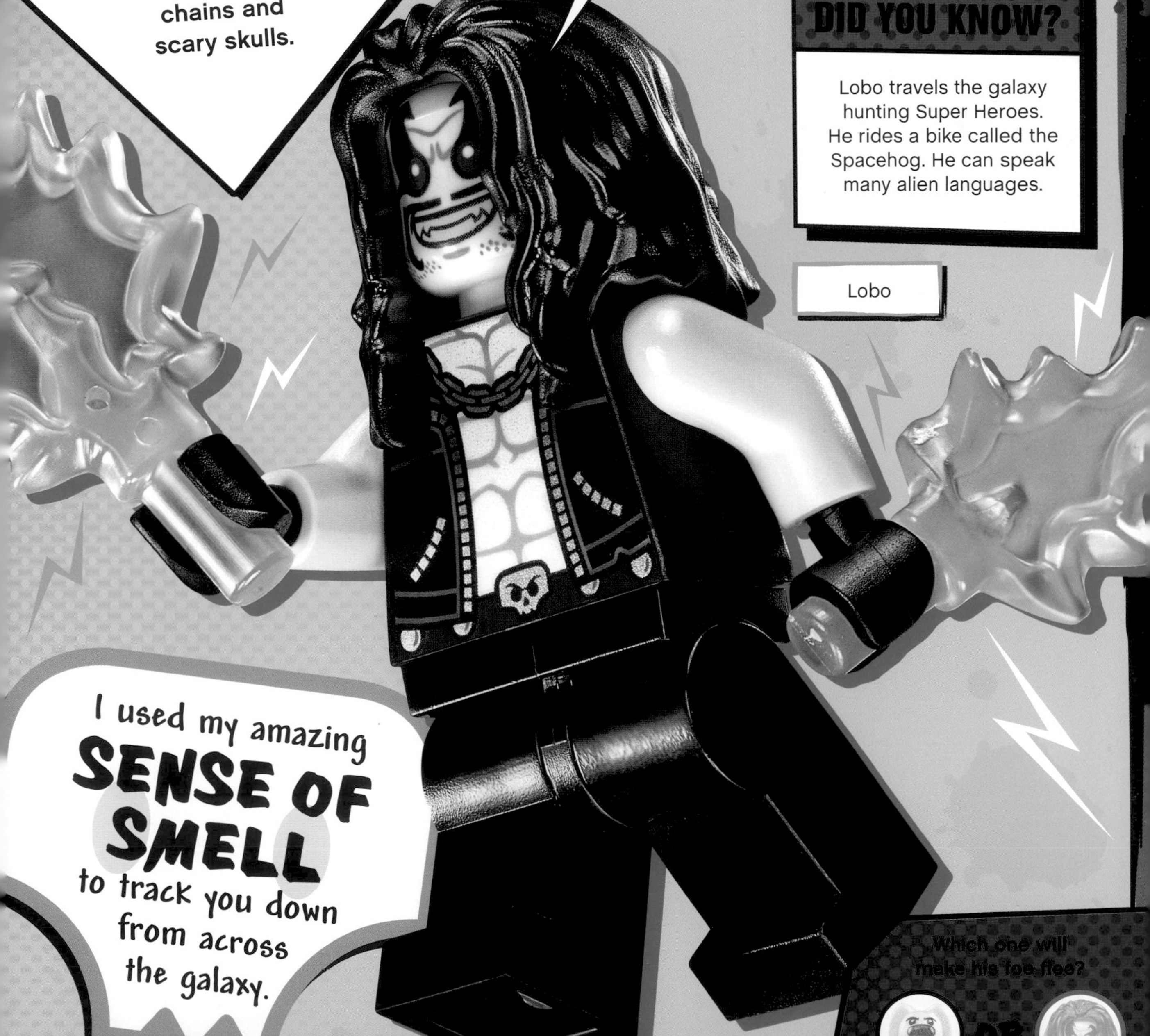
HERE'S A DEADLY POWER BURST. FETCH!

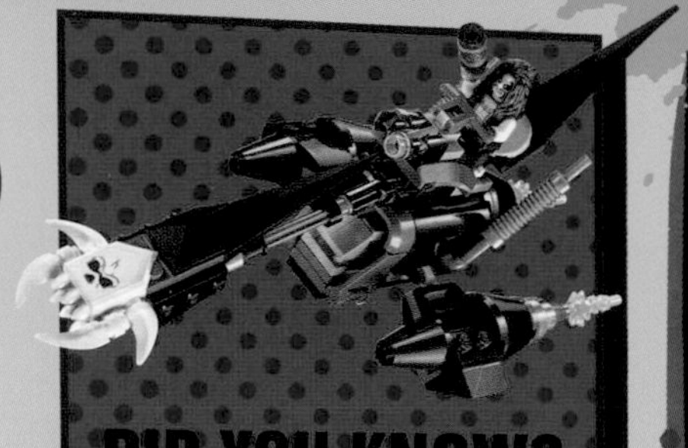

DID YOU KNOW?

Lobo travels the galaxy hunting Super Heroes. He rides a bike called the Spacehog. He can speak many alien languages.

Lobo

I used my amazing **SENSE OF SMELL** to track you down from across the galaxy.

Which one will make his foe flee?

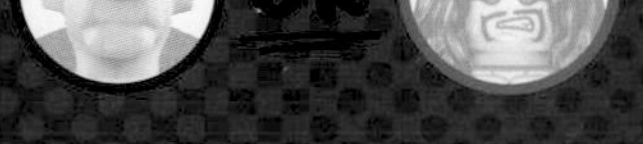
OR

ALFRED VS. CATWOMAN

Catwoman has crept into Wayne Manor. Can Alfred the butler put the cat out before she uncovers Bruce Wayne's secret identity as Batman?

Alfred Pennyworth is Batman's loyal and discreet butler. He's also a medic, a British ex-spy, and a computer expert!

HELLO? I WISH TO REPORT A STRAY CAT ...

I may be old, but I have plenty of **FIGHTING** experience!

Alfred

Like my suit, I always stay **UNRUFFLED**

118

There's nobody as agile as me ... I always **LAND ON MY FEET!**

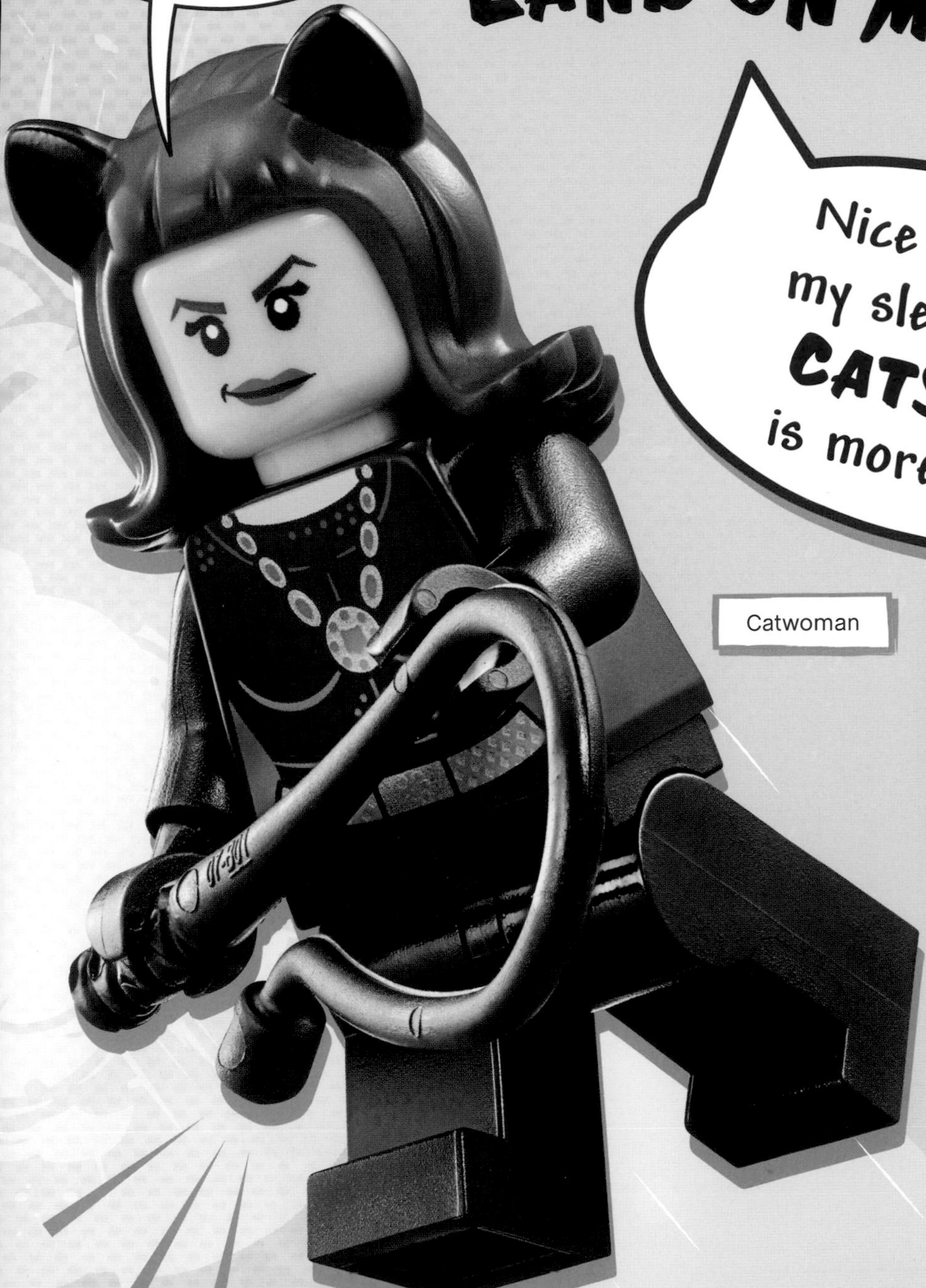
IS THAT A COWL ON THE COAT RACK?
Nice suit, but my sleek black CATSUIT is more chic!

Catwoman

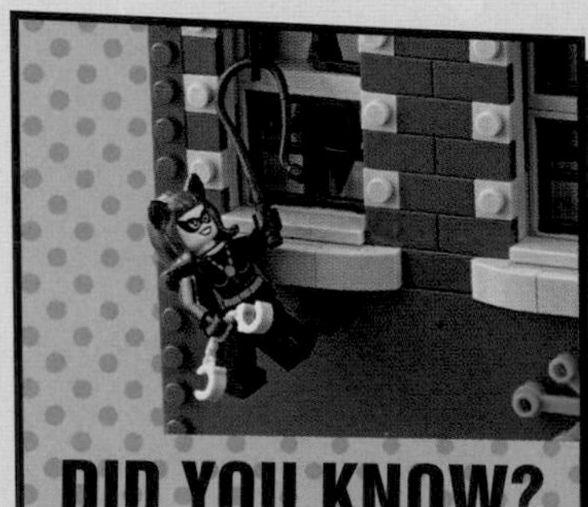

DID YOU KNOW?

Catwoman can easily break into tall buildings. She uses her claws to climb walls and her whip to pull open windows.

Who will win the Wayne Manor stand-off?

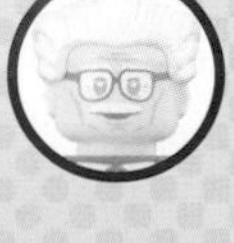

OR

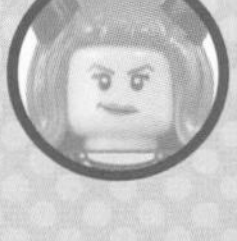

BATMAN WINS!

If you think Batman and his amazing friends and allies won most of the battles in this book, choose this heroic scene.

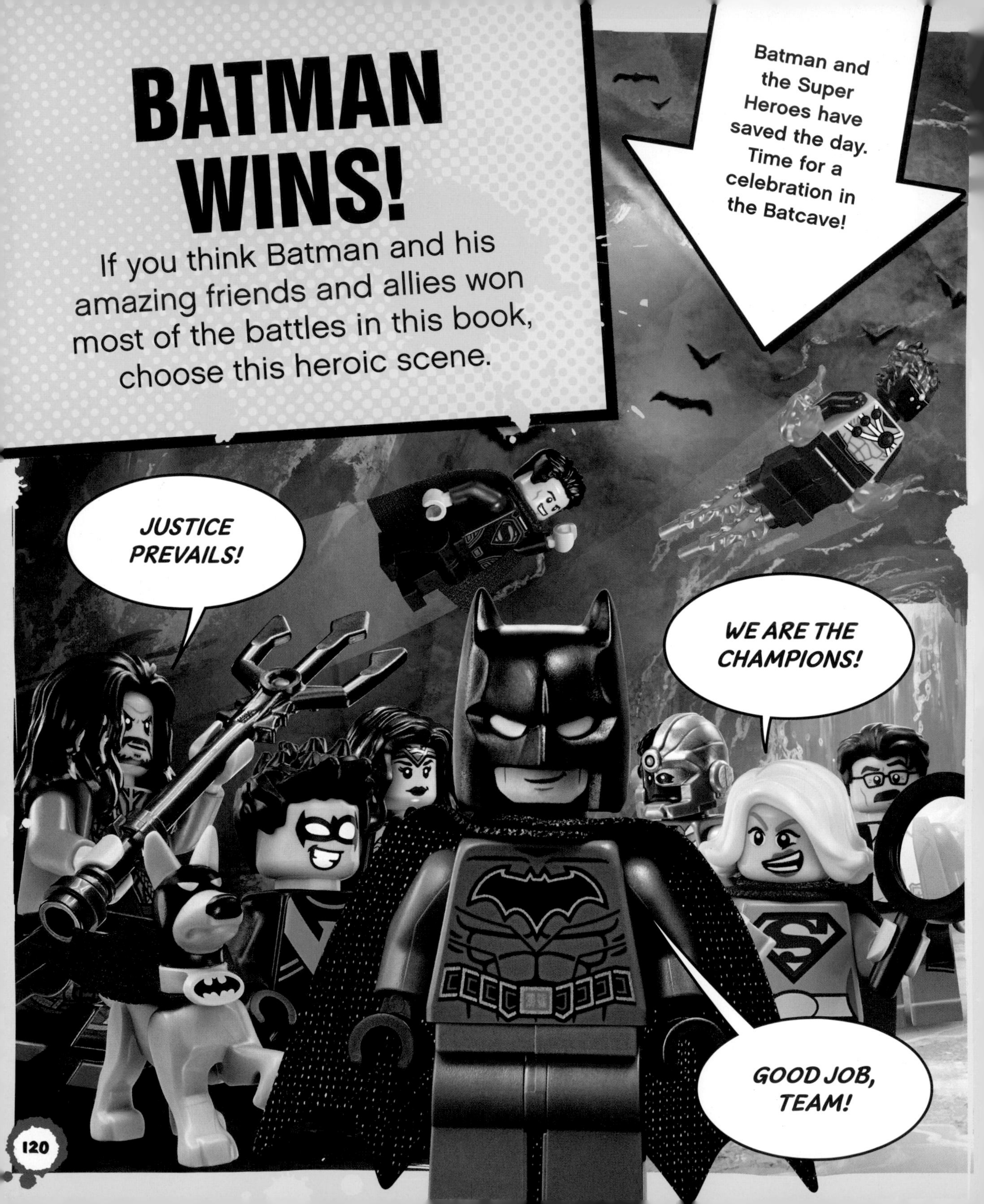
Batman and the Super Heroes have saved the day. Time for a celebration in the Batcave!
JUSTICE PREVAILS!
WE ARE THE CHAMPIONS!
GOOD JOB, TEAM!

THE JOKER WINS!

If you think the Joker and his wicked super-villain pals won more of their battles, choose this villainous victory.

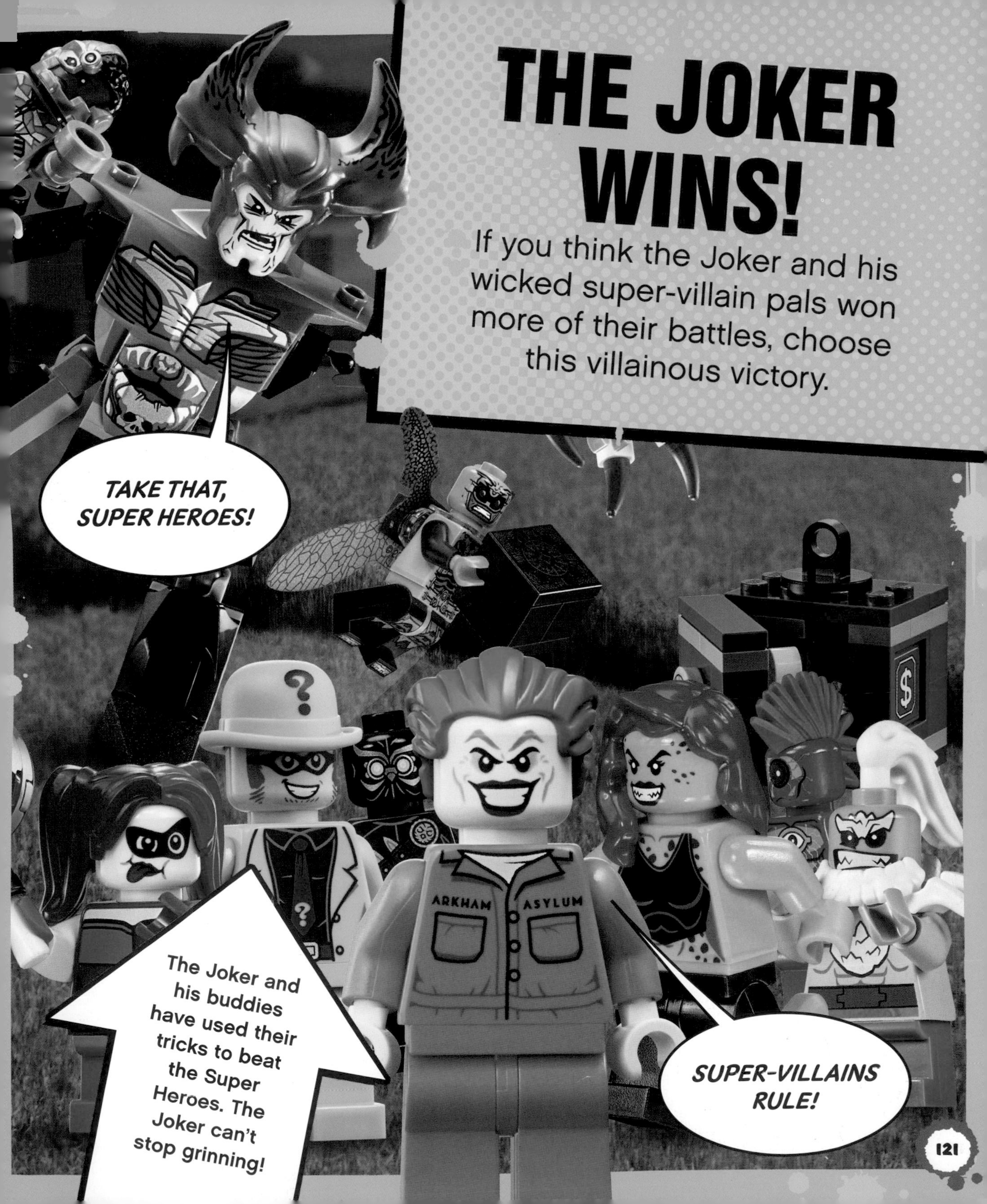
TAKE THAT, SUPER HEROES!
ARKHAM ASYLUM
The Joker and his buddies have used their tricks to beat the Super Heroes. The Joker can't stop grinning!
SUPER-VILLAINS RULE!

INDEX

Editor Rosie Peet
Project Art Editor Sam Bartlett
Designer Thelma Jane Robb
US Editor Kayla Dugger
Senior Production Editor Jennifer Murray
Senior Production Controller Lloyd Robertson
Managing Editor Paula Regan
Managing Art Editor Jo Connor
Art Director Lisa Lanzarini
Publisher Julie Ferris
Publishing Director Mark Searle

Dorling Kindersley would like to thank Randi Sørensen, Heidi K. Jensen,
Paul Hansford, and Martin Leighton Lindhardt at the LEGO Group;
Stefan Georgiou at DK for design assistance;
and Sadie Smith for proofreading.

First American Edition, 2020
Published in the United States by DK Publishing
1450 Broadway, Suite 801, New York, NY 10018

Page design copyright © 2020 Dorling Kindersley Limited
20 21 22 23 24 10 9 8 7 6 5 4 3 2 1
001–316399–Aug/2020

A catalog record for this book is available
from the Library of Congress.

ISBN: 978-1-4654-9239-5
978-0-7440-2145-5 (library edition)

Printed and bound in China

For the curious

www.LEGO.com
www.dk.com

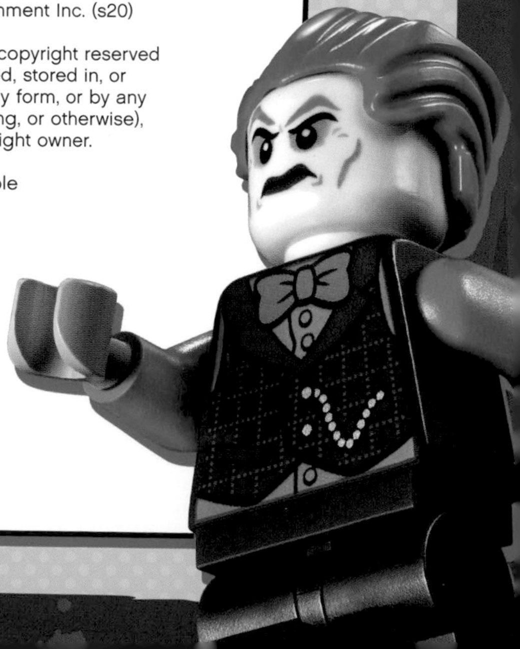